DRAGON HORSE WAR:
TRACKER AND THE SPY

What Reviewers Say About
D. Jackson Leigh's Work

"*Call Me Softly* is a thrilling and enthralling novel of love, lies, intrigue and Southern charm."—*Bibliophilic Book Blog*

"D. Jackson Leigh understands the value of branding and delivers more of the familiar and welcome story elements that set her novels apart from other authors in the romance genre."
—*The Rainbow Reader*

"Her prose is clean, lean, and mean—elegantly descriptive..."
—*Out in Print*

"Leigh writes with an emotion that she in turn gives to the characters, allowing us insight into their personalities and their very souls. Filled with fantastic imagery and the down-to-earth flaws that are sometimes the characters' greatest strengths, this first Dragon Horse War is a story not to be missed. The writing is flawless, the story, breath-taking."—*Lambda Literary Society*

Visit us at www.boldstrokesbooks.com

By the Author

Cherokee Falls Series:

Bareback

Long Shot

Every Second Counts

Southern Secrets:

Call Me Softly

Touch Me Gently

Hold Me Forever

Dragon Horse War:

The Calling

Tracker and the Spy

DRAGON HORSE WAR:
TRACKER AND THE SPY

by

D. Jackson Leigh

2016

DRAGON HORSE WAR: TRACKER AND THE SPY
© 2016 By D. Jackson Leigh. All Rights Reserved.

ISBN 13: 978-1-62639-448-3

This Trade Paperback Original Is Published By
Bold Strokes Books, Inc.
P.O. Box 249
Valley Falls, NY 12185

First Edition: February 2016

CREDITS
EDITOR: SHELLEY THRASHER
PRODUCTION DESIGN: SUSAN RAMUNDO
COVER DESIGN BY SHERI (GRAPHICARTIST2020@HOTMAIL.COM)
ILLUSTRATION BY PAIGE BRADDOCK

Acknowledgments

Thanks again to my amazing editor, Dr. Shelley Thrasher. Her expert hand and patience, as well as her friendship, is appreciated more than I can express.

A special thanks to VK Powell, for the very fun weekends a couple of times each year where we sip liquor and talk out plots and characters. That flow of ideas has helped me let go and give my characters enough rein to guide my plot through some twists I hadn't anticipated.

Also, a debt of gratitude to my super awesome friend, Paige Braddock (aka Missouri Vaun) for drawing Captain Tan for the cover of this book. Thanks, pal.

Finally, a special thanks to my romance readers who trusted me enough to follow me into this fantasy adventure. Thank you very, very much.

Dedication

In loving memory of my father. I still feel his kind
and gentle presence every day.
Ron Jackson, February 1934–June 2015.

A hundred years of peace is shattered when a cult called The Natural Order takes advantage of a series of weather disasters to revive a patriarchal belief that only the strongest should survive. An elite army of dragon horses and pyro-gifted warriors is activated to hunt and destroy the cult before it undermines The Collective culture of embracing diversity and the worldwide sharing of resources. There are lessons for all, however. Even the dragon-horse warriors must learn to embrace the mantra they are defending—stronger together.

CHAPTER ONE

Kyle blocked the doorway into the treatment room. The stream of people seeking medical attention for burns, projectile wounds, or broken bones after being trampled in the melee at the train depot had seemed endless. Some were simply sick from chronic ailments and anxious to receive their share of the medicine recovered from the men who stole it months before.

She was hungry and exhausted but had been assigned to protect the First Advocate, and as long as Alyssa treated patients in the room behind her, Kyle would stand guard. She scrunched her shoulders back until her blades nearly touched in an effort to relieve their ache, but resisted her desire to sag against the doorframe. She might fall asleep standing up if she did, and she needed to stay alert. The hallway of the small medical clinic overflowed with people coming and going or standing and waiting.

Alyssa was apparently someone important. Otherwise, why would the First Warrior—who seemed to be in charge of everything—have ordered Kyle to guard her? Her mind wandered. During the past twenty-four hours she'd seen other pyros like herself; winged, fire-breathing horses; and the First Warrior standing fierce and fearless and glittering in her silver battleskin. She'd dreamed of such things. Last night, those dreams had become real.

Kyle's heart quickened with a forgotten memory—her mother's bedtime stories. Her younger brother and sister would fall asleep, but Kyle always listened until the end. Then her mother would tuck the covers around Kyle's sleeping siblings before turning to her. Laine would kiss her cheek and look into Kyle's eyes. *You are special, my daughter, and destined for great things.* Afterward, Kyle would dream of the fantastic creatures in her mother's stories—warriors and winged horses that breathed fire.

Was it a mother's wish or a seer's premonition? They didn't speak of her mother's and her sister's gifts, just like they hid Kyle's pyro talent. Kyle didn't know why they should hide theirs when so many others didn't. Her mother said all would be revealed when the time was right.

She shook herself from her daydream when the human traffic in the crowded hallway seemed to tense and shift. People thumped against the walls with small exclamations as they moved back to make way for someone headed straight for where Kyle stood. Fatigue forgotten, she felt every fiber of her body vibrate. She raised her hands, palm up and readied to ignite flame and defend the First Advocate.

Predator. Sleek cat. Coiled snake. Dark, angry eyes stared out from a stripe of black that ran from temple to temple above slashes of blood-bright and lightning-white that marked high cheekbones of smooth, rich brown. The well-shaped head was shaved smooth except for a four-centimeter strip of tight curls from forehead to nape. Was the cape draped from shoulder to hip hiding weapons? Kyle's fingertips ignited—reflex rather than conscious thought— when she straightened to fill the doorway as much as her wiry frame allowed.

The figure stopped and regarded her with a curious tilt of the head.

"Identify yourself." Kyle's order rang with a confidence she didn't feel.

"And if I don't?" The resonant alto was punctuated with a snarl, white teeth against full, sensuous lips. "Will you burn the clinic down around our heads, Sparky?"

Kyle stiffened but extinguished her flame. "Identify yourself."

"Get out of my way." A shrug of lean shoulders parted and folded the light cape back to reveal a silver battleskin that clung to every sculpted muscle.

Kyle stared at the dragon-horse insignia emblazoned between perfect breasts but stood firm when the warrior tried to shoulder past her. "I have my orders. Anyone could steal one of those suits. Identify yourself."

The warrior eyed her with disdain. Her hands twitched in a movement familiar to any pyro, and Kyle readied to reignite her own. They would both be burned in a fight at such close quarters. The warrior stepped even closer, her face inches from Kyle's. "I am Tanisha of The Guard. Now, do you know anything more than you did a moment ago?"

The hand that touched her back stopped Kyle's answer.

"Tan, thank the stars. We desperately need your surgery skills. Are you free to help?"

Tan continued to stare down the young woman who had challenged her but stepped back as Alyssa squeezed around the upstart. Few had the backbone to take her on when she was wearing war paint. She liked to intimidate, to dominate. It kept everyone at a safe distance, except for this sparkler. Okay, maybe her flame was blue-white hot. Not a novice, but Tan didn't know her, so as far as she was concerned, this rangy kid was still a novice firecracker who needed to learn her place.

"Stop it. Kyle is a friend."

Tan relented, shifting her gaze to Alyssa, but only because of the weariness in her voice. The First Advocate's cheeks, normally colored by swatches of sunset rose, were pale. Fatigue dulled her vibrant green eyes and shadowed her face. Even the normal spikes of her short, fiery red hair lay limp and dark with sweat. Tanisha's respect for the young first-life had grown over the months they'd worked side by side in the clinic at the dragon-horse army's camp, even if she did miss the occasional jump she once shared with Jael before Alyssa laid claim to the First Warrior's heart and bed. "Are you okay?"

"Yes." Alyssa sighed. "No, but we don't have the week I'd need to explain all the reasons why." She rubbed at her eyes. "Right now, we need another pair of hands in surgery."

She nodded, a conciliatory gesture since she reported to the First Warrior, not the First Advocate, no matter how high her rank. "I've got some time. Diego and I were tracking the bastard that caused all of this, but he's gone underground for now, so I can help out here while Diego works some of his local sources and we wait for nightfall."

"Brasília."

Tan turned slowly back to Alyssa's guard. Alyssa had called her Kyle. She was lean, her dark hair cut androgynously short and her eyes blue flames.

"I don't know where they might be going now, but they were headed to Brasília to meet some believers there."

Everything in Tan went still.

"Kyle was with the people on the train. She helped me escape," Alyssa said, moving to stand between Tan and Kyle.

Tan narrowed her eyes and circled around Alyssa toward Kyle. Maybe the trail wasn't as cold as they thought. "What do you know about this?"

"You don't need to—" Alyssa held up her hand and closed her eyes for a long moment. Then she blinked, as if to regain her focus. "Jael is busy interrogating a group of women and a few men who were captured. Seventeen hundred at the temple. The Guard will gather to debrief then."

Tan straightened. Just because Alyssa was bedding the First Warrior, The Guard didn't take orders from her.

Seventeen hundred, Tan.

Jael's voice echoed in her brain, and she realized that Alyssa had been communicating with Jael telepathically. *You trust this sparkler who's trailing Alyssa?*

I assigned Kyle to that duty.

Tan had her own opinions about things, but she was a soldier and an order was an order. *As you command.* She nodded to Alyssa, giving Kyle one last grudging glance. "Good enough, eh? Until then, point me to the surgery rooms."

❖

The man and woman abandoned the gurney they were guiding toward an operating room and plastered themselves against the wall to move as far away as possible when Tan pushed through the doors to the clinic's small surgery suite. Across from them, a woman who sat behind a scheduling desk slid her rolling chair back slightly, as if preparing to sprint away to safety.

Tan cocked her head and bared her teeth in a snarl of a smile. Reaction to her fierce appearance always amused her, and she was tempted to toy with them a bit. But a small whimpering sound drew her to the gurney.

"Dr. Tan?" The boy's pupils were dilated with the medication he'd been given to relax him, even though a nerve block was stopping pain from reaching his brain. Cyrus, leader of The Natural Order, had severed his hand as a message to Jael when he fled his cult's first clash with The Collective's dragon-horse army. Tan had found the boy in time to save his life, then handed him over to Diego to deliver to the clinic while she chased Cyrus. "Did you catch him?"

"Not yet, Ari." She bent over him and soothed his damp hair back from his forehead, mentally cursing that she had the rough fingertips of a pyro. "But I have his trail. I came to put your hand back on your arm first."

He blinked drowsily and licked at his dry lips. His eyes wandered to the dragon-horse insignia emblazoned on her chest. "You're magic. I saw you at the train on a flying horse."

Tan smiled. "Don't let her hear you call her a flying horse. She's a dragon horse."

"But she can fly."

"Yes, she can. Maybe when you're all better, I'll ask her if she'll take you on a short flight. She does that for very brave boys like you."

His eyes filled with tears, and his face contorted with the effort to hold them back. "I wasn't brave. I cried and begged when they cut off my hand." A sob, then another escaped until he was quietly crying.

Tan stroked his cheek. "The First Advocate said you are very brave. She personally sent me to fix the damage this bad man has done."

"You can really put my hand back?" His eyes were hopeful.

She cocked her head. "Yes. I'm magic, remember?"

He nodded solemnly, then shivered.

Tan pulled back the thin blanket that covered him and took her cloak from her shoulders to lay it over him, then re-covered him with the blanket. "There. I will shield you with some of my magic while I reattach your hand, just for good measure."

His smile was weary, and his eyelids drooped. "Mami will be worried when I don't come home tonight."

"Don't worry, young warrior. I'll have someone go for your mother so she'll be here when you wake up."

"Okay." His eyes closed and Tan started to straighten, but his soft words called her back. "Dr. Tan?"

"Yes, Ari?"

His eyes remained closed, and she put her ear close to hear his whisper. "I like your face paint."

"Sleep now. All will be well."

Tan straightened and strode to the scheduling desk. The three adults had edged forward to eavesdrop on Tan's conversation with their patient, but immediately moved back when she approached again.

"Changing room?"

The woman behind the desk silently pointed to a door down the hall.

"Spare scrubs?"

"O-on the rack to your right, just inside the door," the woman said.

Tan picked up the med scanner lying on the desk next to the scheduling tablet and held it to her neck so it could read the identity chip imbedded there. "I'm Dr. Tanisha of Third Continent, and I'm a qualified fifth-level surgeon. I understand you're shorthanded and I'm here to offer my assistance."

The woman cautiously scooted her chair forward to read the credentials that popped up on her tablet screen. She blinked up at Tan. "I—" She cleared her throat. "I'll notify Dr. Mendez right away."

"Thank you."

❖

"Kyle! It's good to see you safe."

She hadn't expected her eyes to tear, but his presence brought a wave of homesickness and worry. She stepped into Furcho's open arms and buried her face in his shoulder. "You smell like home," she said, her voice wistful and muffled by his shirt.

He chuckled but held her tighter and stroked her back. "It's only the soap I use. The scent reminds me of home, too." Furcho was physically little more than a decade older than she, but his soul was much older. Her father had barely tolerated him, jealous because Furcho was promoted over him at the university. But Kyle's mother and Furcho had been good friends.

Reluctantly, she slipped from his arms and stepped back. Her throat was so tight, she didn't know if she could speak the words. "Thomas is dead, isn't he?"

Furcho's eyes were kind. "Yes, but he died a hero, saving hundreds as the mountainside collapsed and buried half the town."

Somehow, she had known her brother was gone. Her father's anguish was too great for it to be a lie. She didn't know how to ask the next question. "Mom?"

"Alive and well when I saw her last. Your father was so overcome with grief that he was sedated and hospitalized, so I stood with her at your brother's funeral pyre."

The great weight lifted from her, and Kyle made no attempt to brush away her tears. "Father said they were both dead and that he'd buried their bodies."

Furcho clasped her shoulder. "No. Your mother and I saw to it. Your brother's soul has many incarnations yet."

She nodded, then gathered herself to cast about for Alyssa. Stars, she was supposed to be guarding the First Advocate, but she was standing here blubbering. She relaxed when she saw her going into the temple. "I have to leave," she said, squeezing Furcho's hand and then gesturing toward the temple. "I'll see you around?"

"Looks like we're going to the same place," he said.

Only then did the flash of silver where his shirt was open at the neck register with her. "You...you're—"

He grinned and nodded. "Furcho, Third Warrior of The Guard."

"You have, you have a—" What did you call those beasts?

"Yes. I'm bonded to Azar, a dragon horse."

"Amazing."

He laughed at her breathy exclamation and nodded. "Yes, it is amazing. I'll introduce you later, but we need to hurry. The others have already gone in."

Kyle glimpsed Alyssa in the temple and trotted to follow her down a hallway, but when Alyssa turned to enter the room where a handful of people were gathering, Tan stepped into the doorway, cutting Kyle off.

"This is Guard business, Sparkler. You wait in the hallway."

"Let her in, Tan." Jael's voice came from inside the room.

Even with her war paint washed off, Tan's glare was still intimidating. Kyle lifted her chin and met Tan's stare as she slid past.

Alyssa sat at the head of a conference table. Jael, First Warrior and commander of The Collective's dragon-horse army, stood behind her. They were a striking contrast. A crown of dark, fiery spikes framed Alyssa's fair features, and though her emerald eyes bespoke a young soul, the room seemed filled with her calm presence. Jael radiated a deadly, coiled power. Kyle found everything about her imposing—her tall, battle-honed frame, the contrast of her wheat-colored hair against her tanned skin, and especially her eyes that were warm summer sky one minute and searing blue flame the next. She would've thought Jael completely intimidating if not for the tenderness she'd witnessed between the couple and the devotion on the faces of the elite Guard seated around the table, awaiting her debriefing.

Among the others, she knew only Tan and Furcho. Three more stood around the long table—a stump of a man with dark features and a goatee; a woman who looked like a rubber stamp of Jael, blond and tall, except for eyes that were brown; and another woman whose tattoo on the left side of her face and neck identified her as an Advocate like Alyssa.

"Sit."

Jael's call to convene the meeting was simple, but Kyle didn't think it included her. She stood as unobtrusively as possible against the wall near the doorway and carefully made mental notes. She ignored Tan's gaze boring into her as if she were counting Kyle's every breath.

"Although our new army is still untrained and last night was our first battle, we obtained our immediate objective. We reacquired the food and medical supplies, and they're being distributed to their intended destinations. Many children will go to bed tonight with full bellies for the first time in several months. Our new warriors and their mounts performed well. We had no fatalities and only a dozen or so injuries, none critical." She crossed her arms over her chest. "However, several civilians died, including Chief Advocate Camila." She paused for a few seconds of respectful silence. "Also, we did not realize our prime objective. Cyrus, the man who calls himself The Prophet, escaped with the help of his core group of men and apparently some locals lured by his ranting."

The woman who looked like Jael shook her head. "I just don't understand how anyone with a conscience could buy into that survival-of-the-strongest dogma. How can the women with them swallow the servitude that cult espouses? They basically view women as housekeepers and breeding stock."

"They're desolate people in desperate times," Furcho said. "The human instinct to survive is strong. This latest series of weather disasters has hit our food-producing regions hard. People are afraid of going hungry, and fear often overcomes reason. This self-proclaimed prophet has convinced them that to feed their children during this food shortage, they must join his group and keep the food we do have for themselves."

Kyle tensed as Jael's piercing gaze raked the room and settled on her.

"Kyle lost her brother and mother when a mud slide buried their town, and she's known hunger," Jael said. "Yet she stands with The Collective."

Kyle's insides went cold. She'd given her thoughts to Jael but hadn't stopped to consider everything she'd see. She didn't want Jael to know her shame for giving in to her hunger and pretending to go along with Cyrus until she could escape. Everyone turned to her, and she deflected her embarrassment with an update. "Furcho told me a few minutes ago that my mother is alive. He stood with her at my brother's pyre. I…I don't know where she is, but she's alive."

"That's wonderful, Kyle." Alyssa's face lit up at the news, and a wave of emotion washed through Kyle—something she hadn't felt in many months. Joy.

Jael rapped her knuckles lightly on the table. "Second, report."

Jael's near twin responded. "All rations have been divided and are on their way to the various distribution centers. Word's traveling fast about The Collective victory, and people are already gathering to receive the supplies they need."

Jael nodded and moved to the next. "Diego."

The man with the goatee spoke. "Cyrus has gone underground. We rounded up only two of those who escaped with him. Apparently, they've split up and are disguising themselves as locals to leave town in pairs or alone. It's easy enough to slip out that way. The roads are crowded with people packing supplies back to their villages. They probably plan to meet somewhere else in a day or two."

"Bring the two you've captured to me. I'll probe their minds for a rendezvous point."

"One put a gun to his own head when we confronted him, rather than being taken prisoner. A couple of the local peace-keepers took the other to clean him up." Diego chuckled. "Tan spotted the rifle he carried sticking out from his poncho and jumped out of an alley to grab him. That war paint of hers scared the dung out of him… literally. The peace office is only a block away. They're holding him in a cell for you."

"Anything else?"

"Did you learn anything from the women left on the train?" Second asked.

"Nothing useful," Jael said.

"What will you do with them?" Furcho asked.

Jael looked each of them in the eye. "Judgment is mine on the battlefield. Outside the battlefield," she said slowly. "Outside of battle, the First Advocate and I will rule together for The Collective."

Tan shrugged. The rest nodded agreement to this new division of authority and looked to Alyssa for an answer to Furcho's question.

"We'll leave them with the peacekeepers here to complete a sentence of community service, helping the people hurt by their misguided beliefs," Alyssa said.

"If they are judged to be unrepentant at the conclusion of their retribution, then they'll live the rest of their lives in captivity until their souls can be properly released at death," Jael added.

Alyssa stood. "Fair to all."

"We have a little more than four hours until dark. I want everyone to catch a nap," Jael said. "We'll meet at dusk in the field across from the train depot."

Finally. The room was too warm and Kyle's eyelids were heavy. She was beginning to think these people never slept.

"Advocate Emilia has lodging for us here in the temple." Jael gestured to the Advocate Kyle didn't know.

"Farther down the hallway, a room with bunks has been prepared for you," Emilia said. "You'll also find food and drink. The accommodations aren't fancy but should be adequate."

Kyle was sure she could sleep anywhere, even on the bare floor, at this point.

"What about the sparkler?" Tan had been silent until now.

"I'm putting you in charge of her," Jael said. "You and Phyrrhos can give her a ride tonight when we all return to camp."

Tan stood and stomped toward the door, then back again. "That's not a good idea."

Kyle didn't think much of it either. She didn't know why this warrior had taken an instant dislike to her, but she'd rather walk alone to wherever they were going than have Tan as her traveling partner.

"Phyrrhos has been a bitch lately, sort of like her bonded," Diego said, glaring at Tan. "She kicked Bero yesterday when we were gathering for last night's raid."

Wait. Were they talking about riding dragon horses to their camp?

"Kyle can ride with me," Furcho said. "Azar never minds carrying two."

Yes! She was going to fly on a dragon horse. She'd never be able to sleep now.

"Very well." Jael stared at Tan, her expression flat. "But starting tomorrow, I'm assigning Kyle to you."

Tan threw her hands up. "Be reasonable, Jael. I can't track Cyrus and wet-nurse a sparkler at the same time."

"She's going to help you find Cyrus."

Kyle tensed, a small kernel of fear knotting her gut. She'd just escaped him. She wanted to stay with the army and become a dragon-horse warrior. She and Tan finally agreed.

"Do you really think she has more information about The Natural Order than the female prisoners whose brains you've already dug through? Men run The Natural Order. Why would they discuss anything of importance in front of women, in front of her? When I track, I track alone."

The muscle on Jael's jaw jumped. "You'll follow orders." Her words were a low growl, her glare a blue laser aimed at Tan.

Alyssa closed her eyes, her face a study in concentration as though she was meditating or maybe just trying to shut out the ass-chewing that would surely follow if Tan didn't rein in her insubordination. Then Kyle felt a sudden sense of calm. Though their gazes still locked, Jael's glare lessened and Tan's defiance melted away. Kyle relaxed, too, when Tan inclined her head and saluted, her right fist thumping again her left shoulder. "As you command."

"Stronger together." Alyssa's gentle reminder of The Collective mission salved all of their battle-raw emotions.

Tan turned to Kyle. "At least tell me why you think you can help me find him."

Her own objections forgotten, Kyle realized she could help. She could identify the people her father kept close if they saw them, and, if she thought carefully, she probably had other useful information in her head. She looked into Jael's eyes, a calm swath of clear sky, to answer Tan's question.

"Because Cyrus is my father," she said softly, realizing that only Furcho and Jael, who had searched her thoughts before trusting her with Alyssa, already knew this fact. Her relationship to Cyrus was Kyle's secret to reveal or keep. She cleared her throat and spoke louder. "The Prophet of The Natural Order—the man we're hunting to exterminate—is my father."

CHAPTER TWO

Jael slipped into the darkened room, pausing to let her eyes adjust so she wouldn't have to strike a flame to find the air pallet where Alyssa slept. The probe of the prisoner's mind didn't take long. The rendezvous point for the fugitives had been too easy to extract, which made her suspicious that Cyrus and his bodyguards were headed for a location not shared with the larger group. She pulled off her boots at the door to soften her footsteps and padded toward the dark shape in the center of the room.

"Take off those smoky clothes before you get in bed with me."

She smiled. "I thought you'd already be asleep."

"I need more than sleep. I need you."

Jael gripped the collar of her battleskin and yanked open the Velcro closure that ran down her back, then quickly pushed the fire-retardant suit and her briefs to the floor and stepped out of them. She slid under the light sheet and pressed her overheated body against the cool skin of her lover. "I need you, too."

Alyssa's hands were soft against her face but her lips fierce and possessive as they took hers. Though the clash between The Natural Order and The Collective's warriors had ended just before dawn, the residual battle lust still burned in their veins.

Jael rolled over to cover her, urging Alyssa to open to her. Alyssa spread her legs wide and pulled her knees up. Jael nearly ignited as Alyssa's swollen sex, despite the dim lighting, glistened with arousal. Jael's own flesh throbbed almost painfully.

"I want to feel you against me," Alyssa said. "I want to feel how wet and hard you are."

She spread her own sex, her clit distended and firm as though straining to meet Alyssa's. They fit together perfectly as she thrust and rubbed, slick and hot.

"Yes, like that." Alyssa pulled her knees higher, against her breasts. "Oh, yes."

"Not...going...to last." The pressure gathered in her belly and grew with each tantalizing stroke of her hips.

"Oh, stars. Oh, baby."

Alyssa softly keened as she came, her nails biting into Jael's arms. Jael thrust hard, again, again, then let go to ride out their orgasms together.

"More," Alyssa panted. "I want you inside."

She flipped herself over and Jael groaned at the familiar position they both enjoyed. She stretched over Alyssa's back and sucked at her throat as she slid two fingers easily into her and pumped.

Alyssa trembled beneath her. "Feels good, so good, but I need to come, I need to come again now." She reached behind, her hand open, fingers reaching. "Give yourself to me."

Jael already had given herself, heart and soul. Now she gave her flesh, shifting so that Alyssa's fingers found her still-hard clit. She pulled her fingers out and thrust inside with her thumb, curling her fingers so they stroked Alyssa's clit as her thumb massaged the right spot within. Alyssa's fingers were firm against her need, stroking with each pump of Jael's hips and hand. She rode Alyssa's hand and crested on the wave of pleasure Alyssa projected as she screamed her climax into her pillow.

She collapsed onto Alyssa, the sweat of their exertion slicking their naked bodies. Her hand twitched with the after-spasms that grabbed at her belly, and Alyssa groaned with the movement against her sensitive flesh.

Jael gently pulled her hand from between Alyssa's legs. "I love you," she whispered into Alyssa's ear before rolling off to face her.

Alyssa moved onto her side and pulled Jael's hand to her lips to kiss it. "And I love you."

She entwined her fingers with Alyssa's and they both stared at their joined hands, silent for several long moments. Normally, they lowered their mental and emotional shields when they were alone, but it wasn't possible to do that while they were still in a city with the voices and emotions of thousands swirling around them. So, Jael, a telepath, and Alyssa, a unique empath who could project as well as sense emotions, ironically had to communicate like any other couple.

They hadn't been alone to talk since Alyssa had seen Jael pass judgment and instantly execute a spy in a fiery inferno on the night of the army's chaotic mass bonding with a wild herd of dragon horses. Alyssa knew the nature of their mission. She knew the role of the First Warrior to lead an army of pyros, and they both had hoped she'd come to terms with the use of force to break up The Natural Order cult and hurl its leader to a fiery exit from this life so that he might make restitution in the next. But Alyssa, an empath whose very core fed on peace and light, faltered when faced with the righteous darkness Jael summoned to carry out her duty. Alyssa had fled their camp—fled Jael's darkness—and nearly fell into the hands of The Natural Order.

The silence between them now, the struggle for words was deafening. After a few minutes, Alyssa sat up and placed her hand between Jael's breasts. "Open a little? Enough so I can feel you." With her other hand, she lifted Jael's and pressed it to her lips in a brief kiss. "I'll open my thoughts to you, in turn, because I know you won't listen in without permission."

Jael nodded. They needed to talk about the bonding night, but warriors didn't talk about their feelings. Never in her many lifetimes had she found any reason to compel her. Until Alyssa. And, since she seemed incapable of conversing like a normal person, she would try to do as Alyssa asked. She unconsciously began to sort her feelings as she slipped into Alyssa's thoughts.

Filtering. She's filtering what she doesn't want me to feel.

Alyssa's sharp thoughts of disappointment sliced through Jael. She sucked in a breath and tried again. She covered Alyssa's hand with hers and pressed it tighter against her breast as she exhaled and let Alyssa experience everything as she had the night of the bonding—

Grief, heavy and suffocating, grew with each of the twenty-five pyres torched for the warriors who didn't survive the perilous bonding. They burned all around her, searing her skin and scoring her soul.

There were so many. Too many, Jael.

The deepest rend belonged to her young protégé. Irreparably injured, she had begged a warrior's death. It ripped out a piece of her as she and Specter granted the request and incinerated the mangled young woman to release her spirit.

Bast was so young. This shouldn't have happened to her, or to you.

The pyres' flames were fuel to her fury when Michael and Diego dragged an accused spy before her, and she found betrayal in the thoughts of the man to whom they had given work and food for his family. He had dishonored the very lives of those burning on the pyres behind her, and more of her warriors were in danger because of his treason...because she had let him slip into her camp undetected. Her warriors.

The betrayal was personal for you, wasn't it? You still carry the weight of each death. You can't. You can't. It will crush you.

Her warriors. Red fury boiled and roiled into the deadly darkness that over many lifetimes had mindlessly guided her blade as she slashed her way through many battlefields, swiftly and accurately sighted her target to release a barrage of bullets or a deadly laser, or fueled the white-hot fireballs flung from her fingertips.

Where did you go? So dark. Where were you, Jael?

The spy was guilty. Death was his sentence. Not the instantaneous death of honor Bast had earned. The darkness tempered her flame and gloried in his scream.

Oh, stars. His pain. Burning, burning. I couldn't bear it. I couldn't.

It was finished. She felt nothing. The darkness was a void of emptiness as she stared at the pile of ash where the man had knelt less than a minute before. Something niggled at the void, and she raised her eyes to a woman at the edge of the field, her expression horrified and filled with fear. The darkness feeds on that terror.

You looked at me like a stranger. So cold. No recognition. Is my hold on you so tenuous?

Breathe, she couldn't breathe. The darkness she'd always embraced was choking her, constricting her chest. She fought it. Then she was aloft, with Specter's wings sweeping cool night air against her heated skin and into her ravaged lungs. The darkness was receding. She was on a cold mountain ledge now, angry and... empty. She longed for her mountain and peace. She longed for her lover.

Our field of wildflowers. Oh, Jael. I want that, too.

Lust normally followed her rage, but the darkness this time had given way to a different hunger. She needed Alyssa's light to

banish the black remnants clinging to her soul. She found only an
empty tent. A hollow ache replaced the anger, the righteousness,
the sense of honor and duty. She was drained and surrendered to
exhaustion.

I failed you. Again. I am not worthy to be at your side. You
need someone stronger.

Alyssa pulled away, withdrawing her hand from Jael's chest,
but Jael refused to let her go. She sat up cross-legged, facing
Alyssa, and drew both her hands up to her chest.
"One more thing you need to see."
Jael gently positioned her fingers along Alyssa's temples.
"Close your eyes." Instead of thoughts and feelings, she projected
scenes, from her point of view, like she did to communicate with
her dragon horse.

Tan lifts her hand, then concludes her conversation with some
medics and strides over. "I know your brain has been controlled
by your ovaries lately, but I need Alyssa at the clinic today, not
warming your bed."
"You haven't seen her?"
"No. And I was hoping to catch a few winks—" Tan stops.
"Wait. She hasn't been with you?"
"No. I haven't seen her since last night." A visual sweep of
the temporary camp shows everything has been disassembled and
loaded onto transports to return to the main encampment. A cold
weight is forming in her chest. Where is Alyssa?
Second hops off a chow wagon and waves the driver on down
the mountain. "You look better." Her steps slow. "What's wrong?"
"Alyssa's missing," Tan says.
"Missing?"
Nicole is on the edge of the meadow, shooting nervous glances
their way as she shoulders her personal pack and starts toward
them. They jog to meet her. "Where's Alyssa?"

"I was hoping she was with you." Nicole looks worried. "Last time I saw her was last night. She was, uh, she was—" She stops and bites her lip.

The coldness in her chest expands, its weight crushing her lungs. She grabs Nicole's head and tears into her thoughts. Nicole gasps, and Tan wraps a supporting arm around Nicole as she sags.

"Stop it." Second is pulling her away, shaking her. "You could have hurt her."

Her thoughts are spinning, nausea rising. She grabs the only solid thing under her hands, fistfuls of Second's shirt. "Something's happened to her."

"This is my fault. I shouldn't have let her go off alone." Nicole's face is pale.

Second covers Jael's hands and gently pulls them from her shirt. "This is nobody's fault. Alyssa is an adult. A very resourceful adult. She traveled more than half a continent alone to find you. She bears the Advocate mark, and the locals will honor that."

Her gut is churning with so much nauseating fear that she barely feels the tap of Second's finger against her head and against her chest. "Trust me. If something had happened to her, you'd know it."

She'd faced battle and death over and over in her previous lifetimes, and she'd often faced seemingly insurmountable odds and certain massacre. But she'd never felt the paralyzing, all-consuming emptiness that threatened to drown her if Alyssa was truly gone.

"Don't leave me." Jael flinched at the sound of her own choked voice. Her hands were wet with Alyssa's tears, and she realized her own tears were dripping from her jaw onto Alyssa's hands, where they rested on her chest. The only tears she could remember shedding in this lifetime were as she stood beside a funeral pyre with Second, who was distraught at the loss of her mate, Saron.

Alyssa shook her head. "I should love you enough to give you up to someone stronger, more worthy to be at your side."

"If I were stronger, I'd send you away before I contaminate the purest, most talented soul I've ever encountered."

Alyssa blinked, her eyes beginning to dry. "Meeting you, all of The Guard, has opened my eyes and my mind. You are so much more than war and violence. You're honor and duty, loyalty and pride. You haven't contaminated me. You're teaching me wisdom."

Jael lifted Alyssa's hand to her lips for a brief kiss. "And you're the only light that has ever pierced my darkness. I would've wrongly executed Kyle if you hadn't brought me back to where I could reason."

Alyssa's eyes grew unfocused, and Jael fought the itch to listen in on her thoughts. Maybe she shouldn't have reminded Alyssa how close she had come to executing Kyle. Maybe Alyssa was thinking of what could have happened if she hadn't been able to stop Jael. Maybe she was having second thoughts about their relationship again. "Alyssa?"

Alyssa returned her gaze to Jael, her eyes softening. "Don't." She entwined her fingers with Jael's, and Jael felt a surge of affection wash away her insecurity. "I was thinking about gray."

"As in the color gray?"

"Han was trying to help me see that everything isn't as simple as good and evil, black and white." She smiled. "It was a lesson in the art of compromise." She grew serious again, her eyes searching Jael's as if she might find the key there. "He said he had a message for me from The Collective Council."

Jael straightened, surprised. A message from The Collective Council? It was Alyssa's to keep or share, but a communication from the Council was so rare she'd expect Alyssa to have shared it with her. On the other hand, she'd withheld things from Alyssa, too. "When was this?"

"Before the bonding. Right before I came to you and...you know. I didn't tell you because, well, I suddenly had other things on my mind, like you, hot and naked." She stroked along Jael's collarbone and between her breasts, then pulled her hand away and refocused on Jael's eyes. "Mostly, I didn't understand it."

"But you do now?"

"Maybe part of it. Not all. It might make more sense to you. We're stronger working together, right?" Alyssa smiled at the play on The Collective mantra.

A breeze ruffled the curtains drawn to darken the room, and a sliver of late-afternoon sun flickered across Alyssa's face as the smile softened her features and lit her green eyes. Red spikes of her short hair poked out in an erratic disarray, and her cheeks were still flushed from the heat of the room and their recent lovemaking. Sun and stars, she was beautiful.

"Jael?"

"Huh?"

"Don't you want to hear the message?"

Jael shook herself mentally. Message. "Yes, if you're comfortable sharing it."

"Only with you." Alyssa closed her eyes, her brow scrunching together.

"If you can't remember the exact words, I can extract—"

Alyssa stopped Jael's offer with an upraised palm before she began to speak. "War and peace may seem like night and day. But without the dawn, day would not break. Without dusk, night would not come. The Collective can only be restored when the warrior finds peace and an Advocate takes up her mantle."

"What do you think it means?"

"The message contains many meanings. You and I are light and dark, day and night. We must use our skills together to protect The Collective."

Jael pulled Alyssa into her lap. Stronger together, their destinies entwined. "Agreed. Together."

"There's also a greater meaning." Alyssa settled against Jael's chest. "I believe The Natural Order is a catalyst, a test meant to strengthen The Collective if we are successful. Without dusk, there is no night, without night no dawn, and without dawn, day will never break."

Jael absently rubbed her cheek against Alyssa's shoulder. "This feels like the night. This enemy has no army I can march against. He utilizes small pockets of soldiers disguised as believers and hides among legions of misguided innocents." She thought of the spy who had infiltrated her own camp. "When I walk through town, I don't know if a person I meet on the street is loyal to The Collective or secretly part of The Natural Order."

Alyssa cuddled into Jael, stroking absently along the arms that embraced her. "The warrior and the Advocate could be referring to us, but I'm afraid to try to interpret that. It could mean many things. Some of them I don't want to consider."

Jael felt uncertainty, then fear, then deep sadness. "Stop." She tightened her arms around Alyssa and cupped Alyssa's cheek, finding her gaze and holding it. "We are soul-bonds. I can feel it. And when this is all done, I want to make it official."

Alyssa choked out a half laugh, half sob and smiled. "Are you asking me to officially bond with you? It sounded more like an order than a proposal."

Jael returned her smile. "I haven't had much practice at asking for things." Her smile faded. "If I ask properly, would you say yes?"

"Even if you don't, I'll say yes." Alyssa kissed her, deep and sweet. "Yes, because I am only a half-soul without you."

CHAPTER THREE

Kyle stood next to Furcho and thought her heart would burst as five lean dragon horses, wings spread like great birds of prey, drifted downward in the dying light. Furcho murmured their names to her as each of them touched down. Specter, ghostly in the moonlight, pressed his forehead to Jael's. Titan, a dusky buckskin, danced his last steps to Second. Kyle imagined calling one of those beautiful beasts to her side, pressing her forehead to the ridged head, sharing thoughts, riding the wind. Furcho's Azar, a shimmering silver dapple, touched down lightly next to them, while Diego's black, Bero, landed with a snort and jerked his head impatiently. He moved away when Diego stepped toward him. Diego cursed.

Tan stood apart from the rest, watching Phyrrhos circle overhead.

"Call her in, Tan," Jael said.

"I'm trying." Fists clenched at her sides, Tan didn't take her eyes from the circling animal. "Get down here, you daughter of a dung eater, or I'll singe your wings from here."

Phyrrhos lifted her head and screamed into the night, spewing a column of flame.

Kyle was fascinated. What happened when a warrior couldn't control her dragon horse?

Another scream, so close that Kyle's ears rang with it, and Bero launched into the sky.

"Bero! Get back here, you black devil." Diego might as well have been talking to the wind.

"Oh, this isn't good," Furcho muttered.

"What's happening?" Kyle didn't know anything about dragon-horse armies, but it looked like the beasts were breaking rank. The words were barely off her tongue when Specter launched into the sky, and Jael's curses rang out across the meadow.

"Guard, hold your bonded." Second's command was unnecessary since only she and Furcho still had their dragon horses at their sides.

The moon hid behind a blanket of clouds as the dark night lit up with a burst of fireballs sparking like strobe lights. The three dragon horses appeared in different positions with each flash. It was impossible to tell who was attacking whom. Phyrrhos. Kyle blinked. She needed to protect Phyrrhos. Where was that coming from?

Jael stood ramrod still, her focus intent on Specter's dodging, darting form. Tan, too, watched the sky but paced restlessly. "Phyrrhos has gone in season."

"Your bitch better not hurt Bero. This is all her fault." Diego shoved Tan hard, then grabbed his hip as if something unseen had struck him. He whirled on Jael. "Specter. Son of a dung beetle."

Jael turned to him, her hard stare immobilizing Tan and Diego where they stood. Second grabbed them both by their collars and shook them.

This was the elite Guard of The Collective? Kyle had seen schoolyard brawls less chaotic.

Bero landed heavily next to them, a swath of scorched hide on his hip and a portion of his tail burned away. Diego swore.

"Second, you and Furcho escort Diego to the main camp before Specter decides to singe off the rest of Bero's tail." Jael's order was curt, her eyes following Specter's shimmering figure in the night sky. She glanced at Tan, her tone softening a bit. "I think if the rest of you clear out, we can get Phyrrhos under control and back to the main camp, where we can confine her until her heat is over."

Kyle started at the choked sound that came from Tan, but the enigmatic warrior had turned away. For the first time, she wished she were more than a pyro—that she was also a telepath—so she could hear what was going on inside Tan's head.

Furcho clapped his hand on her shoulder. "Ready for your first flight?"

❖

A few smooth sweeps of his wings, and Azar lifted them easily from a canter to airborne. Kyle had never felt anything like it. Her blood sang with each slide of his shoulder muscles under her thighs. Furcho had let her mount in front so she could get the full experience of seeing nothing but stars beyond the ears of the dragon horse. The warm Gulf crosswind ruffled her hair. She was born for this. She knew it. And she knew other things, things niggling at the edge of her consciousness just beyond her grasp.

Things happen when they will, Kyle. You can sometimes change what happens, but not when. She smiled at the sudden memory of her younger sister. Maya was always making statements like that. At first, they'd thought it just the prattle of a child who spent too much time around adults, but as Maya grew, it became evident that she was a gifted seer. A pang of guilt pierced her. She was flying around on dragon horses without a thought of finding her sister. Cyrus claimed that he had her, but where? Had he starved Maya into submission like he did Kyle?

She grabbed at Azar's mane when he dipped to pick up a different airstream. She'd expected to be queasy at that height with nothing but Azar's slim shoulders under her, but she felt completely at ease in the sky and wind. She wondered, not for the first time, if human souls lived previous lives as animals. Perhaps she'd been a hawk or some other bird.

"Ready for your own dragon horse?" Furcho balanced effortlessly behind her. She was surprised to hear him so easily over the wind, then realized the complete absence of life's white noise.

"Yes."

"They'll test your DNA at the main camp, but you'll qualify."

"Being a pyro automatically qualifies you?"

Furcho was quiet for a long moment. "No, Kyle, it doesn't. Your mother carries the gene. That's all I can say. Anything else, she'll have to tell you."

There's more? Hope flared. Could Furcho be hinting that Cyrus wasn't her biological father. Could she even hope? She hated that any part of her could have come from him. Maybe Furcho was her father. He and her mom were close. Uh, no. He was too young, and she looked even less like Furcho than she did Cyrus. Besides, she could only hope she'd see her mother again. With her brother gone, she was sure Laine would be trying to find where Cyrus had taken Maya.

"Can I ask something else?"

"No. I'm not your father."

"I kind of figured that out already."

He chuckled. "Ask away, then."

"Is Tan a bitch to everybody? Or just to me?"

"Tan's strongly under the influence of Phyrrhos right now. Don't judge her yet."

"I don't know much about her."

"After hours of intricate surgery to reattach a boy's hand this morning, she found out the man assigned to bring the child's mother to the hospital didn't go. So, she commandeered a transport, got the GPS coordinates of their coffee ranch, and went herself. She'd promised her patient that his mother would be there when he woke, and she kept that promise. That's the Tan you should get to know."

That certainly didn't sound like the person Kyle had met. Still, Alyssa seemed to respect Tan, so she must know a different side of her.

"What's the deal with Alyssa? What exactly is First Advocate? Isn't she really young to be in charge? I know she's a healer, but what else? Is she gifted?"

"Yes. She's a very powerful empath." He hesitated. "I guess that as her personal guard, you should know. Only a handful of people are trusted with this information, but she can project as well as detect feelings."

Kyle thought back to the standoff between Jael and Tan at the debriefing earlier and the warm feeling that had washed over her before both Jael and Tan relaxed and Tan backed down. Was that Alyssa? Had Alyssa defused the confrontation between her and Tan when they first met in the hallway of the clinic and were about to throw fireballs at each other? Stars. She was one big ball of world peace all by herself.

"I know what you're thinking. It's not that easy."

"What's a First Advocate?"

"I can never recall one in any of my lifetimes. From what I understand, she answers directly to The Collective, as does Jael, the First Warrior of The Guard."

"Explain The Guard to me."

Titan and Second dropped away, gliding downward. Then Bero and Diego followed before she felt Azar also shift to descend.

"That's our valley below, so I'll save the long version for later. Three units exist around the globe, each with seven members. If they were to unite, Jael would be in charge of all because she is the highest ranking, the oldest soul of all The Guard. Danielle, her cousin, is Second Warrior—that's why everybody calls her Second. I am Third Warrior. The next highest-ranking Guard members lead the other two units in other parts of the world."

Kyle took a mental inventory. "I counted only five of you."

"You haven't met Raven and Michael. They returned here with the rest of the dragon-horse army as soon as the train was recaptured, before the animals transformed at dawn."

She's running atop the length of the train car as pandemonium erupts. Cyrus is jumping down from the next car, chased by Jael's fireball. She gathers herself to tackle Alyssa and hurl the two of them over the side and beyond the spray of bullets. Everything slows and she realizes the night sky is filling with dragon horses carrying warriors who are hurling fireballs at the believers firing upon them and the citizens storming the train.

"Stars. How big is this army?"

"Fewer than a hundred."

"Seemed like a thousand when they filled the sky over the train depot."

Furcho chuckled. "Good to know we make that kind of impression."

Only a few lights shone in the valley below them as they touched down in a large hillside clearing nearby, but Kyle could tell from the shadowy outlines of buildings and the movement of livestock under the weak moonlight that the encampment was the size of a well-established village.

Second waved them over. "Diego and I will fly down to the stables and get a ration of fire rocks for Bero and Titan. He can feed them there and send them to their day meadow. You two wait for Jael and Tan while I find someone to ready the cave stable. I'll hike back with fire rocks for the others. We'll probably have to wait until daylight, when Phyrrhos transforms from dragon to horse, to isolate her. Even then, she'll be a handful."

Furcho nodded. "We'll wait."

Azar raised his head and snorted small puffs of white smoke from his nostrils as the others left. Furcho smiled. "Your rocks are coming, my friend."

"Rocks?" What exactly were fire rocks?

"While they are in dragon form, they crave sulfur and phosphorous to supplement their pyro ability. In the wild, they seek and eat rocks containing those minerals. We, however, feed our dragon horses a concentrated phosphorous manufactured into a hard form that also satisfies their natural desire to crush rocks. That's what those big teeth are for...not eating people or other beasts."

Kyle laughed. "I was wondering about those teeth."

Furcho laughed with her. "You don't want to feel them close around your arm or leg, but they normally use them to crush rocks. Anyway, the fire rocks we feed produce a hotter, blue-white flame. When you have a chance to see a wild dragon horse, you'll notice their flame is the red-yellow flame of a campfire. Not as hot. That's because they're eating the volcanic rocks around here that are mostly just sulfur."

Furcho stood, and Kyle was almost startled as Specter and Phyrrhos dropped from the sky into the clearing farther downhill. Jael dismounted and reached up to help Alyssa down. Specter shook out his wings impatiently, strolling uphill to join Azar in staring at the path that led to the encampment. Second appeared with two buckets, handing one to Furcho and the other to Kyle. She reached in the bucket and held up a hard chunk bigger than her fist.

"Don't get too much on your hand," Second warned her. "Light a fireball with a palm full of that dust and you'll burn your eyebrows off." She gestured toward Specter. "Give this bucket to him. Furcho will walk Azar over there to feed him. They get possessive over their rocks, and you don't want to feed them too close together."

Kyle glanced downhill. "What about Phyrrhos?"

Tan had dismounted but paced a jerky disjointed path between them and Phyrrhos, as if she couldn't decide where she was needed most. Her expression was as fierce as the flame-colored dragon horse that bucked, wings unfurled as she trotted back and forth.

"She won't eat while she's in season, and the last thing we want is to fuel her flame right now."

"Okay." Kyle turned toward Specter but stumbled and fell when Phyrrhos screamed. Stars, that was loud. Her ears still ringing, she scrambled to pick up the rocks she'd spilled while keeping an eye on the agitated mare. Second stooped next to her and scooped up a few rocks. "Sorry."

Second's smile was easy and reassuring. "Don't worry about it. She made me jump out of my skin, too."

Kyle approached Specter cautiously, but he seemed concerned only about the bucket of rocks she carried. He plunged his nose into it before she had a chance to settle it on the ground, and she laughed. "Easy. Nobody's going to take your rocks."

The grinding sound was awful, but she closed her eyes and pretended for a moment that the sound was her own dragon horse chowing down. She moved to Specter's shoulder and scratched the top of his withers with her nails. Most horses liked that, so she figured dragon horses would, too. He twitched a wing and lifted it, so she took a chance and scratched under where it joined his shoulder. The crunching stopped for a second, and he made a contented noise before he resumed eating. She smiled and scratched some more.

The moon slipped behind clouds again, and Kyle squinted to make out the shapes of the others in the clearing. One of those shapes approached.

"The night is always darkest just before dawn," Furcho said.

"That's what Mom used to say," Kyle said. She missed her mother. And her sister. Everything was happening, changing so fast, she hadn't even had time to mourn the loss of her brother. "What's the big discussion about?"

Jael and Second were arguing with Tan while Alyssa watched. Tan repeatedly broke away, pacing between them and Phyrrhos. The mare's agitation grew with Tan's distress.

"Dragon horses aren't like regular horses. They rarely cycle into breeding season if they are bonded, and, well, it's a difficult time for their warrior, too. It's hard to think clearly. Jael doesn't feel this is a good time for Phyrrhos to breed. She needs all of The Guard battle-ready, not pregnant and unpredictable. But Tan is influenced by Phyrrhos, and she's resistant to confining her until her heat passes."

"How long will that take? We're supposed to be tracking Cyrus." Maybe Jael would come up with a different plan. That would be fine with her. She'd rather just bond with a dragon horse and melt into the army. She'd be happy if she never had to see her father again. She certainly wasn't looking forward to going on assignment alone with the volatile Tan.

Furcho shrugged. "Two weeks, maybe three. If she were to breed, the heat could subside in a few days. That's what Tan is arguing for. Come on. Let's see who's winning."

They joined Alyssa, who stood, arms crossed over her chest, expression grim as she watched Jael and Second argue with Tan. Kyle felt protective, possessive…no, jealous. Of what? She followed Alyssa's gaze and watched the body language between Tan and Jael. The First Warrior was shifting away when Tan approached, her eyes following Jael's every movement. It was Second, not Jael, who put a hand on Tan's arm, wrapped an arm over her shoulders, then discreetly stepped between Jael and Tan as the three negotiated.

Furcho's glance held a warning. Kyle was about to hear something else she should keep to herself.

"Alyssa, their history together was only physical. Tan knows Jael's soul belongs to you," he said. "You know she respects that. Tan respects you. It's just that her bond with Phyrrhos is keeping her from thinking clearly."

Alyssa's shoulders sagged and she dropped her arms. "I know."

The moon reappeared, and Phyrrhos glittered as she fluttered her wings and pranced in an odd but beautiful display. Her scream was met by one from Specter, who chased Azar until he rose into the sky and disappeared. Specter flashed his wings at Phyrrhos and spit a stream of fire into the night.

"Son of a volcano," Furcho muttered. "This is not good."

Kyle had grown up in an agricultural community. It was pretty clear what was about to happen if they didn't do something. She thought quickly. Tan did respect Alyssa. She'd seen it in the clinic and again in the debriefing. Alyssa had been able to calm her. "So, maybe Jael isn't the best one to handle Tan. Maybe Alyssa should try. Maybe that would settle Phyrrhos down enough for Jael to get Specter to the day meadow before we have a breeding right here."

They stared at her.

"Out of the mouths of babes," Furcho said.

"It might work," Alyssa said, taking a deep breath and leading them to the arguing trio.

Tan's dark eyes were glassy bright, and sweat beaded along her scalp and dripped from her jaw. Second stood between her and Jael, both her hands on Tan's shoulders, pressing her back. "Think, Tan. Think. You do not want them to breed. Calm Phyrrhos."

Alyssa stepped forward and took Tan's clenched fist in her hands, pulling the fingers open and stroking them. She spoke quietly. "Tanisha. We are all your friends. No one wishes any harm for you or Phyrrhos."

Kyle could swear that if she closed her eyes, the clearing around her would burst into sunshine and wildflowers. How did Alyssa do that? She felt drowsy but fought to watch Tan's face relax. Alyssa edged between Second and Tan.

"You are important to us, as a friend and an important officer of The Guard. You're a talented physician. You're a loyal warrior and intelligent leader. And you're the best tracker in The Guard. We need that skill more than ever right now. The Collective is counting on you. Your friends are counting on you. I'm counting on you. Please, calm Phyrrhos and let us do what's best for her in these unusual circumstances."

Furcho tugged Kyle from the spell Alyssa was weaving, and she shook herself to concentrate on his whisper. "Go get the buckets and wait by the path to the encampment. Jael is going to deal with Specter. Second and I will take up position to engage Phyrrhos if we need to distract her until sunrise."

The night was still very dark, but a faint light shone toward the east. The dragon horses would transform to normal horses soon. The moon showed from behind the clouds again just enough for her to see the two buckets, now empty and turned on their sides. She hurried toward them but snagged her boot on a rock or a root. Her momentum tumbled her a few yards down the incline of the hillside before she managed to catch herself. Sun, she needed some sleep. She was never this clumsy. They must think her a bumbling idiot. Something jabbed into her ribs, and she tugged an uneaten fire rock from under her body. She stood quickly and brushed the grass and damp soil from her clothes. Nothing seemed to be hurt. Maybe it was still dark enough that nobody saw her fall. A loud snort sounded directly behind her and she froze. She could see Specter's pale form several meters uphill. The other dragon horses had all left the clearing. That left only—

Kyle turned slowly. Phyrrhos towered over her, a bare half meter away with her wings fully extended and canted forward as if intending to swat Kyle like a pesky fly. One exhale would incinerate her before she could raise her hands to block it with a firewall of her own. The red slits of the dragon horse's pupils pulsed, and Kyle felt a strange pull. She closed her eyes and tried to focus, to latch onto it. The stench of sulfur breath made her cough, and she opened her eyes to find Phyrrhos' nose centimeters from hers. Ears working back and forth, Phyrrhos snuffled along Kyle's neck and sleeve, then her hand where she'd scratched Specter. Her wings fluttered faintly and lowered, and then Phyrrhos carefully took the fire rock from Kyle's other hand.

"I'm sorry. They said you wouldn't want any rocks, or I would have saved you more," Kyle said. Her words were lost amid the crunching and grinding of teeth against rock, but Phyrrhos' head bobbed as if she understood.

The sky was growing lighter, and as soon as Phyrrhos ate the fire rock, she folded her wings. They seemed to shimmer and gradually disappear, along with the horny ridges running down her face. Her pupils morphed from red slits to dark, round pools. All that remained of the dragon was the coppery hide that glittered even brighter under the rising sun as she trotted over to her bonded.

Tan, her expression unreadable, stared at Kyle. Alyssa still stroked Tan's back and talked in soothing tones. Furcho and Second were converging on them from the edges of the clearing, but Kyle hesitated. She was uncertain of her place among them, or if she belonged among them at all. She stiffened when a strong hand gripped her shoulder.

"For a minute there, I thought you were cinders."

Kyle's face grew warm as Jael studied her with questions in her eyes, but Kyle didn't feel a mental probe she knew Jael was capable of initiating.

"Me, too." Should she tell Jael about the strange pull she'd felt? Stars. She didn't even know what to call it. It was probably just Alyssa's calming influence on Tan flowing through Phyrrhos. Yeah. That was probably it. "I guess Alyssa calmed Tan just in time."

"Maybe." Jael's gaze didn't waver. "Let's hope that's all it is." She gave Kyle's shoulder a rough pat. "Let's join them."

Kyle fell into step behind Jael. What did Jael mean? What else could have caused Phyrrhos' reaction? She had so many questions, but she'd always been an observer rather than an interrogator. She'd hold her tongue until she had more information and could ask better questions. She didn't want them to think she was a klutz and an idiot.

"What did you do to her?" Tan stepped around Jael and snarled at Kyle.

"I let her take the fire rock that was in my hand. Second said she wouldn't eat, but didn't say not to feed her."

Kyle exceeded Tan's height slightly and didn't back down as Tan came chest to chest, nose to nose with her. Their voices rose with each exchange.

"I shouldn't have to tell you not to touch another warrior's dragon horse. You were lucky she didn't fry you."

"If it were up to you, I'd probably be a pile of ashes right now."

"You're right about that."

"Son of a dung eater. What have I done to make you hate me?"

"You're breathing my air."

A loud snort sprayed both of their faces and they instantly broke apart, wiping away wet sooty horse snot with their sleeves or shirttails—anything available. Jael crossed her arms over her chest, looking amused while the others laughed.

"Phyrrhos, that is so nasty." Tan glared at her bonded, who stomped her front hoof and swished her tail impatiently. "Okay, okay." They pressed foreheads together, and Phyrrhos swished her tail angrily several times at the mental pictures Tan was showing her.

"Sweet feed," Kyle whispered to no one.

Jael glanced at Kyle.

Show her there'll be a bucket of sweet feed in the paddock.

Kyle blinked, nearly missing Tan's signal that Jael's telepathic message had been received. How did she do that? Had Jael broadcast that to everyone standing there or just to her and Tan—like copying her on a forwarded d-message?

Tan pulled back at last, her shoulders sagging. "She'll go."

Second stepped forward to slip a rope over the horse's head. "I'll take her up. Furcho's going to drive you to the village and put you on the train to San Pedro Sula."

Tan tensed, instantly vibrating again like a taut bow string, and snatched the rope from Second. "No. I'm not leaving Phyrrhos."

Alyssa put a hand on Jael's arm to stop her from going to Tan. Kyle didn't know these women well enough to understand what to do if a disagreement erupted. Jael was obviously in charge. But, for reasons she couldn't imagine, her every instinct screamed to protect Tan.

Furcho defused the confrontation, flinging a casual arm over Tan's shoulders. "Diego has arranged everything—a very private luxury house where you can relax for a week. It has a hot tub and sauna."

"No. I'm not going anywhere." Tan pushed his arm from her shoulders, but Furcho was quick. He grasped her jaw firmly and brought his face close to hers, but his voice was gentle.

"You need to separate from Phyrrhos. It will be better for both of you." He smiled. "Besides, Anya is waiting for you in San Pedro."

"Anya's here?" Tan's rich brown eyes grew bright, and her pink tongue swiped over her lips as though tasting something unseen. Kyle's body heated and her belly clenched. With everything that had happened in the past months, she couldn't remember the last time she'd felt aroused. But the raw need in Tan's expression had instantly jerked her to the edge.

"In San Pedro Sula. Are you ready?"

Tan glanced at Phyrrhos, who was grazing quietly. In horse form, she was calm and only excitable in the presence of a stallion.

"She'll be fine," Second said. "We'll put another mare in with her, so she'll have company." She gently took the rope from Tan.

Tan nodded wordlessly, then trotted toward the path that led to the encampment and transportation to the train. Furcho followed close behind.

When they disappeared down the trail, Second let out a loud breath. "That was easier than I thought."

"Who's Anya?" Alyssa looked from one warrior to the next when no answer was forthcoming. Furcho made an "X" sign over his mouth. Jael scratched her ear and stared at the ground.

Was the prickly Tan soul-bonded to someone? Hadn't Furcho said Tan and Jael used to have a casual arrangement? If she was bonded to another, she shouldn't desire Jael, unless she was polyamorous. They weren't a huge percentage of the population in the area where she lived, but in some parts of the world this practice was fairly common because of an imbalance in the gender ratio or customs of the local culture.

Second cleared her throat. "She's, uh, a therapist that can help, you know, during this kind of thing. I mean, well, any time really. She and Tan have had a professional relationship for, I don't know, years. You know how wound up Tan can get. A few sessions with Anya, and she purges all that built-up tension." She looked to Jael. "Right, cousin?"

"Right. A therapist." Jael's sarcastic tone was clear. Subject closed.

Second shrugged. "Kyle, why don't you come with me to put the mare up? Then we'll find you a bunk to call your own. I'll write some orders to get you outfitted, too, since all you seem to have are the clothes on your back."

"Thanks, that'd be great." Kyle struggled to stand upright as Phyrrhos rubbed her nose up and down her back. Jael and Second stared for a moment, then shared an unreadable look but said nothing about the mare's sudden affection for Kyle.

"We're going to get some rest," Jael finally said, taking Alyssa's hand in hers. "I want you to do the same, Second, as soon as the mare and Kyle are bedded down."

Second started to protest, but Jael held up her hand. "That's an order. I don't want to hear you prowling around until noon. You might be able to keep me out of your thoughts, but you know I can still feel you."

Second smiled and dipped her head in acknowledgement. "As you command."

Chapter Four

The surgeon carefully wrapped a fresh bandage around Simon's damaged right hand. "You'll need another seven days of treatments to form new skin over the burns, especially over the knuckles of the three fingers that were burned off." He finished the bandage and gave his handiwork a satisfied nod.

Simon grimaced. The anesthesia was wearing off and his hand throbbed. If he ever saw Cyrus's pyro whelp again, he would slice her to pieces with the new laser gun holstered backward in front of his right hip. He was already practiced at drawing and firing with his left hand.

"I can't stay. I have to be in Brasília in three days." It wasn't difficult to find a doctor who would accept a generous amount of credits to fix his hand without questions, but he didn't need to waste time searching again in Brasília. "You can come with me and bring the equipment you need."

The man stood, cleaning up the instruments and procedure's detritus on the metal table next to them. "I'm sorry. I have patients no one else will help and a full surgery schedule. I can't leave. Not even for a few days."

In one quick movement, Simon pulled the laser and used the forearm of his damaged appendage to pin the doctor's hand as he reached for some soiled gauze. He held the weapon over the man's fingers. "You know about lasers, don't you, Doctor? I'm sure you're still allowed to use them in surgery."

The doctor stared at the weapon but didn't speak.

"This is a much bigger laser. Instead of skimming off a cornea or sealing a bleeder, this one will cut right through this table. In fact, right through your wrist. I could cut your hand into so many pieces there'd be no hope of reattaching it."

The doctor jerked when the laser activated and its red beam silently sliced through the metal exam table. He tried to pull away as the beam inched toward his hand. "Do you understand?"

The doctor nodded, and Simon extinguished the laser but still held the man and weapon in place.

"My guard will accompany you to your office, where you will instruct your assistant that you will be gone for at least a week and your schedule must be cleared. Then you will call your wife and tell her to pack you a suitcase. I'll send someone to pick it up. You will take whatever supplies you need from the clinic here. You will stay with my people tonight. We leave in the morning." He released the man and stepped back.

The doctor met Simon's gaze, but his voice held a faint tremble. "I don't want to inconvenience you. My wife can bring my bag to me."

"It's no trouble. We already know where your family lives. You have two lovely daughters, Doctor. My people, of course, will look after them until my treatments are complete and you can return home." Simon smiled. Credits could buy a lot of things, but only fear could buy absolute loyalty.

❖

"Jael, honey?"

"Hmm?"

Alyssa was half draped over Jael's body, both naked as usual. The mild winter was short in this region and still another month away. "Can you turn it down a notch or two? You're making me sweat."

"Oh, sorry." Jael consciously lowered her body temperature. "Better?"

"Yes." Alyssa propped up on her elbow. "What are you worrying about?"

"I don't worry."

"Yes, you do."

"I evaluate scenarios."

Alyssa smiled and dropped small kisses along the top of Jael's shoulder. "My mistake. Let me rephrase. What are you evaluating?" She continued her kisses across the opposite shoulder.

Jael stroked her hand along Alyssa's back while she searched for the words to explain her thoughts. "I was wondering about Phyrrhos' odd behavior. She should have incinerated Kyle for stumbling between her and the stallion she was courting."

Alyssa looked up, surprise flickering across her face. "You sound disappointed that she didn't."

Jael chuckled. "No. Of course not. *Why* Kyle isn't a pile of ashes is what worries me...I mean, what I'm evaluating."

"So, what are the possible scenarios? You must have seen something like this before. How many lifetimes have you been a dragon-horse warrior?" Alyssa yawned. They'd had only a few hours of sleep in the past two days, and Jael now regretted stealing these precious minutes of rest from her.

"As many as I can remember." Jael didn't want to put ideas in her empathic lover's head, but she was honestly trying to be more open. "It happened once with two warriors who later soul-bonded. It seemed the dragon horse recognized their chemistry before they did."

"That one's hard to believe. I don't know why, but Tan has taken an irrational dislike to Kyle."

"Tan is hardly herself right now. She's heavily under the influence of Phyrrhos' fever to breed."

"Will she be okay?" Alyssa lightly bit the soft skin at the top of Jael's breast. "Who's Anya?"

Jael sighed. "She's a professional."

"I'm guessing you don't mean professional therapist."

"Uh, not the way you mean it."

"Just tell me, Jael."

"Some things aren't mine to share, babe, even with you. But I'll tell you as much as possible without violating Tan's privacy too much." She took a deep breath. "Tan has certain sexual appetites that require special handling. She's a complex person, much more sensitive than people realize. She internalizes everything like a pressure cooker. And when she's about to explode from the pressure, she blows off some steam with Anya."

Alyssa considered this explanation for a moment, her expression and her thoughts suddenly unreadable. "Did you…did she ever blow off steam with you?"

Jael smiled and shook her head. "Not my style."

Alyssa's expression, her body, and her shields relaxed again. Right answer. "Good. That's good. Next scenario." She yawned out the words and laid her head on Jael's shoulder. Jael stopped her stroking and settled their bodies comfortably together as she felt Alyssa go limp.

"Kyle had been touching Specter. Phyrrhos could have just been responding to the scent of Specter on Kyle's hands and clothes."

Alyssa's slow, even breathing filled Jael with a lethargy she hoped would also lull her brain into the sleep she needed. She whispered the last possibility so she didn't rouse Alyssa. Or maybe she didn't want to give substance to this final daunting theory. It was only legend. But the situation could be delicate even in normal times, and now, given Tan's current dislike for Kyle, it could be disastrous.

"It could be the first salvo of a prenatal bonding."

❖

"I don't know why you're flying to Brasília and I'm going to be stuck on some stinking fishing boat for a week to cross the Gulf back to the Third Continent." Cyrus was The Prophet. The One spoke to him, lived in him. They were becoming the same. Simon was a credit-grabbing, soulless husk of a human. Cyrus wanted to take Simon's bandaged hand, that reminder that his own daughter was a deviant pyro, and cram it into his big mouth the next time he started ordering the men around like he was in charge.

Simon tapped the digital gauge of the medical cuff on his forearm. The device partially interrupted the nerve impulses traveling from his hand to his brain, dulling his pain without mind-numbing drugs. Cyrus took some perverse satisfaction in knowing that the hand was bothering him enough to increase the scrambling voltage. He'd heard the doctor warn Simon that becoming dependent on the cuff could damage the nerves permanently and atrophy his arm. But Simon always thought he was smarter than everyone else, even doctors. Simon turned to him, his expression akin to a parent placating a sulking child. Cyrus hoped his stupid hand curled up and fell off.

"It isn't a fishing boat, Cyrus. It's an eighty-four-foot sailing yacht. It's like a floating hotel with your own quarters. The three-man crew will be running the boat, so you and your two guards will have to cook your own meals. But think of this as a vacation. You can try your hand at deep-sea fishing. Relax in the sun. Get a tan. I'll take care of things in Brasília and then let you know when we're ready for the next step."

Cyrus stood, pushing his face close to Simon's. "I will not rest until The Natural Order has been restored to this world. I am the one who is chosen. I will tell you when and where our next step will be."

The four men trusted to travel with Simon and Cyrus shifted uneasily at the other end of the long room. They were believers. They belonged to him. Simon glanced at them and sighed. Cyrus swelled with victory.

"I can fly because the authorities aren't looking for me," Simon said. "They're looking for you. You can't get through an airport or travel by train or transport through the Third Continent checkpoint. The only way is by water. I didn't want to tell you yet, because I wasn't sure we could arrange it soon enough, but it looks like we'll have the digital net hacked by the time you arrive at the new headquarters, uh, temple. You can use the time at sea to prepare the messages you want to broadcast."

Cyrus stared at him. Maybe he would keep Simon around awhile longer. He did have skills and contacts that were moving their plan along faster than Cyrus had ever imagined.

"Very well. I'll expect to hear from you after you've secured the Fourth Continent's main supply house in Brasília."

Simon nodded. "It should be about two weeks. When you go ashore, a team will meet you and escort you to your destination in the Rocky Mountains." He smiled. "You'll love the City of Light, Cyrus. It was designed and built at the top of a mountain, fit for The Prophet that you are."

"City of Light," Cyrus said. "I like that."

❖

Second looped the soft cotton rope into a slip halter over Phyrrhos' head but chuckled as she handed the lead line to Kyle. "I'm not sure this is even necessary."

After rubbing her entire face along the back of Kyle's shirt, Phyrrhos rested her chin on Kyle's shoulder and began lipping playfully at her collar. Kyle grinned and waved her hand in front of her face. "I'm glad she likes me, but, whew, that sulfur breath is something else."

Second laughed. "You'll get used to it."

They took a different path through the forest that led to a hillside on the southern end of the valley, opposite the direction the others had taken. Some distance above the training fields and livestock pastures, a large paddock—enough room for a restless horse to have a good trot or roll in the grass—extended from the mouth of a shallow cave.

A lone figure waited at the gate of the paddock, holding the lead of a dappled gray draft mare. Kyle thought it was a dark-haired boy at first, then realized it was a young woman. Her short, lean frame was coiled tight, brown eyes defiant as they met Kyle's.

"Good morning, Corporal Antonia." Second snapped a salute, right fist to left shoulder.

The young woman reddened, straightening her posture and executing a belated salute. "Commander." Her voice was edged with bitterness.

Second looked over the mare. "Good choice. Very good choice."

Toni didn't answer, but the muscles in her jaw worked as though only her clenched teeth were holding back a reply.

Kyle looked from commander to corporal. What now? Hanging out with this group was worse than walking through a minefield. Big horse lips closed on her ear, and she pushed Phyrrhos' nose away when sharp teeth tested the durability of its cartilage. "Ow. Stop it, sulfur breath. That's my ear, not a fire rock." She stopped, realizing she'd spoken aloud. She sighed. She was never going to learn to act like a warrior. But when she looked up, Second's expression was amused. Toni's scowl was unchanged.

Second turned back to Toni, her expression softening. "Did you want to ask me something, Toni?"

Toni stared straight ahead. "Am I being assigned back to the stable, ma'am?"

Second smiled. "No. I'm sorry I didn't make that clear. The First Advocate would be very unhappy if I reassigned her most trusted assistant, and then I'd have to answer to the First Warrior for making her bond mate unhappy. I only requested you for this duty as a favor...in addition to your duties at the clinic."

Toni's posture relaxed, and she gave Kyle a curious look. "That's Captain Tan's mare, isn't it?"

"Yes," Second said. "And I'm afraid her dragon is going into season, which is really bad timing."

Kyle pushed Phyrrhos' nose away again and held her hand out to Toni. "Hi, I'm Kyle."

Second rubbed at her temple. "Sorry. I'm so tired, I forgot to introduce you."

Toni took Kyle's hand in hers, hesitating a split second before squeezing a bit too firmly, then immediately disengaging to step back.

Second didn't seem to notice. "Captain Tan will be gone for a week. So, I need you two to listen very carefully and do exactly as I say."

She opened the gate and gestured for them to release the horses into the enclosure. The gray mare, older and more sedate, began to munch on a patch of tender clover. Phyrrhos stood erect, head raised to survey the valley below. She called out in a loud whinny, but when no answering call came, she settled down to graze alongside the other mare.

Second led Kyle and Toni to the cave. The ceiling was high enough for a horse to move about comfortably, but the cave wasn't spacious enough for a dragon horse to fully unfurl wings. A thick, sliding double door of fire-resistant metal covered the entrance, except for a narrow strip left open at the top to let in fresh air and moonlight.

"Kyle, you'll put Phyrrhos in here every night before dark. Toni, you'll take the gray down to the stable. Once Phyrrhos transforms, she'll be crazy with hormones and could hurt the old mare. You both will return after sunrise and put Phyrrhos and the mare in the paddock for the day."

"I can handle it myself," Kyle offered. "I don't have anything else to do until Tan returns, but Toni has other duties."

Second contemplated Kyle, then turned to Toni. "Corporal?"

"Yes, Commander."

"Kyle, here, wants to be a dragon-horse warrior. But she's just coming on board, so she's missed a lot of the training. I'm hoping you can help her catch up on the basics of military life."

"Me, Commander?"

Second smiled warmly and clapped her hand on Toni's shoulder to take any sting out of her words. "Well, I figure if there's something that'll trip her up, you've already found it. So, who's the best person to show her the ropes?"

Toni's ears reddened, but the corner of her lip quirked up in tiny smile. "That would be me."

"And what'd she just do wrong?"

Toni looked up at Kyle, tossing her head to flick her overlong bangs out of her eyes. "Never interrupt until your commander has completed her instructions."

Really? This kid was going to teach her to be a warrior? "I was just—"

Toni held up a finger. "Never interrupt." She looked to Second, who nodded for her to continue. "You are questioning the efficiency of the commander's plan before you have all the information. You are allowed to suggest alternatives, but don't make yourself look stupid by doing that before you know everything that has to be considered."

Second nodded. "Well said, Corporal."

Exhausted, Kyle felt her anger start slowly and crawl up her spine. She wasn't in the mood to be lectured by a low-ranking corporal. Her hands itched to flame, until Toni shrugged and grinned.

"Took me several times to get that one through my head. I'm not called Toni the Pony just because I'm short." Toni knocked her fist against her skull. "It's mostly because I'm a bit hardheaded."

Second clapped her hands together. "Back to why you both need to be here." She slid the doors to the cave so that they nearly closed. "A dragon horse and its bonded warrior can become irrational for several reasons. That's why this enclosure was built. The locking mechanism requires two people to operate it simultaneously. That way a frenzied warrior can't release his or her dragon and endanger the rest of the camp."

She positioned Kyle on one side and Toni on the other, showing them three digits each must alternately tap in for the locking mechanism to lock, then reverse the numbers to release. "It's simple. The code isn't mysterious. You just have to type the numbers in one immediately after the other, so it's impossible for one person to do it unless they have an arm span of ten feet. The easiest way to do it is to call your number out as you punch it in so your partner can immediately press the next number. One-two-three-four, and so on." She signaled them to each push from their ends, so that the doors closed together with a click. "Let's give it a try."

Kyle and Toni failed the first time because Kyle hesitated once, but Second encouraged them. "That's good. Now you know how quickly you have to respond."

They had a few failures trying to count backward to open the gate, and Kyle was surprised that Second let them dissolve into hysterical laughter at their own bumbling before she quieted them, coached them to take a few deep breaths, and congratulated them for completing the next three attempts successfully.

She was startled when Second grabbed them both by the shoulders of their shirts and pulled them close. All trace of their easy-going commander disappeared, replaced by a hard edge. Jael seemed to have surfaced in Second's body. Kyle's hands heated in a defensive response. "I don't care what you're doing. Do *not* let time slip up on you. Be up here every day *before* dark."

"Sure, Commander," Toni said. "We won't forget."

❖

Toni stood outside the quartermaster building with Second, wondering again why the commander didn't go with Kyle instead of sending her inside with a list of clothing and other necessities for the sergeant on duty to fill. Second was in charge of the entire quartermaster unit. She could have fifteen people scrambling to stuff two duffels full in under a minute. Instead, Commander Second sat propped against a porch support with her eyes closed and face raised to the morning sun.

Toni stared down the wide dirt lane that was the main artery of the camp. The line into the dining building was fairly short. She shifted her feet, unsure why she hadn't been dismissed to go about her day. Stars, she'd been summoned at daybreak, sent to the cold stables to get a horse and haul it up the hillside. She hadn't had a shower or breakfast, and she would be expected at the clinic in another hour.

"I want Kyle to bunk with you."

Toni jerked in surprise. "With me?"

"You moved out of the barracks into the Advocate's cottage, right?"

"Alyssa, I mean the First Advocate, thought it would be better since my schedule in the clinic is so different from that of the people assigned to the barracks. I stay up really late some nights working on their inventory." She felt pathetic. They both knew that Alyssa had rescued her from the barracks. But Second only nodded.

The cottage had three bedrooms. Nicole and Uri lived in the two small bedrooms, and Alyssa had occupied the large one. But when she moved in with Jael, they'd changed the large room to twin beds for visiting Advocates. Of course, they'd never had any, so Alyssa had insisted that Toni bunk there.

"Kyle won't be here long. As soon as we get Phyrrhos straightened out, she and Tan will leave on assignment."

"She's a pyro. Wouldn't she be more comfortable with the warriors?"

Second sat on the steps of the building, and Toni suddenly felt she was speaking with a friend, eye to eye.

"She's a very potent but untrained pyro." Second lowered her voice. "And she might have a bit of a problem fitting in."

Toni stared at the ground. Like she couldn't seem to fit. But Kyle? She couldn't see it. "She's built like a warrior, great looking, and you say she's a blazer of a torch. Why wouldn't she fit in?"

"That's her story to tell." Second glanced toward the door Kyle would exit. "I grabbed you both by the collar a while ago for a reason."

"I thought she might combust."

"Exactly. She needs to learn more control. If I bunk her in the barracks and some smart-ass starts in on her and decides to test her flame, she'll fry 'em."

"She's that hot?"

"Yeah. With a little training, she might be as hot as Jael."

"Wow."

Second grinned. "So don't make your new roomie mad, okay?"

"Thanks a lot." Toni tried to scowl, but she was sure she didn't quite pull it off. Inside, she swelled with pride that Second had chosen her for this special assignment. "If she wants to leave the light on all night to read, I guess I'll have to sleep with a pillow on my head."

Second stood and clapped her on the back. "Nah. I'll requisition you a sleep mask."

They both turned at the sound of cursing and jumped onto the porch to help Kyle with the two fully packed duffels she was struggling to drag through the doorway.

"I've got this, Commander," Toni said, shouldering one of the duffels while Kyle took the other.

Second smiled. "Then I'll leave you in good hands, Kyle. Get some rest. Come up to the headquarters building for lunch if you don't sleep through it. If you do, then dinner is at seventeen hundred. We drill at night, so the warriors sleep most of the day." A jaunty salute and she was gone.

"Come on. It's your lucky day," Toni said. "You're assigned to bunk with me."

Kyle raised an eyebrow. "You're not really my type."

Toni eyed her. Not flirting, she decided. Just joking. Like a friend. She didn't have any real friends. Well, Alyssa, Nicole, and Uri. But Alyssa and Nicole were occupied most of the time with Jael and Furcho. And Uri? He kept to himself a lot. "You're not my type either, but Commander Second says we're kind of alike."

"Yeah? How's that?"

"We're both outsiders." Toni let that remark sink in, but Kyle's face was a mask. "She didn't tell me why you're an outsider."

Kyle sighed and rubbed her face. "Then we're even. She hasn't told me anything about you either."

They stepped onto the porch of the cottage, and the weariness that shadowed Kyle's gaunt features now that they were out of the bright sunlight surprised Toni.

"Are you hungry? The dining hall's open for breakfast."

"I'm past hunger. I'm just so tired I could fall down."

Toni led her inside and showed her the bed, already made with clean sheets and a soft blanket. A fan whirled quietly overhead. "I meant that you were lucky to be bunking in my room because the cottage has its own personal facility, right down the hall. You don't have to walk four buildings down the street to the communal facility."

"Sweet. I'm dying for a shower if I can stay awake ten more minutes."

"I'll head out then. If you need anything, the headquarters building is next door on your left, or I'll be at the clinic. It's down the lane on the right. There's a sign."

"Thanks." Kyle fiddled with the closure on her duffel. "We'll talk later, okay?"

"Sure. If you want. See you before dark, if not sooner."

Kyle, panic flickering in her eyes, scanned the room. "You have an IC to set a wake-up?"

Toni shook her head. "Forbidden in camp. Don't worry. I'll check to make sure you aren't still sleeping."

When Toni started down the lane to the dining building, the sun seemed brighter, the sky a brilliant blue and the surrounding hills still lush despite impending winter. She'd never thought she'd meet someone with more baggage than she carried. But this Kyle, she had real problems. A pyro warrior without training or a dragon horse, she carried a secret that made her an outcast in her own camp. Why was Phyrrhos, a dragon horse bonded to Captain Tan, acting lovesick over Kyle? Could Kyle be tangled up with

Tan? Stars. Tan could be prickly, but Toni liked her. Still, if the rumors were true about Tan's proclivities, she wouldn't want to be in Kyle's boots.

❖

A single bead of sweat dripped from Tan's chin onto her chest and trickled slowly between her breasts. She could feel everything with acute clarity. The leather biting into her wrists and the painful stretch of her shoulder joints as she hung blindfolded and naked from the sturdy metal rack. The teeth of the clamps biting into her swollen nipples. Every raised, stinging welt striping her back. The throbbing of her clit against the clip holding back the rush of blood that would finally deliver sweet release…and, hopefully, elusive relief.

"Anya knows your shame, Tanisha."

Tan bared her teeth at the low, taunting voice close to her ear, and the excruciating pain of a bamboo cane immediately radiated across her buttocks. She clenched her teeth against the agony but cried out when a second blow followed across her thighs.

"Only Anya knows the dominatrix really wants to be dominated. Isn't that true, Tanisha?"

Tan's refusal to answer earned several more blows on her upper back, and she yelled through the pain, then panted through the aftershocks.

"Isn't that why you follow the First Warrior through lifetime after lifetime, hoping she'll give you what you seek? Because she's the only one who can judge and punish you?"

"No." They both knew she lied.

"You are pathetic." Two more blows.

"Ye-yes." A broken whisper was all she could choke out.

A fingernail raked over the line of agony the cane had cut across her back, then traced over her bottom lip and poked into her mouth. Tan tasted the salt of her sweat and metallic tang of her own blood.

"Tell Anya what you want."

She pulled at her bonds, but she was too tired, too weak, too needy.

"Tell Anya what you need."

Two more blows on her back and buttocks. Still, the pain inside burned greater than what Anya inflicted. She was unable to hold back a weak sob when Anya released the clips and blood rushed into her tortured nipples. "Please."

"Tell me." The whispered demand was gentle this time.

"Fuck me. I need you to fuck me until I'm raw." The call to give herself was so incredibly strong, she felt raw inside. But for the first time, it wasn't Jael who drew her.

CHAPTER FIVE

Try again. It's easy for a pyro with your power to project a hot flame, but you have to learn enough control to also project low flame." Jael set up another row of square wood targets covered by cloth against the stone fence six meters away. She returned and tapped Kyle's temple. "Picture only the cloth burning away."

Kyle stared at the first target, palmed a fireball, and threw it. The fireball struck with a whoosh and only ashes remained. She grumbled under her breath as she palmed another fireball to fling at the next target. "I don't know why I have to learn to turn my flame down. Plenty of low-grade pyros are around if you need somebody to cook dinner."

Kyle's frustration had been growing and gnawing at her since she'd awakened refreshed but inexplicably restless the afternoon before. At loose ends until Tan was ready to travel, she had only to guard Phyrrhos' cavern prison at night. Toni had lingered for several hours after they had locked Phyrrhos in, but she'd worked all day in the clinic and needed to sleep, so Kyle sat the night alone with Phyrrhos' frequent angry screams. Jael had checked on Kyle once, briefly. But Kyle thought it was more to connect with Specter, who flew constant patrols in the sky above to chase off other studs drawn there by Phyrrhos' calls.

Most of the night, Kyle stared at the stars and thought of the others up there training to be dragon-horse warriors, and her anger festered. She would be with them if Cyrus hadn't kept her prisoner in his ridiculous cult. She would be a dragon-horse warrior. She wanted to scream her frustration like Phyrrhos. She was still edgy when she'd released Phyrrhos after her post-dawn transition to a wingless horse, and maintaining control of any kind felt as difficult as wading through knee-deep mud. She'd intended to take a good long run to work out her tension, but Jael had appeared out of the morning mists and escorted her here for fire training before the rest of the camp was awake and moving about.

Jael closed her hand over Kyle's, extinguishing her flame. She grasped Kyle's shoulders and turned her so that she faced an open field. Then she walked six meters away. "Shoot me your hottest flame," she said.

Confused, Kyle glanced to the targets at her left.

"No. Throw your flame at me. Give me the best you've got."

She'd already shown Jael she could burn through wood and bone, and melt almost any metal. What more did she want? She palmed a hot fireball and threw it off center. Jael casually flicked a fireball that intercepted and exploded Kyle's.

"Come on. You can do better than that," Jael said.

Kyle scowled and threw another, this time straight at Jael. Again, Jael deflected it. Kyle threw another, and another in rapid succession, each hotter than the last. Her anger rose with each that Jael nonchalantly intercepted until a red haze filled her mind. She sucked in a deep breath and yelled her frustration, raising her hands over her head and turning them inward. A blue-white column of flame sprouted from each palm and joined into one inferno that shot straight and true. Jael straightened and threw up her hands, palms out. Flame met flame in a broiling firestorm midway between them for a long moment before it moved slowly toward Kyle. Sweat ran down her face as she worked to sustain her flame. Her hands burned. It was too hot, too much.

She'd stupidly challenged the First Warrior, the greatest pyro that walked the earth in this lifetime. The commander to whom she'd pledged her life and service. She deserved the penalty for her insubordination. She dropped her hands and hoped Jael's torch would be quick, but the incinerating heat receded so quickly it merely licked a long painful streak along her cheek. Her face burned with shame more than injury. She couldn't meet Jael's eyes as she approached, even when her overly warm hand settled on Kyle's shoulder.

"Feel any better now that you got that out of your system?"

"I'm an ass."

"In the military ranks, the customary response is 'Yes, First Warrior.'"

Kyle looked up. Jael's eyes were serious but held no judgment. "Yes, First Warrior."

"You're carrying a lot of anger, Kyle. There's a fine line between losing your control and using your anger to your advantage." Jael touched the blister forming on Kyle's cheek. "If I didn't have control of my flame, you'd be ashes right now." She took Kyle's hand and turned it palm up. "Your flame is as hot as any of The Guard, and we're all purebloods. None of the new warriors can produce a flame that hot. How can I let you train with them if you can't temper your heat?"

"I hadn't thought of that."

Jael dropped Kyle's hand and stepped back. "You'll come across other situations, unpleasant ones, when you might need to injure but not kill."

What? Oh. "Like when I melted the gun in Simon's hand so he couldn't fire at the First Advocate again?"

Jael shrugged. "I wouldn't have held back in that instance. Firing on the First Advocate of The Collective is punishable by death. But it's not your burden to judge."

Kyle wondered at Jael's choice of words—burden to judge.

"While on your mission, you might need to disarm a believer who has helpful information. You wouldn't want to turn him to ashes before you question him. Ready to try again?"

"Yes, First Warrior." Kyle turned to the targets and closed her eyes for a moment. She imagined a knife in the hand of a believer, formed her fireball, opened her eyes, and threw it at the target. The cloth burned away, leaving the wood intact but charred.

"Better," Jael said. "Much better. Again."

She closed her eyes again. This time, the image of Tan, dangling at the end of a thick rope tied around her hands, which were encased in fire-retardant gloves, popped into her head. Where had that come from? She opened her eyes as Jael's hand on her shoulder jerked her to the right.

"There." Jael pointed.

Without hesitation, Kyle aimed her index and middle fingers at the sand-filled duffel hanging from a wood frame. A laser-like flame shot from her fingers to burn neatly through the rope where it fastened around the neck of the duffel, and the bag fell.

Silence stretched between them, and then Jael cleared her throat. "Even better than a fireball."

They walked together to the bag and examined it. The rope was burned clear through, but the canvas of the duffel wasn't even scorched.

"I think you've figured it out."

Kyle fingered the canvas and frowned. "I thought I saw—"

"I put that image in your head. Dragon horses think in pictures. If you bond, you'll learn to think like that, too. And since I'm a telepath, I can project my thoughts in pictures."

She frowned. The reminder of Tan had that jumpy feeling eating at her again. She didn't want to be touched right now. Having Jael in her head felt like touching.

"Go to headquarters and tell Second I said to feed you. I want you taking all your meals at headquarters from now on."

Kyle gritted her teeth. She just couldn't stop screwing up. She wasn't certain what she'd done wrong this time, but it must be something if Jael didn't even want her around the other new warriors. Still, Toni had told her that soldiers weren't supposed to question their superiors. "Yes, First Warrior." She couldn't keep the edge out of her voice.

Jael stared across the field long enough that Kyle followed her gaze. People were awake and forming lines for showers and chow. Several had stopped along the lane and were watching them. They were too far away to see insignia, but some wore the black armbands of the dragon-horse warriors.

"Most of The Guard can't do what you just did—shoot a straight, narrow flame from just their fingers," Jael said. "You'll likely be here only another week before you and Tan go after Cyrus. We've already found one spy in camp. I don't think it's a good idea to let it leak out that your father's The Prophet. So, it's probably best if you don't mingle a lot and give people a chance to ask questions."

Kyle nodded. Wow. The knot in her stomach loosened a bit. She could do something some of The Guard couldn't? "Yes, First Warrior."

"Good. Go. Eat. Sleep. That's an order."

❖

Tan crept through the forest, a silent shadow slithering from tree to tree. Not even Anya could cool the fire that still burned inside her. So when she'd slept, Tan had gnawed through her bindings like an animal and slunk back to camp. Phyrrhos' heat called her. Laser-blue eyes called her.

She'd been watching since before daylight. The new sparkler kept a restless guard at the mouth of her dragon horse's prison. The screams of her bonded tore at her. She licked her lips. The sparkler was tall and leanly muscled. Her short dark hair set off a long jaw and handsome features. She would like to have that under her or between her legs. Her sex, raw and tender from Anya's treatment, burned as she slickened with arousal. Focus. She needed to focus.

The first rays of dawn filtered over the mountains. She'd need to free Phyrrhos at twilight, not dawn, when Specter was flying about since she'd clearly chosen him to sire. There were things she'd need to do to prepare.

Tan watched Toni trudge up the hill, leading the old mare who would be Phyrrhos' daytime companion. After checking the high, narrow window in the gate, Kyle and Toni activated the dual controls to release Phyrrhos into the paddock with the mare. She raced around the enclosure a few times, then settled down to graze.

Tan watched the two young women. The sparkler was in constant motion, her movements jerky and quick. Tan considered this activity. Was Phyrrhos' heat affecting her, too? Her blood quickened, her own breathing loud in her ears. She felt exhilarated and a little possessive—of Phyrrhos, of course. She had no real interest in the sparkler, although a jump with her could be pretty hot. She licked her lips, imagining the taste of that long, firm torso under her tongue. Would the sparkler seduce Toni the Pony into a little ride? Maybe she'd sneak along behind them to watch.

While the sun warmed the mountain peaks around them, a thin, cool mist had settled over the valley the same way the breeding fever was clouding Tan's normally logical mental processes. That's why she nearly missed Jael striding up the hill toward the younger women. Tan twitched. Her need hadn't lessened when Phyrrhos transformed to her daytime wingless form, and Jael's appearance amped the pressure.

Tan hesitated when Jael led Kyle to the far end of the training fields. Jael normally shielded out random thoughts of the people around her, but Specter's interest in Phyrrhos obviously affected Jael. Would she sense Tan's need if she got too close? Still, Tan paralleled them, staying just inside the woods, and climbed a sturdy tree to observe.

Sun and moon. This sparkler had real heat. Tan watched Jael coach her, like she'd schooled each of them in this and past lives. She leaned forward, nearly losing her footing when Jael walked several meters away and challenged Kyle. The name formed in her mind like a pearl, perfect and iridescent. Sun and stars! She was holding back Jael's flame. Tan tightened her hold on the branch to steady herself and silently rooted for Kyle. When Jael won out but extinguished her flame at the last nano-second, Tan felt every muscle in her body relax in relief.

For a moment, her head cleared of Phyrrhos' frenzy, and she felt ridiculous sitting in a tree when she should be starting rounds in the clinic below or, more importantly, gathering information to go after Cyrus.

It was only a brief respite. Tan's breath caught as Jael jerked Kyle to face the canvas duffle. A razor-thin stream of fire shot from Kyle's fingers to cleanly burn through the rope that held it suspended. Dung. Not a sparkler. A blazer.

❖

"Whoa, whoa, whoa." Second wrapped an arm around Jael's shoulders and steered her toward the headquarters' prep area. "Yes, she's still up there. I think you wore the poor woman out last night."

Jael shrugged her cousin's arm away. "Shut up." She was edgy. She'd expected the backwash from Specter's desire to breed Phyrrhos. That was simple to remedy with Tan gone and her soulbond, Alyssa, more than willing to quench her sexual thirst. But she hadn't expected to feel Phyrrhos' call to Specter so strongly through Kyle. She'd just made two loops of her usual morning run to dissipate some of the sexual tension, and she was still throbbing so bad Second was starting to look good.

"I don't like that look," Second said, grabbing Jael's hand and turning it over to plop a small dark cake in her palm.

"I'm not eating that." Jael stared down at the chocolate treat. "That's one of your specials, isn't it?" When they were young and reckless, Second would mix the herbs and bake them into a chewy chocolate-cake batter. Then they'd eat a few and lie in the meadow for hours to stare at the stars as the herbs slowed their brains and dulled their focus.

"You need to calm down. Just one piece, a cold shower, and a good jump will take your edge off. Then eat another piece and try to sleep so Alyssa can come down and get some breakfast. I know you walked the camp half the night after you exhausted her. You're no good to us like you are."

Jael rocked on her feet. She couldn't stand still for even a few seconds.

"Kyle's already been through here. She looked exhausted but as tense as you, so I gave her a huge breakfast burrito and a couple of my specials for dessert so she'll sleep."

Jael considered admonishing her cousin, then relented. The herbs were harmless—both medicinal and recreational. She popped the treat into her mouth and then scooped up two more while she chewed.

Second pointed to the stairs. "Straight to the shower. Do not touch her until you stand under that cold water and give the special time to work."

"Have Uri and Nicole bring Toni here for breakfast." Jael tried to sound casual, but each word came faster than the one before. Knowing Alyssa was upstairs in their bed, naked, was driving her into a near fever. "Tell everyone. In case there's another spy in camp, I don't want anyone else to know who Kyle is. The less she mingles, the fewer questions she'll be asked, so she'll be taking all her meals with us until Tan returns and they head out." Jael sprinted up the stairs, pulling her T-shirt over her head and popping the other two specials into her mouth before she reached the top.

She forced her eyes away from the sleeping figure still huddled under the blanket. Alyssa was a very deep sleeper and had adapted to Jael's habit of getting up during the night to fly with Specter, then returning to their bed a few hours before dawn. But it was almost zero-seven-thirty, and her responsibilities as a healer usually had her up and on her way to the clinic by now. Alyssa murmured in her sleep, and Jael belatedly reinforced her mental shields so that her need didn't disturb her slumbering bond mate.

The icy water sizzled against her overheated skin, filling the room with steam. Dung. If she didn't pay attention to her core heat, she'd combust like a novice pyro. She stood under the spray, head down and hands braced against the thin waterproof sheeting of the temporary shower. She longed for the cool tile of her cabin on the mountain. She'd had too many lifetimes of camps and marches and battles. She'd like to be able to relax and enjoy just one breeding cycle with her bond mate—with no war or no responsibilities demanding that she suppress it or cut it short.

Had they used the eggs she'd contributed yet to produce embryos to continue her pure bloodline? Surrogates might already have birthed little clones. She'd never been interested enough to ask. Maybe Alyssa would want to surrogate a child for her. Alyssa pregnant with her child. Jael's sex pulsed like a drum. She closed her eyes and groaned. A hand touched her back and slid around to her belly. Alyssa, naked and soft, pressed against her back as she reached around with her other hand and turned the water dials to a warmer temperature.

"While cold water might shrink a penis, it does not shrink girly parts. The brisk temperature will only refresh and sharpen your libido. Warm water and a few orgasms will relax you."

"Alyssa."

"Hush. Let me in. Drop your shields for me."

Jael's head buzzed with the herbs in Second's cakes. The shower felt like a warm summer rain on her skin, and Alyssa's fingers like delicate blades of grass tickling across her belly. She fathomed the sweet ache of Alyssa's desire to have her and instinctively pushed her hips back against Alyssa's.

Inside. I need you inside. Now.

Alyssa laid her cheek between Jael's shoulder blades as she slid her thumb into her from behind. Her fingers stroked Jael's distended clit with every thrust of her thumb, and Jael gasped. Even though the herbs dulled her response, orgasm bowed her body after only a few strokes. Alyssa slowed her thrusts as Jael trembled through the aftershocks. But instead of withdrawing, she turned off the water and began to pick up the pace again. Jael groaned but didn't protest.

"Baby, can you do something for me?" Alyssa's breathless whisper was urgent.

Jael nodded. Her head was fuzzy, her focus centered on the fingers stroking across the bundle of nerves that were singing with pleasure between her legs. "Anything."

"I'm going to make you come again, but I want to come with you. You're too tall though. Can you get down on your hands and knees so I can rub against you?"

Jael hesitated. She wasn't sure. But this was Alyssa. Trust and affection infused her. Alyssa was projecting. Jael's impulse to resist softened. Alyssa's hand felt so good between her legs, massaging her need. "Anything," she whispered to herself more than to Alyssa. She sank to the floor and felt Alyssa go with her, never faltering in her thrusts. Then she felt Alyssa pushing, sliding against her hip, and she reached behind to find Alyssa's wet heat. Alyssa gasped and pumped harder with her hips and her hand.

Jael felt the sweet pressure boil up from her belly. Or was it Alyssa's belly? It was impossible to tell because their orgasm felt like one huge tsunami building, building, building, curling and hanging for a long exquisite moment, then finally crashing and crashing and crashing until it lapped at the other side.

She was barely aware of Alyssa rousing her, drying her, and leading her to bed. At least for now—with Tan miles away, Phyrrhos wingless for the rest of the day, and Kyle asleep in her bunk—she could finally get a few hours of rest.

Tan's entire body ached. Her shoulders were sore from the hours Anya had left her hanging. The weeping welts on her back, buttocks, and thighs were sticking to her clothes and pulling open again when she moved. Her jaw was sore from the ball gag and her ass from—well, something Jael would never do for her. She was tired, but she had to take care of the one person who could stand in her way tonight.

It was mid-morning before Alyssa and Second finally left the headquarters building. It'd taken every ounce of her control not to follow Kyle when she'd headed to the Advocates' cottage to sleep. Her brain was too muddled by Phyrrhos to figure it out now, but something was drawing her to the blazer. She forced her attention back to the headquarters building. If her count was correct, only Jael remained. It was chancy. If Jael was alert, Tan could be toast. Instead of sending her to Anya, they could restrain her and put her in a medically induced coma until Phyrrhos' heat subsided. That would be dangerous for her dragon horse. Their bond would be temporarily silent, and Phyrrhos might go mad.

She positioned a crude ladder she'd lashed together from saplings so she could reach a second-floor window on the back of the building. It opened into the communal personal facility The Guard shared. She knew the window wasn't locked because they raised it often to let the shower steam escape. She moved inside cautiously, glancing into the rooms as she crept down the hallway to be sure they were empty.

She readied the short blowgun and a feathered dart filled with tranquilizer. She had to knock Jael out long enough for Phyrrhos to breed without interference. Jael would be furious, but she'd deal with that later. She froze when she saw the blond mane, the long naked back and sheet drawn up to barely cover the slim hips. Jael, not Second. She'd seen Second leave. Besides, she bunked in this building, too, and knew Second slept in the common room with the rest of The Guard now. Why would Jael be sleeping late in the day? Her brain and body warred as the fever screamed for her to jump the sleeping figure. *Take her.* No, she belongs to another. *Bite her. Claim her.* She has claimed another. *You want her.* No. Not her. Not anymore.

Before she could examine this last thought, Jael stirred. She pushed up with her arms and groggily turned to face her. Tan reacted without thinking, lifting the blowgun and sending the dart on its way.

"Tan, no." Jael's hand never made it to the dart embedded in her throat.

Tan dropped the blowgun and caught her to extract the dart before she fell on it and broke the point off in her skin. She straightened Jael's arm into a more comfortable position. Her hand trembled as it hovered over Jael's back. One small indulgence. She touched the hair that reminded her of wheat fields, stroked her fingers down the strong back that carried the weight of The Collective, and bent to lightly kiss the broad shoulder. "I'm sorry, my friend. This is as it must be."

❖

Kyle practically inhaled the food Second gave her. Her cooking was way better than what they'd eaten in the dining hall the day before. In fact, she could have eaten an entire plate of those little chocolate cakes. Second had warned her not to share because they had herbs in them to help her relax and sleep, but she wouldn't have shared anyway once she tasted them.

She'd taken a hot shower and settled into bed and fell asleep with the help of Second's special cakes and a little right-hand rendezvous. The image of a brown-skinned warrior with deep-chocolate eyes materialized as her orgasm gathered and burst through her. It was just the herbal haze. She shrugged it off and drifted into a sound sleep with her fingers still resting against her pulsing clit.

She was awake and restless again after only four or five hours. Jael said mingling would invite too many questions, but she was too restless to sit in her quarters. So she dressed and slipped between the temporary buildings into the forest beyond.

Kyle skirted the camp, staying several meters off the faint path that appeared to be the perimeter patrolled by the nightly guard. Most of the trees she'd seen near the villages were scrubby by Third Continent standards—coffee trees, slender banana trees with large fronds, or avocado orchards. But, in addition to the banana grove at the other end of the valley, a forest of tall mahogany trees surrounded the camp.

She paused at the bottom of one particularly large tree with a double trunk that seemed to call to her, then scrambled up to a sturdy perch well concealed by the tree's foliage. She could see almost the entire camp. People were streaming out of the dining facility, and she glanced up at the sun, realizing it was well after the noon hour. Her stomach rumbled at the thought. Dung. She wished she'd thought to bring a pro-chow bar from her pack. And a water bottle. Some spy she'd make. She squinted at the hillside where Phyrrhos and the old mare were grazing, barely able to make out their shapes. She began to make a mental list of the things she should take on their trip if she was going to be a successful spy.

She was about to climb down when she heard someone coming down the trail. It was a woman, wearing the white armband of a medical worker, rather than a patrol guard. Kyle frowned when the woman left the trail and sat on a large fallen tree right below her perch. She opened a green backpack and pulled out a poncho that she draped over the log to sit upon. Then she drew out a white cylindrical item and stood, unfastening her pants and dropping them to her ankles. Kyle froze. Surely she wasn't—Geez, in the woods? A low hum began, and the woman's groan when she touched the vibrator between her legs confirmed her intent.

Kyle shifted uncomfortably. She wanted to look away, to put her hands over her eyes and ears, but Phyrrhos' call was pulling at her again. Maybe because it would be dark in a few hours. Maybe because she had yet to satisfy her agitation from the night before.

The branches on the opposite side of her tree shifted. Dung. Was an animal in the tree with her? The hair on her nape prickled. The hum of the woman's vibrator and her soft moans seemed to grow louder. There. It moved again. Kyle sucked in a breath. The penetrating, dark eyes that stared at her were familiar. The face paint was camouflage this time. Dressed in a dark green T-shirt and ragged cargo pants, Tan was barefoot. Had she been there the whole time? Had she watched Kyle climb up?

Tan climbed stealthily down the tree—soundless and hardly stirring a leaf. Kyle wasn't sure why, but she didn't make a sound either.

When Tan reached the ground, she slid a hand around the woman's face to stifle her scream, pressed her mouth to the woman's ear, and spoke words too low for Kyle to understand.

The woman clutched at her chest and turned her face to Tan. "Stars, you nearly frightened the life out of me."

Tan glided like a jungle feline over the downed tree and snatched the vibrator from the woman. "What do you think you're doing, half naked out here in the woods?"

"There's no privacy in those barracks, you know?" The woman sounded like a petulant child. "I've got needs." Kyle nearly lost her balance when the woman shook her foot loose from her pants and spread her legs wide. "You haven't been around the past week, and I've been a very bad girl."

Kyle could almost see, feel Tan vibrating with tension. Her irritated tone changed to a smooth purr. "What have you done?"

"You know that black-banded boy who's been drooling after me? I popped his cherry for him."

"You slut."

"I should be punished." The woman slid off her seat onto her knees.

"It's not exactly punishment when you like it."

"I fucked him on your desk at the clinic."

Tan's eyes narrowed. "On my desk?"

"Yes. Because I knew you wouldn't like it, and I was missing our special kind of fun."

Tan held the vibrator under her nose, then licked the length of it. Without a word, she pointed to the log and the woman scrambled to drape herself over it, bare ass displayed to receive her punishment.

Kyle was sure Tan had forgotten her, but she looked up and they locked gazes as Tan slowly removed her belt. She doubled it and jerked it taut to make a loud popping sound. Kyle flinched and the woman whimpered. Tan smiled and turned her attention back to the woman. "Didn't I tell you to leave that boy alone?"

"Yes."

"But you didn't listen, did you?"

"No."

"How many?"

"Ten. No. Twelve."

"Count them." Tan picked up the discarded panties and stuffed them into the woman's mouth. The belt sang through the air to slap against the woman's fleshy buttocks, but the panties muffled the woman's cry of "one."

Kyle shifted on her branch, uncomfortably aroused. She'd never witnessed anything like this. She should scramble down the tree and intercede, but the woman obviously desired what Tan was doing. Sweat tricked down her back and her crotch grew damp.

Six more lashes and Tan paused to run her hand over the reddened ass. She looked up at Kyle and held her gaze as she dipped her hand between the woman's legs. When Tan withdrew, her fingers glistened with the woman's juices, and she stared at Kyle as she licked them clean.

Then, as suddenly as she'd stopped, she delivered five hard, quick blows with the belt before shoving the thick vibrator into the woman and pumping into her.

When the woman began to tremble and her muffled voice grew shrill, Tan stopped and threw the vibrator on the ground.

The woman yanked the panties from her mouth. "No. Don't stop."

"Did I say you could come?"

"Please, please let me."

Tan pushed her hand where the vibrator had been and began to thrust again. "I want you to take it all."

The woman closed her eyes. "Yes. I can do it."

Tan probed, slapping the reddened butt a few times, and then her hand seemed to disappear to halfway up her forearm. The woman grunted each time Tan pumped into her, grabbing her own nipples and pinching hard.

"I'm going to come. Tell me I can, please."

"Put those panties back in your mouth. I don't want half the camp to come running when you scream. Then come while my hand is inside, while I'm fucking you."

The woman stuffed the panties in her mouth and screwed her face up as she pinched her nipples while Tan pumped. A few more slaps to her tortured cheeks and she screamed out her climax.

Kyle released a ragged breath. Stars. She wanted to put her hand in her pants and relieve the throb in her crotch. No. If she was truthful, she really wanted to swing down out of that tree and have a good jump with the judge and jury in camo paint and fatigues.

But Tan withdrew from the woman and stepped back.

"Give me a minute to recover, baby, and I'll suck you off."

Tan picked up the woman's pants and used them to wipe off her arm. "No. I have to go."

"I know you gotta need—" When the woman slid off the downed tree and turned, Tan was already gone. She shrugged. "Or not." She rubbed her inflamed bottom. "If she had a real penis, I'd have to bond with her." She stared toward the trail. "But then, she's not the bonding type, I guess. Maybe I'll just have to find a man who can give me the treatment she does." She gathered her things slowly, hissing when she pulled on her pants, then smiling. "Won't be sitting down for supper tonight." She laughed as she made her way back to the trail.

Chapter Six

Tan was hidden in a lair of limbs and brambles, sweat beading along her forehead and upper lip, trickling into her ear and down her neck even as the late-afternoon temperatures cooled. The scant hour she'd slept was tortured with images of Anya's punishment, Jael's disappointment when she realized Tan had darted her, and Kyle's brilliant blue eyes watching as she made use of the camp masochist. She woke mired in shame so deep she would have drowned if the persistent breeding fever hadn't redirected her focus.

She'd felt Phyrrhos' need, her need building, like the ticking of a clock, the kind from a past life where a pendulum swung back and forth, advancing the second hand with each completed arc. She could hear Phyrrhos calling for Specter and imagined her already pacing the paddock. Kyle the Blaze and Toni the Pony would have a tough time trying to corner her to get her into that cave prison. She bared her teeth at the thought. Maybe she wouldn't have to intervene. She could just watch Phyrrhos dodge them until dark descended and she transformed to fly off with Specter.

Tan shifted her screen of foliage to slide from under it. Dusk was imminent. She drained her last bottle of water. Her body temperature was rising beyond her control. Her T-shirt was dirty and soaked with her sweat. Even so, her clothes were starting to smell faintly scorched. She had no idea what would happen to her when Phyrrhos bred. She'd never been through a breeding with a bonded before. But she was more afraid she would spontaneously combust if Phyrrhos didn't breed soon.

❖

Kyle emerged from her second shower of the day. Her body was cleaner but her mind no clearer. Even two orgasms couldn't dim the erotic images of what she'd seen in the woods. Toni burst into the room, and Kyle turned and glared at her.

"Don't you know how to knock when a door is closed?" Still being nude from her shower wasn't an issue, but she was half a second away from flopping on her bed and going for a third orgasm. That would have been embarrassing.

Toni looked surprised. "Why would I knock on the door to my own room?"

"What if I wasn't alone?" As soon as the words left her mouth, Kyle regretted her outburst. Toni was younger, but Kyle didn't know how much younger and had no idea if she was sexually experienced. The deep red flushing Toni's face seemed to indicate she wasn't. "Forget it." She rubbed her face, then reached for her clothes to dress. "I just flashed back for a minute on my younger brother barging into my room. He used to do that all the time."

"Oh." Toni stood in the doorway as though she'd forgotten why she was there. "Does your family live near here?"

Kyle fastened her fatigue pants and pulled a black T-shirt over her head. "I don't know exactly where my mother is. Maybe still Third Continent, Region Five, where we lived. But I doubt it." She sat on the bed to put on her socks and boots. "She's probably trying to track down my father because he's taken my younger sister away."

"He didn't take your brother, too?"

"My brother is dead."

Silence hung between them. Then Toni spoke, her voice soft. "I'm sorry, Kyle."

Kyle shrugged. "I'm trying to track down my father, too."

"To find your sister and mother?"

"Yes, but for another reason." She raised her eyes to Toni's. "My father is Cyrus, the leader of The Natural Order, and I'm here to help stop him."

"I knew they didn't want us to tell that you came from the cult, but, stars, I didn't know their leader was your father."

"Now you know why they won't bunk me with the other warrior trainees."

"You're not missing anything but a lot of strutting and bragging." Toni's tone was bitter. "I was glad to get out of there."

Dressed now, Kyle stood. She didn't know where she was going, but she couldn't sit still. Toni still blocked the doorway. "You coming or going?"

"Oh, yeah. Alyssa sent me to get you. We're supposed to go to headquarters for an early dinner."

"How come?" Did they know Tan was here? She should tell them, but something held her back.

"Diego is headed back from San Pedro Sula, and Second's cooking early in case Jael wants to hold a strategy session when he arrives. You missed lunch anyway. You've gotta be hungry."

Kyle rubbed her stomach. The ache inside was growing. Maybe food would help. "Yeah, I guess I am."

❖

Second slid two platters of food on the table. "Where's Jael? Has anybody seen her today?"

Kyle shook her head and took the basket of bread from Alyssa and set it on the table. "Not since early this morning."

"She hasn't been by the clinic today," Alyssa said. She walked over to the door of Jael's office and looked in. "She isn't in here." She cocked her head. "She's not far. I can feel her."

Kyle wondered if that was because they were bonded or because Alyssa was an empath. Had she climbed that tree because she unconsciously felt Tan already among the same branches?

Images of the forest encounter flashed through her, and her core temperature surged.

Alyssa sighed. "She's been shielding really tight lately to try to block out Specter. I miss our mental conversations."

"I couldn't find her to tell her Diego was coming, but I didn't worry about it," Second said. "She always seems to know what's going on all the time anyway. She'll show up."

Had Jael discovered Tan? Kyle clenched her jaw at the thought. Sweat trickled down it, and she shrugged to wipe it onto the shoulder of her T-shirt. Second glanced at her, her brow furrowed.

"Check upstairs," Second said to Alyssa. "Maybe she decided to take another shower." She gestured to the rest of them. "Sit. Eat before it gets cold."

There were still empty seats, even though Uri, Nicole, Kyle, and Toni had joined the headquarters group. The other Guards were camping on the next mountain, keeping their dragon horses clear of Phyrrhos and Specter as they flew out at night to gather intel on The Natural Order. Diego was traveling into camp by transport to report their findings. Vid conferencing was too risky.

The food looked good, but the knot in Kyle's stomach wouldn't make room for it. She shoved it around her plate, arguing with herself about revealing what she knew. She had pledged her life and her service to Jael and The Collective. Was she betraying that vow? Tan was part of The Collective. Logically, she should tell. But something deeper told her keeping this secret, protecting Tan, was meant to be. She felt Toni watching her, so she speared a large piece of meat and shoved it in her mouth.

"Second!" Alyssa stood at the top of the stairs, her alarm flooding the room. "She's still here. I can't wake her up."

Second bounded up the stairs three at a time. Nicole hesitated, then put her fork down and slid her chair back. "She might need some help."

Uri shoved another forkful into his mouth and followed, too, leaving only Toni and Kyle at the table. They looked at each other, then scrambled after the others.

This was bad. Kyle slipped down the hallway, checking the rooms on either side. A few muddy footprints below the window in the shower room confirmed Tan had been here, but Kyle saw no sign of her now. She rejoined the others, and only a quick glance from Toni gave any indication she'd been missed.

"Roll her over on her back," Second said calmly, directing Nicole to the other side of the bed to assist.

Alyssa stood at Jael's head, her hands fluttering over Jael's cheeks. "Jael, baby. Wake up." She stroked her hair, bent to kiss her forehead. Jael stirred but didn't wake.

Nicole pressed her fingers to Jael's throat, and Second gently pried Jael's eyelids open.

"Her pupils are dilated but equal," Second said.

"Her pulse is strong and regular," Nicole added. "She just seems to be in a deep sleep." She looked at Alyssa, her eyes full of concern. "I do sense some sort of tension, like she's fighting to wake up and can't. Can't you feel it?"

Alyssa glared at Second. "What did you drug her with?"

Second straightened. "Just a mild herb. She's had it plenty of times when we were younger. It never hurt her before. Unless—" Second turned to the doorway where Uri, Kyle, and Toni stood watching. "Kyle. Go to the prep and see how many of my special cakes are still in the pan. The ones like I gave you this morning. I left them in the cold storage."

Kyle hurried down the stairs and opened the cold storage. The pan of cake was cut into twenty-four neat squares. Six were missing. Second had given her three, and she was fine. She must have also given Jael only three. Tan was a physician. She must have surprised Jael and injected her with a knockout drug. Even caught up in a breeding fever, Tan wouldn't do anything to hurt Jael. Kyle opened drawers until she found a box of food bags. She quickly scooped half the pan of cakes into one of the bags, stowed it in the backpack she carried everywhere, and hurried back upstairs. She ducked into the large room sectioned into cubicles that were labeled with names. Tan. The bunk was neat, and a large, low trunk was stowed underneath. She slid it out and lifted the lid. A stack of T-shirts covered the box that held everything she needed. She didn't have a complete plan yet, but one was beginning to form.

❖

"No. I just can't believe Jael would go downstairs and eat half a pan of your special cakes. She hates any kind of medication."

"You didn't grow up with her like I did. She wasn't always so rigid about rules." Second stared at the pan Kyle held and shrugged. "But I have to admit, this surprises me. I guess none of us anticipated this situation."

Alyssa frowned. "What do you mean?"

"Well, the only other time Specter ever bred, it was brief, and not with another dragon horse of The Guard. Jael rode it out with, uh—"

"With Tan?"

Uri cleared his throat. "I'll wait downstairs."

"Me, too," Toni muttered, trailing after him.

Second glanced over at Kyle and Nicole, who made no move to leave, then turned to Alyssa and nodded. "It was purely a physical release and only lasted a night. It got kind of rough and frantic, though. She knew Tan could handle it." She took Alyssa's hand in hers. "But this time, she is bonded to you. Maybe she could feel Phyrrhos' fever and Specter's need to answer peaking tonight, so she decided to knock herself out to spare you. If she sleeps until morning, maybe everything will be back to normal."

Alyssa's eyes filled with tears. "She didn't have to."

Nicole put a hand on her shoulder in support.

"I know," Second said. "But she's so afraid of hurting you."

Jael moaned, and Alyssa laid her hand along her cheek. "She's burning up. She shouldn't be this hot, should she?"

Second and Alyssa turned to Kyle, and she shifted uncomfortably under their scrutiny, suddenly aware that sweat beaded on her brow in a near mirror image of Jael's. Did they realize she was somehow caught up in this crazy circle of breeding frenzy?

Second straightened. "Nicole, get some cooling packs from the clinic to lower her temp." With Jael incapacitated, Second was in command. "Alyssa, until she returns, you need to project anything you can to make her cool herself down. Think of glaciers, rolling in snow, swimming in ice water...anything." She grabbed Kyle by the arm and pulled her toward the door. "Kyle and I need to talk with Diego. Then I'll be right back."

Alyssa only nodded, her eyes on Jael's face as she murmured words into Jael's ear too low for Kyle to decipher.

Second released her grip on Kyle's arm as they descended the stairs. Only Toni and Uri sat at the table. "Diego isn't here yet?" She walked to the door without waiting for an answer. "He should have been here an hour ago."

"I can check the equipment barn for some news about his transport. Maybe he had mechanical problems," Uri said.

"Yes. Do that. He would have contacted the dispatcher there since Jael wasn't awake to respond to a mental message." Second watched him leave, then turned to Kyle. "I don't like this. You and Toni go secure Phyrrhos now."

Kyle swayed. The room swam around her. Her insides burned. She reached for something to anchor herself, and Toni's shoulder slid under her hand, solid and strong.

"Sure you didn't eat a few more of those special cakes?" Toni's tease was tinged with worry.

"She wants fire rocks."

"Who wants fire rocks?"

"Phyrrhos. She wants fire rocks."

Her focus returned as Second and Toni shared a look Kyle didn't have time to decode. Phyrrhos was calling her. Or was someone else?

The fire rocks were stored in a metal shed away from any other structures because of their flammable nature, and the shed was in the opposite direction of the stone stable. Going there first would mean penning Phyrrhos as sundown approached.

"You two go pen Phyrrhos. I'll send somebody to get a bucket of fire rocks," Second said. She glanced upstairs. "I don't want to leave Jael unprotected."

"Tan wouldn't hurt Jael," Kyle said. Dung. She had to open her big mouth. They'd never trust her now.

Second closed her hand around the nape of Kyle's neck and gave her a hard shake. "What do you know?"

"I...I saw her. In the woods earlier."

Second paced, cursing under her breath. She stopped and looked at them. "Don't stand there staring. Go. Get that dragon horse locked up tight." She started toward the office but stopped and pointed at Kyle. "I'm going to d-message the rest of The Guard to get here as fast as their transports can carry them. Then I'll help you stand watch. If Tan shows up, *do not* engage her. If at all possible, stall until I can stand with you."

"Yes, Commander."

❖

Phyrrhos paced, kicking her heels as the sun dropped lower in the sky.

"Stars, we need to hurry," Toni said. "If she sprouts wings, she'll be gone before we can blink."

"You get the other mare out of the way. I'll try to calm Phyrrhos," Kyle said, opening the gate and stepping inside the large paddock. "I'm not sure why, but we have some kind of connection."

"Be careful. Those guys are fast and unpredictable."

"Don't worry. I grew up handling livestock." Kyle approached cautiously, but Phyrrhos whirled away. She tried again, arms spread to gently corner her, but Phyrrhos turned to slip past her.

"Hold on, and we'll try that together." Toni was at her elbow, holding the lead of the large old mare.

Kyle frowned. "I thought I—"

"That's the trouble with you warriors. You're all action and not enough thought." Toni's grin took the sting from her words. She led the mare to the cave stable, angled her to stand at the entrance, and dropped lead. The mare obediently stood in position. "Bella ground-ties better than a granite statue. Nothing can move her. If we both spread our arms out, we can span the rest of the entrance. Phyrrhos will have to run over one of us or go inside. I'm betting that even in her frenzy, she's too well trained to run us over."

Kyle gave her new friend's shoulder a squeeze. "I'm thinking that Pony isn't a bad nickname, because every pony I've known was really smart."

Toni chuckled. "We have to use our brains to make up for our lack of height."

The two of them circled around behind Phyrrhos and spread their arms, drawing closer together as they slowly moved her toward the cave's entrance. She whirled in panic when she realized they'd trapped her, then finally darted into the cave. They scrambled to opposite sides of the cave, pushed the two sides of the thick metal door closed, and locked eyes, their fingers on the keypads.

"Ready?" Kyle asked.

Toni nodded. "On my mark. One."

They punched the keys as they counted out the sequence together, and both visibly relaxed at the loud click of the lock sliding into place.

Toni joined Kyle and slid down to sit in the dirt with her back against the metal door. "Stronger together, right?"

Kyle nodded and flashed a brief smile but didn't sit. She shifted restlessly, scanning the darkening horizon. Phyrrhos' hooves thudded dully against the stone floor inside, and her shrill whinny clawed at Kyle's ears.

"Even if Tan shows up, she can't release Phyrrhos by herself," Toni said, nervously flicking the laces on her boots.

"No. Not by herself," Kyle said absently. She scanned the wide lane that wound through the encampment to their end of the valley. What was keeping Second?

They silently watched the sun disappear behind the mountain peaks, and darkness fell around them like a cloak. Phyrrhos' whinnies turned to dragon screams, and her hooves drummed against the door of her cave prison. Sweat ran down Kyle's neck, her back, her belly. Her skin felt as if it would sear her clothes.

Tan was near. Kyle could feel her. She turned to scan the mountainside at their backs. Would she need the things she'd hastily stuffed into her backpack? She had no idea what she'd do when Tan appeared, but she wouldn't be caught unprepared this time. Not like she was in the woods earlier. She glanced at Toni. "I think you should leave."

"No way. I'm staying until the commander gets here and tells me to leave."

"You should listen to The Blaze." The voice, low and rich, deadly and quiet, came from behind Kyle. "Second isn't coming."

Toni scrambled to her feet as Kyle turned slowly and held her hand low, palm up to ignite a low, nonthreatening flame for illumination. "Captain Tanisha."

Tan stepped into the light. Her clothing was stained with dirt and sweat, but her eyes were bright, muscles taut and beautiful sliding under perfect bronze skin. She cocked her head as she regarded Kyle. "You can do better than that. You're not a sparkler after all, are you? A real blazer, eh? Looking to test your flame?"

"I'm not here to challenge you, Tan," Kyle said, keeping her voice soft.

Phyrrhos screamed and pounded the gate with her hooves. Tan's eyes glittered; she rocked from foot to foot and her hands twitched. "My bonded calls, and you're the only one left. Are you going to stand in my way?"

Would she stop her? The rich timbre of Tan's voice, the sway of her shoulders, the arousal dilating her pupils into dark pools was a mesmerizing, inviting vortex. Phyrrhos called to Specter. Tan called to Kyle. Every cell in her body yearned to answer.

"Where's Commander Second?" Toni's voice broke the spell and doubt speared into Kyle. Maybe the connection wasn't real.

Maybe Tan also had the talent of illusion, or hypnosis. Or maybe she was just rationalizing to give in to her own desire.

Tan's eyes never left Kyle's. "She's taking a nap. Just like Jael and Diego."

Kyle didn't respond, even when Toni's sharp elbow nailed her in the ribs.

"What's the matter with you?" Toni kept her voice low, edging close to present a united front against Tan.

Another dragon scream echoed through the valley but from outside the cave. Specter, his eyes glowing red and huge wings ghostly in the moonlight, dropped to the ground at the other end of the paddock. He spewed a stream of blue flame toward the stars. Phyrrhos answered his call and again drummed her hooves against the gate.

Tan's calm façade was fading. Sweat poured from her scalp and dripped from her chin. She began to pace. "Get out of my way."

Specter screamed and Phyrrhos answered. Tan grunted and clutched her side. Kyle's belly churned and her sex pounded with the two beasts' desperate calls. She couldn't imagine what Tan must be experiencing.

"It takes two people to open the gate," Toni said.

"Move." Tan's eyes were black, her face contorted in a pained grimace. Kyle was amazed at her control as she fired a stream of flame just to the left of Toni's head. Not meant to hit but to scare. Still, Toni threw up her hands and mysteriously deflected the flame skyward.

Sun and stars. It was like an invisible shield. She didn't know Toni was gifted. She'd never heard of such a talent.

"What the jump?" Tan's growl choked off and she dropped to her knees, clutching her belly, when Specter screamed and a column of blue-white flame barreled toward them. Kyle met his flame and stopped it with her inferno. She walked slowly toward him, her flame backing him away until he extinguished and she stood next to Tan.

Specter screamed and reared. Phyrrhos' answering call was followed by flame pouring forth from the narrow transom of the stable. A choked sob rose up from Tan's bowed head. Kyle knelt next to her and cupped Tan's face in her hands. Tan's eyes swirled with desire and misery, urgency and longing.

No words, no mental telepathy, no empathic impressions passed between them, yet they had complete understanding. Kyle knew it as sure as the certainty in Tan's eyes. She felt it as real as the need churning in her belly. She knew what must be done. This was as it should be.

She rose and turned to Toni. "We have to release Phyrrhos."

"Are you kidding me? Commander Second will have our hides."

Kyle laid her hand on Toni's shoulder and held her gaze. "She's going to hurt herself if we don't. It's going to hurt Tan if we don't."

Toni glanced at Tan, on her knees with hands pressed over her ears to shut out the continuous screams of the two crazed dragon horses. Flames licked again at the transom of Phyrrhos' prison. That door had to be red-hot, and the stone of the cave would trap the heat, too. If she kept it up, she would cook herself.

"If Jael was awake, I'm sure this is what she'd do, too," Kyle said. "I'll take responsibility."

Toni stared into the darkness for a few seconds, then stared hard at Kyle. "I'll do it, but you have to do something for me."

"Name it."

"What you saw earlier...me deflecting Tan's flame. Don't tell anyone."

Kyle blinked. What? Why would she hide this talent? She was among people who valued gifts. "Toni—"

"No. Swear it or I won't help. You have to make Tan promise, too, when she's sane again, or you have to convince her that she imagined it."

She didn't have time to argue. "Yes. I swear. Not a word. I'll make sure Tan says nothing, too."

Toni nodded. "Okay, then."

Kyle helped Tan to her feet. "Try to get through to Phyrrhos. Tell her we're opening the door, but she has to stop heating it. I just hope she hasn't already melted the mechanism." Tan nodded and leaned against Kyle as they moved to the keypad on the right side of the entrance. Toni stood next to the left keypad.

"On my count," Toni said. "One."

The keys were hot, but they punched them quickly and the lock thankfully clicked open when Kyle called out the last number. They met in the center to slide the two sides of the door back, but the calluses of Kyle's pyro hands sizzled against the heated metal. It would surely damage Toni's thinner skin. "Don't touch it," she said. "Take Bella down to the stable, then go to the headquarters to check on Nicole and Alyssa. Tell them everything is okay, but I don't want anyone else coming up here tonight."

"What are you going to do?"

"I'm staying to take care of Tan."

Toni's eyebrows shot up. "I don't know, Kyle. I've heard stuff about her."

Phyrrhos had gone eerily quiet, while Specter strutted the width of the paddock, fluttering his wings in an erotic display. He spit a fireball into the sky, impatient with the delay.

"I don't have time to argue. You shouldn't listen to rumors."

Toni looked around Kyle to Tan. She was pacing again, halfway to Specter before turning back to test the heat of the door before snatching her hand back when her sweaty skin audibly sizzled. Toni didn't look convinced.

"I know more about her than you think. I'm prepared," Kyle said, holding Toni's gaze.

"Okay." Toni went to Bella and gathered the mare's lead in her hand before turning back to Kyle. "Just be careful."

"See you in the morning," Kyle said as Toni and the mare started down the hill. Kyle pulled her T-shirt over her head. The night air felt good against her bare chest.

Tan stopped pacing. The urgency, the need driving her stilled like a stalking predator suddenly motionless as its prey turns.

Kyle was primal under a backdrop of stars. Lean muscle etched across her shoulders and torso. Her blue eyes glinted gray in the moonlight, framed by the sweat-dampened strands of her dark hair plastered across her forehead. Tan's mouth was a desert. She licked at the perspiration salting her lips, but she really wanted to taste, to drink from the bead of sweat that was making a path between Kyle's small breasts, aiming for the ridges of her abdomen and ultimately the belt of the utility pants slung low on her slim hips.

"Take your shirt off," Kyle said. "We can open the gate and release Phyrrhos if we use our shirts to protect our hands."

Kyle's words were fast and urgent, but Tan savored each like the last swallows of water in barren desert. She tugged her shirt over her head. She was more full-breasted than Kyle and wore a support band underneath. She pulled that off, too, and was rewarded when Kyle's eyes flicked downward.

"You're beautiful," Kyle said, lifting her hand.

Tan burned when Kyle's hand hovered and dropped to her side without touching her.

Specter screamed and flames licked at the grass near their feet. They ran for the cave. The stallion's patience had run out. They used their shirts like hot pads to grasp the door's handles and slide it open. Phyrrhos shot out into the paddock and launched skyward with Specter close behind.

Tan expected they would court briefly midair, then settle on a private mountaintop to breed. A shudder ran through her. Her bonded might be out of sight, but she wouldn't be out of mind. Tan closed her eyes against the frenzy building in her gut. Her core temperature was rising. Phyrrhos might survive this breeding, but she wasn't sure she would.

She swayed. Sun, she was burning. Her mind was filled with stars. She couldn't sort her thoughts from the images Phyrrhos was feeding her. Hot flesh burned against hers. Kyle? She sagged against Kyle's body and the arm that held tight around her waist. They were moving, moving backward.

"Sit." Kyle knelt to put food and a bottle of water in her hands. "Eat. And drink this."

Tan blinked slowly. "What is it?" Her voice was rough and sounded loud inside the cave.

"Water with some electrolytes, and a couple of Second's special cakes. They'll help."

She tensed, her spine bowing at another barrage of images from Phyrrhos and a sharp spasm of pain along her neck. Specter was a rough sire. But then she had no doubt Phyrrhos would mark him with a few love bites, too. She stuffed the cakes into her mouth and chewed, then washed them down with half the bottle of water before the spasm released her.

"I don't understand why you don't just knock yourself out until it's all over," Kyle said.

"Can't," Tan said, panting through another spasm that raced through her loin. She rolled on her side, holding her crotch and squeezing her legs together. "If I'm…unconscious…will break… the bond…Could…hurt Phyrrhos."

Kyle left, and Tan heard the clang and click of metal. The cave went dark as her spasm eased again.

"What are you doing?" Panic rose in her throat, a hot bitter bile, but Kyle was back. Tan's skin tingled where Kyle's hands stroked along her arms and chest.

"It's okay. I locked the door to give you some privacy, but I can open it when we're ready. I know what you need, Tan. Let me help you."

She rolled onto her back, the stone floor cool against her overheated shoulders, but her pants burned her skin and were too tight against her throbbing sex. The dark was disorienting. She needed to get out of her clothes. She was so empty inside. She needed to couple. No. She needed to get out of here. Nobody knew what she needed. Not Anya. Not Jael. Certainly not this stranger. "Because of what you saw in the woods today? You don't know anything, Blaze."

Something soft wrapped around her waist and wrists and tightened. A cuff belt. She was trapped. The only thing she could reach was her own clit. As if that would be enough.

"I'm going to roast your heart right out of your—"

Another spasm bowed her body and she fought to breathe through it. Air at last filled her lungs again, and she found her hands encased in fireproof gloves they used to keep pyros on the mental ward from hurting themselves. Tan's fury exploded. She screamed into the pitch. "I'll kill you. I'll jumping kill you, Blaze."

Her angry words still reverberated off the stone walls when a flame lit the cavern. Kyle flicked the switch on a solar lantern hung from the hay manger and extinguished the fireball in her palm. She was naked, her eyes blue jewels even in the muted light. Her short black hair was plastered against her skull, and sweat poured down her lean form. Tan groaned and clutched at her pulsing crotch as much as the cuff belt allowed. She closed her eyes. Phyrrhos was breeding now. She could almost feel it. Almost.

Kyle was beside her. "I need to help, Tan. As much as you need it, I need you." She was tugging at Tan's pants. "Sun, you're burning up."

Tan moaned. "Inside. I need you inside me."

"I need that, too, but we need to cool you down."

Her pants gone, Tan felt Kyle lift her as if she weren't equal her weight. Then she gasped when Kyle dropped her into the icy water of the drinking trough and slid in after her. The water sizzled against their skin, steam rising as it cooled their heated bodies. Tan wrapped her legs around Kyle's hips, and Kyle buried her fingers in Tan's Mohawk, yanking her head back to claim her mouth in a rough exploration of teeth and tongue. Tan growled, struggling futilely to free her hands. She bit Kyle's lip in frustration, and Kyle pulled back. Tan feared for a second that she would leave her wanting. She was even more afraid she would beg. She was on the verge of it now.

Instead, Kyle held her gaze as she slipped an arm under Tan's lower back and jerked her up so that her tender clit rubbed against the stiff curls of Kyle's sex. She undulated against her until Tan felt her eyes start to roll back at the sensation. She groaned and tightened as Kyle filled her with two, then three fingers and thrust with a steady pressure that pushed her instantly to a racking orgasm. Before the first orgasm subsided, Kyle lifted her higher to the surface of the water and bent over her. One long finger penetrated her ass as Kyle's thumb pushed into her again. Tan found footing on the sides of the trough and pushed upward to meet Kyle's renewed thrusts. When Kyle's hot mouth closed on her distended clit and sucked, she soared. She sang. She burst forth inside and out until she was limp and panting. Still, she needed more.

"More," she moaned.

"I know, baby." Kyle climbed out of the trough and moved Tan to one end so that she sat up with her elbows on the edge. "Can you sit here for a minute? I need to get some things ready, but I don't want you slipping down under the water."

"Free my hands."

Kyle stroked her face. "Not sure I can do that just yet."

"I suppose I deserved that after drugging half The Guard." Tan did understand, but she'd never taken orders from anyone but Jael, never taken punishment from anyone but Anya.

Kyle's lips were soft and searching against hers, no desperate clash of teeth and tongue. When she withdrew, she gently fingered a ragged welt that marred the smooth skin of Tan's shoulder. "I'm not Anya, Tan. Please understand that you're shackled for your safety and mine. I trust you, but I don't know—you don't know—how Phyrrhos' breeding will affect you tonight." Another brush of lips, and Kyle fed her two more special cakes and helped her down another bottle of water before moving away. Tan frowned. The brief break in Phyrrhos' breeding felt like she was finally swimming to the surface for a big gulp of air, but Kyle was muddying her water.

Tan hadn't realized she had drifted until she felt Kyle lift her from the water. She tried to rouse, but she was very relaxed after four of Second's cakes. She was vaguely aware of Phyrrhos. Images of a clear night, a million stars, and wings that fluttered like a heartbeat seeped into her brain. Kyle's body was smooth and firm, her nipples hard. She smiled when a gentle bite elicited a low groan.

"I might drop you if you don't stop that," Kyle said, but her warning held little force.

Then she was lying on a cooling mattress covered by a soft cotton blanket. The scent of forest and smoke, sweat and pheromones filled her senses. Kyle or Phyrrhos? She was hungry, but not for food. She blinked sleepily at Kyle.

"Something's bunched up under me," she said, squirming her right shoulder. When Kyle stretched over her to tug at the blanket, Tan locked her legs around her and flipped Kyle over onto her back. Kyle gripped Tan's hips, encouraging her when she massaged her swollen sex against Kyle's taut belly. A spasm grabbed and held her. "Mother of Dung." The first breeding hadn't taken. It was starting again. She moved lower and ground against the hard bone of Kyle's pubis.

"Lift yourself up, baby, and let me get inside you."

It wouldn't be enough this time. "I need more," she moaned.

"I've got more." Kyle sat up and gently reversed their positions. She reached to the side of the bed and retrieved a phallus, large and black, and a harness that she quickly strapped onto her hips.

Tan's muscles clenched and her body bowed upward with a second spasm. "Stars, hurry."

Kyle popped a tube, and Tan thought she'd orgasm as Kyle's hand pumped up and down to spread lubricant liberally along the latex phallus. "Mother jumper. Don't bother with that." A third spasm brought her shoulders off the mattress as her hands, held tight by the cuffs, clenched into fists.

Tan sucked in large gulps of air when the spasm began to release. Kyle's face was close to hers, her eyes laser bright. Wordlessly, she moved over Tan. She felt the phallus bump against her cuffed hands. She pulled her knees up and guided it, slick and fat, to ease her tortured ache. She needed her hands. She wanted to dig her nails into Kyle's ass and yank her forward. Instead, she dug her heels into Kyle's thighs. "Please. Fill me. Fuck me. Harder."

Great wings fluttered around her, and dragon calls tore at her ears as Kyle filled her again and again. Kyle's sweat dripped down to mingle and run with her own. Her hot mouth and burning tongue covered hers, but Tan broke away. "More." She growled and dug her teeth into Kyle's shoulder until she tasted blood. Kyle's thumbs dug into her jaws and she released the flesh in her mouth. The cavern was a dizzying jumble of light and dark, images and reality, need and emptiness...Kyle was gone. "No, please." Did that sob come from her?

Rolling. Hands were rolling her onto her stomach. Kyle's breasts pressed into damaged skin on her back. The salt of their sweat stung anew. An arm around her waist raised her hips, and she cried in relief as she was filled again.

"You are mine." Kyle's primal growl called to something deep in Tan, and she gave herself up willingly. Every stroke pushed her higher, brought her closer to that place she knew she had to reach. When their chorus of cries rose above the slap of flesh, a great beating of wings and triumphant dragon screams two mountain peaks away joined them.

Chapter Seven

Cyrus stood on the dock and eyed the eighty-four-foot yacht moored in the bay. A short, deeply tanned man in white pants and a white epaulet shirt was tying up a skiff that had arrived from the yacht. This might not be so bad after all.

He was tired, though, and unhappy that Ruth and the other women had been left behind. Simon said they would rescue them later, once the furor died down, but Cyrus doubted they were high on Simon's list. He wouldn't forget. No, sir. A man couldn't easily find a woman who understood her place like Ruth did. He would personally send someone for her once he had settled in the City of Light.

"I'm Robert," the man said, extending his hand. "You are Moses?"

Cyrus nearly rolled his eyes at the fake name Simon had given him for the trip, but he answered. "Yes. And these are my assistants." He turned to indicate his two guards, but only one was visible. He stood nervously by the open door of a warehouse and yelled inside to the other guard, who came out a minute later, hastily fastening his pants. They approached, red-faced.

"Had to take a leak," the missing guard mumbled, avoiding Cyrus's glare.

"The boat is this way," their escort said, picking up Cyrus's duffel and leaving the guards to carry their own.

Cyrus didn't miss the young woman who slipped out of the warehouse, glancing their way and checking her IC. Cyrus shook his head. His guard had probably paid her credits for quick sex in that dark warehouse. When would women stop enticing men to soil their souls? That was where it all began to break down, wasn't it? If women could be brought back to their natural purpose, then men would again respect them and resume their natural purpose as protectors and providers rather than abusers.

He sighed. He would call these two men to him tonight and counsel them. Then they would pray for the wayward man's soul. The Prophet would have no rest until he had shone his light into every corner of this dark, misguided world.

❖

"The Natural Order appears to be sticking to the plans Kyle said they have to take the central warehouse in Brasília. We know that Cyrus's second in command, a fellow named Simon, has secured air transport here." Diego pointed to the halo map. "We just have to figure out who his contacts are there and when they plan to hit the warehouse."

"It could be a decoy," Second said.

"Possibly, but we won't know unless we have someone on the ground there," Furcho said.

Jael remained as still as stone when five of The Guard looked to her for instructions. She followed the debriefing with her eyes but hadn't spoken since they entered the room.

Tan dropped her gaze to the table before her. She couldn't look any of them in the face. She had violated both her oath to The Guard and her friendship to Jael. Breeding frenzy was no excuse. Kyle and Toni also had been summoned but waited outside the headquarters office.

"What about Cyrus?" Second asked when Jael didn't respond.

"We lost him in San Pedro Sula," Diego said.

Silence again hung heavy in the room. Finally, Alyssa spoke. "Could all of you give us a minute? We won't keep you waiting long."

Jael didn't move, but her eyes flicked to Alyssa.

Tan stayed in her chair as the others filed out. Jael's silence was about her, and she might as well face it now. She was an impediment to their mission, so she must resign and leave The Guard, who had been her family for several lifetimes. She withdrew her hands clasped before her and slid them under the table to hide their shaking.

"Tan?" Alyssa's voice was soft.

She just shook her head. No words could repair what she'd done. If they existed, she couldn't have spoken them around the tightness in her throat.

"Oh, Tanisha." Alyssa rose from her chair. Her hands were cool on Tan's neck, stroking the bare part of her scalp. "Jael knows your heart. The Guard knows the captain to whom they have always trusted their lives."

Pride and respect permeated her. Thank the stars Alyssa hadn't projected sympathy. She already felt pitiful enough after awakening that morning naked and sore with Kyle fully dressed and watching her from where she sat on a feed bucket in the corner of the cave.

The gate was unlocked and sunlight shone through where it had been opened wide enough for a person to exit. Her hands were no longer shackled. The thin blanket covered her, and her clothes were folded neatly beside her. The memory of giving herself wantonly to this pup of a warrior—a blazer for sure, but pup nonetheless—was a deep wound in her sizable ego. She pulled on her shirt and realized that Kyle had dressed the welts on her back and thighs while she slept. The scabs were softer and no longer wept. She felt Kyle watching as she dressed. She looked around. Everything but the mattress and blanket where she'd slept was stowed in a pack.

"Are you okay?" Kyle's words were soft and careful.

"Fine." Her answer was harsh and clipped. What did this puppy expect? A scratch behind the ears? A treat for a trick well played?

"Second is waiting for you outside."

Tan stiffened. "Does half the camp know what we were up to last night?"

Kyle stood, her arms crossed over her chest. "She only knows that I managed to restrain and drug you to keep you safe after releasing Phyrrhos." When Tan finally met her gaze, Kyle's lip twitched as if she wanted to smile. "And that you're probably pretty pissed about it."

Tan didn't answer. She walked past Kyle into the sunlight and silently down the hill with Second.

Jael, however, wasn't some pup she could ignore. She was the First Warrior. They'd trusted their lives to each other in many lifetimes, and Tan had fractured that bond when she'd darted her. She shook her head again, finally finding her voice. "No, Alyssa. I've violated our trust, and you can't go into battle next to someone you can't trust." She stood and straightened her shoulders to finally face her old friend. Jael's face was stone, her laser-blue eyes unreadable. "I'll track your Prophet and send him to his next life myself as penance, but I'm clearing out. Take Kyle to the wild herd. I have little doubt she'll bond and easily take my place in The Guard." She turned to go but paused without looking back. "I'm sorry, my friend. I would rather have cut off my arm than defy you."

She was almost to the door when Jael spoke. "I'm still First Warrior, and you're still a member of The Guard. I have not dismissed you, Captain."

Tan turned back to them, her relief tentative. Jael sighed and scratched at her belly. She indicated for Tan to sit, then stood and lifted her T-shirt to expose an angry red rash. She scowled at Tan. "As soon as I sort this all out, your first orders are to go get another antihistamine injection for me from the clinic. I'm apparently allergic to whatever you had in that dart."

"And please make a note in her medical records so you'll remember to use something different next time."

Jael's intimidating glare apparently was wasted on Alyssa, who added a grin to her cheeky comment.

Tan relaxed a bit. She still had a lot to mend, and she could sense that Jael had lost her taste for righteous executions. "Let me go after him alone, Jael. This is like the later wars—no front lines, no battlefields. Take the army to protect the supply lines, and let me hunt Cyrus for you."

Jael walked to the window. She stared out for a long moment, then turned back to the map and studied it. "Could you bring Kyle and Antonia in?" she said to Alyssa.

The two young women filed in, only their white faces giving away their nervousness. Kyle stood tall and met Jael's eyes. Toni glanced about, her eyes holding only when they found Alyssa's warm gaze.

Jael sat at the head of the table and indicated for them to also sit.

"Tell me why you released Phyrrhos when your orders were clearly to keep her in the cave." Tan was surprised to hear no accusation in Jael's query. Did Jael know something she'd missed in her frenzy?

Toni seemed surprised, too, by Jael's tone, but Kyle's answer was immediate.

"I was convinced, and persuaded Toni, that Phyrrhos was going to damage herself if we didn't release her. Specter was in the paddock throwing flame, and she began breathing flame inside the cavern. The door and the cave were superheating. I could smell singed hide." Kyle paused, glancing at Tan. "Captain Tanisha was present outside the stable, but her skin was also superheating because of her bond with Phyrrhos. I concluded that, under the circumstances, release was the best option to keep them both from harm."

Jael nodded, steepling her fingers before her and contemplating them. "Corporal Antonia, do you concur?"

"Yes, First Warrior."

Jael scanned the faces of each, and Second quietly entered the room. She'd been summoned telepathically, Tan assumed, because Jael was about to issue orders she wanted recorded.

"The frenzy of Captain Tan's bonded obviously would have affected her judgment, and Kyle hasn't been with us very long," Jael said. "But I've observed Corporal Antonia quietly make several sound decisions for the good of the entire unit. So, I'm going to trust that you did what was necessary." Her mouth relaxed into a faint smile as she looked over at Alyssa. "Commander Second, although Toni already has been acting as The First Advocate's assistant, I want you to promote her to the appropriate rank that will give her the authority she needs to fully function in that capacity. Those duties should also include official hospital quartermaster. She seems to have a knack for keeping track of things."

"As you command," Second said.

"Thank…thank you, First Warrior," Toni said, looking from Jael to Alyssa and back to Jael. "I won't let you down." She looked to Alyssa. "Or the First Advocate."

"It's well earned, Toni," Alyssa said, smiling.

"You are dismissed," Jael said. "Kyle and Tan must remain for their orders."

Second led Toni from the room, and Jael's hand moved over the controls at her end to project a holo map over the table. San Pedro Sula lit up in red.

"Cyrus was last seen here. It's a big city with lots of places to hide, an airport, train station, and lots of roads leading out. We also know that his second in command is headed in the opposite direction to Brasília, which Kyle said was their original destination." Jael highlighted another location, this one in the Rocky Mountains of the Third Continent. "In addition, we have reports of some kind of activity here. If you are unable to locate him in San Pedro, you may want to consider travel routes toward the activity in the Third Continent. We suspect they may be building a stronghold there."

"Jael, let me hunt alone." Tan felt Kyle tense next to her but still refused to look her way. "I can be quicker and less conspicuous than two people. I'll find him and be in and out before his ashes cool." It was a callous thing to say, considering the man was Kyle's father, but the rookie needed to face the hard reality of the mission. To her credit, Kyle showed no reaction.

Jael shook her head. "The mission is more than just about Cyrus now, Tan. Some information Furcho gathered from a clinic where Simon, the man Kyle injured, sought treatment indicated that he might be a new threat as well."

"Simon's never pretended to buy into my father's ranting, but he's the general organizing the war," Kyle said. "And, he's a dangerous man with no conscience."

Kyle's scowl and the darkness growing in her eyes surprised Tan. This blazer could be an intriguing puzzle if she didn't have more important things to do. At the moment, she was just a complication.

"He's also proved to be a good strategist so far, so we have to anticipate that he has another mouthpiece ready to put in place should Cyrus fall," Jael said.

Kyle stood as Jael approached her, and her cheeks flushed when Jael reached up to clasp her shoulder.

"Trust Tan to find Cyrus. And when she does, I want you both to follow him to his destination. We suspect it will be their stronghold. I saw your thoughts, so I know how much you hate the role, but we need you to go back into their fold and find out as much information as possible."

"And Cyrus?" Tan would prefer to incinerate the man the instant she found him.

Jael gazed down at Tan, her eyes serious. "You are to summon me. It's my duty, not Kyle's and not yours, to judge and sentence her father. You are authorized to take matters into your hands only if circumstances demand it."

Tan stood and nodded briskly. She wouldn't screw this up, like she had everything else lately. "As you command."

"You are dismissed to prepare for departure tonight. If Pyrrhos still won't accept a second rider, another of The Guard will fly Kyle to San Pedro with you." She waved them toward the door. "Please send the others in for their orders."

If Tan had any doubts about her place in The Guard, those fears were erased when each offered words of solidarity as they filed back into the office.

"Good hunting, amigo," Diego murmured.

"Go get 'em, Tan," Michael said, touching her arm briefly.

"Eyes of a hawk, wind at your back, my friend," Raven said quietly, her gaze steady and sure.

Furcho and Second stopped together and addressed both Tan and Kyle.

"Take care of my young friend," Furcho said to Tan. He grasped the back of Kyle's neck and gave her a soft shake. "And you take care of Tan. She'll never ask for your help, so you'll have keep your eyes open for opportunities to assist." He looked at Tan but spoke to Kyle. "And don't let her bully you. She's all bark and no bite."

Second chuckled. "Some people might dispute that, Furcho." Then her expression grew serious. "Tan, I know Kyle is green, but she's got skills and a good head on her shoulders. Use her. Let her watch your back." She turned to Kyle. "A military operation is not a democracy. You are to do everything she orders. Do you understand?"

"Yes, Commander."

She clasped both their shoulders. "Go get a shower and a few hours of bunk time. I don't care if you just lie there and stare at the ceiling. Report here at zero-five-hundred for chow, and I'll have light packs ready for you. Bring two clean T-shirts, two changes of underwear. You can also bring one small personal item."

Kyle looked confused. "Like what?"

"You'll be issued a wrist IC," Second said. "Tan, I know you'll want to take your own...so, something you might need."

Tan studied Kyle, thinking of the pack she'd brought to the cave. The sparkler had obviously put some thought into being prepared, and she'd seen the disassembled lock that had allowed Kyle to open the gate from the inside the next morning. "I'll bring a medical kit."

Kyle nodded. "I have a small set of tools that could come in handy."

"Good," Second said. "Zero-five-hundred."

❖

Kyle stared up at the ceiling. She sure couldn't sleep.

How could she go on a mission with Tan after what had happened between them? She'd never intended to lose control like that, to be so rough. That's not what Tan needed, what she intended. Tan seemed to feel she needed punishment to achieve release, but some instinct told Kyle that she needed tenderness instead. That wasn't what she'd given her last night. Then she'd dressed and sat like a lump in the corner until Tan woke, instead of waking her with caresses and apologies like she should have. Who could blame Tan for giving her the cold shoulder now? She'd used her to sate her own urges. Her face burned with shame.

And her belly burned with the memory of Tan's beautiful, smooth brown skin, the arch of her back, the curve of her hip, the scent of her arousal, and the soft brush of her Mohawk. She closed her eyes and recalled Tan's—fierce one minute and pleading the next. After she'd opened the gate, she'd watched the rays of the sun slowly find the elegant planes of Tan's profile, lips slightly parted, in soft repose. Kyle was certain her high cheekbones and fine brow must be from the bloodlines of African royalty. She was strong yet elegant, and unlike any woman Kyle had ever met.

Her hand crept down her belly. It wouldn't take much. Images of Tan filled her mind.

It didn't help that Nicole and Furcho were in the room across the hall. It was no secret that they'd become lovers, and from the sounds filtering under Nicole's bedroom door, they were making the most of their final hours before Furcho's departure. He, Diego, and Raven were also leaving at dusk to track Simon to Brasília and assess the threat to the central warehouse there.

The moans and steady creaking of Nicole's bed drew Kyle back to the cave and the rhythm of Tan's hips rising up to meet her thrusts, Tan's dark-honey eyes searching hers. Her hips moved under her fingers as if they remembered, too. One stroke, two, three, and her shoulders jerked up as orgasm gripped and held her for a few brief, powerful seconds. She fell back to the bed, drained and hollow. Her memories might be all she'd ever have with Tan.

She had failed her when she'd slunk away before Tan woke, and Tan didn't seem to be the kind to give anyone a second chance. Kyle sighed and stared at the plain tiles of the ceiling. She would not fail her again. No matter how hard Tan pushed her away, she would do her duty—to The Collective, to The Guard, and to this woman to whom she seemed inexplicably connected.

Restless, Kyle arrived a half hour early, but Second already had a light meal ready and her supplies spread across the floor of the main room.

"Geez, can't either one of you tell time? Tan just picked up her stuff and left."

"She's already headed up to the meadow?"

"No. She said she wanted to stop by the infirmary and check on a few patients before she went up."

Kyle was amazed at the efficiency of her pack. Log shaped, it contained pro-chow bars, a liter of water, a handy multi-task tool, and room for her clothing. She added the small set of tools stored in a long shank of cloth dotted with neat pockets and rolled into a compact tube, and a small jar of ointment. She didn't know if Tan would add any salve to her supplies, and the wounds on her back would need to be dressed again.

Second watched but didn't comment. She took the rucksack and laid it alongside two short tent poles positioned on top of a thin bedroll that lay on a waterproof sheet.

"This waterproof sheet serves as a rain poncho or converts to a one-person tent by using these two poles and this little pouch of stakes and nylon twine," Second said. At the last minute, she seemed to remember something and went into the office. She opened Kyle's rucksack and added some folded clothing when she returned. Then she rolled the rucksack up in the bedroll and sheet, which made a long cylindrical pack with straps on either end so the wearer could position it diagonally across her back and, at the chest, snap the straps that came over the shoulder and hip.

"What was that?" Kyle asked.

"Furcho had one of the women from the train retrieve some of your belongings. It didn't look like there was anything you'd want, but you will need the proper uniform when you return to them."

The hated skirt? "I hope you appreciate how humiliating it is for me to wear that."

Second cocked her head. "I was a Scottish warrior in one of my lives. A man. And I proudly wore my kilt with nothing under it. Nearly froze my nuts off in winter, but it was considered unmanly to wear undergarments."

"It's not the same," Kyle said. "Dung. I'm going to have to put this on in front of Tan."

Second smiled. "Don't worry. Our Tan is something of a chameleon herself. You just haven't seen the red-hot-cocktail-dress Tanisha yet."

Kyle stared at her in disbelief.

"Hard to picture, isn't it? Believe me, once you see it, you'll never get it out of your head or catch your breath." Second winked. "It's a rare occurrence but one you'll never forget. She totally rocks it."

Kyle tried to wrap her brain around that image. "Red dress? Tan?"

Second laughed. "You won't figure Tan out tonight."

"Where's she from?" Kyle's tone was casual, but Tan fascinated her.

"She's genetically African but has lived this life in the upper Third Continent, so she speaks with that area's accent and cuts her hair like she belongs to a First People tribe." Second reached for Kyle's arm and strapped an individual computer to her forearm. "You're all set. You can hang out here for a while or head on up."

"I'll go," Kyle said. She was too itchy to stand around inside. She needed to be outdoors and moving, doing something. The waiting was driving her nuts. Was Tan feeling the same restlessness?

❖

Furcho sat on a large boulder near the meadow where he and Kyle would rendezvous with the dragon horses at dusk.

"Hi," Kyle said. "I thought you'd be spending every possible minute with Nicole."

"She had to work at the clinic." Furcho grinned. "I'd apologize for maybe keeping you awake. But if you haven't figured out how vocal Nicole is by now and found some ear plugs, that's your problem."

"Too much information." Kyle put her hands over her ears. "You're my mother's friend, you know. You're like an uncle to me."

"I'm not that much older than you, Kyle. Maybe twelve or fifteen years?"

She shrugged her pack off to drop it onto the grass and climbed onto the broad boulder with him. It was warm from the sun, and she dangled her legs over the side as she lay back to stare up at the sky and let the heat soak into her tense back muscles. "How old were you when you met my parents?"

"I was twenty, a new doctoral graduate from a university on the Fourth Continent." Furcho leaned back, propped up by his hands. "Your father was very kind and opened their home to me until I could find an apartment to rent."

"Cyrus? Really?" Kyle did have vague memories of a man who smiled and played with them when they were small, but more vivid was the stern man who looked at her with constant disapproval as she grew taller and stronger, and her sexual orientation developed toward women rather than men. Tension had built between them and filled their home. Then it grew until it tainted his view of his marriage, his relationship with his other children, and the one with his coworkers. "He hates you."

"Don't judge him too harshly, Kyle." Furcho's soft, even voice and the warmth of the rock felt like a brief shelter from the storm she was about to breech. "I'm not at liberty to reveal everything. That's for your parents to explain, but your father has struggled for a long time with feelings of inferiority. He's aware that you and your sister are gifted." He looked at her. "Your mother, as well."

"I knew about Maya, but Mom? She never told me. What about Thomas?"

"In a way." Furcho smiled at her. "Your brother was gifted with one of the bravest, purest hearts I've ever encountered."

Kyle didn't try to hide the tears that dripped down her temples into her hair. "When I heard what had happened to our town, I went to my aunt's house to find my family, but she said Father had taken Maya and left. She said he'd gone mad, and she'd been trying to get in touch with Mom to tell her that he'd taken Maya."

She sat up and wiped her eyes, her voice growing strong and bitter. "So I found Cyrus, only I wasn't prepared to stand against him, not the madman he'd become." She looked at Furcho. "He had me shackled to a post in the middle of a courtyard like a dog. I had six feet of chain. I was taken to a restroom twice a day, given one bottle of water and a half cup of pro-chow a day. Day and night, I was chained there…for weeks until I pretended to break and join his cult. Who does that to another person? What kind of father does that to his own daughter? I hate him, Furcho."

He grasped the nape of her neck. "Hate will eat your soul, Kyle, just as fear has eaten your father's. Don't let it. Your brother's death crushed Cyrus. Try to see your father as ill rather than evil.

He needs treatment. The kind soul your mother married is still inside that tortured man."

"How can he fill people with all those lies about a vengeful deity and a single life that will be judged when we know that souls reincarnate?"

Furcho released her neck and gave her a one-armed hug before releasing her. "When the world was divided by the great religions—Christianity, Islam, Buddhism, Judaism, Hinduism, and so forth—they had similarities because they all contained pieces of earlier ancient beliefs. Perhaps the beliefs we hold today as The Collective are only a piece of the big picture, too, and we're off the mark a bit as they were. Maybe the entire concept isn't for us to know and understand at all."

"But—"

"Do you have past lives that you recall, Kyle?" His eyes were suddenly sharp with interest.

"No, not really. Sometimes I think I have flashes of something, but it feels just out of my grasp."

Furcho nodded. "It could be a past life, or you could have a bit of your sister's talent for seeing the future."

"I'm not anything like Maya, or Mom." She looked at Furcho. "Am I adopted?"

"Can you stand in front of a mirror next to Laine and seriously ask that question?"

She shrugged. "We could be related in some other way."

"You need to talk to your mother if you have questions."

His evasion irritated her. She wasn't a child. She didn't need to ask her mother about anything. And, if she wanted to hate her father, who was he to question her? "You can recall past lives, can't you? Can't you say with certainty that our belief in The Collective is the real truth?"

"I can say that it's my truth," he said. "Does my truth apply to the entire universe? Who can say?" Furcho swept his arm toward the darkening sky. "When you look up at the stars, do you believe there might be other inhabited worlds out there?"

"I'm sure there are, even though we stopped trying to explore that possibility long ago."

"Then perhaps our Collective is but a speck in a huge infinite Collective. When we fully evolve into one Collective soul, what happens then? Does the chaos repeat itself and we fight our way back to unity, or do we evolve onto a higher plane in a huge universal Collective?"

Kyle never wasted much time thinking of such things. What would be would be. These circular discussions of philosophy that Furcho and her father were so fond of only made her tired. "I don't know all the answers. I just want to make it through this life."

Furcho chuckled. "And so you will. Nobody has all the answers, Kyle, but each person must live true to what their heart feels is right. The only way to keep your soul pure is to keep your heart and mind open."

She shrugged. "I'll try." That seemed an impossible task.

Movement at the edge of the meadow silenced them as Raven, Diego, Tan, Jael, and Alyssa emerged from the path. Dusk was descending and the dragon horses would be flying in from their high daytime pasture soon. They jumped down from the boulder and secured their packs over their shoulders.

They all met in the center, and Alyssa gave Kyle a reassuring smile. "Ready?" she asked.

Kyle glanced at Tan, who was still ignoring her. "Ready as I can be." She watched Alyssa move next to Tan and pull her down for a hug. She held Tan's face in her hands and said something Kyle couldn't hear, and after a hesitation, Tan nodded slightly before Alyssa released her. Tan shot a look at Jael, and Jael shrugged. What was all that about?

Then the sky was filled with great dark shadows as Bero, Potawatomi, and Azar landed lightly and trotted over to their bonded warriors. Kyle was relieved to see everybody calm after the chaotic scene caused by Phyrrhos being in season.

Only thirty seconds after the first three, Phyrrhos and Specter landed together and ambled quietly to their warriors. Phyrrhos' normally concave belly was full and slightly rounded. Sun and stars. How could she be visibly pregnant in less than twenty-four hours? The gestation for a dragon horse must be much shorter than that of a regular horse. Should she carry two people? Phyrrhos let out a huge smoky sigh and closed her eyes as she pressed her ridged forehead to Tan's. She glittered as the moon rose and its light played across her coppery hide.

When they parted, she turned to Kyle, her dragon eyes blinking. Her ears moved back and forth, she walked haltingly to her, turning sideways to rest her belly against Kyle's chest. Kyle stood very still and felt her chest warm as something niggled at the edge of her brain. She closed her eyes and tried to focus, but, like a weak signal, it faded in and out and then was gone.

When she opened her eyes, Jael was watching her. Their eyes held for a moment, and then Specter nudged his head over Jael's shoulder to sniff at Kyle. Phyrrhos moved away and stretched her wings in pleasure as Tan scratched her withers, the two relishing their contact after being separated.

"Specter and I are going to give you a ride to San Pedro Sula tonight. Phyrrhos would probably carry you, but it isn't wise this early in her pregnancy."

Wow. Specter. She stared at him, tall and ghostly in the moonlight. His reptilian eyes glowed red, and he snorted short blue flames from his nostrils.

"Stop showing off," Jael said, backhanding him in the chest. "He's full of himself since he knocked up Phyrrhos."

Alyssa slid her arm around Jael's waist. "Will you be all night?"

Jael hugged Alyssa against her side. "No. I should be back shortly after midnight."

"Good. I won't have to drag out the extra blanket, then."

Kyle stepped back and looked away to give them some privacy when Alyssa pulled Jael down for a farewell kiss, but she laughed along with Alyssa when Specter pursed his big dragon-horse lips and presented them for a similar kiss.

Jael swatted him away. "Go kiss your own girl, you big Romeo," she said, pretending to scowl. "I used to get more respect around here." Her grumbling, however, had a good-natured tone. She'd never seen Jael so relaxed and casual. If there was any warrior she'd want to emulate, it would be the First Warrior. But then every dragon-horse warrior in camp probably felt the same.

Jael sprang onto Specter's back and reached down to pull Kyle up behind her. When she was settled, Jael waited for Tan to mount, and they turned to face the other three of The Guard.

"I'll check in with Tan and Furcho twice daily, telepathically. I don't want any IC communication that can be intercepted or hacked," Jael said. "And I'll always be listening so you can contact me anytime in the event of an emergency." She searched each of their faces. "Be careful, my friends. Do not engage the believers unless you must protect yourself or an innocent. Wait until the army can confront them."

They acknowledged her orders with sharp salutes.

"Good speed," Jael said, returning their salutes.

"Guard. Aloft," Furcho shouted.

The three dragon horses reared and spread their great shimmering wings, then lunged in unison into the night sky. Kyle's heart caught in her throat. She'd never seen anything so beautiful. Specter and Phyrrhos moved restlessly, eager to also be flying.

Jael bent to take Alyssa's hand once more. "Second is waiting to walk back with you."

Alyssa glanced across the meadow to the path that led to camp. Second was propped against a tree, smiling. "You didn't have to summon her, Jael. I traveled halfway across the Third Continent to find you. I think I can follow a path." Her admonishment, though, was warm with affection.

"I know. Indulge me, okay?"

"Don't get used to it." Alyssa released Jael's hand and rested hers on Kyle's leg. Kyle filled with confidence and pride she suspected came from Alyssa. "Trust your instincts, Kyle. And trust Tan."

Kyle nodded. Getting Tan to trust her was the issue.

Alyssa backed away and waved to them and to Tan.

"Hold tight," Jael said.

Aloft.

The command was silent, but Kyle had barely tightened her arms round Jael's waist when it rang in her head as clearly as Furcho's shout.

CHAPTER EIGHT

The flight was short, but they hovered over the city awhile before landing on a tall building to leave Tan and Kyle on foot. Phyrrhos would fly back with Specter but would return every few nights as their bond demanded.

Kyle looked up and down the busy square. Transports and people hurried between shops and restaurants. The city, with no shortage of goods, was nothing like the rural villages. A couple hurried past and something seemed familiar to Kyle. She scanned the passersby again. Why hadn't she seen it before? A man passed by them and stared disapprovingly at Tan, who glared back at him.

"What's his problem?" Tan said.

"You have on pants rather than a skirt." They both wore loose cotton drawstring pants and hooded pullovers common in the rural areas over their cargo-style military pants and T-shirts.

"What? Women can wear either."

"Look around." Kyle gestured to the busy square. "These shops are open and doing business because they're getting merchandise from The Natural Order. The women are *all* dressed appropriately in dresses or skirts, and escorted by men. That's your first clue."

Tan gave her a sidelong look. "That guy didn't stare you down. You're wearing pants, too."

Kyle cleared her throat. "I think it was your, uh, chest that gave you away as a female. I'm not so well endowed. He probably thought I was a guy."

Tan cocked her head, and for the first time since the cave, her gaze fell fully on Kyle. She warmed under the scrutiny. "I don't think you look like a man."

Tan's matter-of-fact tone instantly deflated Kyle's swelling expectation. Expectation of what? That there'd be something more between them? That whatever connected them before was more than temporary breeding frenzy?

Kyle shrugged, trying to cover her disappointment with nonchalance. "I doubt he approved of your haircut either. Hair should be long. It's the adornment of a woman, according to The Natural Order. My father's going to freak when he sees I've cut my hair again."

But Tan was no longer listening. She was staring across the square where a group of four young men had cornered a couple of teen girls in tattered clothes. Before Kyle could speak again, Tan was striding toward them. Kyle hurried to catch up.

Two girls were backed against a storefront, one obviously scared and the other defiant. One of the young men toyed with a strand of the scared girl's hair. "You're very pretty. If you'd join The Natural Order, you'd have a husband to care for you and children as The One intends."

"We take care of each other," the defiant one said, swatting his hand away. "We're loyal to The Collective."

"You mean the starving Collective?" another said. The men laughed.

A third man clutched his crotch. "Then maybe you'd like to earn a few credits so you can eat. We can help you with that, too."

Tan slipped behind the young man and slid her hand under his. "Maybe I could help you with that, stud." Her other arm held him tightly around the chest. The man began to squirm and pull at her hand where she grasped his crotch.

"Stop it. Son of a dung eater, you're burning me. Stop."

After a moment, Tan released him.

Kyle stepped up beside the two girls and faced the men. "I think you guys should move along, before I report you for offering to defile these girls for credits. That's a direct violation of The Natural Order."

"She's unnatural," Tan's victim said, pointing to her and clutching his scorched crotch.

The other men ignored their friend, sauntering off and pretending they were bored with their prey rather than intimidated. "No harm intended, friend," one said to Kyle as they departed. Tan's victim followed, then turned back and spat one last insult. "Witch."

"Are you okay?" Kyle asked the girls.

"Yeah, we're good," the defiant one said. She peered up at Kyle and wrapped her arm around the other girl. "They thought you were a guy."

"I get that a lot," Kyle said, smiling at the girl. "I'm Kyle." She gestured to Tan. "This is Tan."

"I'm Haley. This is Oni, my girlfriend." She gave Tan a skeptical once-over. "I'm guessing you aren't from around here."

Tan's smile surprised Kyle. "We're looking for someone who might have passed through here or could still be here."

Haley looked at Oni. "What do you think, babe?"

Oni's soft brown eyes searched Kyle's face, then Tan's. Then she nodded. "They're good," she said.

"The network pretty much knows everything that goes on in the city," Haley said. "Maybe we can help."

"The network?" Kyle was doubtful tracking could be this easy.

Tan grinned. "Thought I spotted you." She pulled up her sleeve to reveal a round tattoo on her upper forearm. "Third Continent, Montreal."

"Sun, you're a long way from home." Haley said.

"I'm hunting a man, possibly with two others as guards. We know he was last seen in this area of San Pedro, but our people lost him here. He's the leader of The Natural Order."

Haley exchanged a look with Oni, who nodded at whatever thought passed between them. "Come with us. I'll see what I can find out for you."

Kyle had a million questions, and they multiplied as they left the thriving square for neighborhoods that looked increasingly poor and deteriorating. Tan, however, seemed confident enough in these young women to follow them, and she was the tracker. Finally, they entered a vacant multiple-story building. Most of the windows on the front of the building were broken out, and the staircase was dark as they walked up four flights, then down a long hall. Doors stood open to cold, empty apartments where moonlight exposed dirty, ragged carpet and broken glass.

At the end of the hallway, Haley opened a battered door labeled MAINTENANCE, and they stepped into a small room that had a single mop and bucket. She pressed her hand to a dirty spot on the wall, and when it began to move Kyle realized it was an elevator. Haley opened the door at the back of the room when they stopped, and they stepped into a bright, warm room where a dozen people of all ages milled about.

Haley turned to them. "Welcome to the San Pedro network."

Kyle stared. "What is this place?"

Tan dropped her pack on the floor and shucked off her outer clothes, obviously making herself at home. "The network is in almost every large city. The people you see here are probably all gifted in one way or another and have been rejected by their families or found it impossible to live in regular society because of their gifts. Not all of the gifted find their way to a temple and understanding mentors like Alyssa or have other nurturing gifted in their families like you. Some of us, like me, end up on the streets. That's where the network finds us and gives us a home and a family that understands us."

"Oni is an empath," Haley said. "I'm a shield."

Tan looked at her curiously. "A shield?"

"I can put up a force field that can deflect practically anything."

Kyle's eyes met Tan's. That's what Toni had done. She must be a shield. If Haley had the same gift, there must be others.

"I'm guessing you have telepaths to pass the word along about the guy we're searching for?" Tan asked.

Haley grimaced. "We have one. But he's a pain in the butt. He runs things just because he's the only guy who can tap into what this cult is doing."

"I'll take my chances with him," Tan replied mildly.

Kyle was suspicious of this calm, relaxed version of Tan that had replaced the intimidator, but she'd wait and follow Tan's lead since she obviously knew more about this network than she did.

They walked through several small rooms where people of various ages sat on loungers, engrossed in their digital tablets, networking or watching news vids or reading or answering d-messages. In the third, much-larger room, Haley led them to a dark-haired young male Kyle judged to be on the cusp of his third decade, still more boy than man and probably ten years her junior. He was handsome, with a sparse stubble of dark beard and huge blue eyes. He stood when they entered the room, his eyes roving over Tan's muscular yet womanly physique.

"Who do you have here, Haley?"

"This is Tan and Kyle," she said. "Tan is network. Third Continent, Montreal. Ladies, this is Zack."

Several inches taller than Tan, he circled and looked her over. "What beautiful skin. Darker than most of the women here. Love the hair. It's so retro."

Tan stared ahead, her expression amused, as he murmured his appreciation. Zack paused and looked puzzled. Tan raised an eyebrow. "Problem, thought-stealer?"

His eyes narrowed. "Either you know how to shield your thoughts, or there's a steel plate under this lovely skull of yours." Zack lifted his fist to knock on the shaved side of Tan's skull, but a hand closed firmly around his wrist.

"Show some respect, boy." Kyle's growl was low as she twisted his hand away from Tan. "You're addressing a captain of The Guard, an elite unit appointed to protect The Collective."

Zack's face contorted, and the young man turned into a whining boy. "Ow, let go. You're burning my arm."

Kyle released him. She hadn't realized she'd turned up her body heat. Isn't that what Jael had cautioned her about? She had to learn better control. She glanced at Tan, expecting a rebuke. But Tan's expression was smug.

"You'll have to excuse Blaze. She's a pyro with a short fuse." She laughed at her own bad joke and slapped Zack on the shoulder. "You should never probe someone's thoughts without asking permission, pup."

He shrugged. "People just make it too easy for me to hear." He cradled his right hand, the wrist red and blistering, against his belly and glared at Kyle. "I can hear everything you're thinking. You think she's—"

A blue flame flared from Tan's palm and licked at Zack's nose, making him yelp.

"You also don't announce what you hear to general audiences." The relaxed, friendly Tan was gone. She moved in front of him, nose to nose, and backed him up a step. "Did I mention that I'm also a pyro? My fuse is even shorter than hers."

Others had drifted in from the other rooms, watching the exchange. Tan turned to them. "We're looking for a man named Cyrus. He calls himself The Prophet and is the leader of The Natural Order. He was last seen in San Pedro, but he might have left here. We believe he's traveling with two or four bodyguards. If any of you have any information that could help us track him, or know anyone who might have information, you would honor The Collective by coming forward."

Kyle activated her IC to project a hologram of Cyrus.

A man stepped forward. "And what is your intent?"

"We're an advance team of an army recently formed to stop this cult from its aggression on society," Tan said.

A woman spoke from near the door. "They're hoarding food and medicine, and other supplies. We've managed to jam some of their communications and intercept some of their shipments and return them to the population, but not nearly enough."

"Everything you do helps," Kyle said. "It's good that people are fighting back now in the cities and towns, while The Collective's army goes after the core group."

Zack still scowled, his arms folded carefully over his chest in deference to his blistered wrist. "How do we know you aren't just double agents trying to infiltrate our network?"

Tan walked over to him and knelt. "Look into my memories and behold The Guard and the dragon-horse army they command."

Zack hesitated, then slowly reached for her, his fingers lightly touching the smooth skin on either side of her Mohawk. He closed his eyes for several moments, then drew in a long breath. When he opened his eyes, they were full of wonder. "Sun and stars. Do such beasts really exist?"

"Phyrrhos might take offense at the term 'beast,' but yes."

The others crowded closer. "What'd you see?" Haley asked.

Zack waved his arms in a wide gesture. "An army of pyros riding flying horses. No. Not horses. Dragons. Or half horse, half dragon. They were incinerating these believers and sending them to their next lives right where they stood. It was like something out of a fairy tale."

"They're very real," Kyle said. She looked to Tan and, receiving a nod of permission, spoke to her IC. "Show Phyrrhos."

Those in the center of the room stumbled backward and gasped as a holo of a stunning copper-colored dragon horse, wings spread, glittered before them.

"This is Phyrrhos. She's bonded to Tan," Kyle said. She allowed the image to remain for a minute, then withdrew it.

Zack looked at Tan with new respect. "We'll help." He looked at the rest gathered in the room. "Let's get the network humming. Circulate the holo of this man, Cyrus. No one has more eyes than we do."

The others scattered, tapping away on their digital tablets. A young boy about eight years old tugged at Kyle's pants. She bent down so she could hear over the shuffle of feet and chatter as people connected with others via their tablets.

"My cousin was supposed to get married, but her boyfriend says he don't want to marry her now."

Kyle scanned the room for a parent or older adolescent who might be responsible for the boy. "Oh, I'm sorry. Your cousin must be very upset."

He nodded solemnly and touched his chest. "I can feel her sadness here."

Ah, an empath. She took his hand and led him over to a lounger, where she sat and patted the worn seat next to her. "It's important that you don't let her sadness overwhelm you. Is it your gift to be able to feel what others do?"

He nodded.

"People decide not to marry for lots of reasons. But it's better that they discover those reasons before they marry than afterward. Your cousin will meet someone else she'll like better."

He shook his head. "She loved Felipe with all her heart. But my auntie needed medicine real bad. My cousin went to the docks where a man said he could give it to her if she met him there. But he didn't have any medicine. He made her touch him, and he touched her. Then he gave her credits to buy the medicine. Auntie's better now, but Felipe said the man made my cousin dirty and he won't marry her." He looked as if his heart would break, and Kyle wondered how it must feel to be an empath, shouldering the sorrows of so many others. "Felipe wanted to kill him, but he got on a boat with the other men and they sailed away."

"I'm so sorry," Kyle said, wrapping her arm around his slim shoulders. They sat for a moment in silence, and she wished she could somehow absorb his sadness and leave him clean again. Then it came to her. "Would you like to hear about my first ride on a dragon horse?"

His serious eyes met hers. "You rode on a dragon horse?"

"Yes."

"Can I see the holo again?"

Kyle hesitated.

"Maybe smaller."

Kyle smiled and spoke to her IC. "Display desktop Phyrrhos."

The boy studied the small holo. "It sparkles."

"They're descended from the Akhal-Teke horse, know the metallic-like coloring of their hide."

He frowned. "They're skinny."

"I suppose they have to be, so they can fly."

He looked skeptical. "How come nobody's ever seen them

"During the day, they look like regular horses, but at sundow. they grow great wings and ridges down their neck and faces. The breathe fire like pyros project flame from their hands."

"Doesn't the fire burn their feathers?"

"Look closer. They don't have feathers. Their wings are more like bat wings."

"Do you have a dragon horse?"

"Not yet. I hope to. You have to bond with one, and it's very dangerous. If they don't like you, they can burn you up." She produced a small flame in her hand and extinguished it with a clap. "Poof."

"Wow." He stared at her. "But you said you rode on one."

"I did. I rode with a dragon-horse warrior, a friend."

"Were you scared?"

"No. It was wonderful."

She closed her eyes to fill her mind with the memory and felt him press close to absorb her emotions. "I could feel his muscles gliding under my legs as his great wings moved up and down, lifting us almost effortlessly from the ground. And then, it was as if the wind just picked us up and carried us. We glided through the wind currents like an eagle does, smooth as glass. It's not so scary at night because you can't really see the ground, only tiny lights below. But the stars, the stars seem so close you want to reach out and touch them." She opened her eyes and looked down. His were closed and his hands clutched her T-shirt.

"I want to ride a dragon horse," he said, his voice a whisper.

Finishing her impromptu conference with Zack and Haley, Tan knelt next to them. "What's your name, little man?"

He opened his eyes and looked up at Tan. "Pete."

"Where's your family, Pete?" she asked.

"My mom died, and my father took my sisters and brother and joined The Natural Order because they were hungry. He left me with my uncle because he said I was unnatural and I couldn't go with them. But my uncle barely makes enough credits to feed his own family since The Natural Order stopped people from getting basic rations. Zack knew my cousin, so he brought me here. He's teaching me how to build shields so I don't have to feel everything around me."

"That's very good, Pete. It's important that you learn that."

"I know."

"Do you mind if I steal your new friend away for a few minutes?"

Kyle was surprised the boy wasn't intimidated by or at least shy of Tan because of her uncommon appearance. Then she realized that he must be reading her as an empath. She was relaxed and smiling at him, her brown eyes soft in the diffused lighting.

"It's time for me to go to bed anyway." Pete smiled, too, and touched Kyle's arm after he stood. "Thank you. I think I'll dream about dragon horses now." He ducked his head in a shy gesture. "You can sit with me at breakfast if you want, at Zack's table."

"Thanks, Pete. We'll look for you," Kyle said, grabbing his hand and giving it a quick squeeze before he turned and trotted toward the door.

Kyle studied Tan. She'd been as gentle with Pete as she'd been intimidating with Zack. But as she watched, Tan's face returned to a stoic mask and her expressive brown eyes shuttered, becoming dark, unreadable pools.

"Haley says they have a place we can bunk for the rest of the night," Tan said, rising and gathering her pack without looking at Kyle.

"We aren't going out to look around for Cyrus?"

Tan turned to her and raised an eyebrow. "Where? Do you think Cyrus frequents bars? They're the only places open at night."

"No. Father wouldn't, but we could—"

"Diego knows where he and Simon sought medical help. We'll go there tomorrow when the day-shift people—the ones we'll need to question—are working."

"Right. Makes sense." Kyle felt foolish. Tan was right. She hadn't been any help at all.

Oni led them to a tiny room that had two thick sleeping pads on the floor with only about a half meter of space between them. "It's not much, but it's got a door you'll probably want to close so you can sleep. People are always up walking around out here. There's a personal facility just down the hall." She glanced toward the room where Haley was talking to Zack. "We're a little short on blankets, but I can see if I find a couple."

"This is great. Thanks," Kyle said. "We've got our bedrolls, so we don't need blankets."

Oni looked relieved. "Okay. Well, breakfast is at zero-seven-hundred. We don't have much, but you're welcome to join us."

Tan pulled a sack from her pack and handed it to Oni. "We have our own rations, but let me contribute coffee for everyone."

"Wow. This is kind of hard to get in the city. Thanks." She waved as she headed toward the food-prep area, clutching the bag close.

They both stripped off their boots but didn't undress. After separate trips to the personal facility, they closed the door and settled in the dark.

Kyle listened to Tan's soft breathing. She could see Tan's profile in the faint light that filtered under the door. The memories of that dark cave, of Tan naked and so beautiful squeezed the breath from Kyle's lungs. The silence was crushing her.

"Are we ever going to talk about it?" she asked.

"No." Tan's abrupt answer turned the knife of guilt that'd been sticking in Kyle's gut all day.

"I...I just wanted...I need to say I'm sorry." She tensed for the explosion of temper she expected. Instead, Tan opened her eyes and stared up at the ceiling, her brow furrowing. Kyle rushed to explain. "Somehow, I got caught up in the frenzy. I never meant to lose control and be so rough." She paused, her next words almost a whisper to herself. "You're so beautiful. I wanted to go slow and be gentle."

Tan frowned, her eyes still fixed on the ceiling in the dim light.

Kyle started to rise on her elbow. "Tan—"

Faster than Kyle could draw a breath, Tan rolled across the narrow space and pinned her to the pallet. Her eyes were fierce, but all Kyle could think about were the hips pressing against hers, the hard nipples she could feel through the thin cotton of their T-shirts. Tan's hand was in her hair, jerking her head back. She claimed Kyle in a hard, rough kiss of teeth and tongue, and scraped her nails over Kyle's taut left nipple. Kyle groaned with the onslaught of arousing sensations and writhed under Tan's weight. She was taller, but Tan was strong, much stronger.

"You think because you caught me under the influence of Phyrrhos' breeding frenzy that you know what I want?" Tan pinched Kyle's nipple and twisted hard. Kyle reflexively tried to pull away from the pain, but Tan tightened her grip on Kyle's hair and forced her thigh between Kyle's. "Maybe I like it rough." She jerked her thigh hard against Kyle's wet crotch and twisted her nipple again.

"Tan." Kyle wasn't sure if her strangled word was a plea to stop or continue. Tan didn't seem to care. Sweet tension began to build low in Kyle's belly as Tan continued to pump against her crotch. She pushed Kyle's T-shirt up, nipping and sucking her tender breasts.

"Tan." She groaned out her name when her body bowed tight as orgasm bloomed and held her there for several incredible seconds. She collapsed to the pallet again, her heart pounding, and Tan abruptly rolled off.

"That's what I do. I top. I jump and run. I don't cuddle and plan a bonding ceremony the next morning." Her words were hard and bitter. "If you want to apologize for something, it should be for taking advantage of me when I wasn't in control of myself."

Kyle flushed hot—with anger or embarrassment—it didn't matter. She had never, she *would* never take advantage of any woman. To her dismay, her eyes filled with tears as she lay there still wet and panting. Stars, warriors didn't cry. Kyle tugged her shirt down to cover her breasts and the hollow ache in her chest. Still, she felt so exposed. "I was trying to help, not take advantage." The words came out as a whisper, but, thankfully, her voice held no tremor.

"If I ever hear you've been bragging about it, I'll burn your tongue off."

Kyle should be furious. She should stab Tan with angry words. She should tell her that maybe Tan was the bragging type, but she wasn't. Anger was Kyle's usual response. Yet instead of rage, her heart bled for the fear at the root of Tan's mistrust. Tan didn't need the resentment she sought to provoke. She needed understanding.

"What happened is only between us. It will always be only between us, Tan."

Azar circled high on the edge of the great city of Brasília, with Bero and Potawatomi trailing his path. Furcho activated his earpiece and signaled the others to do the same, necessary equipment without Jael present to communicate orders telepathically.

"We could spend a lifetime trying to find them in the city. The warehouse is near the rail station on the other side of town. Our best bet is to start there and hunt outward. We'll skirt the city to the north to avoid air traffic."

"Check," Raven said.

"Confirmed," Diego said.

Unlike the villages, which were quiet in the long, cool hours before dawn broke, the city never slept. They finally found a muddy lot between two abandoned warehouses, inhabited only by a couple of men sitting against one building and passing a nearly empty bottle of tequila between them. They landed and each pressed their foreheads to their bonded dragon horse, then released them to go find safe pasture for their daytime transformation into horses.

The two men stared at them with bloodshot eyes.

The first man wiped at his eyes, as if to clear them. "Did you see—"

"No, man. I didn't see nothing. The tequila must be bad. You just think you saw flying horses," the second man said. He poured the few remaining drops onto the ground.

"You saw them, too," the first man said, turning to him.

"Nope. Didn't see anything."

"Then how'd you know they were flying horses?"

"Just a guess." He rose unsteadily to his feet. "I'm gonna surprise my old lady and go home. Flying horses. You must be crazy. I must be crazy."

The first man staggered to his feet, glancing at Furcho, Diego, and Raven as they approached. "Wait. I'm coming, too." He jogged to catch up to his departing friend.

Diego picked up the abandoned bottle and sniffed it before walking to a nearby waste receptacle to discard it. "Smells like perfectly fine tequila to me."

Furcho smiled. "But flying horses? Really, Diego. What will they think of next?"

They chuckled as they strolled down the dimly lit street, trailed by Raven, dark and silent.

❖

Simon's transport slowed to a stop in front of an expensive Brasília hotel. "Finally, some decent accommodations." He climbed out of the transport as his assistant came around to unload their luggage. "Make sure we have a suite and aren't disturbed before noon. I need to sleep." It was well after midnight, his arm ached, and he was bone weary. "Have our local guy come for a meet at one o'clock and order food for everybody."

"You got it, Boss."

"You're with me, Doc," Simon said. "I need something more to dull this pain." He pressed the digital gauge of the medical cuff again. "This thing isn't doing the job."

"You're doing that too often," the doctor warned him softly. "You've probably already damaged the nerves in your arm."

"Shut up." Sweat trickled down Simon's temple as he clenched his teeth and waited for the fire in his arm to abate. If he ever saw that pervert Cyrus had sired again, he'd make her pay for burning his hand to a crisp. He rubbed his face. The pain was wearing him down, and he needed to be sharp. It was time to form a plan to get rid of Cyrus and take over this operation. He'd had enough of these Natural Order freaks. The world he'd raise up from these disasters would be every man for himself. The guy with the most credits has the most power. That was the real natural order of things.

And he'd be the guy on top of it all.

CHAPTER NINE

Tan spotted Kyle hunched over her coffee, her pro-chow bar only half eaten.

"Finish your breakfast. Time to mount up, Blaze," she said, standing and waving Haley over. "Diego received some new information this morning, so we're going to pay a visit to a couple of believers who are holding a doctor's family hostage."

Although Tan had turned toward the wall, she'd lain awake and listened to Kyle toss and turn for several hours. When she heard faint talking, she rolled back to find Kyle had fallen into an exhausted slumber that made her jerk and mumble indecipherable words. Tan wanted to go to her, to soothe her troubled dreams. But she couldn't. Finally, she'd settled into a light, restless sleep, too.

Jael was the only person to whom Tan had ever wanted to completely give herself. But the soul-bond was missing between them. Although she was inexplicably drawn to Kyle, Phyrrhos was the only bond she was capable of making. Blaze deserved more, just like Jael deserved the mate she'd finally found in Alyssa. Tan knew she would never be worthy. She was stained from many lifetimes ago. That's why she still punished herself with Anya. That's why she could not soul-bond.

She wished Kyle had just let what happened between them stay in the cave. So, when she insisted on bringing it up, Tan didn't even think. She just reacted. She didn't want to hurt Kyle, but she needed Kyle to see they could only be colleagues. Yesterday, it seemed like they might become a workable team in this hunt. But now they weren't speaking again. So, her plan was the same as with everybody she pissed off—which was just about everybody she knew. She'd just act like nothing happened and give Kyle the chance to do the same.

Kyle rose without a word, draining her cup and stuffing the rest of the pro-chow bar into her pocket. "I'm done."

Tan sat on the table and put her booted feet on the bench next to where Kyle had been. She pointed to the bench, pulled out a bar for herself, and set two bottles of water next to her. "Sit back down. First rule of tracking—take care of your body. You may not feel hungry, but your body needs fuel to burn for energy." She held up her bar and peeled back the wrapper before shoving one of the water bottles over to Kyle. "Stay hydrated. Drink all of that and finish your bar while I eat mine."

Kyle complied without protest, finishing before Tan did. Haley joined them, and Tan chugged the last of her water. She took both water bottles and deposited them in a recycle bin, then looked at Kyle and Haley.

"Okay. I'm not your mother, but does anybody need to go to the personal facility? Because the first person who says 'are we there yet' or 'I've got to pee' is going to get left behind."

Haley laughed at her joke, but Kyle's eyes narrowed before she turned and walked away.

"Hey, where's she going?"

Tan shook her head. "She doesn't trust me and probably thinks I'm planning a long trip. So she's gone to the personal facility, just in case."

"But we're just going across town."

"I haven't told her exactly where we're heading."

Haley stared at her. "You guys are kind of weird together. I thought she was going to fry Zack when she thought he was disrespecting you yesterday. And you almost burned Zack's nose off when he started to tell everybody what she was thinking. But in the next minute, you act like strangers."

Tan shifted under Haley's scrutiny. What did she care what this kid thought? "I usually track alone. I'm not used to having to haul somebody else along with me." She shrugged. "Maybe I forget to share stuff sometimes, and she gets all bent about it."

Haley looked skeptical but shrugged. "Not any of my business."

Kyle was striding toward them, their two featherweight rain ponchos folded over one arm. She handed one to Tan. "It's raining outside." She looked at Haley. "Sorry. We don't have a third."

Haley waved her off. "No problem. I've got rain gear."

❖

Raven rested a shoulder against the side of the warehouse. There was absolutely no security. She'd walked in freely and seen stacks of crates labeled for rural destinations that should have been transported out within days of their arrival. Their shipping labels, however, indicated they'd arrived at least two weeks ago.

While she was checking the warehouse, Diego and Furcho paid one of the workers to use his solar cycle to go into the city. Diego planned to meet a local contact, while Furcho visited the Chief Advocate at the Cathedral of Brasília, an impressive structure that remained from before The Great Religion Wars. She peered up at the sun, already so bright it pierced through the dark glasses screening her eyes. It had to be at least zero-nine-hundred.

She was hungry and hoping for something better than the pro-chow bars they'd been eating for the past two days it took to fly the dragon horses from the base camp. She wondered, not for the first time, about their disadvantage. The Natural Order guys could hop in a solar plane and cover the same distance in hours. Was The Collective's downfall going to be its adherence to ancient methods? She had to believe the First Warrior had considered this possibility.

Raven abandoned her ruminations when she spotted Furcho and Diego motoring toward her. She jumped out of the way as Diego brought the cycle to a jerking, wobbly halt.

"I told you I should steer." Furcho raised his voice over the noise of his boots scraping across the gravel as he put his feet down to steady them.

A couple of men peeked out from the warehouse entrance to see who was yelling.

"You're too tall. I can't see anything when you're in the front," Diego said, matching Furcho's volume and irritation.

Furcho hopped off the cycle and began brushing dust from his clothes. He was very fastidious about his appearance. "Unfortunately, I can see over you—everything we're about to hit."

"We didn't hit anything. That man jumped up on the curb."

"Gentlemen," Raven said, hoping to quiet them. She'd rarely seen Furcho rattled.

"You ran over his chicken." Furcho's face was red, and he practically sputtered as he stared incredulously at Diego.

"He was taking it to the butcher anyway. Dead now or dead later. What does it matter?"

Raven held up her hands and shouted. "Guard." They looked at her. She gestured toward the warehouse where a group of men stood, still watching them. She lowered her voice to a normal tone. "You're acting like a couple of schoolboys, and your playground audience is starting to lay bets on who's going to throw the first punch."

"You're right, Raven. Thank you." Furcho closed his eyes, and his shoulders slumped. "Sorry, Diego."

"Yeah, me, too," Diego said. "We're here in one piece, right? No problems."

"I have no idea what's gotten into me. I think—never mind. It's nothing." Furcho rubbed his face. "Tell me what you found."

"Lots of crates that arrived several weeks ago and haven't been shipped out to the rural distribution stations."

"What did the quartermaster say?" Diego asked.

"He hadn't arrived yet when I asked," Raven said. "I just walked right in, looked around all I wanted, and nobody even asked who I was or what I was doing."

"That's odd," Furcho said. "If The Natural Order has control of the warehouse, there'd already be security in place. But if they don't, those crates should have been shipped."

"Maybe the quartermaster is here now," Raven said.

Furcho hesitated. "We don't have the authority to demand an accounting."

"Didn't you see the Chief Advocate of the city?" she asked.

"No. The Natural Order believers have taken over the temple. We still need to find out what happened to the Advocates who lived there."

"My contact has lodging for us and has arranged a gathering this afternoon," Diego said.

"Then we should get a few hours of sleep," Furcho said. "I'll report to Jael, and then we'll meet with the other citizens."

A man approached from the warehouse. "You're back, I see."

"Yes," Diego answered. "Thank you for the use of your cycle. We've returned it without a scratch on it."

"Only a little chicken blood," Furcho said under his breath.

"Good, good." The man nodded. "I see the credits are already transferred. Thank you very much."

"Say, friend." Raven stopped the man as he started to wheel the cycle toward the warehouse entrance. "Can you tell me why the crates for the rural distribution centers haven't been shipped out?"

"No. Can't say." The man glanced toward the warehouse.

"The shipping labels indicate they arrived several weeks ago, but they're still sitting there," she said.

The man shifted nervously. "You want to know, go ask the head quartermaster. I just do what I'm told to do."

"People need the food and medicine that are in those crates," Furcho said. "What if it were your mother or child who needed medicine or was hungry?"

"Go away. Quit asking questions. It'll get you in trouble." The man began backing away. "I don't want trouble. I'm trying to keep my job so I can feed my family, okay?"

❖

Cyrus stared at his plate. Fish again. Was that all they had on board to eat?

"What's the matter, Boss?" Luke, one of his guards, picked the white, flaky flesh from his fish and arranged it on a large flour tortilla with beans, avocado, and salsa.

"I'm sick of fish." Cyrus pushed his plate away and went to the cabinet for the bread. "Make me a grilled-cheese sandwich."

"You ate that for the last three nights," Luke said cautiously, buying time so he could finish creating his fish burrito and take a big bite before rising to go to the stove.

"It's better than eating stinking fish." Cyrus stabbed at the one that had been dished up for him. "How do you even know that's a fish that won't poison you? That idiot Bobby is still sick after eating that stupid fish he caught the first day."

"That's because he listened to those crew guys when they told him eating barracuda would make him more virile." He turned on the stove and started cooking Cyrus's sandwich. "Those things are full of bones and don't even taste that good. He's an idiot. He's probably got a stomach full of bones." He eyed Cyrus. "You know that girl in the warehouse?"

Cyrus glared at Luke. Yes, he knew about Bobby soiling himself with that girl.

Luke flipped the sandwich in the frying pan. "One of the crew guys told me she was the niece of the first mate. They're afraid he's going to throw Bobby over the side before we reach Galveston. Maybe they figured if they made him sick, he'd stay down below and the first mate would leave him alone."

"Will he be able to travel when we arrive?" Cyrus was eager to make port and travel to this City of Light Simon had promised him. It was imperative to get his message to the world. He was wasting time on this boat, surrounded by morons.

"If he's not, we'll leave him at a hospital," Luke said, shoveling Cyrus's sandwich onto a clean plate and returning to his burrito. "We'll meet other believers in Galveston who'll have our travel arrangements ready from there."

Cyrus nodded. "Good, good." He bit into his sandwich. At least he had one competent person with him.

❖

Haley's rain gear consisted of a sombrero and piece of waterproof tarp with openings cut for her head and arms, but Tan thought it blended better with the city's population than her and Kyle's hooded camping ponchos. She was getting sloppy in this lifetime. Would memories of being warriors be enough to carry them successfully through this crisis? At least the network's beat-up transport, with a roof but no doors and sprayed with graffiti, was the norm among local teens.

The deteriorating buildings with broken-out windows gave way to a retail district, and that gave way to a patchwork of multi-family housing. Children roamed the streets because they had few open places to play. Haley drove cautiously, yelling at the older kids who were belligerently slow to move out of the way. The residential area evolved into a business and industrial district. Haley turned into a narrow alley that was mostly blocked by a large delivery transport. She waved at the man sitting in the open rear of the transport.

"I've got your customers," she told him.

Tan met his gaze when he looked them over with a critical eye. "Twenty credits each just to drop you off, right? I don't wait and don't come back to pick you up."

She nodded curtly. "That's the deal."

Kyle tapped the information into the IC on her forearm, then touched it to the man's IC when he held out his arm. He watched the transfer, then jerked his head toward his transport. "Get in."

Tan gave Haley a small wave. "We'll find our way back later to see what your team's turned up."

They climbed into the back of the transport, and the man pulled the door down to seal it. The only seat was for the driver, and since they preferred to stay out of sight they sat among the boxes in the back.

"That street has twelve houses, and I have deliveries to make at two. These are nice houses, so I deliver to the back doors, using an alley." He kept his eyes forward on the road as he spoke over his shoulder. "The house you want will be the third on the right. I'm delivering to the fifth on the right and the last on the left."

"If you don't see anyone around when you stop for the first delivery, we'll be gone when you get back to your truck," Tan said. She shed her poncho and folded it to fit into one of the cargo pockets of her pants. "The poncho material makes too much noise," she said. Kyle nodded and did the same.

They drove for about twenty minutes before the truck slowed and swayed as it bounced. Tan could see the narrow alley of pitted dirt through the windscreen. Neat fences and stone walls topped by silver coils lined the lane, interrupted by an occasional garage.

"What's that on top of the fences?" Kyle asked.

"Razor wire," Tan said. "It's very sharp and keeps burglars from climbing over the fences and stealing what they want."

"People are stealing to survive," the driver said, turning to look at Tan for the first time. "The peacekeepers are overwhelmed, so the citizens with pantries full of food and medicines are putting locks on their houses and walls around their courtyards."

"How can one man destroy decades of relative peace in a matter of months?" Kyle's words were bitter.

Despite Tan's determination to hold Kyle at arm's length, her heart hurt for her. She knew, too, the relentless gnawing of guilt in her belly. "If not Cyrus, some other disease would have eventually exposed the weak immune system of The Collective," she said, hoping to ease Kyle's pain a little.

They stopped, and the driver checked his IC, then selected a box from the shelf beside Kyle. "The house you seek has an iron-post fence. No one's in the yard, but the gate has an electronic lock."

"The lock's no problem for me." Kyle took a tiny tool set from her front pocket.

"I have to ring a bell at this gate, and they'll unlock it remotely. Once I go in, you can slip out." He scanned the area through the windscreen, then paused in the doorway of the truck, as if checking his address.

"All clear," he said, stepping out and pushing the bell beside the gate.

Tan slipped silently out of the door on the other side of the truck as soon as she heard him push through the gate, with Kyle on her heels. They walked casually to the wrought-iron gate, and Kyle removed the plate on the locking mechanism. Tan surveyed the house. All looked quiet. She was about to tell Kyle to hurry when the gate swung open.

Tan nodded and led the way in a crouching run around a pristine pool to the back of the house, where they knelt against the brick exterior. The house wasn't a mansion, but those were few in this new era of more evenly distributed wealth. Tan peeked into the window of the rear door. A woman was facing away from the door, stirring something on the stovetop. She ducked down and put her mouth close to Kyle's ear.

"You go in the back door and try to get to that woman without alerting the two men guarding her. I'll go around front to take a more direct approach. If I can distract the men, see if you can sneak the woman and two girls out the back and away from harm."

Kyle nodded and Tan started to move away, but Kyle's long fingers wrapped around her forearm. "They're probably armed with projectile weapons. You won't have time to melt a bullet at that close range, so be careful."

The snarky retort making its way from Tan's brain to her mouth evaporated when she looked into Kyle's eyes, impossibly blue in the sunshine. "You, too, Blaze," she said.

Kyle drew a deep breath as Tan disappeared around the house, then peeked into the window. The woman still had her back turned, busily chopping vegetables she was adding to the pot on the stove. Kyle used her magnetic tools to disengage the lock and silently opened the door to slip inside. The woman chopped noisily. Kyle closed the door and attached a small magnetic box to the locking plate, then easily moved behind her unnoticed. She covered the woman's mouth with one hand and grasped her knife hand with the other—just in case the woman reflexively swung the blade at her rather than the vegetables. She whispered into the woman's ear. "Don't scream. We're here to rescue you and your daughters. Do you understand?"

Kyle could feel the tension coiled in the woman's small frame, but she nodded her understanding.

"My name is Kyle. I'm going to let you go. You should keep chopping while I ask some questions." Kyle released her, but the woman's eyes were bright with panic.

"You must disarm the alarm or it'll go off," she whispered. "They don't guard it because they changed the code. I don't know it."

"Relax." Kyle pointed to the box attached to the door plate. "That box fools the alarm into thinking the door is still locked." She gestured to the counter. "We don't have much time. Chop."

The woman put two more tomatoes on the chopping board and began cutting.

"How many guards and where are they?"

"Two. They're both in the living room watching the d-vids."

Kyle could hear the sounds of an action vid playing, and she snuck a look. A dining room separated the food-prep area and the living room, but the wall between the two other rooms was little more than open shelves holding decorative items. She could see the back of one man's head and the profile of another sitting in a chair. A hallway was immediately to the right.

"Besides you, how many hostages?"

"My two daughters. One is ten, the other sixteen. They're down the hallway in the last bedroom on the right. We've been staying together because I don't trust those men."

A loud knock sounded at the front door.

"That's my partner," Kyle said.

"They'll expect me to answer the door."

"Go into the dining room and ask them to see who it is. Tell them you can't leave your cooking right now." Kyle ducked behind the cold storage, peeking around it for a clear line of sight to the front door.

The woman took a few steps into the dining room. "Hey, I'm frying tortillas. It's probably my daughter's boyfriend. If you tell him she's not here, he'll go away."

She came back into the kitchen as the man in the chair stood and went to the door. Kyle nodded and signaled for her to turn off the stove. The man's big body filled the doorway so she couldn't see Tan, but she was speaking loud enough to be heard clearly.

"Simon says he doesn't need you guys to babysit any longer. His hand is all better and he's sending the doctor home on the next plane," Tan told the guard.

Kyle bent close to the woman's ear. "Go quietly and get your daughters. Don't stop to get anything. Just them. Then come back down the hall, but stay back enough so they can't see you from the living room, and wait until I wave for you to come this way and out the back."

The woman slipped silently into the hallway while the second man paused the vid and rose to stand in the middle of the living room. He had a projectile weapon at his side.

The big man turned to the first man and smiled. "Hey, did you hear that? That's good news. I'm sick of sitting here."

The second man stared at Tan, then also smiled. "Come on in, friend." He backed toward the dining room and swept his hand toward the lounger where he'd been sitting. "Maybe you'd like to have a seat while we ask a few questions."

Tan smiled a predatory smile. "I'm in a bit of a hurry, if you don't mind, but I'm supposed to confirm that the doctor's wife and daughters are unharmed."

"Yeah, about that."

Kyle cursed under her breath. The man had moved so that she couldn't see his gun hand. The woman and her daughters were now waiting in the hallway.

"Why would Simon send a woman to tell us?" the gunman asked.

Tan shrugged. "Less threatening to the lady and her daughters, I guess."

The big man laughed. "Sun, you nearly scared the dung out of me when I opened the door, dressed like a man and shaving your hair off on the sides."

"Now I remember where I've seen you." The gunman raised his weapon.

Kyle stepped out while the men's backs were still turned and motioned the hostages to slip out behind her.

The gunman glared at Tan. "Grab her hands. Now!"

Everything happened at once.

Tan ignited her hands, but the big man grabbed her forearms, stopping her from flinging a fireball and swinging her toward the gunman. Tan used their momentum to continue their spin as the gunman began firing. The spray of bullets tore into the big man's back before two narrow blue-white columns of flame from Kyle incinerated the gunman's head. His gun and body dropped lifelessly to the floor.

Tan pried her arms free of the big man's grasp. He lay on the floor, a pool of blood widening around his upper torso. A fine bloody mist coated his lips with his last breaths. He blinked once, then stared blankly into his next life.

The other man was facedown. At least he would have been if he still had a face. His head was a blackened husk, the skull cracked open like an egg from the intense heat and his brain charred black. Dung, she'd never even seen Jael do that before. Not that she couldn't. She just had more control than this untrained blazer.

Souls above. Jael wasn't going to be happy about the mess they'd made here. She'd have to see if the network could haul the bodies out after dark and get them to a rooftop tonight. She straightened and looked around. Kyle stood in the dining room. Behind her, the woman stood in the food prep doorway, her wide-eyed daughters peeking around her. The woman's gaze was calm.

"Ma'am. I'm very sorry for the mess."

The woman walked forward and lightly touched Tan's shoulder. "You're bleeding."

Probably the adrenaline flowing. She hadn't even felt the bullet graze her shoulder, slicing a shallow seven-centimeter cut in her deltoid muscle. That would smart later. "It's fine. Just a graze."

"My husband keeps some supplies here. Before we had children to raise, I worked as a nurse."

"Thank you, but I'm a physician. I'll take care of it when we return to our base. We need to clear out in case someone heard the weapon fire and calls the peacekeepers. Is there somewhere you and your daughters could go for the night? The house of a friend or a relative?" Tan asked. "We'll have someone come after dark and clean this up, if it's safe, so you can return to your home tomorrow."

"I'll take the girls to my sister's home. Then I'll come back and stay with my neighbor until your people arrive. I'll help them clean."

"You don't have to—"

"I want to scrub every trace of these filthy men from my house before my family spends another night here."

"I understand." Tan did understand. She recalled many places she wished she could scrub clean, memories she wished she could erase. But some stains would always remain. "Do you have a transport?"

"In the garage."

"Could you wait outside for us and drop us off in the city?"

"We owe you much more than a ride into the city. It would be my honor."

The woman ushered the girls out the back door, but Kyle stood rooted in the same spot. She was pale and silent, her eyes fixed on the man she'd incinerated.

Tan picked up the weapon the man had used. She superheated her hands until it was a useless lump of metal that could never be fired again, then threw it onto the belly of the big man. It didn't seem decent, no matter their crimes, to leave them sprawled about the room, and it would be easiest to drag the gunman alongside the larger man to cover them both with her poncho. She went down the hall to the personal facility and found a towel that she used to tie around the gunman's charred head. She didn't want to trail pieces across the floor while Kyle watched, looking like she was barely holding together. Then Tan gently lifted his shoulders, dragged him next to his friend, and covered them.

She went to Kyle and examined her hands. She'd seen pyros burn themselves by using too much heat, but Kyle's hands seemed fine. The rest of her wasn't fine though. Her skin felt clammy, and her pulse beat too fast when Tan held her wrists to turn her hands for examination. She grabbed Kyle's shoulders and shook her gently. "Kyle, take a few deep breaths."

Kyle's eyes remained on the covered bodies as if she hadn't heard.

Tan firmly cupped Kyle's face with both hands and moved so close their noses were inches apart. "Deep breath, Kyle. Take a deep breath."

Kyle blinked, then sucked in air as if she'd suddenly remembered to breathe.

Tan released her face and stepped back but gripped her shoulders. Kyle closed her eyes and a fine shudder ran through her, but she took a few more deep breaths. "That's it. A few more, but slowly and through your nose." Her skin was still clammy, but they needed to go. "You okay now, Blaze?"

Kyle opened her eyes and nodded but avoided Tan's gaze. If it was possible to turn any whiter, Kyle's face did, and she bolted for the back door. Tan let her go. She needed to check in.

Jael.

Here. What do you have to report?

The doctor's family is safe and has been retrieved. We have two believer casualties, however, and will need a rendezvous tonight to pick up the bodies. I'll let you know coordinates later.

Any word on Cyrus?

I've made contact with some old friends with many eyes on both continents. They're looking. I think we might find them a very useful tool in our fight.

Excellent. You and Kyle are unharmed?

Nothing that will impede our mission or fail to mend. But there's no time to elaborate. We're still on location and need to get the family to a secure place and return to base.

I'll expect a more thorough report when you rendezvous tonight.

As you command.

Tan sighed and walked to the cold storage. She grabbed a bottle of water and followed Kyle, whom she found doubled over, emptying her stomach into the flowers planted at the base of a banana tree. Tan offered the water, and Kyle rinsed her mouth and spit that among the flowers, too.

"Ugh. Not sure regurgitated pro-chow mixed with stomach acid is appropriate fertilizer for perennials," Tan said, trying to break the tension.

Kyle blinked at her, the attempt at humor obviously not registering.

"They're waiting for us," Tan said, pointing toward the transport idling in the alley just outside the open gate. The woman and girls were watching them. She closed her hand around Kyle's bicep and guided her toward the car.

"It might kill the flowers, but banana trees thrive on acid," Kyle mumbled.

Tan looked at her, surprised that she'd finally spoken, but Kyle's face held no expression. So which was Kyle—a flower or a tree? She'd taken a life today. Would this experience damage her or make her stronger?

Chapter Ten

I did as you suggested, Simon. We gave supplies to the believers and sent them over to the Cathedral to get the Advocates out of the way. Then, all it took was a few bribes to have the shipments held in the warehouse."

"Excellent." Simon eyed the man who had spoken. He was dressed in a fine suit, his dark hair slicked back like the mobsters in one of Simon's previous lives. This man had a lot of potential. Simon sat back in his chair. His body felt numb and his thinking a little slow from the narcotics, but at least he *could* think now that he wasn't consumed with pain. And his plan was so brilliant Cyrus would never know he was being undermined. While he and his misguided believers were making themselves a huge target for that infernal unnatural army, he would be quietly taking control simply by manipulating man's baser nature—greed. "Xavier, isn't it?"

"Yes."

"I'm putting you in charge of the Brasília operation, Xavier. You'll be given access to a credit account to recruit a core group of enforcers you can trust. Those men—dung, I don't care if they're women as long as they're tough enough—will be the people who make sure the quartermasters at the central and outlying warehouses aren't giving away or skimming any of the merchandise or credits. The enforcers must make an example of anyone they catch doing that. Do you understand?"

Xavier's gaze was unwavering. "Perfectly."

"Good. You'll receive forty percent of all profits. However, once the initial credits I'm giving you for start-up are gone, you must finance your own operation from your cut of the profits."

Xavier tilted his head. "Once I've repaid the start-up cost, we can talk again about the division of percentage," he said.

Simon narrowed his eyes. He'd expect no less from a man who was ideally suited for the job. "Agreed," he said. "But first, we'll have to get those pesky pyros out of your hair."

❖

Furcho toed off his boots and stretched back on the bed in the room he and Diego would share. He was alone with the door closed for quiet while he spoke telepathically with Jael.

We need to find Cyrus's second in command. Cyrus is an expert in cultural history, not military and political strategy. I think Simon could be directing some of their moves now, especially in Brasília.

Tan contacted me about an hour ago. The family of the doctor Simon forced to go with him is safe now. See if you can rescue him, too, before things get too hot.

I'll assign Raven to that task.

Furcho rolled onto his side and reached into his pack to take out a silk scarf. He held it to his nose and closed his eyes. It smelled of Nicole. The silk felt like her hair trailing across his bare chest. Sun, he missed her. She was smart and sweet and sexy, but fiery when she saw injustice.

Furcho! Sun and stars. Can't anybody keep their mind on business?

Sorry, Jael. I drifted off course for a minute.

That was the trouble with telepathic reporting. He'd forgotten she was in his thoughts. He wasn't sorry, though. He knew Alyssa had softened the previously single-focus First Warrior. He smiled to himself.

Has Alyssa been by to make sure you're taking time for lunch? Of course not.

A long moment of silence.

Well, not yet.

Furcho had known Jael for many lifetimes and was her third in command, but he sat upright at the unfamiliar feel of her chuckle vibrating in his thoughts. He smiled, picturing her in her office, her eyes closed as she concentrated to project over such a great distance. Most people took her powerful gifts for granted, forgetting what it cost her to perform the feats no one else could.

We meet with Diego's contacts in an hour. I'll report back afterward.
Take care, my friend.
Don't worry. I have a very good reason to keep my hide in one piece.

The chuckle again.

Looks like my lunch steward has arrived. She says she'd appreciate it if you'd d-vid with her assistant Advocate so she'll quit worrying and get some work done this afternoon. I'll message her to sign on the d-tablet in Alyssa's desk.
As you command, First Warrior.

❖

Jael opened her eyes as Alyssa slid into her lap.

"No, don't open your eyes yet," Alyssa said.

Jael closed her eyes again and smiled as Alyssa nestled into her arms, her short, spiky hair tickling her neck. She smelled of warm vanilla and cocoa butter from the poultice Jael knew she mixed for burns. She dropped her mental shields and formed the picture. It was always the same—their place.

The field of wildflowers rippled like a flag of red, yellow, blue, and orange. The sky was an impossible blue and the sun warm on their skin. Sometimes they just sat in the field, holding hands or each other. But today, Alyssa stood to her left and bowed slightly to her. Jael instantly understood and returned the gesture. Then they began a flowing twenty-four-movement tai chi. No one else—not even Second, who as her clone was almost physically identical—matched her in such perfect unison. The last move executed, they bowed, and the mental image faded.

Jael let out a long, contented breath, then kissed her mate. "Thank you."

"I could feel your tension all the way in the food prep while I was making a tray for us."

Jael noticed, for the first time, a tray on the long conference table that doubled as her desk in their temporary encampment. It held a simple lunch of fruit and a couple of sandwich wraps. She realized she was hungry and picked up one of the wraps. "This looks good. But where's Second?"

"She and Michael are sleeping. They've been training the army with you at night and working all day to get the medicine laboratory up and running, and I think it finally caught up with them."

"I would have made myself something as soon as I finished with Furcho's report."

Alyssa slid off Jael's lap and into the chair next to her. "Sure you would have. Remember who you're talking to."

Jael smiled and shrugged. As an empath, Alyssa could almost always detect when someone was lying to her or even to themselves.

"Okay, maybe not. But if I always ate when I'm supposed to, then you might not come visit me at lunchtime."

Alyssa swallowed the food in her mouth and stretched to touch her lips to Jael's. "Honey, I'd still have lunch with you whenever possible. Now, tell me what's got you so worried."

Jael chewed her food while her mind chewed over her thoughts. She normally discussed her battle-strategy concerns with Second. Alyssa had no experience in such matters. And yet, she should share everything with her partner. Something else tickled at the back of her mind. Then she remembered what the most ancient of The Collective Council had said.

Open your mind, First Warrior. You will need to look through both old and new eyes for what is coming. We are stronger together.

"Our force is young and untrained. I don't like splitting up the handful of experienced warriors I have." She stood and paced by the windows. "I have a roaring lion headed north and a slithering snake headed south. Should I pursue both at the same time, or first one and then the other? But who is the greatest threat?"

Alyssa shoved her plate away. "Can I ask what Furcho reported from Brasília?"

"They haven't met with the local contacts yet, but believers have taken over the Cathedral of Brasília. They don't know what happened to the Advocates. The warehouse doesn't seem to be under any guard, but shipments aren't going out to the rural distributors for some reason, and the workers won't tell them why. I've d-messaged the World Council for credentials that will allow Furcho to demand access to the quartermaster's record-keeping."

Alyssa stood and tugged at her right earlobe, a familiar gesture that meant she was thinking, as she stared out the window. "We should have sent Nicole with them."

Jael snorted. "Right. I need Furcho's mind on his work."

Alyssa gave her a dismissive wave. "Right before we came back here, when we spent a few hours reconnecting, do you remember what you told me was the toughest thing about this uprising?"

Jael thought back to their conversation.

This enemy has no army I can march against. He utilizes small pockets of soldiers disguised as believers and hides among legions of misguided innocents. When I walk through town, I don't even know if a person I meet on the street is loyal to The Collective or is secretly part of The Natural Order.

She nodded.

"Furcho, Diego, and Raven should have an empath like Nicole or Uri or me with them. How else will they know who to trust?"

She hadn't considered this point. She'd never thought of empaths as soldiers, but how many lives could have been saved in past wars if gifts had been acknowledged? Suicide bombers could have been detected before they walked into crowds or soldier patrols. "You're right. He plans to report again later. If we have time, maybe we'll send her to join them. But that still doesn't solve the problem of splitting my army."

Alyssa pursed her lips. "I was in fairly close proximity to both men that night of the raid. Cyrus is truly insane. But Simon—" She shuddered. "He's worse than badly born, Jael. His soul is horribly dark."

Jael wrapped her arms around her mate, as if she could shield her from any evil the world still held. "We'll go after the first one to surface. If they both surface at once, Simon will be our priority."

❖

Cyrus made a diving catch to save his d-tablet with one hand and grabbed for something solid to anchor himself with the other. "Isn't anyone driving this boat?" Not long after they rounded Cancun and left the Caribbean Sea to enter the Gulf, the sea had grown increasingly rough and the sky heavy with swirling clouds.

He repositioned his d-tablet to continue his reading, but the yacht pitched again, and he had to cling to the table to stop from being tossed to the floor. "Stars above!"

The deck pitched dizzily under his as he stumbled through the galley to his cabin. He put the tablet away and braced himself against the bulkhead or anything else solid to make his way topside. He wasn't prone to seasickness, but his stomach was beginning to feel a little uncertain. He needed some air.

The smell that wafted out when he struggled past Bobby's and Luke's cramped cabin didn't help. Bobby lay in his bunk, delirious and mumbling incoherently. He was dangerously dehydrated after days of being unable to keep even water in his stomach. But they could do nothing more for him on the boat, so Cyrus tuned out his moaning and started up the narrow stairs.

A powerful gust nearly threw him back down the stairs when he emerged on the outside deck. The air was heavy and lay on his skin like a warm, wet cloth. He spotted Luke starboard about twenty feet, arguing with the captain of the yacht. Now that he was topside, he was adjusting to the roll of the boat and walked carefully toward them.

"What's the problem?" He had to shout to be heard above the wind.

The captain turned to Cyrus. "You and your man should get below. Secure anything that's loose in your cabins and put on the life vests stored under your bunks."

"I'm not sure I want to be down there if we could possibly sink."

The captain nodded curtly. "You'd be welcome to my office. I'll be at the helm or in the communications room."

"We could have already been in Galveston if this numbskull hadn't been slowing us down." Luke glared at the captain.

The captain shook his head at Luke, then explained as if he were speaking to a child. "The sea anchor has been keeping us steady in these heavy seas."

"If that's so, then why'd you just pull it out of the water?"

The captain turned to Cyrus, ignoring Luke's accusing tone. "The weather conditions have suddenly changed. The storm has strengthened and moved our way. We're now northwest of a category-two hurricane, where the winds are most treacherous. It'll continue to gain strength as it crosses the Gulf. Our best option now is to outrun it."

Cyrus wasn't a physically powerful man, but he and his mate, Laine, had enjoyed hiking and camping when they were young. He'd grown a little soft over the past twenty years in a classroom, but these recent months of traveling from one disaster to another and then skulking through the Sierra Madres to elude The Collective Council's trackers had returned some of his previous vigor. He was not afraid. He was The Prophet, filled with The One. Nothing could harm him.

"Let's go below and prepare, Luke," he said.

CHAPTER ELEVEN

Kyle stared at the passing houses, but all she saw was the charred remains of the believer's head. It had happened so fast. The deafening blasts of the repeating weapon were bombarding her ears one nanosecond, and then a laser-like inferno was shooting from her fingers to explode the man's skull.

Her stomach roiled again, and she put her hand over her mouth. She didn't think anything was left in her stomach, but she didn't want to find out in the back of this woman's transport. Her fingers trembled against her lips, and she tucked both her hands between her legs to hide their shaking. She closed her eyes and felt smaller hands gently tug her left hand free. She looked down into the ten-year-old girl's dark, sympathetic gaze. Her voice was soft.

"When my stomach tries to come back up, my papa tells me to press here." She used both her thumbs to apply pressure to Kyle's wrist. "He's a doctor, so he knows."

Kyle closed her eyes and sucked in a breath. She was about to break into a million pieces, and the girl's kindness was a chisel wedging into the fractures she was barely holding together. She jerked and opened her eyes at the touch of something cool against the back of her neck. Tan, also in the rear seat of the transport, was reaching over the girl and holding a damp cloth against her.

"She's right about the wrist thing, but this'll also help the nausea," she said.

Kyle nodded. She reached back, and Tan gently positioned Kyle's free hand to hold the cloth. But Kyle didn't look at her. She couldn't. She couldn't bear the pity or, even worse, disdain for a want-to-be warrior with no stomach for battle. She should have gone home and searched for her mother instead of coming here. She could have taken her brother's place as an emergency responder, cowered under her mother's wing like the weakling she was. Then she'd still be able to close her eyes without seeing that man's charred brain smoldering in his shattered skull.

"My sister's house is a few blocks from here," the woman said, stopping outside the flow of traffic.

The older girl, who sat up front with her mother, pointed past Tan to a bench on the other side of the road. "My sister and I catch the public transport that stops there to go downtown. From there, you can board another or hire a personal transport to go wherever you like."

"Thanks," Tan said. "If nobody calls the peacekeepers, we'll have someone clean your house tonight so you can go home tomorrow."

The girl released Kyle's hand. "When's Papa coming home?" She looked up, and Kyle saw in her hopeful eyes the expectation of thousands—millions, if word continued spread via the d-net—that The Collective's contingent would right their world again. More lives would be taken and lost before that could happen. Panic swelled in her chest until Tan's hand clamped firmly on her shoulder to ground her.

"I can't say exactly, but we have people in Brasília working to rescue him, just like we rescued you today," Tan told the girl. "They have to wait for just the right minute so your papa isn't hurt. Okay?"

The girl nodded.

Tan turned to the mother. "It should be soon—within the week. You'll hear from someone before they put him on the plane for home."

"We owe you so much. Are you sure we can't do more?"

Tan smiled. "Share what you have with others, and teach your children to do the same. We are stronger together."

She exited the transport, but Kyle couldn't seem to move. The woman and her daughters stared at her. She told her arms to move, her legs to move, but her body remained frozen. The door opened and Tan was there, grasping her arm and urging her up. Then she was standing on the side of the road with no idea how she got there. She felt like she was watching a vid rather than being actually present.

Tan was beginning to really worry. They crossed the street, but instead of going to the bench the girl had pointed out, she led Kyle to the shade of a tree on the opposite corner. They sat and Kyle slumped against the sturdy trunk. Kyle moved like she was sleepwalking, her eyes vacant. Tan knew she needed fluids and rest, in a bed rather than under a tree on a busy street corner.

Zack.

She had no idea if he was telepathically strong enough to hear her summons as Jael would. They weren't mentally in tune like The Guard was to Jael, but they had left their ICs at the network quarters in case they were captured, and Tan didn't think Kyle was in any shape to take public transport.

Zack.
Geez. You don't have to yell. Woke me out of a dead sleep. What's up?
We need transport. We're at the corner of 11 Avenida Southeast and 8 Calle Southeast.

She could almost hear his mental yawn. *I'll see who's around.*

Quick, if possible. Kyle needs attention.
Functioning now.

His casual tone had disappeared.

I'll get somebody to you.

She was surprised when Haley arrived fifteen minutes later in the same battered transport from that morning.

"Rough day?" she asked as they maneuvered Kyle into the vehicle.

"Not too bad," Tan said.

"Looks like somebody cut you pretty good," she said, eyeing Tan's ripped and bloody sleeve.

"You should see the other guy."

Haley climbed behind the controls and slipped smoothly into traffic. "Kyle get hit, too?"

"No. She took out the guy that nailed me." Tan glanced back where Kyle was curled into a ball on the rear seat. "She saved my skin. It's her first time…taking another life. She's still processing that."

"Man. That's real darkstar."

"Yeah. Darkstar." The popular slang for "the worst that could happen" could have been an appropriate nickname for Tan. She seemed to carry and spread the worst karma of anyone she knew. She mentally rewound her entry into the house and tortured herself with a dozen scenarios of what she could have done differently to spare Kyle. The truth of it? Kyle was destined to be a warrior and would eventually have taken a life at some point. She glanced back. Kyle's eyes were open and unblinking, even though she was curled up as if to sleep. Tan recognized what lurked behind Kyle's blank eyes. She'd felt it in many lifetimes.

When they arrived, she guided Kyle toward their room, waving off Haley, Zack, and others who wanted to swap information.

"We need some downtime. It can wait."

Zack looked to Haley for a few seconds, obviously reading her thoughts, then nodded. "It'll keep."

"Thanks." She dug through their packs for the things she needed. "Haley, can you clear out anyone in the personal facility down the hall so we can have some privacy for about thirty minutes?"

"Sure. We've got two others people can use." Haley eyed Kyle, still silent as she slumped against the wall. She was pale and sweating. "Is she going to be okay?"

"Yeah. She needs to hydrate and rest, but she'll come around." She opened her med-pack and filled a hypospray injector from several of the medicine canisters. "While we're cleaning up, can you drop off a couple bottles of water here in the room? She needs fluids."

"You got it."

Haley left, and Tan gently grasped Kyle's arm to press the hypospray against the vein at the inside of her elbow, where it would enter her bloodstream quickest. Kyle blinked, panic again flooding her eyes. At least it was emotion rather than that disturbing flat, vacant stare.

"No."

The hoarse plea tore at Tan. "It's not a sedative, Kyle. It's only something for nausea and electrolytes. You need the electrolytes to balance your body chemistry so you can raise your temperature. You're too cold for a pyro." She gathered the clothing and the med-pack. "Let's go shower. We both need to clean off, and it'll help you warm up."

Tan made a mental note to find a way to thank Haley when she found the personal facility warmer than usual and empty. She locked the door and started the jets in the first shower stall to let the water heat. Kyle stood listlessly as Tan carefully undressed her, then shed her own clothes. She hissed in pain when she tugged her shirt over her head and her wound reopened where sleeve, blood, and damaged tissue had dried together. The sight seemed to wake Kyle from her sluggish state.

"Stars, Tan. You're hurt."

"It's just a graze."

"You're bleeding."

"Let's get in the shower, eh? We'll clean up, and you can help me seal it."

The wound seemed to give Kyle a sense of purpose as they moved under the gentle spray. Tan watched her face as Kyle filled her hands with body soap and carefully washed the blood and dirt away from Tan's shoulder. Her hands were sure and gentle, and were beginning to warm. Kyle would need to deal with her feelings at some point, but perhaps this respite from thinking about taking the believer's life was what she needed right now.

She filled her hands with soap and began to wash Kyle's body. Kyle's gaze jerked up to meet hers. A million questions swirled in the blue depths of her eyes. Tan had no answers, only that—for this moment—it felt right. She touched her cheek against Kyle's, wordless, and they continued bathing each other until both were clean. They stood under the drying vents together side by side, and then Kyle held Tan's wound together while the adhesive bonded.

"I love the color of your skin," Kyle said, releasing the sealed wound and trailing her fingers across Tan's bare shoulders.

Everything in Tan went very still. Kyle's touch was different than any she could remember. Each of her senses strained to decipher the reason for this without visibly reacting and revealing her confusion. Then the rough pad of Kyle's index finger traced the curve of her ear, thumb joining to tug slightly on her sensitive lobe. An involuntary shiver ran through her.

"Everything about you is stunning."

Tan turned to face her. They were still naked. She'd seen many magnificent warrior women in their natural state—ranging from heavily muscular to voluptuously curvy. Kyle's body was leanly muscled, almost boyish with her small breasts and narrow hips. But the smooth, flowing lines of her face and body were too graceful to be anything but female. "Kyle." Her wistful tone surprised her and erased anything further she'd thought to say.

It didn't matter because Kyle seemed to be fading again. She pressed her cheek against Tan's, then kissed her neck and rested her forehead on Tan's uninjured shoulder. "I'm so tired." Her words were faint and shaky.

Tan embraced Kyle, stroking her hands along her back to comfort her, to assure that Kyle's temperature was returning to normal. Or was it to reassure herself, to feel the odd combination of exhilaration and calm that she experienced every time she opened herself even a small bit to this unexpected enigma?

She reluctantly released Kyle and dressed them both in soft T-shirts and boxers. Kyle needed to rest, and, even though Tan needed to check in with Jael and Zack, she wouldn't leave Kyle to wake up from the inevitable nightmares alone.

Tan closed the door and extinguished the light to their room as Kyle stretched out on her sleeping pad without protest and rolled onto her side facing the wall. Her eyes remained open, but Tan hoped the dark room and fatigue would win out and Kyle would eventually sleep. She settled onto her own pad and listened in the stillness. She'd drifted into that drowsy twilight between waking and sleep when something catapulted her to full alert. She listened, barely breathing. The distant sounds of footfalls and voices beyond their door were normal background noise. Then she heard it—a faint hitching breath. She waited. Even in the dim light, Tan didn't miss the slight spasm in the outline of Kyle's back that came with the next muffled sound. Kyle was still turned toward the wall but curled into a tight ball like in the transport.

Tan rolled to her knees and crawled the short distance to her. Kyle shrank away when Tan's fingers met cool, bare skin because Kyle's shirt was pulled up and bunched in her hand to cover her mouth and muffle another choked sob. Something Tan couldn't define flooded through her. She wanted to absorb Kyle's pain into her own body, to melt into Kyle's wounded places and heal them. Kyle apparently didn't want anyone to see her so emotionally exposed. Tan understood. She'd felt the same when Kyle came to her in the cave. Still, Kyle had ignored her efforts to shut her out and met her need with no judgment, only passion and caring. She wanted, no, needed to do the same for her.

Tugging her shirt off, she raised her body heat and curled against Kyle's cool back. She stroked Kyle's short hair and gave in to her impulse to kiss the smooth curve of her neck. She spoke low and soft. "I've been a warrior for many lifetimes but didn't start to remember previous lives until I reached adulthood in my first life as a pyro. I was twelve in that incarnation when I first took another life, and it's that moment that's burned in my memory for all of time."

Kyle stiffened and edged away as her body jerked with another strangled sob, but Tan dropped her arm down and held her in a tight hug.

"I knew I had some pyro ability but had hidden it because I thought it was black magic. Then one day, a very bad militia group, Boko Haram, came to the village where I lived. They killed the men—my father and brothers—and forced the women into slavery they called marriage. The man who claimed me dragged me away from my mother and sisters to a hut on the outskirts of the village. He threw me on the dirt floor and ordered me to take my clothes off. I was only twelve and so scared, I just cowered. He slapped and kicked me, then began to tear my clothes off. Then he took his clothes off to show me his erection. I remember crying for my mother, but he only hit me more."

Another sob escaped, but Kyle's hand slid down to cover Tan's. Her chilled hand trembled, and Tan entwined their fingers to steady her.

"Then he pushed me facedown to the floor and climbed on top of me." Tan paused and took a deep breath. The memory from several lifetimes ago was vivid. "The next thing I remember is standing in that mud hut with blood running down my legs and his charred corpse on the floor. My hands were in front of me, flames still shooting from my fingers. I was so afraid for what I'd done. As bad as he was, I was scared that I was even worse to have taken another life. I fled because I was terrified I'd be executed as a witch. But they did worse. They tortured and murdered my mother and sisters as punishment for me killing that man."

Kyle made a strangled noise and vehemently shook her head. She turned in Tan's arms, her eyes finally meeting Tan's. Her gaze was bright and fierce again, and Tan's heart soared to see it. "You were a child. Sun and stars, he violated you. You only defended yourself." Kyle's voice was hoarse and tight. "I would have killed him for you if I'd been there." The fire in her eyes died as soon as she realized her words.

"Don't." Tan stroked Kyle's cheek and gave in to the need to touch her lips to Kyle's. "Don't punish yourself for wanting to protect a child, for protecting me today. If you hadn't reacted as quickly as you did today, his bullets would have hit me, too, when the big man fell. I would have bled out on that floor along with his friend."

This time, she lingered as she gently caressed Kyle's lips with hers, then tasted Kyle's mouth when she opened to her. She gently disengaged and held Kyle's gaze. "What happened today will never go away, Kyle. But when it haunts your dreams, I want you to dream about this instead, because I wouldn't be here if you hadn't protected me."

Tan rolled slowly to hover over Kyle. Sun and stars, she was both handsome and beautiful at once. Her eyes were a swirl of emotion. Desire? Fear? Self-incrimination? Tan hesitated. She wished she were empathic or telepathic. Was this what Kyle needed or what she needed?

"Please."

Kyle's whispered plea and the lift of her hips affirmed Tan's decision. Despite Kyle's disgust with what she'd done, the adrenaline of the morning was likely fueling some residual battle lust. Still, Kyle was fragile. Tan traced a finger along her thin brow, then across her smooth cheekbone. She looked into Kyle's eyes and smiled. "You're a very striking woman."

Kyle's face flushed, and she averted her eyes.

"No one's ever told you?" Tan asked softly.

Kyle gave a slight shake of her head. "Too tall. Too boyish."

"No. You're a magnificent warrior woman." She tilted her head to capture Kyle's elusive gaze and held it. "You're so beautiful, you make me ache inside." She hadn't realized the truth of it until her words hung in the air between them.

Naked vulnerability flared in Kyle's eyes, and unfamiliar panic rose in Tan's gut. Dung, she'd said too much, revealed too much. She couldn't blame this situation on breeding fever. She wanted to bolt for the door, summon Phyrrhos and fly very far away from this blazer who somehow made her burn hotter, purer inside than ever before.

Kyle's fingers trembled as they touched Tan's cheek. "The first time I saw you without your war paint, I couldn't take my eyes from you—so elegant, so exotic. Like pureblood royalty." Kyle's eyes—irises blue as a cloudless sky, pupils dark as starless midnight—reached out to Tan in a way that felt familiar and right. She pushed the panic away. She wanted this as badly as Kyle needed to replace her memory of incinerating the believer's head.

She captured Kyle's mouth again, drinking in her sweet taste, breathing warmth into Kyle's chilled body. The delicate curve of Kyle's ear, the soft throb of her neck and strong slope of her shoulder enticed Tan, and she savored each until Kyle moaned and her hands clutched at Tan's hips. Tan gently massaged Kyle's small breasts, then used teeth and tongue to torture the dusky pink nipples into rigid peaks. She rose to her knees and curled over to tickle her soft Mohawk along Kyle's taut belly and smiled at the shiver it produced. Tan lifted Kyle's legs and shouldered under her knees. Kyle's arousal filled her senses, moist and musky. She breathed her in and stared down the length of Kyle's long body, into her eyes, dark with desire.

"Please, Tan." Kyle's eyes were iridescent, begging in the dim light.

Tan took her carefully in her mouth, bathing every inch of Kyle's sex with the flat of her tongue except where she needed her most. Kyle writhed and whimpered, but Tan held fast to her hips. When Kyle's moans changed to a broken sob, she relented and raked her teeth against the engorged clit. She sucked the bundle of nerves hard and slid one long finger inside to massage that rough spot she knew should send Kyle rocketing to release.

Kyle grabbed her T-shirt and bunched it over her mouth to muffle her cry when Tan felt her body go rigid with orgasm. She watched the muscles in Kyle's abdomen tense and define as she peaked. But she felt cheated because the shirt had hidden Kyle's face from her. She wanted, needed to see Kyle's eyes when she came. Tan dropped Kyle's hips down to the sleeping mat and straddled her thigh. Kyle was slick and open as she shuddered through the last waves of climax, and Tan couldn't wait. She filled Kyle with two, then three fingers and thrust rhythmically in and out as she rode Kyle's thigh.

"Tan, Tan." Kyle's words came in short pants. Her body was warm now, her temperature still rising as she hooked her free leg around Tan's hips, opening herself. "Oh, stars. I'm going to come again."

Tan, her voice tight with the effort to hold off her own climax, stared down at Kyle. "Don't cover your face, baby. I want to watch you come."

Kyle blinked, and then her eyes lost focus and began to roll upward. "Oh, stars. Tan. I'm—"

Tan stroked deeper as Kyle's body closed around her fingers, and she bore down as she slid her hypersensitive flesh along Kyle's slick thigh. She could let go now. Kyle had let go. Kyle had seen her weakness in the cave. But she'd seen Kyle's now, too. Kyle bowed under her, her cheeks flushed, mouth slightly open in a silent cry and half-lidded eyes soft and unfocused. So incredibly beautiful. The thought barely registered when the air was sucked from her lungs and her belly balled into a fist of pleasure so intense she thought her heart had stopped beating. Then the fist let go, and she jerked and shuddered with wave after tingling wave of sensation.

She collapsed onto Kyle, breathless and trying to sort out what had just happened. Kyle stirred under her and Tan rolled off to the side. Kyle was taller, but Tan's muscle probably weighed a bit more and was likely squishing Kyle.

"Don't go," Kyle said, her voice low and sleepy. She turned on her side and snuggled against Tan, resting her head on Tan's shoulder. Tan tentatively wrapped an arm around Kyle's shoulders, then relaxed when she felt Kyle do the same.

"I've got you, Blaze baby." She stroked her hand down Kyle's long, naked back. "We'll dream together, eh? Picture you and me on Phyrrhos, gliding along in the warm jet stream under a midnight sky and a trillion stars."

"I'm on my dragon horse," Kyle muttered.

Tan chuckled quietly. "Okay. I'm on Phyrrhos, and you're riding your dragon horse, eh?"

"Sunfire. Her name is Sunfire. She says she can fly during the day, too."

Tan played along. "And when did she tell you this?"

Kyle's deep, relaxed breathing was the only reply. Tan kissed the brow of the woman resting safe in her arms, the woman who had earlier kept her safe, and joined her in sleep.

CHAPTER TWELVE

Fifty dragon horses and their silver-clad warriors gathered on the training field was an impressive sight, no matter how many times Alyssa sat on the overlook to watch Jael, Second, and Michael guide the recruits through maneuvers. While huge solar spotlights illuminated the field where more mundane instruction was given, the aerial exercises were fantastic displays of flame against the night sky. That's what she came to see. Well, that and the First Warrior commanding her troops. Jael had an instinct for leadership, when to be tough and formal or when to offer personal instruction and an individual word of encouragement. She made sure her officers identified the individual talents of each soldier and made the best use of them.

"Alyssa?"

She twisted toward the trail at her back and squinted to adjust her vision to the darkness. "Toni, hey. Were you looking for me? Everything okay at the clinic?"

Toni glanced around the large, flat stone outcropping that overlooked the dragon-horse army's encampment. "Oh, sure. Everything's fine. I was just, uh—" She looked up at the sky again and adjusted the straps of a backpack she was wearing.

Alyssa stood and brushed the dust from her pants. The backpack looked heavy. "Are you going somewhere?" She didn't like the nervous, secretive emotions she was sensing from Toni.

She was fond of the young woman and had hoped Toni had finally felt accepted in her role as Alyssa's assistant and hospital quartermaster.

Toni averted her eyes.

"Toni?" Alyssa spoke softly. "If there's something wrong, I'd like to help."

Toni sighed and dropped her pack to the ground. Before she could speak, stiff gusts of wind swirled dust and dirt around them. They both shielded their eyes and crouched to keep their footing since they were standing very near the outlook's edge. The wind abruptly stopped, and a familiar blowing sound broke the sudden silence. Alyssa slowly lowered her hands.

"Sun and moon." He was magnificent. Black as a moonless midnight. His wings, still unfurled as if he would take flight given the slightest cause, spanned nearly the entire width of the rock outcrop. She'd seen him before in flight, but not up close. How had she mistaken him for Bero before? He had the wide chest and thick, arched neck of a breeding stallion. And he carried the scars of past challenges. She frowned. Some appeared to be still-healing wounds. She wasn't sure, but she thought she sensed pain coming from him. She projected a calming, friendly emotion.

He shook his head, then stretched his nose toward them and blew out a breath, small licks of flame shooting from his nostrils as he scented them.

Although it was unusual for her to so clearly sense an animal, she definitely felt him. "He's hurt," Alyssa said, lifting her hand toward him.

He jerked his head back, and the red slits of his dragon eyes dilated as his chest expanded.

"No!" Toni threw herself in front of Alyssa and raised her hands, palms out. The column of blue flame that the dragon stallion spewed seemed to hit an invisible wall and dissipate. The stallion shook his wings and stomped his feet.

"Don't scream, don't scream, don't scream." Toni chanted urgently, her hands still raised.

"Are you talking to me or yourself?" Alyssa blinked at the tremor in her voice and suddenly felt rather silly. She was hiding behind a woman at least a head shorter, gripping the back of Toni's T-shirt like she was her only lifeline.

The stallion pawed the ground and tossed his head, his ears working back and forth.

"I was talking to him. If he lets loose one of those dragon screams, the entire army will come up here, and he'll be toast." Toni slowly lowered her hands. "Calm. I need you to project calm. But don't approach him. That's what nearly got you fried. He won't hurt you if he doesn't feel threatened."

Alyssa released Toni's shirt but kept her hands on Toni's back. The surprising steadiness of her assistant seemed to anchor her. She conjured a picture in her mind of a field lush with clover, a horsy favorite, and pushed it outward. The stallion lowered his wings a fraction, then a bit more.

"Good. That's right. You're hungry, aren't you, boy?"

The stallion loosely folded his wings, and his elliptical pupils pulsed as he watched Toni. Not anxious to be an exposed target, Alyssa squatted with Toni as she slowly reached for the backpack and tugged it in front of them. She opened the pack and waited while the stallion blew out a few breaths, scenting the air to check the contents of the pack. He snorted blue flame, as if in warning, then folded his wings tight against his body and backed up to the edge of the woods. Tony nodded and stood.

Alyssa grabbed the back of her shirt again. "What are you doing?"

"It's okay. He's hungry." She glanced over her shoulder at Alyssa. "I've got fire rocks in the backpack. I'm just going to empty them out over there and come right back. You stay here and don't move." She took a few slow steps and looked back. "It's really important that you don't move, no matter what. Okay?"

Alyssa nodded. "Okay." She watched Toni walk slowly but confidently to the other side of the outcropping and dump the fire rocks onto a small depression in the stone. When she returned, they quietly moved as far away as possible, considering he blocked their path to the woods on their left and the edge of the outlook was on their right. They sat and he watched them for a few more seconds, then ambled over to munch the rocks.

"This isn't the first time you've fed him, is it?"

Toni shook her head. "No. I was looking for a plant to make an analgesic you needed at the clinic and thought I'd seen it on the way to the wild nest. It took less than a day when we took a whole caravan, so I figured I could get up there and back easily before dark."

"You went alone?" Alyssa kept her voice low so she didn't spook the dragon horse but added a disapproving glare. She didn't expect it would be very effective, given the dim lighting, so the spike of bitterness that radiated from Toni surprised her.

"Yeah, well, my millions of friends were all busy."

Alyssa laid a reassuring hand on Toni's leg and squeezed. "You're wrong about that, but it's a subject for another day." She gave her another squeeze and withdrew. "So, you went to their mountain?"

Toni nodded, her eyes on the stallion. "I left really early and by midday was near where we'd camped. Then I heard these awful screams, and I ran to the edge of the forest." She nodded toward the stallion. "Dark Star—that's what I call him—was fighting with another stallion. Since it was daytime, they weren't in dragon skin, and Dark already looked pretty beat up and skinny. He had a couple of big burns and bad-looking wounds." Toni was quiet for a moment, and Alyssa could feel her wrestling with a swell of emotions. "The other horse, a big bay, won and chased him off." She turned to Alyssa. "That was his herd."

"Nature can be cruel," Alyssa said quietly.

"Why?" Toni asked. "Why does one animal have to die to feed another? Why do animals and humans have to hurt each other?"

She thought about her struggle to come to terms with the violence of Jael's mission. "Why must we have day and night, light and dark, life and death? Do we need pain to know when we're without it? Must we know sadness to recognize joy? I don't have answers to those questions, Toni."

Toni shrugged. "Anyway, I still get up early like I did when I worked in the stables, and I noticed him flying around the edges of our valley an hour or so before dawn. So I started leaving fire rocks up here. After they disappeared a few times, I stayed to make sure it was him eating them."

"Weren't you afraid he would—" Alyssa suddenly realized why they hadn't been burned before. She poked Toni in the side. "You've been hiding a gift, my friend."

Toni looked away. "It's nothing much."

"Nothing much? You kept us from being tomorrow morning's toast."

"It's not cool like being a pyro or a telepath."

Alyssa nodded. "Yeah. Being an empath isn't all that exciting either."

Toni chuckled. "Yes, it is. You know it is." She grew serious. "People can't lie to you."

Alyssa felt a wave of old pain, and she projected what she hoped would be a soothing balm to whatever hurt Toni carried that brought that emotion to her surface.

"Many things that hurt us also help prepare us for our purpose, our destiny. We can't see the destination but can only trust that our path is as it should be."

Toni sighed. "Are you going to tell Jael about Dark Star?"

"I have to. We let our shields down when we're together, so it's impossible to keep secrets. She hears my thoughts, and I know her feelings. And she would know if I was trying to keep something back. It would damage the trust we have in each other."

Toni grimaced at one particularly loud grinding noise as dragon teeth broke up the hard phosphorus bricks. "What do you think she'll do?"

"About the stallion or you saving my life?"

"She'll probably point out that I wouldn't have had to shield you if I hadn't been feeding him up here."

Alyssa smiled. "It's all in how you present it. Trust me. I know how to handle the First Warrior."

❖

"Who is this?" Simon didn't like interruptions, and he was engrossed in the weather reports scrolling across the large d-screen in his suite while this fool of a doctor pretended to administer to his hand. Simon wasn't stupid. The hand was useless. He hadn't even felt the cut on the underside near his elbow, and that stupid doctor hadn't found it until it started to smell.

Xavier led a man dressed in work clothes, nervously twisting a knit cap in his hands, forward. "This is Juan. He works in the central warehouse." He clamped his hand on Juan's shoulder, and Juan looked up at him. "This is *the man*. You understand?"

Juan nodded. "Yes, yes. I'll tell him everything I know. Only the truth."

Xavier released him. "Good man." He patted Juan's shoulder. "Strong, too. I'm looking for strong, loyal men to hire for very good jobs."

Juan straightened. "That's me. I know how to keep my mouth shut, too."

Simon wiped at the sweat that beaded on his face. How could he be sweating? It felt like the Alps in this hotel, and he was tiring of the chatter. "Xavier, call the front desk again. I swear the climate control in this room isn't working right." The doctor lifted his injured arm to secure the bandage around the elbow and blocked his view of the weather report for several seconds. "Enough." He jerked his body away, his arm flopping uselessly against his stomach. The doctor reached to secure it in the protective harness that looped over his shoulder and around his torso. Simon pushed him away. "I'll do that. Just leave it."

"The room temperature is fine. You have a fever from the infection in your arm. The hypospray antibiotics I have with me aren't working. You need to go to a hospital."

"I don't have time."

"You're running out of time," the doctor said.

"You let me worry about that."

Xavier studied Simon as the doctor gathered his instruments and bandages. He'd never been a big man, but he seemed to have shrunk over the past few days. His face was gray and damp with sweat. He didn't like Simon, but he respected him. He could learn a lot from him, make many contacts through Simon. He would stand in Simon's place one day, but he still needed him awhile longer. He touched the doctor's arm as he walked past. "Doctor?"

"If he won't go to a hospital, you'd better get a local doctor over here with a super-antibody infusion pronto."

"I can arrange it." Xavier waited while Simon stared at the screen a moment longer. He seemed to have forgotten about them. He moved close and whispered to Juan. "Go to the bedroom on the right and get something to cover him."

Juan nodded and moved around the long leather couch where Simon sat, ignoring them. Xavier stepped out onto the balcony and slipped a receiver in his ear. He keyed the IC on his forearm. "Report." He listened. "They're gone? Maybe they moved them to another place. Let me know if they contact you. Yes. Contact me, not Simon. He's still not well, but he'll be okay. I'm going to arrange for another doctor here, and the fellow Simon brought with him is going to mysteriously disappear. Yes. They've already been sniffing around. Soon."

He clicked off and keyed a different contact. "Have they arrived? Where did they last report from?" The smile grew on his face as he listened. "Excellent. I want eyes on that coast from New Orleans to Tampico." This was the news he would give Simon. The disappearance of the doctor's family, he would keep to himself for now.

He went back into the suite where Juan stood uncertainly, holding a light blanket. Xavier took it from him and went to Simon. "The hotel manager says they're working on the climate-control problem. Until it's fixed, Juan has brought a blanket. We must do something about your fever."

Xavier spread the blanket over Simon's legs and bunched the rest in his lap.

"I'm not going to any dung-eating hospital. I have an operation to run." Despite his protest, Simon shivered and tugged the blanket up over his chest.

"No hospital. I can arrange for a doctor to bring what you need here."

Simon scowled at the d-screen's weather radar but nodded.

"And, I have news you will want to hear."

Simon glanced up in irritation.

"Cyrus's boat has been delayed by the bad weather and has not arrived in Galveston." He had Simon's full attention now. "Unfortunately, the captain last reported their location northwest of the storm, which is now a category-two hurricane. I'm told the northwest edge of a hurricane is the worst place you can be. I'm afraid their situation is dire. We must pray for a miracle that they'll survive." He offered a small smile as he mimicked the believers' signature gesture of touching their foreheads, mouths, then chests when they ended a prayer—dedicating their thoughts, words, and hearts to The Natural Order.

The corner of Simon's mouth lifted in a half smile that looked more like a sneer. "Yes. That's terrible news."

Xavier waved Juan over. "Juan, tell Simon about the people you talked to at the warehouse."

Simon seemed to brighten with the news about Cyrus, and Juan stepped up boldly to give his report.

"There were three of them—two men and a woman two nights ago. The men were brown-skinned, like most in this region, dark hair—one young and handsome, one short and stocky. The woman was tall with long dark hair. The two men paid to use my transport to go into town, but the woman stayed and walked around the warehouse to look at shipping crates. We let her look, like Xavier told us. When the men came back, I heard them talking. They had been to the Cathedral. The woman told them about the crates that hadn't been shipped, and then they all left."

Simon nodded, lightly tapping his fingers on the arm of the couch.

"Did they ask you any questions when they returned your transport?" Xavier asked.

"Yes, but I did as you said. I told them nothing and acted scared. They didn't press the issue."

"Did you hear them say where they're staying?" Simon asked.

"No, I'm sorry. They only said that someone had arranged it for them."

"I can help with that." Xavier smiled. "That someone would be my second cousin's girlfriend."

CHAPTER THIRTEEN

Tan would have yelled at whoever was hammering somewhere outside their room, but the warm lips tasting their way along her neck were too pleasant to interrupt. The lips found her earlobe and sucked it into a hot mouth. She moaned, drowning out the noise for a few seconds.

"Good. You're awake," Kyle said. "I was beginning to think your heart had given out during that last orgasm." They'd awakened earlier and, their battle lust previously sated, made love slowly before falling asleep again.

Tan didn't open her eyes but couldn't stop the smile that pulled at her mouth. "I'm not awake. My heart did stop, and I need mouth-to-mouth."

Kyle's mouth covered hers, her tongue pushing, stroking against Tan's. She drew Tan on top of her and stroked overheated hands down Tan's back.

The racket grew louder. Not hammering. Someone was persistently knocking on their door. Tan broke off their kiss. "Son of a dung eater. If you don't stop that infernal banging, I'm going to come out there and burn your knickers off."

A giggle. "Oni says to tell you dinner's being served, and Zack needs to talk to you before it gets dark," Pete, the boy who'd talked with Kyle, said through the door. "That's only about an hour from now."

"Tell them to jump off. We're busy."

"Kyle said I could see the dragon horse." More banging.

Tan stared down at Kyle, who smiled and shrugged. Tan closed her eyes. Stars, her crotch was throbbing. "Your hand, quick. It won't take but a couple of strokes," she whispered. "I don't think I can walk if you don't."

Kyle glanced at the door. "Okay, Pete. We need to get a quick shower and dress. We'll see you in the dining area in about fifteen minutes."

Tan felt for Kyle's hand. "Just a few strokes, baby." A few thrusts of her hips against Kyle's thigh would do it, too, but she wanted to feel those long, warm fingers.

"What are you guys doing? It feels like fun. I can wait for you."

"No, you go ahead," Kyle said loudly.

"Let him wait," Tan said. Sun, she was almost whining, but she might combust if Kyle didn't touch her.

"No. He's an empath. He'll feel it." Kyle raised her voice again. "Go save seats for us—and you—at Zack's table."

That had the desired result. "Okay, Kyle."

His footsteps were still echoing in the hallway when Kyle flipped them so that Tan's back was to the floor. Watching Tan sleep for a few minutes had been a gift. Awake, Tan exuded the defensive wariness of a strikingly gorgeous but dangerous predator. Sleep relaxed, softened, and transformed her features into a beauty that made Kyle ache inside...ache so badly she hadn't been able to resist a brush of her cheek against a puckered nipple, a taste of the tempting brown skin that smelled of the Shea butter moisturizer Tan preferred. She straddled Tan's thigh and rode to her own climax as she stroked Tan inside and out with long, sure fingers.

Though they needed to be quick, Kyle still mourned their fast rise to orgasm and the lack of time to hold onto Tan a bit longer. She was afraid once they turned on the light, once they left this room, this new bond between them would vanish. For a few hours, she'd belonged with someone. She'd never had that before, even as a child when her family was happy together. She'd always felt as though her mother was preparing her for some mission away, while grooming her brother and sister to stay close at home. She'd always been the outsider. Maybe that's why she felt a kinship with Tan. She was an outsider, too. She was the rogue member of The Guard. When they'd all waited outside the headquarters office while Jael and Alyssa dealt with Tan about drugging Jael, Diego had had plenty to say about her.

"She's had a jump with half the countryside and a temper so quick, I'm surprised she hasn't fried some innocent and sent the locals running from us with that ridiculous war paint." Diego waved his arms dramatically but kept an eye on the door to Jael's office and his voice low.

"Her skills as a physician are an asset and her talent as a tracker invaluable to The Guard," Second said. Her words, however, held a sliver of uncertainty that pervaded the mood of the group.

Only Diego was bold enough to speak it. *"She's unstable. She shouldn't be treating patients, much less leading an army."*

"Han says Tanisha's soul still carries deep guilt from a previous life. She seeks redemption, and it will tear at her until she finds it." Kyle knew that, as a teacher, Furcho believed knowledge assisted understanding, but it wasn't exactly an endorsement of Tan's stability.

Michael, who'd flipped a dining chair backward, listened with his chin resting on his arms crossed atop the chair's back. Kyle had never heard him speak when the entire group was together.

"Do not judge, for you also could be judged," Raven said softly.

The others stared at her.

"I didn't know you were a student of religious history," Furcho said.

"Many truisms are much older than how history remembers them, and their meaning transcends one culture or system of beliefs," she said.

"Treat others as you would want them to treat you," Michael said, standing up from his chair and holding Raven's gaze.

"Michael speaks the truth, and of Guard loyalty," Second said firmly, meeting each of their stares. She stepped forward and held out her fist. "Stronger together."

One by one, they stepped forward and added their hand atop Second's fist without hesitation. Despite their freedom to speak their reservations and who they were individually, they knew their purpose in this life and any that followed. They were a unit that included Tan.

"Guard," they chorused quietly.

Kyle withdrew her fingers gently and kissed the soft skin of Tan's breast. She wouldn't care if Tan was one of The Guard or not. She was simply mesmerized by the most complex and beautiful woman she'd ever met—a fierce warrior, a passionate lover, a skilled and tender physician. "I don't want to leave this room." She brushed her lips against Tan's. "I don't want to leave this here."

Tan's dark eyes narrowed. "I am Guard. We've got a job to do, Blaze. I won't stop until I find Cyrus. And I track a lot faster alone." One corner of her full lips hesitantly twitched into a half smile. "But you're kind of growing on me." She stroked her fingers along Kyle's bare shoulder. "I'm thinking that maybe the perks of having a sidekick outweigh the inconvenience." The smile spread across her face. "And it doesn't hurt that you're blazing hot... Blaze."

Kyle grinned. "Yeah?" She liked the nickname Tan had given her.

"Yeah." Tan tugged her down, and they moaned together as their lips met and tongues caressed. Tan's hands were on her breasts, then dropping lower to grasp her ribs, and she was suddenly flipping in the air. "Get off me or that kid will be back and banging on the door."

Kyle laughed and scrambled for her clothes and toiletries. "Race you to the shower."

❖

They stepped into separate showers to curtail the temptation to linger and were in the dining room within minutes. Everyone was in high spirits. Dinner was an uncharacteristic feast of meaty chili that Tan thought was excellent use of the luxury credits she'd donated to their group. Her credits also purchased several crates of bottled ale, which were rationed one bottle per person of legal drinking age.

Zack stood as they approached his table. "Ah, our honored guests." He cocked his head and smiled. "I trust that you are rested and all other, uh, needs satisfied?"

Tan raised an eyebrow at his insinuation. "Food and information still on the check list."

Zack swept his arm toward three empty seats where Oni was placing full steaming bowls of the chili. Pete carried a large plate of thick soft tortillas and set it on the table, then climbed into the middle chair and smiled up at them. Kyle looked at Tan and shrugged. Tan shook her head but sat in the nearest chair as Kyle sat on the other side of Pete.

She was hungrier than she realized and wolfed down a few mouthfuls of the hot, tasty meal before looking up at Zack. "So, you have some information for me?"

Zack sat forward in his chair, his eyes gleaming. "We found your man." He shrugged. "Well, at least we know he's on a boat in the Gulf and sailing toward the Third Continent." He frowned. "Turns out that one of his guards was the jerk that took advantage of—" he glanced at Pete. "He hurt somebody we know."

"Satellite of the boat's location?"

"Oh, yeah. He's about 200 kilometers off the coast just east of Matamoros."

"Then we'll leave tonight."

"Will the dragon horse come here to get you?" Pete nearly bounced in his seat. "I want to see him. Kyle said maybe you'd take me for a ride."

Kyle looked up from her food with an exaggerated expression of surprise. "I did?"

Pete ducked his head. "Okay. Maybe she didn't." He looked up at Tan, his eyes big and pleading. "But it would be the best thing in the world for a little boy whose family deserted him."

Everyone at the table stilled, and Tan knew her mouth was hanging open at the blatant play for sympathy. Then Kyle barked a laugh and Tan joined her. Tan laughed until she was wiping tears from her cheeks. Sun, she hadn't laughed like that since...well, since she was a kid.

"That performance has to be worth at least a short ride," Kyle said, still grinning.

"Maybe." Tan held up her finger to belay Pete's victory cheer. "Her, my dragon horse, is a her. And she's pregnant and very moody. We'll have to see which way her mood is swinging tonight. Okay?"

Pete nodded vigorously.

"But only a very short ride, because we've got to be on our way," Kyle said.

"You might want to hold up, hoss," Zack said. "You're not the only one hot on this man's tail."

Tan was instantly alert. "Someone else is tracking him?"

"A category-two hurricane. It's looking like his boat might never make it to shore. Nature could solve your problem for you."

Tan glanced at Kyle. She seemed to be contemplating the geometric design on the tablecloth and chewing her bottom lip.

"Can't trust the weather," Tan said mildly. "So we won't count on that." She stood and reached around Pete to lay her hand on Kyle's back. "Ready to roll, Blaze? Phyrrhos is already tap-dancing on the roof."

Pete looked up. "You can hear her?"

Tan watched Kyle carefully. She stood, seemed to shake herself from her thoughts, then smiled and nodded. Tan turned her attention back to the boy, but part of her remained tuned to Kyle. "I can feel her, Pete, because we're bonded."

"Wow."

"Yeah. Wow. Come on. You can carry my pack for me."

❖

Normally, Tan wouldn't let a bunch of strangers anywhere near Phyrrhos. She could be as temperamental as Bero, even when she wasn't pregnant. But the feelings flowing through their bond were happy and affectionate. Were Phyrrhos' pregnancy feelings inflating her own feelings toward Kyle? The thought brought a mixture of relief and disappointment, but she didn't have time to decipher it and wasn't sure she wanted to sort it out.

Still, she was sure it was safe to take a small group up to meet her. After all, this network had helped them, and she intended to talk to Jael about engaging the other networks of gifted that spidered across the continents to be their eyes and ears against The Natural Order. Cyrus had a growing grid of believers. Why shouldn't they have their own embedded in the communities?

Tan pushed through the entrance to the rooftop but motioned for Zack, Pete, Haley, Oni, and Kyle to wait by the door until she checked with Phyrrhos. She'd only taken four or five steps when Phyrrhos ambled over, casually stretching first one and then the other of her wings as she walked. Her red eyes glowed in the half-light of the city as she pressed her forehead to Tan's. She showed Tan some confusing pictures of Specter and the black stallion from the wild herd. Tan wrote it off to hormones. Then a clear picture formed of Second aboard Titan, his powerful shoulders flexing as his wings pumped to keep altitude while carrying the extra weight of two heavy bags of fire rocks. Tan stepped back and scanned the skyline. Second was coming. They were flying slower but would be here soon.

She ran her hand over Phyrrhos' swelling belly. It'd grown noticeably larger even in the past twenty-four hours. The foal moved under her hand, and she jerked back. She must be mistaken. She thought she'd glimpsed a mental image. But that was impossible.

"Everything okay?" Kyle's voice was low and soft. Tan hadn't heard her approach.

"Yeah. It just surprised me when it moved."

Phyrrhos made a low rumbling noise and brought her wings forward in an uncharacteristic move that embraced both Kyle and Tan and drew them to her in an odd dragon hug. When she released them, she proceeded to examine Kyle from head to toe, snuffling noisily from her hair, down her neck to her armpits, and—reddening Kyle's face and ears—lower to a thorough scenting of her crotch, then all the way to her feet. Finally, she resumed the rumbling noise and began to bathe Kyle's neck and cheek with her tongue.

Tan was stunned. Phyrrhos had only shown irritation toward other humans. She was respectful of The Guard but ignored any others. What was that hugging thing? And that new noise she was making—was she...purring? Kyle shot her a helpless look as she tried to discreetly dodge Phyrrhos' ministrations. Tan only crossed her arms over her chest and raised a challenging eyebrow. Phyrrhos never purred for her or went all mushy like that. Not that she'd want to have a neck and face full of dragon slobber. But that was her bonded lavishing attention on another pyro.

"Urk." Tan barely heard the swoosh of the great wing as it circled behind her to slam her against Phyrrhos' side in a rib-crushing hug. She could feel the foal moving again in Phyrrhos' belly. It was very active. "Okay, okay. I love you, too. But let me go. You're crushing me."

Phyrrhos released her and abandoned her attention to Kyle as Titan's hooves sounded against the rooftop. He held his wings extended until Second dismounted with her two heavy sacks, then folded them to his body and obediently waited while Second dumped out a small pile of fire rocks from one sack as his reward.

Second smiled as she approached. "I brought you some extra dragon rations." She returned Tan's salute and Kyle's hesitant one. "We got your report, and I figured your friends here can ship these rocks forward when you know where you're going. Jael, by the way, is very interested in hearing more about this network you have and how they can help The Collective cause."

"Thanks. I can introduce you to some of them now." Tan waved to summon the small group gathered by the stairway. They walked in a careful arc outside of Phyrrhos' reach as she extended her head, red eyes pulsing and nostrils flaring to check their scent. Apparently finding them of little interest, she swung around to press her side against Kyle and rest her forehead against Tan's shoulder. "This is Zack, telepath and leader of the network here. Also Haley, her bondmate Oni, and this young man is Pete. He's an empath, like the First Advocate." She gestured to Second. "This is Danielle, Second Warrior of The Guard."

"Only my mother still calls me Danielle. I go by Second," she said, bumping her fist with each of theirs in the common greeting of their generation.

A rude nip at her sleeve nearly tugged Tan off balance. "And this is the beautiful Phyrrhos, my bonded." The introduction earned her a slobbery brush of dragon lips against her cheek.

Second laughed. "Pregnancy sure has changed her personality."

"You're telling me," Tan grumbled. Dung, that dragon breath reeked of sulfur.

"Can I pet her?" Pete asked, shuffling cautiously to the front of the group.

"Let me ask." She pressed her forehead to Phyrrhos' while Second explained how warrior and dragon horse communicated.

"Neat," Pete said, his eyes wide.

When Tan drew back, Phyrrhos thrust her face inches from Pete's. He froze. Her head was almost as large as he was tall. Two ridges of hard spikes ran down her forehead in a V-shape, and her dark eyes had red elliptical pupils that pulsed as she examined him. Her ears worked back and forth.

"She says you can touch her if you want," Tan said.

Pete extended his hand to carefully feel one ridge of spikes, then trailed his fingers down her flat forehead between the ridges.

"She's beautiful and scary at the same time," he said. "And she's got really big teeth."

Tan squatted to his eye level and dragged over one of the bags Second had dropped nearby. She dug a fire rock from one and held it up. "They eat these rocks to enhance their fire-breathing ability. The big teeth are to grind up the rocks, not eat people or other animals. They become regular horses during the day and eat stuff other horses eat." She handed the rock to him. "Here. You can feed it to her."

Pete took the rock and held it out to Phyrrhos, who neatly plucked it from his hand. Pete grimaced at the grinding and cracking sounds as she pulverized the rock into bits. "Yuck. That must be why her breath stinks like rotten eggs." He jumped when Phyrrhos snorted little blue flames from her nostrils.

Tan laughed. "Careful. You don't want to insult her. She's being very sweet now, but pregnant females can have huge mood swings."

Pete looked up at Phyrrhos. "I think she's the most beautiful dragon horse I've ever seen."

Tan formed a mental picture for Phyrrhos of her carrying the two of them on a short ride. Phyrrhos nodded as she crunched the remnants of her fire rock. "Would you like to take a ride on her?"

"Yes!"

"I need to brief you," Second said.

The picture that formed in Tan's mind was of Phyrrhos carrying Kyle and Pete. Tan frowned. Then a picture of Kyle looking down and Phyrrhos descending flashed in her mind. Was she saying—? Phyrrhos swallowed the last of her fire rock and grabbed a mouthful of Kyle's shirt, nearly jerking her off her feet.

"Phyrrhos has agreed that Kyle can go up with Pete for a short ride while Second and I confer," Tan said slowly, trying to understand this new development.

Kyle blinked at her. "Me. By myself?"

"You can ride a horse, can't you?" She mentally flinched at the edge in her voice, but dung, she'd only let Kyle take a tiny step inside her personal boundaries and she already was pushing her way into Tan's only real relationship. She forced a small smile and lightened her tone. "Or should we get a safety harness?"

"I grew up in an agricultural community. I can sit a horse very well, thank you. But—" Kyle's eyes darkened, and her expression hardened like it was before they'd opened to each other.

Tan hesitated. She wasn't sure why, but she wanted to be honest with Kyle. She wanted to look into Kyle's eyes and see the same. "I'm not sure how, but I think Phyrrhos is saying that she understands what you're thinking. Not clearly, like when she and I share thoughts, but a general impression. So just think of this rooftop when you're ready to return, if I haven't already called her back. You'll be fine."

Kyle's blue eyes cleared as her gaze held Tan's. "You'll fill me in later?"

"Yeah." Tan pressed against Phyrrhos, centering herself in their bond, while Kyle carefully levered herself onto the tall mare. Then she handed Pete up to Kyle, making sure his legs were tucked securely between Kyle's and Phyrrhos' wings. "Hold onto her mane, Pete. It won't hurt her. Kyle will also hold onto you."

The boy's eyes shone with excitement. "I'm not scared. She won't let me fall."

Tan winked at him and sent Phyrrhos a mental picture of a low flight around the city rooftops. Then she stepped back and watched her trot across the rooftop and right off the edge with a gentle sweep of her magnificent wings.

"Wow!" Haley stood with her arm around Oni, watching Phyrrhos ascend into the night.

Tan gestured to a small building in the center of the rooftop that housed the mechanics of the building's solar panels and handed each of the women a pair of night-vision binoculars from her pack. "Why don't you guys climb up there and keep an eye on the other rooftops for me? It's not likely, but I wouldn't want some believer to pop up and start shooting at them from one of the other buildings. Zack needs to meet with me and Second for a few minutes."

"Sure, Tan. No problem," Haley said, already headed to the assigned lookout post.

Tan waited while Second finished explaining the fire rocks to Zack and transferring to his IC the encryption code for the message she would send with their location when she needed them shipped.

"It'd be easier if I could just contact her telepathically," he groused.

Tan narrowed her eyes. This boy needed to know the ground rules up front. "You're not wandering around in my head."

Second's hand on her arm stopped her. "You've done an amazing job establishing this underground army with no mentor, no blueprint to guide you," she said. "Your network and those across the continents could be valuable eyes and ears for The Dragon Horse Army. In exchange, The Guard can offer mentors for your gifted—people who have spent many lifetimes exploring the possibilities of their gifts, learning the limits, and…" she glanced pointedly at Tan, "establishing the ethical boundaries."

Zack scowled at Tan. "We've been fine on our own."

Second, taller than the young man by several inches, laid her hand on his shoulder. "The Collective stands stronger together, Zack. If The Natural Order is allowed to spread, do you think they'll embrace you and your gifted friends?"

Tan sighed. "This isn't about a couple of hardheads like you and me, Zack. It's about Pete, Haley, Oni, and lots of others. What would happen to them?"

Zack lifted his chin and straightened his shoulders, giving Tan a curt nod. "You're right." He turned to Second and imitated Tan's earlier salute. "The San Pedro Sula network is at your service."

Second squeezed his shoulder and nodded before dropping her hand. "Tan, tell me what you know."

"The doctor's wife and daughters are safe, but we had two believer casualties. We think Zack's people were able to clean up after us—the bodies are being incinerated—without any other believers being alerted." She deferred to Zack. "I'll let him report what his people dug up."

"We tracked Cyrus and two of his men to the coast," he said. "We know he hired a private yacht to sail him to Galveston, but a hurricane is crossing the Gulf that's probably going to sink him or force him to put in somewhere much more south, probably on the Tamaulipas coast."

"What do you know about the boat and crew?" Second asked. "Do they have a chance in a hurricane?"

"The yacht is big—eighty-four feet, and the captain and crew come from generations of sailors. Several d-weather models give them at least a thirty-percent chance of survival at sea. Better if they reach shore before the outer bands catch them."

"Excellent work," Second said. "Tan, can you contact Jael? I think we need a change of plans."

Tan closed her eyes—not that she needed to, but Zack's curious stare was distracting.

Jael.

Here, Tan.

Can you review my thoughts from the past few minutes?

I'm fine, thank you. Alyssa's fine. How are you and Kyle? You haven't damaged her, have you?

Tan chuckled at Jael's teasing admonishment, forgetting for a moment that Second and Zack were watching her.

"I didn't think she was telepathic," Zack said.

"Tan isn't, but First Warrior Jael is the most powerful telepath of this lifetime, as far as we know. She can get into anyone's head—well, anyone but mine."

"Not yours?"

"She can when I consciously open to her, but it's much more taxing, especially at a distance. That's my secondary gift. Tan also trusts that Jael will review only the thoughts she's given permission to probe. You apparently haven't earned that same trust from her."

Tan?

Sorry, distracted by the conversation around me.
Review complete. Tell Second I'm listening with you. She
wants to change plans?

"You want to change our plans?"

Second acknowledged the indication to proceed. "I think it's imperative that we immediately pursue Cyrus. If the yacht sinks, our time frame to recover his body so his soul can be properly released this time will be narrow. If he makes it to shore, our chances of intercepting him will be greater if we can find him before he has a chance to melt back into the population."

Tan shrugged. "Kyle and I will leave within the hour."

"Phyrrhos is heavily pregnant. More than we anticipated," Second said. "I doubt she can carry both of you very far."

Tan scratched at her scalp. She needed a trim. The smooth sides of her Mohawk hairstyle were filling in with soft, tight fuzz. "She's been acting weird, too."

May I?

Tan hesitated.

Only those memories of Phyrrhos, Tan. What's between you
and Kyle is only for you.
Sounds like you've already seen enough to satisfy your
curiosity.

They'd once been mutually dependent, filling each other's physical needs because neither was capable of soul-bonding. Then Jael found Alyssa, and Tan still fell pitifully short.

Tan. No. You know I wouldn't. Alyssa can't see, but she feels.
It was unintentional. Every day, her gift grows stronger. She was
gathering some things at the clinic to be laundered. She had a
jacket Kyle left in the storeroom, then a lab coat you'd left on a

hook in your office. That's when she felt your bond, as she held both in her hands. She could feel it from here. She says it's good, and I've learned not to argue with her.
I don't know, Jael.

Faint laughter filled her head.

Neither did I, my friend. If it's meant to be, then it will happen no matter what you think you want. Now, Phyrrhos?
Yes, of course.

Jael's review took only a blink.

I suspect Kyle's bonding with the foal in utero.
Is that possible? I wondered, but I've never heard of such a thing.
And I've never witnessed this shield gift I'm hearing about.

Tan didn't respond. She trusted Jael hadn't culled that information from her thoughts without permission. Toni had likely revealed herself to someone else who told Jael about her gift.

Second is waiting, I'm sure. Ask that hardhead to open up and I'll include the young man, too. I can feel him probing. Not bad, but he's got a lot to learn.

Tan tapped her temple.

"Go ahead," Second said, acknowledging the signal to join Jael's part of the conversation.

"Then I'm to track Cyrus on my own from here?" That should have been good news. It was what she'd initially demanded, but she was suddenly reluctant to leave Kyle behind.

"No," Second said. "We still need Kyle at hand to keep our options open. Titan can carry two of us. Instead of shipping those fire rocks, we'll each carry a quarter load. Phyrrhos should be able to handle that."

"Will this disrupt the plans in Brasília?" Tan asked.

Michael can hold the camp while I join Furcho, Diego and Raven. Something's off down there. Shipments aren't leaving the warehouse, but we didn't see any guards like on the train.

Hooves clattered against the roof, and Phyrrhos arrived with a grinning Kyle and a breathless Pete on board. Time to wrap this up.

Report your location at sunrise.

Tan and Second spoke in unison out of long habit. "As you command, First Warrior."

"That was star-tastic," Zack said. "It was like she was standing here. She was in all of our heads at once. How does she do that?"

"Maybe you'll get the chance to ask her once we get this Cyrus business all straightened out," Second said, smiling. "Hate to chat and fly, but we need to get as far up the coast as we can tonight."

Tan was ready. She needed some Phyrrhos time, and then she needed some Kyle time. She didn't care if Second was along or not. She'd bedded in plenty of barracks with no privacy, so she always just turned her back to the soldiers trysting in the next bunk. She shouldered her pack, but a sharp tug stopped her. Pete's face was flushed, his eyes shining. She knelt to his level. "I don't have much time, but how'd you like flying, buddy?"

"It was amazing. Thank you for sharing your family with me."

She blinked at him. "My family?"

"Kyle, Phyrrhos, and Sunfire."

"Uh, right. They're not exactly—" She stared into his young face so full of joy and awe. Family meant a lot to these network kids, because theirs had rejected most of them. "You're welcome, Pete. Thank you for sharing your family with me and Kyle."

"My family?"

"Sure. Families come in all shapes and forms. A network just like this one was my first family. Then I bonded with Phyrrhos, and The Guard became another family to me."

"And now you have Kyle and Sunfire, too. I see."

It would be silly to get into a discussion with a kid about whether Kyle and a foal that wasn't born yet were actually family to her. "So, the network here is probably just your first family. You'll have more, too, like me. But right now, you have Zack, Haley, Oni, and the rest."

"Zack takes good care of me." His face was serious now.

"You do everything he says because, as of tonight, this network is officially part of The Collective's Dragon Horse Army."

"Really, Tan?"

She stood. "That's Captain Tan to you, soldier." She thumped her right fist to her left shoulder in salute and waited while he straightened and snapped a return salute. "Carry on, Private Pete."

"Yes, ma'am, Captain Tan."

She turned on her heel and went to Kyle, who was stroking Phyrrhos' distended abdomen while she watched her exchange with Pete.

"You're really good with kids." Kyle smiled at her. "They just don't know how scary you can be."

"I like kids. Most haven't learned to be dung wipes yet. If they do get out of line, all you have to do is bark a little bit." Tan conjured up her best scowl. "I only bite adults."

On the pretense of measuring Phyrrhos' girth with her arms, Kyle bent forward, bringing her face close to Tan's. "I like it when you bite me."

Tan's breath caught as a shudder ran through her belly. "Thank the stars you're riding with Second, or we'd surely be joining the thousand-mile-high club tonight, and I'm not at all sure Phyrrhos would appreciate it."

Kyle grinned and quickly brushed her lips against Tan's. Before she could protest such a public display, she was staring at Kyle's back as she sauntered toward Titan and the Second Warrior, who had discreetly turned away.

Chapter Fourteen

I t's not that serious, is it?"
Alyssa looked up from her d-tablet. "Just trying to figure out why I've treated fifteen people today with sore throats, stuffy heads, and a fever."

Jael ignored the smile that was a reflex to her presence, dropping her mental shields to get a full measure of her bondmate's concern. But even she wasn't prepared for the rapid-fire churn of Alyssa's thoughts.

I have no idea where to begin. The symptoms are so general. I have no clue as to how dangerous this could be, or how contagious. Should I quarantine? Stars, I need Tan here. No, I need a historian, not a physician or a medical analyzer.

"Alyssa." Agitation, laced with urgency, filled Jael, and she knew the emotions were not her own but projected by Alyssa. "Hey, deep breath."

"The disruption of supply shipments isn't just leaving people hungry. It's endangering the health of everyone, Jael."

Jael circled behind to grasp Alyssa's slender shoulders.

"There are so many illnesses we haven't treated in years because preventatives have been routinely distributed in the bottled vitamin water that goes out worldwide," Alyssa said.

Jael warmed her hands a bit and began a firm but gentle massage of the tense muscles.

"I have no idea which infection I should be fighting." Alyssa dropped her chin to her chest. "Stars, that feels good."

They were silent for a long moment while Jael massaged and mentally projected their favorite escape—the field of vibrant wildflowers on her mountain, basking under a brilliant-blue summer sky. Alyssa sighed, and Jael felt a bit of their distress drain away.

"I'm not a historian, but I have memory of several fairly recent lives. Describe the symptoms for me."

"Headache, body aches, head cold, coughing, sore throat, and fever. From the med scans, it appears to be a virus."

"Sounds like the flu to me."

"Flu?"

"Yeah. It was fairly common in the twentieth and twenty-first centuries. I remember yearly inoculations for it. It was mostly just annoying, but there were always some fatalities every year—mostly very old people, babies, or people with already compromised immune systems." She closed her eyes, reaching farther back. "But before they had the right medicines to treat it, a lot of people died."

"We might not have the medicines we need available now either. We might need to quarantine, or your whole army could come down with it."

Jael stilled her hands. Dung. The memory was strong now—the stench and misery of hospitals filled with so many soldiers suffering and dying the weary medical staff barely had a path between the makeshift beds to maneuver. It was the fall of 1918, and more men were dying of influenza than on the battlefields of World War I.

Michael, report to the clinic office.

"I'll take care of that and leave the medicine part to you. If you need to consult with Tan, I can link you telepathically. I don't want to risk messaging her in case Cyrus has someone monitoring the d-net."

"Reporting." Michael stood in the door. He shrugged when Jael looked up. "I was in the building, calibrating some equipment."

Toni edged past him and looked to Alyssa for permission to enter the small office they shared. Entrance granted, she quietly went to her desk and began syncing information on her tablet with the clinic's intranet.

"Issue an urgent order."

Michael lifted his left arm and tapped the controls on his IC, then nodded for her to begin.

"This is First Warrior Jael. Tonight's training exercises have been canceled. Troops are immediately confined to barracks until further notice. Dinner and every meal until the confinement is lifted will be served at the barracks. Barrack commanders are to query each warrior and make a list of anyone reporting the following symptoms: headache, sore throat, body aches, chills, diarrhea, or fever. Anyone reporting those symptoms should go immediately to the clinic. Also, a second list should be made of any warrior who has been in close contact with someone from another barrack who displayed any of those symptoms. Your lists should be forwarded to Lieutenant Michael."

Michael ended the transmission. "Jael?"

"It could be an overreaction, but our army is small and our time-frame to act short. We can't afford to spend weeks nursing a fever and runny noses. I want two units healthy and ready to leave for Brasília on short notice. We need to isolate the source of this virus."

"C Barrack."

Jael looked to Alyssa, who shrugged. They both turned to Toni, who was busily entering data into her tablet. She looked up from her work.

"All of the patients admitted to the clinic today are housed in C Barrack. But you should question Private Raynor. A female corporal from D Barrack brought him in, the big baby. I've heard he's very active and multi-oriented, so you may want to find out just how many 'friends' he's exposed in the past couple of days."

"Thank you, Lieutenant Antonia." Jael shook her head. "Your efficiency shouldn't still surprise me."

"Just doing my job, First Warrior." Toni turned back to her tablet, but her mouth curled into a small smile. "Oh, and Private Raynor is in bed twenty-two, if you want to find out who he might have contaminated."

Jael glanced at Michael.

"I'm on it," he said.

Jael bent to kiss Alyssa's cheek. "Mind if I steal your assistant for a bit?"

"Toni?"

"I thought we'd go feed a hungry dragon horse."

Toni's back stiffened, and her hand hovered over her d-tablet.

"Is that a good idea?" Alyssa frowned. "If Toni takes you to see Dark Star, Specter will find him, too."

Jael touched the back of her hand to Alyssa's cheek. "Do you trust me?"

Alyssa pressed into her touch. "You know I do."

"Toni and I'll be fine. If Specter shows, I can hold him off." She brushed her lips against Alyssa's and stepped over to thump Toni on the back. "And rumor tells me Toni can hold off the wild one."

Toni dropped her chin to her chest. "I'm up to my ears in dung," she muttered.

❖

"He hasn't been here the past two nights," Toni said, restlessly shifting the bucket of fire rock at her feet near the edge of the outcropping. "Maybe the other dragon horses found out he's hanging around and ran him off. Maybe they thought he was trying to steal back his mares that bonded with our warriors."

Jael stood, turned partially away from the tree line where Toni said Dark Star usually emerged. "Specter is top dragon and he likes to brag, so I'd know if that happened."

"What about Bero? He can be a real butthead sometimes."

A picture of a dark, winged form gliding down from the sky formed in her mind. Specter was watching? "He's coming." She closed her eyes to focus on the projected thought. Strange. Specter seemed curious rather than guarded. She was still puzzling over this oddity when a rustle of leaves and the sound of hooves on rock alerted her to the wild stallion's presence. The moon was rising, full and bright.

"Hey, Dark Star," Toni crooned to the animal. "Where have you been? I was getting worried." She walked forward slowly with the bucket of fire rocks, then dumped them onto a shallow depression in the stone. "Here you go, boy."

Dark Star stepped out of the woods and raised his nose. Tiny spurts of flame shot from his nostrils as he took in Jael's scent. Blue-white, Jael noted, not the cooler red-yellow his flame had been before Toni began feeding him. He still looked a little beat-up, shiny new skin covering healed burns. He didn't seem nervous, so she faced him and took a few steps for a closer look.

The air stirred at her back.

"Jael."

Toni's warning was unnecessary. She knew Specter was landing lightly behind her, barely making a sound.

Toni slid to the right, positioning herself off to the side but midway between Dark Star and Specter. Alyssa had told her about Toni's gift of shielding, but she was skeptical that she could stand against Specter's flame.

Specter held his wings outstretched but made no move toward the wild stallion. Dark Star's pupils pulsed like red beacons. He slowly extended his wings, matching Specter's display.

Jael had never been this close to the wild dragon horse, and she realized for the first time that his wingspan beat Specter's by several feet. Where Specter had a long back and lean physique made for gliding, this dragon horse had a short back for quick turns and a thickly muscled chest, shoulders, and neck for powerful wing strokes. All in all, he was a larger, more powerful animal. She should be picking up something from Specter, but for the first time since they'd bonded, he was silent to her. She tensed, flicking her eyes from one dragon horse to the other. What in blue blazes were they doing? Two dominant stallions should be screaming at each other.

Dark Star folded his wings. There would be no challenge tonight. Had losing his herd broken his spirit? A picture formed in her head of her—no, not her—of Second riding Dark Star. She looked at Specter. That couldn't be right. He was staring back. The image had come from him. Specter turned away and launched skyward.

"Whoa. That was weird. What'd you say to get him to leave without roasting Dark Star?"

Jael shook her head. "I didn't say anything. He didn't give me a chance."

"You're not in trouble with him, are you? For, I don't know, cheating on him with another dragon horse?"

She could see why Alyssa liked this kid. "I hadn't thought of that, but I don't think so." She stared into the sky where Specter had disappeared. She didn't get the impression he was angry, but something was strange with him.

Nothing about this war was happening normally. Most in The Natural Order weren't soldiers—just hungry, misguided people. The Collective Council had saddled her with a first-life Advocate who'd lit a flame in her heart but put a hesitation in her incineration. And now, the freaking dragon horses had gone crazy. Sun and moon, she longed for the simplicity of a sword and shield against a field of burly barbarians.

CHAPTER FIFTEEN

Cyrus's feet flew out from under him, and he held tight to the railing as the rear of the yacht rose with another huge wave that nearly rolled the ship upright onto its bow. They were losing their race to beat the hurricane to the closest shore. He was no sailor, but it was clear they were being tested. If he was to be a martyr for The One, then he would not shrink from his fate. History would remember him with respect, perhaps sainthood.

He tightened the straps of his life vest and grabbed whatever he could to make his way to the crew's quarters. All hands were on deck, or at least indoors on the upper decks. Anyone down here wouldn't have a chance if they began to sink. That's why he had to get Bobby topside. The crew wouldn't help him because of whatever he'd done to that girl in the warehouse. Luke didn't seem to care if Bobby died down there either. But something deep in Cyrus, the tiny part of him that sometimes missed the days when he and Laine were happy and their children were small, wouldn't let him leave Bobby behind.

Bobby was on the floor, holding to the leg of one bunk. He groaned as the ship pitched wickedly, throwing him against the wall. Cyrus grabbed Bobby's sweaty T-shirt and straddled him.

"Let's get this life vest on you, so you don't drown if we capsize," he said, tugging at Bobby's arms to make him let go of the bed. "I need to get you up top, or you'll be trapped if we go over. And I'm pretty sure the next wave or two will do it."

"Help me," Bobby said.

"That's what I'm trying to do. Can you at least crawl?"

Bobby nodded, and Cyrus secured the vest, then pulled him onto his hands and knees. Together, they made their way across the pitching floor, through the doorway, and to the stairs. The stairway was easier with the rail to grasp, but Bobby's strength was waning. Cyrus had to drag him the last few steps and out onto the deck.

Luke appeared in the doorway of the upper-deck lounge, squinting in the driving rain. He crouched next to Cyrus and set three square plate-sized devices on the deck. A hose attached a rubber mask to each. He shouted to be heard over the raging wind and ocean. "I saw a couple of the crew getting these out of an emergency box and putting them inside their life vests." He demonstrated by stuffing one inside the front of his vest and slipping the strap of the rubber mask over his head so that it hung around his neck. "If you go overboard, try to get to the surface and clear the water from the mask, then pull it up and over your mouth so that it seals around your nose and chin. The box thing will convert the carbon dioxide you exhale back into oxygen so you don't have to worry about getting a lungful of water while you're tossed around the seas."

Cyrus examined the devices skeptically, then scrambled to hold onto them and the railing when the ship nearly capsized and a gigantic, curling wave almost washed them overboard. Luke braced himself in the doorway and snagged Bobby's arm as he slid past. Cyrus pushed the third unit into Bobby's vest. His eyes were wide with fear. Cyrus laid his hand on Bobby's shoulder. "Do not be afraid, brother. The One is with us. Whatever happens is his will."

Bobby looked to Luke for confirmation, but Luke only shrugged. "I hope somebody's looking out for us. If we go over, it'll be every man for himself."

Cyrus dismissed Luke's sarcasm as fear. He'd seen it from many strong men in times of crisis. "Get some rope to tie us together," Cyrus said. "If we go over, you and I will have to pull Bobby between us to get clear of the boat. Stronger to—" He'd almost said it. The Collective mantra had been ingrained since his childhood and still was true no matter what his spiritual beliefs. But he couldn't say their words now. "We got on this boat together, and we'll arrive on shore together."

Luke looked at Bobby, then back at Cyrus. He scrambled over to a locker and extracted a coil of thin nylon rope. They briefly debated how they should be tied together, but another treacherous roll of the yacht ended the argument. They looped the rope around the outside of their vests at chest level, leaving about three meters of slack between them.

Luke was tying the last knot when an earsplitting boom shook the boat as lightning tore through the stormy gloom to strike the main mast in an explosion of sparks. Shouts rang out from the crew that had been strangely absent on the second deck as the yacht wallowed to the port side. The next wave towered over them and the ship began to roll broadside.

"Jump." Luke shouted and pointed to the bow. "Jump off the end and swim away."

Luke began to run, but Bobby's weight jerked him back. Adrenaline fueling his strength, Cyrus hauled Bobby up and over his shoulder, then ran with Luke. They leapt over the side as the furious ocean slapped the big yacht onto its side and it began to sink.

❖

Phyrrhos screamed as a new band of driving rain hit them.

The network's informants said Cyrus was bound for Galveston, and they'd flown a significant distance their first night of travel. While the hurricane was still far from their location, they'd traveled easily in the flowing updrafts and shelter of the mountains all the way to Ciudad Victoria by daybreak. But they'd cut back toward the coast when they resumed their journey tonight and had begun flying into the storm's intermittent bands of fierce wind, stinging hail, and needle-like rain.

Tan could feel Phyrrhos tiring after only a short time as she struggled to keep her additional body weight aloft. She couldn't, wouldn't risk her bonded and the foal in this storm. She spotted a large barn on what appeared to be the outskirts of a research farm. There weren't any residential buildings, only cattle huddled in the woods and under open sheds in the surrounding fields. If she was reading this correctly, the barn would be used for hay storage. A perfect cozy shelter. She signaled toward the ground, and Titan followed as Phyrrhos descended.

Tan studied the lock on the barn's sliding door. She could melt it, but she didn't want to damage the property, just bed here until the storm passed. She waved Kyle over.

"Can you pick this?"

Kyle winked at her. "Does the sun rise every morning?"

It did when Kyle looked at her with those blue eyes warm and dancing. But Tan tilted her head and looked pointedly at the door. "I don't know. The door's still locked."

Kyle only grinned, ignoring the rain pelting them and running into her eyes. She drew a wallet of small tools from one of the side pockets of her cargo pants and extracted a flat, rectangular box. It adhered to the lock like a magnet, and Kyle activated her wrist IC.

"Open lock app thirty-two. Analyze and open."

The digital lock clicked open, and Kyle pulled back the large sliding door. It was, indeed, a hay-storage barn. A small tractor was parked in the center aisle, but there still was plenty of open space for the two dragon horses and three women to move inside.

Tan dropped her pack to the floor and dug out a small solar bulb that produced a wide circle of soft light when she activated it. She wouldn't think of palming a fireball for light while in a barn full of hay. She went back into her pack for a towel and tossed it to Kyle. Her own shirt was soaked through, and she unbuttoned it with one hand while she rummaged for a dry one. She stopped when she felt a familiar mental probe and opened to it.

Jael?

Tan, ask Second to open to me. I need to talk to her.

She swallowed. Jael's curt order and the fact that she was obviously going to exclude her from some information exposed what Tan had expected, despite Jael's earlier reassurance. The trust between them was still tenuous after what she'd done. Her shame that Kyle had somehow managed to push away returned, weighing heavy on her shoulders and choking her heart.

Yes, First Warrior.
Sorry. Alyssa's punching me in the ribs. Could you please let Second know I need to communicate with her? But before you do, how's Phyrrhos holding up? I don't want you to push her too hard. If it takes an extra day or two to get Cyrus, she's more important.

Tan looked up at Second, gestured a half-salute, and pointed to her temple, then to Second, who nodded her understanding.

We had to stop tonight. The storm is too much for her to fly.
I doubt Cyrus is traveling in that weather either, so no worries. Things okay with you and Kyle?
Uh, yeah. Blaze is doing okay.

Tan normally could compartmentalize her thoughts to filter what Jael heard, but the very mention of Kyle sent Tan's thought on a lustful journey that she knew must be flashing through Jael's head, too. Damn her lack of control.

Okay. I need Second back here. Can you two make it okay without her?
Yeah. We're close enough. I'll release Phyrrhos to hover nearby in case I need her, but we'll find other means of travel.
Be safe, Tan.
As you command, my friend.

The band of tension around her chest loosened when Jael discreetly ignored the images Tan knew she must have seen. She took a deep breath as she stood, then forgot everything when she turned to see Kyle stripped down to her skimpy skivvies as she dried her hair. Her long, sinewy body, caught in the lamp's glow, was an artistic study in shadows. Every ropy muscle in her long arms and legs, every ridge of her abdomen was defined.

"Breathe, Tan."

Tan jerked, startled by Second's whisper next to her ear.

"Jael needs me to return rather than go on with you two," Second said, raising her voice to a normal tone.

Kyle pulled on a T-shirt and glanced up while she felt around in her pack for some pants. "You're going back out into the storm?" She laid the pants on a nearby bale and rummaged through the rest of her things. "I know I have some dry socks in here somewhere."

"Titan will be fine. We'll be traveling away from the storm, back to the mountains, then up to Monterrey. I plan to catch a commercial flight to get back faster and let Titan find his way back over the next couple of days."

This *was* urgent. Tan stared at Second. Dung, that woman was harder to read than Jael. Second smiled as she clapped a hand on Tan's shoulder to give her a squeeze and a bit of a shake.

"Don't look so worried. Diego heard rumors in Brasília that Cyrus's right-hand man was cooking up something there. She sent Uri to Brasília because things didn't feel right, and he confirmed it. He can't say exactly what's going on, but he confirmed that a lot of people aren't telling the truth. So she's strategizing her next move, and you know she can't organize anything without my help."

"Yeah, okay." But Tan didn't like it. She followed Second out into the night. The rain had lessened for the moment, but streaks of lightning lit the sky in the distance. They both watched the electric display for a few seconds, and then Tan pointed in the opposite direction. "Good thing you're headed that way."

Second seemed to sense her unease. "Find Cyrus, Tan. That's what Jael needs you to do. Don't worry about the rest." She smiled. "And take care of Kyle. I have a feeling she might be special."

Tan watched Titan lift off, then returned inside and slid the barn door closed. Phyrrhos stood dozing in a pile of hay. She'd obviously broken several bales and scattered them for bedding in case she decided to lie down briefly. It was probably just a wishful exercise. Her belly had grown so large, she was only comfortable enough to sleep while standing.

"What's the plan?" Kyle asked, stepping into her pants and pulling them up her long legs.

Tan shed her wet shirt. "We stay here tonight. Phyrrhos is done. I can't…we can't be separated this late in her pregnancy, so she'll always be somewhere close, but she'll leave just before the dawn transition and find a safe hiding place. You and I will set out on foot to find other transportation." She removed her chest support band and scratched under her breasts where the band irritated her skin.

"So, you're saying that we're in for the night?"

Tan smiled at Kyle's gaze locked on her hands. She stopped scratching and began to massage her breasts. She nearly laughed when Kyle visibly swallowed and licked her lips. "I'm saying you might as well take those pants right back off."

Kyle's eyes flicked up to her face then, and she grinned. "Well, you do outrank me, and I wouldn't want to disobey an order." She shucked off her pants and T-shirt, flinging them onto the hay bales stacked behind her, then stalked smoothly over to Tan. She kissed her way down Tan's neck while her fingers worked Tan's pants open and dropped them to the floor. Then she lifted each of Tan's breasts and kissed the dark nipples. When she raised her head, Tan thought those azure eyes would swallow her.

"Reporting for duty, ma'am," Kyle said softly.

Tan hesitated. "Kyle. You know you don't have to…I mean, just because I'm—"

"Shut up, Tanisha. This is about you and me. Nothing else. Now kiss me. We've only got until dawn, and I need at least ten minutes of sleep."

❖

Cyrus gave up trying to swim. The turbulent ocean tossed and swirled him in so many directions he had no idea which way the surface or the shore might be. He closed his eyes tight against the salty, sand-filled water, reducing his world to each breath inhaled and exhaled into the rubber mask suctioned over his nose and mouth and the constant jerk of the rope that tethered him to Bobby and Luke. His only hope was his faith that their destiny was in the hands of a power greater than the force of the hurricane.

Something big slammed the back of his shoulders and head. Not the hard hull of the yacht. A fish? A whale, maybe? He waited to feel it again. Seconds seemed like hours underwater. What was that old parable about the man swallowed by the whale? His breath swooshed out of his lungs when he was slammed again, this time along his side. When the water lifted him up, something familiar filled his fist. Sand? Before he could ponder this question, he was slammed facedown, and the mask was knocked from his face. He panicked and began to flail. Then his feet touched bottom and he instinctively pushed upward. When his face broke the surface, he sucked in a lungful of air, then coughed and sputtered as another wave tumbled him forward.

He had his bearings now—ground under his feet, waves crashing at his back, and the shore a dim outline in the curtain of rain. He alternately swam and walked, tugging his rope tether along with him. He might be dragging two bodies or two buddies, but he—Cyrus—had survived this test.

He stumbled onto the beach and fell to his knees to catch his breath. A few yards away, Luke emerged from the water, and Bobby washed up between them. He appeared unconscious, but his breathing mask was still in place. Cyrus stood and straightened. He turned his face up to the rain and let it wash the ocean from his skin, then opened his mouth to rinse the taste of the breathing pack from his tongue. He spat onto the sand. No hurricane would beat him. No ocean could swallow him. He dropped his life vest and breathing pack on the beach as he walked slowly to Bobby's prone figure. He knelt and felt for a pulse. Faint, but alive. Bobby's skin was gray. He removed his mask and breathing pack but left his vest. It would make a convenient handhold if they had to drag him across the beach.

Luke stumbled over, stripping off his gear. "I thought that water would be our grave." His hands shook. Fear or fatigue? It didn't matter to Cyrus. Not every man could be as strong as he was.

"We can't be too far from some village or city. This is a very populated coast. There's probably a road just past those dunes." Cyrus sat Bobby up and stooped to slide his shoulders under Bobby's left arm. "Grab his other arm, and let's go."

Luke opened his mouth as though he was going to argue or offer an alternative but closed it when Cyrus glared at him. He sighed and shouldered Bobby's other arm to lift him between them, and they stumbled purposefully through the thick sand of the dunes.

When they reached the top of the second dune, a wide highway stretched out below them.

Luke grinned. "Thank the stars, you were right."

There was never a doubt. He was The Prophet. "Go flag a ride for us. I'll wait with Bobby."

He watched Luke jog down the dune and toward the road, waving his arms at a supply transport headed north. Then he looked back at the beach and saw no sign of the yacht or its crew. Their faith in their precious Collective had offered them no protection. Only The One had true power. Only his believers could emerge unscathed from nature's test. And he was the greatest of the believers.

He had proved himself stronger than the army of The Collective, stronger than the forces of nature, and gloriously filled with the power of The One. He was anointed The Prophet, but he was becoming The One.

❖

Tan woke from the light doze that'd overtaken her after the second...no, her third and Kyle's fourth...orgasm. The night was cool, but neither she nor Kyle needed anything other than the blanket under them that protected their skin from their itchy bed of hay. She usually liked the feel of a sheet covering her body when she slept in a bed, but Kyle was currently a more than adequate, if not overly warm, blanket draped over her.

She stared at the metal rafters of the barn, faint outside the glow of the solar bulb, and smiled as she absently fingered a dark, silky lock of Kyle's hair. It was growing out. Kyle had trimmed it again in the back and on the sides, but it was long and straight on top, falling across her brow in a boyishly sexy style.

They should rise soon and prepare to leave. Farmers began work early, and they couldn't risk someone showing up to feed the cattle and catching them lounging in the buff. Kyle mumbled in her sleep, as though she'd heard Tan's thoughts, and snuggled closer.

Kyle's head rested next to Tan's so that her slow exhales rhythmically caressed Tan's neck and ear. Normally, that would irritate her. But she liked feeling Kyle that close, so close she sprawled half across Tan, one arm over Tan's chest, tucked under her breasts, with one long leg stretched over Tan's hips, thoroughly pinning her. She couldn't move, which usually triggered a defensive response, something next to panic. But rather than suffocated, she felt anchored.

Tan never slept with anyone. She had sex with them. She stayed overnight only if she needed a place to crash, not because she wanted to wake up with them. She'd had a best-friend-with-benefits arrangement with Jael. And with Anya...well, that was more of a service. But Kyle was an itch Tan couldn't stop scratching, a thirst Tan couldn't seem to slake. She feared Kyle would steal her control, taint her decisions. Even as she thought it, she closed her arms around Kyle's shoulders, cradling her close.

Tan needed to be in full control right now because too much was spiraling out of control. They seemed to be constantly chasing rumors and shadows. She found no battlefield honor, no feeling of victory in skulking around, chasing a madman traveling with a bunch of zealots. She was a warrior, trained to fight other soldiers head-on. If Jael was going to Brasília, Tan and Phyrrhos should be at her side. But Phyrrhos could foal in a few weeks, for stars' sake, and was in no condition to go into battle.

She had to agree with Jael. Something definitely felt wrong, very wrong, like something ominous was waiting. She didn't like it.

❖

The ray of sun that broke through the remnants of clouds in the hurricane's wake seemed to seek out Cyrus where he stood on the flat bed of a truck loaded with gallons of fresh water, bags of ice, and boxes of groceries destined for a local store. A man who'd just come from finding his elderly parents crushed to death when the hurricane winds collapsed their home with them inside had been driving the supply transport Luke had flagged down. They'd quickly converted him and diverted his goods to their cause.

Now parked among rows of houses flattened by the hurricane's winds, surrounded by flooded streets and debris, Cyrus looked down at the crowd gathered to get a share of the truck's bounty. First, they'd have to swallow his message.

"Look around you, friends. This is the eighth disaster I have personally witnessed on the Third and Fourth continents. Scientists claim a rare convergence of galactic events and our legacy of environmental abuse is causing these weather anomalies. I am a professor of history, and I'm here to tell you this is simply history repeating a cycle our society is choosing to ignore because we think we've evolved beyond it."

A toddler began to cry, and the crowd shifted impatiently. Cyrus smiled at them.

"Can a few of you men come up and help Luke—he's the tall fellow right there—pass this water out to everybody?"

Luke pointed to two men from the handful who stepped forward, and Cyrus pointed to the woman with weary eyes and the crying toddler.

"Ma'am, can you come on up? That little one must be hungry or maybe needs a diaper change." The crowd parted to allow her through. "Luke, I believe there's a big box of diapers on that other side, and the one next to it has food for babies in it. Can you help her?"

The woman gave Cyrus a grateful smile and hurried to the boxes he'd indicated. He had the crowd's attention, and respect, when he turned back to them.

"All the old religions recognized the truth, and the time has come for us to rein in our pride and acknowledge what we have sought to reject. There is only one true power, one creator of all, and he is angry. It is time we abandon our pride and misguided teachings to return to The Natural Order of things."

"Hey, do you guys know who that is?" A guy on the edge of the crowd waved excitedly. "That's The Prophet. Right here in Matamoros."

Cyrus smiled. "You are right, brother. I was on a ship bound for Galveston, but The One led me here instead to help you."

"I believe." A woman raised her hand. "My husband would be here to get supplies for us, but he was injured, broke his leg. He's an elder among our local believers."

Cyrus clapped his hands together. "Excellent. Perhaps you could take me to him. If he can introduce me to the local elders, we can better organize our efforts to help people here. Also, I'm afraid we lost all of our personal things when our journey was, uh, redirected. If someone can help me with communication access, I can contact our regional center and have more supplies directed to this area."

"I'll be delighted. My husband will think he's hallucinating when I bring The Prophet to his bedside."

CHAPTER SIXTEEN

The rain had stopped, but the air remained thick with humidity. The barn where they'd sheltered for the night was far enough inland and the hurricane's path angled far enough northwest that most of the immediate damage they encountered was limited to flooding, flattened crops, hail-dented transports, and shattered solar panels. The destruction turned catastrophic as they neared Matamoros. Sturdy adobe structures were roofless, their household contents strewn throughout the streets. Animal carcasses—dogs, oxen, pigs, chickens—lay haphazardly in the road or in muddy yards and ditches.

"Tan, look." Kyle's face was white, and her hand trembled where it lay on Tan's forearm.

A row of bodies lay lined up in front of a small café. A mix of blankets, sheets, and a few checkered tablecloths covered their torsos and faces, their arms and legs left exposed to the weak sun and swarming flies. Several small, frail limbs poked out from the hasty shrouds. Children.

Tan had seen much worse. She'd looked out over entire battlefields covered with a tangle of dead and dying men, horses, and war dogs. She'd walked among them as a warrior, slaying still-breathing enemies and driving her sword into the heart of any suffering but fatally wounded comrades. She'd also once lain among them as life leaked out of her. Another life, another time.

"Someone's probably setting up a central morgue somewhere. Those are waiting to be tagged and transported. That's how it works in a disaster zone."

"We have to help. We can't just ignore what's happening around us."

Kyle's grip heated on her forearm, and Tan pried it away, then held Kyle's hand in her own. "Deep breath, Kyle. You're overheating. Cool it down a notch."

Tears filled Kyle's eyes as they fixed on the bodies. "My brother was once one of them—one of those people lying in a row of dead at a morgue. If I'd been there to help, maybe it'd been me, and Thomas would still be here."

Tan grabbed Kyle's shoulders. "Look at me, Kyle. He was destined to transition to a new life. It was his time. You cannot change what is meant to be." She touched Kyle's flushed cheek and finally spoke the truth she'd been afraid to admit. "What would have happened to me if you weren't here? You've already saved me twice from departing this life prematurely. Your destiny and mine appear entwined." Fearless warrior aside, she was too much of a coward to simply confess she'd dreamed of...no, not just dreamed but realized that she desperately wanted many endless nights with Kyle.

Kyle blinked at her, searching her eyes. A myriad of emotions Tan could only guess flashed across her handsome features. She didn't question that Kyle returned the feelings growing between them, but Kyle hadn't yet experienced the things she had. Life changes people. It wasn't that she didn't trust what Kyle felt for her now. She didn't trust what Kyle would feel tomorrow or the next day or in the next life after she'd weathered what might be ahead. They'd have to speak more plainly, but sweating in the middle of a muddy road with the stench of death and exposed sewage plumbing in their nostrils wasn't the place for promises and pretty words.

They heard shouting farther down the road. A woman stood over the carcasses of two dead oxen, using a long staff to fend off three men next to a flat transport loaded with several more animal carcasses.

"Let's see what's going on there," Tan said, leaving the roadway to make her way through the rubble undetected by the group. Kyle stayed close behind her.

"These are my oxen," the woman yelled.

One of the men stepped forward, sneering. "Where's your man? Or maybe that's the problem. You need a man to teach you a woman's proper role in The Natural Order."

The woman raised her staff. "I'd like to see you try." She wasn't a large woman but appeared confident despite the three-to-one odds.

"The carcasses will just rot in the heat," a second man said more calmly. "We're collecting all we find to butcher immediately. The meat will be properly stored and distributed daily from trucks in the downtown plaza."

"I know who you are, and I know who will get the meat. These are my oxen to butcher, and you heretics will not take them to let the rest of us starve."

The third man had begun to move behind her as Tan and Kyle stepped out from a nearby building.

"Is there a problem here, friends?" Tan asked.

The men eyed them. Tan's darker-than-common skin and Mohawk hairstyle always drew second glances. But she'd grown used to the stares as strangers struggled to reconcile her ripped muscular physique with her very womanly assets. While they stared, she evaluated the situation. A quick hand gesture sent Kyle subtly maneuvering to the other side of the man circling behind the woman.

"No problem," the calm man said, smiling. He seemed to be in charge of the trio. "We're part of the disaster-recovery team organized downtown. Somebody was smart enough to suggest we collect the dead livestock as quickly as possible before the meat spoils. A lot of roads and half the airport runways are flooded. They don't know how long it will take to clear all the debris from the train tracks."

Tan nodded. "Good idea." She turned to Kyle. "Maybe we should go downtown to see if we can help."

The woman snorted. "Don't think you two would fit in with their kind very well."

The men looked curiously at Kyle.

"Are you guys believers?" she asked.

"Yes, we are." The calm man said. "You know about The Natural Order."

Kyle nodded.

"Shut up, Kyle. I'll handle this." Tan punctuated her words with a condescending snarl and hoped Kyle trusted what they'd shared the past few days enough to catch on to her act and play along. Kyle's entire demeanor seemed to stutter, then change as she stepped back. Her hunched shoulders and nervous glances perfectly mimicked those of the female believers they'd rounded up from the train raid almost a month ago. Not just blazing hot, but sharp as a laser, too. She would make a good spy.

Tan addressed the woman. "These are your oxen?"

"Yes. My family works the cooperative farm outside of town. They were our work animals." She looked at the bodies. "I don't know how we'll get along without them." She glared at the men. "But their last service will be to fill our bellies, not the warehouse of a bunch of hoarders." She spat on the ground for emphasis.

The sneering man began to advance again. "I don't see a man around to stop us."

When the woman raised her staff, the third man behind her made his move. Tan subtly waved Kyle off and grasped his forearm. "It shouldn't take more than one man to subdue a woman, should it," she said, burning her fingers into his arm when he tried to jerk free. His yelp distracted the sneering man, and the woman swept his feet from under him with one swift swing of her staff. Tan released her victim, and the woman withdrew to a defensive stance rather than follow her attack.

"I want no trouble," the woman said. "Just protecting what's mine."

"That one doesn't just look weird. She's unnatural." Tan's victim backed toward the truck, keeping his eyes on her as though he expected her to launch herself at him. The calm man motioned him over and examined the blisters forming on his forearm.

"We're wasting time here, men," the calm man said. "Get back in the transport."

"I'm not letting a bunch of women run me off," the sneering man said. He charged the woman with the staff, but she was ready. She feinted as though she was going to hit him on the right side of the head, and when he reached up with both hands to grab the staff, she swung the other end up between his legs. His eyes bulged, and he grabbed his damaged crotch with both hands. This time, she did hit the right side of his head with the end of her staff, hard enough to knock him out.

"He's not seriously hurt, but get him off my property before he wakes up and I do have to really injure him," she said to his friends.

"Serves him right," the calm man said under his breath. Without another word to the women, they lifted their unconscious comrade and tossed him into the flat bed of the transport among the animal carcasses, then climbed onto the driver's bench and left.

After the transport disappeared from sight, the woman turned to Tan and held out her hand. "I'm Diana. Thanks for having my back."

"No problem. I'm Tan. This is Kyle."

Diana nodded but didn't extend her hand to Kyle. "I don't hold with what those Natural Order people are pushing on people."

"Neither do we," Kyle said, straightening her shoulders and coming to stand even with Tan.

"I took a chance you'd understand and play along, but—" Tan cocked her head and raised her eyebrows at Kyle. "Wow, what a performance. You almost had me fooled."

Kyle's face darkened, her eyes hardened in a scowl, and Tan grabbed her hand to squeeze it gently. "Hey, that was a compliment."

"I hate it." Kyle looked away, her jaw working. "Having to do it brings up some old stuff." She closed her eyes a few seconds, her face relaxing. When she opened them again, her normally expressive face was blank, her tight smile devoid of emotion. "I'm fine."

Tan knew the look, knew how it felt to bury your self-recrimination just so you can keep moving, keep breathing. When the hole she stuffed her guilt into grew too full, she went to see Anya. The punishment wasn't a purge, never a solution. But enough abuse, bloody welts, tortured body parts, and humiliation gave her breathing room—pain in exchange for the pain she'd caused over many lifetimes.

She clasped Kyle's chin and gave her a little shake when she initially refused to look at her. Finally, Kyle's gaze lifted to hers. "We'll talk about this later, eh," Tan said softly.

Kyle sighed, her eyes softening. "Okay."

Diana was watching them curiously. "You're not believers, then?"

"Mother of a dung beetle, no. Did you miss the part about where women fit in The Natural Order?" Tan gestured to herself. "Do I look like one of those women?"

Kyle scratched her head. "Maybe if we traded those cargo pants and bush shirt for a skirt and blouse…a red blouse would look nice with your skin tone…and maybe braid your Mohawk with some beads and ribbon," she deadpanned.

Diana burst out with a laugh, and Tan gave Kyle a playful shove. "Ha. Very funny, Blaze." She leaned close and whispered. "Careful, sparkler, or I might scorch you in places you'd rather not have blisters tonight." Her threat, however, was hollow because her heart was singing to see Kyle rebound. But Tan knew she hadn't really. Kyle had just closed the door for now, like Tan always did.

Kyle flushed, cleared her throat, and looked at Diana. "I grew up in an agriculture community. I could give you a hand butchering these two unless you have some other help." She hesitated and glanced at Tan. "That is, if we have time."

They should push forward. If believers were gathering in the town's center, there could be news or at least rumor of Cyrus. Duty always had been Tan's first priority, but seeing warmth, life again in Kyle's eyes seemed more important now. Roads were a mess, trains weren't running, and Second was headed for the only airport open within a half-day transport ride. If Cyrus had washed up near here, he wouldn't get far very quickly. They could wait a few hours, maybe even a day.

Tan shrugged. "We've got time. Maybe while we're working, you can fill us in on what's going on in town."

"Sure. I could use the help. The farm's main complex is only about two kilometers from here," Diana said. "A lot of the workers haven't shown up, though, because they have injured or family sick from drinking bad water. My mate's there, but his leg's broken and there's no doctor to set it. That's why I came out to look for our oxen. I was lucky enough to find them a few minutes before those guys did. I'll share the meat with everyone. They've been intercepting shipments for months and only giving it to people to join their cult." She thumped the ground with her staff. "I'd rather starve."

Tan nodded. "Do you have a transport to get these big guys back to the farm to cut them up?"

"Yes. Some of our other workers were using it when I set out, but now that I've found the oxen, we can go get it to haul them back."

Being the ranking member of the team, Tan made a quick decision. "Okay. Kyle, you stay here and guard the carcasses. I'll go with Diana and see what I can do for anyone who needs medical attention while she comes back for you and the meat."

"I don't think we should split up," Diana said, shaking her head. "If those guys come back, she'll be one against three. They might even bring more guys with them."

Tan straightened to attention, then bowed slightly. "I apologize. I failed to fully introduce us. I'm Captain Tanisha, and this is Lieutenant Kyle. We serve in the army of The Collective and are in pursuit of the man responsible for the criminal disruption known as The Natural Order." She held out her hand and ignited a blue-white fireball in her palm. "We both are pyro-gifted and quite able to defend against a regiment of believers if necessary. I'm also a surgeon. I can set your husband's broken leg."

Diana stared, her smile starting slow, then spreading into a broad grin. "Sun and stars. We've seen d-vids of the battle at the solar train." She looked up at the sky. "Where are your flying dragons?"

"Dragon horses." Tan corrected her stiffly.

Kyle chuckled. "Hers is nearby somewhere, but pregnant and grumpy. And mine...well, I'm still waiting for mine."

"Star-tastic." Diana pumped her staff into the air. "That's what my daughter will say when she meets you. Come on." She began to pick her way through the rubble of a house toward a street paralleling the one where they stood.

"Can't wait," Tan muttered.

"So I've been promoted? Star-tastic." Kyle grinned at Tan.

"Field promotion." She narrowed her eyes in a mock glare. "Don't make me take it back, sparkler."

"That's Lieutenant Blaze to you, Captain," Kyle said with a wink.

Tan shook her head and jogged through wreckage like it was an obstacle course to catch up with Diana—or was it to run with the pure joy that was Kyle. Stars, this woman had blazed a trail from her easy-open libido straight into her guarded heart. How did that happen?

❖

Kyle was physically sated but still emotionally desperate for Tan. She swallowed against the tightening in her throat and rubbed her cheek along the soft curls of her lover's hair.

They'd politely declined beds in the bunkhouse and bedded down in another hay-storage barn nearby. The short winter hadn't begun yet so the bales were stacked high. They climbed to the top to spread their blanket. Tonight was different. This wasn't about sex frenzy or about healing raw emotions. Tonight they made slow, careful love in the dim light of Tan's solar bulb. Every kiss, every touch was a shy request, a tentative promise. Every climax was about wanting to belong and trying to hold on to the belief that maybe they did, even while they would be apart.

Kyle stroked her fingers up and down the curve of Tan's strong back. She didn't want to leave her. Stars, she'd miss her.

When she was with Tan, she felt like she was more than the girl who couldn't stand up to her father, more than the sister who didn't keep her younger brother safe. She felt like she could be that heroine in the fantastic bedtime stories her mother had whispered only to her.

She didn't want to go into that believers' camp. They reminded her that she was less than. She was less than the son her father wanted. She wasn't any of the things he wanted—feminine, opposite-sex oriented, yearning to bear children, or any of the usual things that interested most women. She even preferred science over his passion for cultural history.

She closed her eyes and focused on Tan's fingers stroking across her abdomen and tracing the line of her hipbone. Maybe she could burn the feel of Tan's skin, the touch of her hands into her memory and take that with her.

Tan kissed her shoulder. "You'll leave first with Diana's brother. I'll shadow you so we aren't seen together, but I can see where his shop is located since that will be our rendezvous point."

Kyle smoothed her hand along Tan's shoulder and down her chest to cradle Tan's full breast in her palm. "Then I want you to leave, Tan." She thumbed Tan's dark nipple and watched her pupils dilate with arousal. "Promise me you won't wait until I come out of the shop."

Tan's eyes fluttered as Kyle worked her nipple. "Why? What if you run into those guys and they get rough?"

"I can take care of myself. You said so yourself when you left me with those dead oxen this afternoon."

Tan laid her hand over Kyle's to stop the distracting massage of her breast. "This is different. You'll be in the hornets' nest. If something goes wrong, they could swarm you." She tugged Kyle's hand up and kissed her palm, then returned it to her breast. "Why, baby? Why do you want me to leave?"

Kyle stared up at the rafters and sighed. "I'll have to change into a skirt and—"

Surprised amusement lit Tan's face and she chuckled. "You don't want me to see you wearing a skirt? That's what this is about?"

Tan's laugh was a cold blade. Kyle thought she would be the one person who would understand. She started to roll away, but Tan's strong arms clamped tight around hers.

"Kyle, babe? I'm sorry. You're serious." Tan peppered Kyle's shoulder, her face with kisses. "No, don't. I'm sorry. It's much more than that, isn't it?"

Kyle didn't answer. She couldn't answer because of the lump lodged in her throat, the angry tears burning the back of her eyes.

Tan rolled them over, pillowing Kyle's head against her breasts, stroking Kyle's hair and down her back. "I've experienced a lot in my lifetimes, Kyle. I've been a warrior, soldier, and mercenary. I've experienced almost every kind of torture you can imagine. The pain that scars worse than physical abuse, though, is when they shred your dignity."

Tan's soft words, her gentle strokes unlocked the vise squeezing Kyle's chest, and she let go of the sob caught in her throat. "I hate him. He makes me hate myself." She buried her face in Tan's breasts, no longer able to hold back her tears or the angry sobs. "I don't want you to see me cower to him or any of those men, even if it is an act. I don't want you to see me like that. Promise me, Tan. Promise you'll leave once we go inside the store."

"I promise, baby. I swear on Phyrrhos' foal, I'll come back here. I won't hang around. Okay?"

Kyle nodded, relieved to have Tan's promise and a little surprised that admitting what was bothering her had eased the twisting in her stomach. She could do this. She would find her father and help end The Natural Order and bring harmony once again to The Collective.

Tan handed her something soft. "Here, dry your face and wipe your nose so I can make love to you again."

Kyle did as requested, then looked at the material in her hand. "Hey, that's my shirt."

Tan smiled. "You don't think I'd give you mine to wipe your nose on, do you?"

❖

Kyle hunched her shoulders and hurried toward the group of believer women milling about a large outdoor cooking area. She was going to have to dig deep to conjure a shy, lost young woman when she felt more like a cranky, out-of-place warrior. Even with the mid-calf length, she felt embarrassingly vulnerable wearing a skirt. Adding to her discomfort, the numbing agent was wearing off, and her scalp was beginning to itch and her head ache from the shoulder-length hair extensions implanted an hour ago. This spy business wasn't much fun.

She watched the women for a few minutes, then approached a short, full-bodied woman who flitted among the group, chattering cheerfully. She would be the rumor-central type of person—exactly who Kyle needed to befriend. She edged around the group and caught the woman's attention when she came near.

"Excuse me, ma'am?"

The woman stopped and smiled. "Yes?" She regarded Kyle, her expression open and friendly. "I don't believe I've seen you around before." She extended her hand. "I'm Juanita."

She wiped her hand on her skirt and limply clasped the other woman's hand. "I'm Kylie. Some men up the road said you had bottled water." She let her pack slide from her shoulder to the ground as if she couldn't bear its weight any longer, then touched her hand to her forehead and swayed. "And, uh, I thought maybe you could use another volunteer?"

Juanita grasped Kyle's arm and guided her to a circle of folding camp chairs where several women were taking a break from their labors. "Sit here." She opened an insulated chest that sat in the middle of the circle and handed Kyle a bottle. "You must be dehydrated, poor thing. Are you by yourself?"

"Thank you." Kyle drank the entire bottle. She'd been too nervous to eat earlier, and they'd purposely taken all rations and water from her pack in case she was searched. She closed her eyes for dramatic effect before she began her tale. Tan had advised her that the best cover stories were based on truth. "I was traveling by train with my father and a group of believers to Brasília when we were attacked at a town where we stopped to share our message. I'm not sure what happened to my father and the rest of the men, but the women were being held by this army of The Collective."

Juanita nodded. "Yes, we've all seen d-news vids of that attack. I didn't know any women were involved."

Kyle nodded. "A small group of us went to take care of the cooking and laundry needs of the men helping with the mission."

Juanita's eyes were wide. "They didn't, you know, hurt any of you, did they? I mean, some of them are unnatural."

Kyle didn't know if she wanted to laugh or slap the stupid woman, but she had to maintain her cover. "No. They were kind, except they wouldn't let us leave until they interrogated us thoroughly. They said they'd let us go only after The Natural Order had been dissolved and The Collective restored, but I escaped. I wanted to find my boyfriend. He'd been lost at an earlier stop. So I've been traveling north for weeks."

"All alone?"

Kyle nodded. "I've been scared to death, but I've found kind people here and there who helped me with food and a place to stay overnight." She ducked her head and conjured the memory of Tan between her legs, Tan's mouth hot, her tongue teasing against her clit. The flush she sought heated her face on cue. Only she would know it wasn't the embarrassment she was pretending. "I know it was wrong, but I was so hungry and tired that I sometimes went to a local temple and told them I was a stranded tourist. The Advocates never refused to feed and house me. I'm ashamed that I lied and that I had to go to them." She looked up again. "I know their beliefs are wrong."

Juanita patted her leg. "An unaccompanied woman doesn't have a lot of choices, Kylie."

Kyle stared down at her hands. "They said my boyfriend was killed. I had no idea where to look for my father, so I was trying to return to the Third Continent. Maybe my father made it back, too. If I can't find him, I'll go to my aunt's home. I don't have any other family. They were killed in a mudslide."

Juanita squeezed her knee. "I'm going to get you a sandwich and another bottle of water. Once you have some food in you, I'll take you to get a bedroll. We've got room in our single-women's building, right next to me. Then we'll go over and get you a job assignment."

Kyle smiled. "That would be wonderful. Thank you so much."

"We serve The One," Juanita said, smiling back.

"The One," Kyle said, trying not to taste the bitterness.

❖

"Hurry," Juanita said, waving when Kyle stopped to tighten the closures on her athletic shoes. At least she didn't have to wear those girlie sandals that some of the women flopped around in. They were so impractical and impossible to run in. A lot of the more practical women or those with fewer luxury credits opted for more comfortable shoes like Kyle's.

"Where's everybody going?"

"To the central plaza. They're saying there's big news for everyone."

The evening was still early. Kyle had chopped vegetables and meat until her hands felt like they would fall off. And her head hadn't stopped throbbing. She couldn't believe women willingly went through this discomfort just to make their hair appear fuller or longer. She was tired, hungry, and lonely for Tan. Dinner, however, had been postponed until after this big meeting, so bedtime wouldn't be anytime soon either. Being a spy sucked.

The plaza was a city block surrounded by historic buildings and the older business district. A large shade tree stood lone vigil over a handful of fresh stumps—all that remained of the other trees torn apart by the hurricane's high winds. In the center of the plaza, the foundation of a gazebo had held its ground when the supports and roof were torn away. People streamed in from streets in all directions, converging on the gazebo-turned-platform until more than a thousand stood shoulder to shoulder.

"Can you see? What's happening?"

Kyle was as tall as most of the men, but Juanita couldn't see past the back of the man in front of her. "Nothing yet." Kyle wound through the crowd and onto the steps of one building. She put Juanita two steps up and motioned for another woman to take the step between them, so both of the shorter women could see over Kyle. "I'll be right down here," Kyle told Juanita.

Juanita nodded, but she was watching the crowd more than she was listening. "There. Somebody's coming up to the platform to speak."

Kyle could see the crowd stepping back from a spear of big men as they made a path for someone moving toward the platform. A man she didn't recognize hopped up onto the platform, tapped the amplifier on his wrist IC, and spoke.

"Friends." The man paused and waited as the noise of a hundred conversations gradually quieted and he held their attention. "These past few days have been difficult. Many of you have lost your homes. Others have lost their businesses. Some of you have lost family members and friends. We believe, and yet we suffer along with those who defy the power we have just witnessed—judgment by The One. Many of you have questions. The Omnipotent is not uncaring for those who are loyal and has favored Matamoros believers with a glorious miracle."

He raised his hands above his head as the people cheered, even though they had no clue as to what this miracle might entail. He waved for them to quiet after a moment.

"A series of unlikely events placed him on a boat sailing across the Gulf, just ahead of the great storm. Perhaps it was your prayers as the storm upgraded to a hurricane that slowed his ship so that it was caught in the hurricane and capsized. The crew apparently was lost, but The One gave this witness, his spokesman, the courage and the divine strength to dive into that angry sea and save himself as well as the two believers traveling with him. Two days ago, they washed up on the beach just south of Matamoros."

Kyle froze. It couldn't be anybody else. She backed up onto the step behind her, crowding the woman in front of Juanita. "Sorry, sorry. Can we both fit?" She wedged in next to the woman despite the irritated glances from other nearby people. Kyle squinted to see the faces of the men standing next to the platform. One looked familiar and she focused on him.

"This man is here today, sent by The One to speak to you. I give to you the one who awakened the world to our sins and the power of our maker. I give to you The Prophet."

The man Kyle was watching turned and, with another man, cleared a path to the steps for Cyrus to mount the platform. He was tanned and looked leaner than when Kyle had last seen him. She thought of when he was younger, of happier times when her family would hike and camp in the mountains. A wave of longing washed over her for family, home, and simpler times.

The people cheered wildly.

"Oh my stars." Juanita hopped about on her step, her fingernails digging into Kyle's shoulders where she held on to keep her balance. "Can you believe it? The Prophet is here. I've only seen him on d-vids. This is a miracle."

Cyrus smiled broadly as he activated his amplifier and turned in a full circle for several long minutes before gesturing for the people to quiet.

"A living miracle," someone shouted from the edges of the plaza. Affirmations of this declaration rippled across the gathering, and Cyrus nodded in agreement.

"My believers, The One is with you."

"We believe," they said in response.

"I am not deaf to your cries. I am not numb to your pain. Until my word has spread and is accepted by everyone, the evil that poisons this world will taint the lives of everyone, even the innocent." Cyrus's deep voice rang out over the silent square. "It is our reminder that we must not waver in our message, in our purpose. We must not be weak when faced with the suffering The Collective brings upon itself."

Kyle gritted her teeth to squelch the scream that swelled in her chest. He might look like the father she'd once loved, but this man was a stranger who could let children and old people starve or die from preventable diseases just because they didn't share his beliefs. This was the man who'd ordered his own daughter chained to a tree with no shelter and little food or water for weeks until she caved in to his authority. She felt sick to her stomach.

"Just as The One punishes, he also rewards. I'm very impressed with our immediate organization in the wake of this terrible storm. But you need help. My colleague has spoken with our community in Killeen, and a convoy of your brethren believers left yesterday for Matamoros, driving trucks loaded with food, essential household items, water purifiers, and supplies you need to rebuild your homes and businesses."

Men cheered and several women began to weep tears of relief.

Kyle turned and put her mouth close to Juanita's ear to be heard. "I don't feel so good. I'll meet you back at the kitchens to help with the dinner meal."

Juanita looked worried but kept glancing back at platform. She clearly didn't want to miss any of what was happening. "Can you find your way back?"

Kyle nodded but rubbed at her belly for emphasis. "I found my way here from the Fourth Continent. I just need to visit a personal facility right now." Without another word, she slipped through the throng of people.

Cyrus was here in Matamoros. If she hurried, she could leave a message for Tan at the rendezvous shop and be back at the kitchens before anybody missed her.

❖

Cyrus looked out across the plaza into their upturned faces. They were at least several thousand strong in this one seaside city. He was The Prophet, their modern miracle. They didn't even realize that when they looked at him, they saw the face of The One. It didn't matter. They were his army and his greatest weapon. A virus among The Collective, they were spreading his words to their families, friends, and coworkers, who then infected their connections. Their belief, their trust in him would be the sword that would slay The Collective dragon.

CHAPTER SEVENTEEN

I'm Xavier, regional quartermaster. I have a request from The World Council to meet with you. How can I help?"

Furcho bowed very slightly and held out his hand. Cautionary flags already were waving. He'd known men like Xavier, slick in appearance and with moves so smooth you'd never feel the knife sliding into your back until it pierced your vital organs. But that was why Alyssa had insisted they fly Uri to Brasília. They wouldn't have to depend on Furcho's impressions. Uri was an empath and could discern deceit. So he relaxed and concentrated on his job, which was to keep them safe.

"I'm pleased to make your acquaintance. I'm Furcho." He gestured to the three behind him. "These are my colleagues—Diego, Raven, and Uri. We're part of a special task force appointed to secure our shipping routes. It seems a number of shipments are not reaching their rural destinations, and we've been sent to trace some delays at this specific warehouse."

"Ah, yes. Please come with me. I think I can explain the problem."

They followed him inside the warehouse. Transports were backed up to the loading docks, and workers moved up and down the warehouse aisles to check numbers on their d-tablets against crate labels, dodging flats being airlifted to the transports.

"It's very busy today," Raven said. "There was no activity or workers when I visited several days ago."

Xavier held up his finger to forestall her as a foreman brought a d-tablet for him to review. After a moment, Xavier signed his approval on the tablet and the man left.

"I'm sorry. It is busy. We've had shipments backing up for weeks now because we've had several transports hijacked en route to their outlying destinations."

Diego frowned. "We have no reports of hijacking."

"No, there wouldn't be." Xavier smiled indulgently. "If we'd filed a report with the peacekeepers, it would've been on the d-news and everyone would know the shipments were unprotected."

"The shipments haven't needed protection in the past," Raven said.

"Crops weren't failing, and people weren't hungry then," Xavier said.

"But you're filling transports for shipping today," Furcho said.

"Yes. We've had several warehouse positions open here that won't be filled, and I've asked each of the rural centers to sacrifice the salary of one position if they have one open now or when they have one come open in the future. The credits are being pooled to pay for extra security."

"What kind of security?" Diego asked.

"We don't want the details to be public knowledge. If you'll come into the office, however, I can be more specific." Xavier stepped back and motioned for them to precede him.

The office was spacious enough for the three quartermasters who shared it on rotating shifts, but it felt stifling with five adults packed in among the three desks and various electronic records equipment. The oily stink of whatever Xavier used to slick back his dark hair made Furcho want to hold his breath. One of the things he loved about Nicole was her clean, light scent. He'd hoped Alyssa would send her to Brasília, but Nicole was in bed with the flu that was sweeping the dragon-horse-army camp. He hated being away when she was sick.

"Can I offer anyone something to drink?" Xavier asked.

Furcho started to say no, then changed his mind. "I wouldn't mind a bottle of water, if you have one," Furcho said.

The others declined, and when Xavier turned to a cold storage tucked into the corner of the office to get the water, Furcho shot Uri a questioning look. Uri's brow furrowed and he waggled his hand, signaling that he had no clear impression yet.

Xavier handed Furcho the water and stroked his goatee. "Where were we?"

"You were going to explain your security measures," Diego said.

"Ah, yes. Well, we've equipped each transport with a concealed camera that can be activated by either the driver or the guard we're hiring to ride along. Anyone who attacks will be caught on a live feed, so even if they smash the camera, we'll have the recording here."

"They could wear masks."

"They haven't so far. That's another reason this information shouldn't go out to the public. They'll figure it out after we catch a few, but it will work for a while."

"These security guards. How do you expect them to stop the hijackers? You know as well as I do that it's illegal for them to carry arms. Only peacekeepers are allowed to use stun weapons."

"They're all trained in martial arts and hand-to-hand combat. The hijackers are villagers, armed with staffs or, at worst, a jungle machete. Our guards will be armed with the same. Only instead of a machete, they could be carrying a rapier or some other sword. Fair is fair, and those aren't illegal to own."

"Not if you're a licensed collector, but collectors don't take jobs as security guards and carry their prized swords around strapped to their hips," Diego said.

"Would you prefer that we just hand over the shipments?"

"If you're shipping the food for proper distribution, I don't understand the need for theft. Everyone would get sufficient rations."

Xavier shrugged. "People are greedy. They want more than standard rations."

Furcho finished his water and placed the empty bottle on the desk. "At any rate, it seems that you have things moving again here. Perhaps we should report your solution back to The World Council so they might consider implementing it in other problem areas." He nodded to Xavier. "We won't detain you further. Thank you for making time for us."

Xavier watched them file out of the office behind Furcho, then went to the window to make sure they got into their transport and left. He went to a bank of d-screens and activated one that showed the interior of the office, then backtracked the video to show the silent exchange between Furcho and Uri while he was getting the bottle of water.

Juan, who was quickly becoming Xavier's right-hand man, came through the door. "How'd it go, Boss? Do you think they bought it?"

"No. I think our source was right. The big man with the Advocate tattoo is an empath. He knew I wasn't telling the truth. He wasn't sure out in the warehouse, because everything I said was partially true. But he's probably telling them now that I was lying about the guards not being armed." He watched the vid again of them standing in the office. "I'm afraid they're going to have a terrible accident today. It's unfortunate. The woman is quite attractive."

❖

The four of them were quiet as they climbed into the automated multi-passenger taxi. Furcho tapped in the route to the central bus station in the center of town and settled into his seat.

Nobody would discuss what they'd seen until they were safely secluded and scanned for listening devices that could have been planted on them while they were in the warehouse.

They'd stayed a few nights in the home of a local contact until their host's wife became visibly nervous. It didn't matter why she was nervous, whether it was for her safety or because she'd sold them out, but Diego found new quarters for them each night until Tan's friends in San Pedro hooked them up with the local Brasília network, who'd finessed extracting the kidnapped doctor from the men Xavier paid to "dispose" of him and provided refuge for The Guard at their underground quarters.

Still, they were followed each time they ventured out and were careful to make a series of transportation changes, splitting up midway, before they met back at the network. Today, they would separate when they reached the bus station, and each pair would wander around the city, lunch, dawdle, and then slip into the network's underground at two different entry points.

They were lost in their own thoughts when Uri turned in his seat to peer through the rear window. "Something's wrong," he said.

Furcho scanned ahead. Nothing suspicious. "Diego?"

Diego sat forward. "This isn't the route we took before."

"My window won't open," Raven said, pressing the control several times.

The transport turned down a narrow alley between buildings three- and four-stories high. It slowed to a stop, but the door safety locks failed to disengage. As though he'd anticipated it, Diego already was ripping into the door panel with his knife.

"We need to get out," Uri yelled, kicking the windshield with both of his large, booted feet. It popped out in one piece onto the street at the same time Diego's blade disengaged the lock on his door.

"Get out, get out and run," Uri shouted.

Diego and Raven scrambled out of his opened door. Uri grabbed Furcho's shirt and literally threw him through the opening where the windshield had been. It was a tight squeeze for the big man to follow and his belt hung up on something.

Furcho reached for Uri. Damn, he hated being on the ground. He fought from the sky. If only he could summon Azar in the daytime.

"No, no," Uri shouted, swinging his arms to fend Furcho off. "Get away."

Furcho grabbed Uri's arm and held tight. "Raven."

"Got it."

She grabbed his other arm and braced her foot against the transport as Diego slid his knife under Uri's belt and cut it. Uri kicked and they pulled. A loud crack sounded, and they were all on the ground struggling to their feet.

"Run, run," Uri said. He looked up and pointed. "Roof."

Why did Uri sound so far away? Roof? Was he saying run or roof? Furcho could see his lips moving, could feel Uri tugging him to his feet, but his legs felt like rubber. He could walk, just couldn't catch his breath. Each desperate attempt to suck in air brought a sharp stabbing pain. Uri was holding him too tight and the big moose was running. Stars, the jostling hurt. Raven and Diego were running in front of them. Why were they running?

A thunderous boom threw them all to the ground, and Furcho was thankful Uri fell next to him rather than on him. The pain in his chest was red-hot, but he was getting a handle on it. He could manage if he took short, quick breaths.

Uri turned his head, sand and grit clinging to his cheek. It was too hard to talk, so Furcho curled his index finger and thumb in an okay signal. Uri started to smile and push up from the street when his brow furrowed.

"Roof." Uri yelled again and flung himself at Furcho. Another sharp crack sounded, followed by the familiar whoosh of a fireball. The cracking must have been a couple of ribs breaking because Furcho couldn't breathe again. He thanked The Collective when Uri groaned and rolled away. The odor of burning flesh filtered through Furcho's pain. He needed to assess the damage and get The Guard to safety. He gritted his teeth as he rolled onto his side, and then Diego was lifting his shoulders to help him sit.

Furcho focused first on the carnage in front of him. The auto transport was a burning shell. Next to it lay a torched body and a shattered sniper rifle. Blood drenched the right side of his white shirt. That explained the pain in his chest. Diego squatted next to him, his head bowed.

"Diego?" A red mist sprayed from his mouth with the whispered word.

"Raven got him. Too late, though." Diego looked up, his rugged features drawn. He moved aside to reveal what Furcho hadn't yet seen.

Raven knelt next to where Uri was sprawled on his back in the street, a pool of blood seeping from under him and his unseeing eyes turned to the sun. She chanted softly as she dipped her fingers in the blood and painted a bear symbol on his forehead, the eye symbol of a medicine man on one cheek, and a rising sun on the other cheek. She gently closed his eyes as the last soft tones of her chant were drowned by the sing-song siren of the local peacekeepers arriving.

Furcho wasn't sure which was greater, the pain from his wound or the ache in his heart. "When he...jumped...on top...of me—" Each word was a struggle as he gasped for breath.

Diego nodded, glancing away and swallowing hard, then clearing his throat and holding Furcho's gaze again. "Just after he arrived here, Uri told me that Nicole was so upset she was too sick to come, she made him promise to bring you back safe."

"No. She didn't...mean this."

"You'll have to help her accept that," Diego said. "He would do no less than give his life to keep his promise to her." He glanced at Uri. "He was a good friend to her...my friend, too."

❖

Alyssa sank back against Jael's tall form and let her lover's strong arms and impenetrable shields surround her.

The news of Uri's death had shaken the entire camp. The Advocate's easy-going, quiet manner had made him a favorite among the few children who lived there. It wasn't unusual to see several hanging onto his broad hands, sitting on his hulking shoulders, or trailing in his wake.

A chartered aircraft had arrived in the early morning hours, carrying Uri's body and Furcho, feverish but refusing to be left behind. Diego and Raven would arrive sometime the following night with the dragon horses. Nicole and Furcho wept together over Uri's sacrifice, and Furcho had claimed his right to fire Uri's pyre. He was too weak to stand, however, until he could be reunited with Azar and draw strength from their bond, so the funeral had been delayed until Tan could repair Furcho's shoulder in surgery and the others arrived.

When Tan had returned with the details of Cyrus's location and Kyle's infiltration, Jael had decided to take down Cyrus, then clean up the situation in Brasília as The Natural Order began to fall apart. Now that Uri had been killed, that plan had changed. Something in Jael's gut told her that she'd misjudged the threat in Brasília. Perhaps Cyrus was only the bark of the snarling dog. The teeth snapping at the throat of The Collective was in Brasília. The dragon-horse army—or what part wasn't in the influenza ward—would go there first, then after Cyrus. Tan argued heatedly against it, but Jael was firm.

Everyone's emotions were running high, and Alyssa was weary from trying to shield them out. It was a relief to have Jael shield for her, even for a few moments, but it also kept her from feeling Jael.

"Are you okay, love?" Words would have to suffice.

Jael rubbed her cheek against Alyssa's. "I'm fine. Tan's being a pain in the ass. Normally, I'd say it was because she's too eager to see this end." She paused, and Alyssa's skin tingled at the feathery touch of Jael's lips along her neck. "But I think it's about getting Kyle out of the believers' camp and safe with her again."

Elation replaced the weariness that'd been draining Alyssa. She whirled around in Jael's arms and searched surprised blue eyes. "Do you think they've bonded?"

Jael laughed. "I didn't say that."

"But you're thinking that, aren't you?"

Jael narrowed her eyes. "Are you trying to read my thoughts now, too, empath?"

Alyssa smoothed her palms up Jael's chest, lingering over the nipples hardening under the thick T-shirt. Her breasts relatively small and very firm, Jael never wore a support band. "I don't have to read your mind, lover. Your body always tells me what you're thinking."

Jael's pupils dilated slightly and her voice dropped an octave. "What I think about Tan and Kyle isn't what makes me throb inside."

Alyssa cocked her head and smiled at the flush coloring Jael's neck. She rubbed her cheek against one rigid point under the soft cotton. "It doesn't matter what sparks you, warrior, just who stokes your fire and gets to put it out." She jerked her head around to grasp the nipple in her teeth and bite down gently. Jael hissed at the pleasurable pain. "Because that job belongs to me."

Jael cupped her face. "*I* belong to you." Her lips were gentle but her tongue hot and thorough.

Alyssa's belly did a slow, tingling roll, and she pressed her hips into Jael's. Stars, this woman was everything to her—the air she breathed, the very blood that surged through her heart and made it beat. "What were we talking about?"

Jael smiled. "Tan and Kyle."

"Oh, yeah." Alyssa sighed and stepped back. Would there be a day when she could be in Jael's presence and not need to touch her? Sun, she hoped not. But it would be nice to at least stay on track once in a while. "Well, I know you wouldn't probe Tan's thoughts without her permission, but feelings don't work that way. I can't help but pick up on hers. She's an emotional whirlwind."

"A whirlwind?"

"When Kyle comes up, she radiates so much. She's protective, possessive, even tender. Yet I still read a bit tentative."

Jael shook her head. "Tan finds it very hard to trust."

"Someone hurt her before?"

"Not that I know of. It's more like she doesn't trust that she's worthy of anyone's love. I think she punishes herself for something that happened in a past life."

The pieces of the puzzle that was Tan began to click into place. She'd seen the damage Anya had done. Alyssa had gone back to the headquarters the morning before Tan and Kyle departed and heard the water running in the common bathroom. The door was partly open, so she worried that a showerhead they'd had trouble with might have broken again. But when she started to push past the door, what she saw made her stop. Tan stood at the sink, bare from the waist up. Second was carefully cleaning blood-crusted lashes marring Tan's beautiful shoulders and back. She quietly backed away, leaving Tan's privacy intact. "Oh, Jael. That's why she lets that dominatrix abuse her."

"That's what I think." Jael shrugged. "It's not part of her thoughts I've ever been invited to read." Jael's hands were warm as she absently slid them along Alyssa's arms, her eyes distant and sad. "I sincerely hope Kyle somehow has gotten past that barrier. Even so, Tan still has to forgive herself."

Alyssa thought about the emotions she'd read from Kyle the night they'd left for San Pedro Sula. Kyle had been in a deep discussion with Furcho when Alyssa and Jael entered the meadow, and the emotions rolling off Kyle were raw and angry—directed inward rather than toward anyone present. "I think we all need forgiveness at some point."

❖

Furcho instinctively breathed slow and easy, not too deep so the pain in his chest remained only a dull ache as he floated toward awareness. His eyelids were heavy, too heavy. Maybe he'd sleep awhile longer. The tap, tap, tap was persistent, drawing him. Not tapping. Dripping. Something dripping on his hand. Images of the alley in Brasília flashed through his mind. Kicking to get out of the taxi, an explosion, running, burning in his chest, Raven chanting over Uri, blood everywhere. He gasped, bringing a vicious stab of pain. A cool hand stroked his forehead.

"Breathe slow, small breaths."

The soft words were music in his ear. Each breath brought a familiar scent, her scent. Something soft that hovered between powdery and sweet, like sandalwood. He let his body float with the medications still coursing through his blood, and the pain receded. He worked his mouth, but no words came out and his eyes still wouldn't open. Flashes of a plane ride and then Tan bending over him. Bullet. She was going to take a bullet out of his chest. The dripping was back, along his arm now.

He tried again. "Water." He was surprised when a few chips of ice slid into his mouth. He'd barely recognized the word he groaned out. But Nicole always knew what he needed. He blinked, feeling stronger, more lucid with every second. Nicole. Sun and stars, her tear-streaked face had never looked more beautiful to him. Ah, that explained the dripping.

"Don't cry." His voice sounded like sandpaper. He swallowed. "Nothing vital was injured. I can still have children."

"I can't believe that's the first thing you'd think about." Nicole laughed softly, wiping at the tears on her cheeks. "Wait. Yes, I can."

Furcho tried to raise his hand to touch her cheek and grimaced when the movement knifed pain through his side. The sniper's bullet had entered the back of his shoulder, nicked his lung and broken a few ribs. Nicole's warm hands wrapped around his, forestalling any further attempt. He wished for the strength to pull her down next to him on the bed so he could hold her in his arms. "You're wrong. The first thought when I opened my eyes was how lucky I was to find the most beautiful woman in the world at my bedside."

Nicole's tears began again. "I could have lost you, Furcho. I had an uneasy feeling when you were leaving, so I—" She dropped her chin to her chest and clung to his hand as she sobbed. "When I asked Uri...I never meant—" She looked up at him, her blue eyes pale with grief. "I keep telling myself I shouldn't have made him promise to watch out for you. I loved Uri, but I'm glad it's not you on that pyre tonight." She looked away from him. "And I hate myself for being glad."

"Nicole, sweetheart, look at me." He waited until she hesitantly met his gaze. "Everything is as it should be. Uri made a brave, selfless sacrifice few souls ever have the opportunity to make. I haven't forgotten that we talked about this when I first arrived, before my surgery."

Nicole looked down at her hand still entwined with Furcho's. "We didn't have a chance to talk about all of it." She wiped away her tears with her free hand, a small smile forming as she cast a shy glance his way. "Uri was the only one who knew how important it was for you to come back...to us."

"I knew it was important...wait—" Us? Maybe the medication was still making his mind fuzzy. "Us? Who are you talking about?"

Nicole licked her lips, hesitating as though making a decision. Finally, she laid her hand on her stomach and held his gaze. "Me and our child."

He swallowed. His throat was dry again. "I'm going to be a papa?"

She nodded, watching him.

He grinned and squeezed her hand. "This is better than any medicine."

"Really?"

"We have to be bonded. I mean, I knew we were soul mates the first time I saw you, but I mean legally."

Nicole cocked her head, pretending a haughty look that fell just short of convincing. "Warriors. Are you asking or telling me?"

"I'll get down on one knee if you want." Furcho moved his legs a bit and picked at the blanket pulled halfway up his chest as though he was going to get out of bed.

Nicole laughed, not fooled by his weak display. "How about if I do the kneeling and propose to you instead? I don't want you to get dizzy and fall." Her gaze wandered pointedly downward from his chest. "You could damage something essential, and I'm sure I'll want more children later."

He widened his eyes in mock horror. "What if we just mutually agree and seal it with a kiss?"

Nicole's eyes were soft with affection as she bent over the bed. Furcho reached with his good arm to pull her close, and their souls melded as their lips met in a long, probing kiss.

"I'm an even better surgeon than I thought. I'd say the patient is making a miraculous recovery."

Nicole groaned, her face flushing as she straightened to reveal Tan and Jael standing just inside the doorway. Furcho grinned at them. "I'm going to be a papa."

CHAPTER EIGHTEEN

Juanita prattled endlessly while Kyle washed pots, glad for something mindless to occupy her hands since she couldn't think of anything other than Tan. Had she picked up the message she'd left for her yesterday evening? It was a long flight back to the valley camp. Even if Phyrrhos weren't heavily pregnant, it would take more than one night. How long would she have to rest before Tan could return? Would she return? Or would they send another of The Guard whose dragon horse wasn't fat and about to foal?

Kyle rinsed the last pan, braced both hands against the trough that had been rigged as an outdoor sink, and stretched her aching back. She was too tall and the sink's level too low. She hated everything about being a spy in The Natural Order camp—the deceit, the way the men treated the women like servants, watching the spirits of the young girls being crushed as they were schooled to respond submissively, and even the sensitive boys being pushed aside rather than valued like the more aggressive boys. Submitting was hard enough for her, but it was even harder not to defend these young people whose souls might be irrevocably scarred.

"Oh my. I've just been talking my head off about The Prophet, when I should have been helping you," Juanita said. "I'm so sorry, Kylie."

Kyle gave the shorter woman a one-armed hug. At least her chatter had kept Kyle from having to engage in a conversation with anyone. It let her spend the time thinking about Tan. "It's okay. I was so caught up listening to you I didn't realize I'd washed them all until I was rinsing the last one." She offered Juanita the hand-blower. "But if you'd like to dry and store them, I wouldn't mind grabbing a shower. I'm still not feeling all that great. I'd like to stop by the first-aid station for something to settle my stomach, shower, and climb into bed early with a book."

"Sure, sure. You go ahead." Juanita yelled at a dark-haired girl who'd been wiping the same table for the past hour while she talked with two young male believers. "Luisa. Stop flirting and get over here. Help me dry these pots and put them away."

Kyle untied the rubber apron that had kept her clothes dry while she labored and hung it on a hook at the end of the sink.

Luisa sauntered over, eyeing Kyle. "Where's she going?"

Fists on her hips, Juanita gave the girl a steely stare. "Not that it's any of your business, but Kylie washed all these pots even though she isn't feeling well. Now she's going to the first-aid station."

"Excuse me," Kyle said, moving to slip past Luisa. A hand on her forearm stopped her.

"One of my friends is interested in meeting you. They're going to save seats for us at the singing tonight. Your stomach should be better by then, no?"

Luisa's tone clearly wasn't a question, but Kyle gently tugged her arm free. "Tell your friends I'm honored but decline."

"Maybe you don't understand. My friends have secured very important jobs with The Prophet."

Juanita's eyes widened. "Really?"

Luisa lifted her chin and looked down her nose at Juanita. "Did you think I was polishing that table for an hour over two buffoons? The Prophet has chosen a group of men he says will become the business leaders at the City of Light that is being built on the Third Continent. Each has a different area of expertise. That's where The Prophet's headed when he leaves here. They'll go with him and are permitted to take their families or even a girlfriend with them." She jabbed her thumb toward her own chest. "I'm going to that City of Light." She looked at Kyle. "You can stay in this sweaty old town that stinks of sewage and death if you want."

Kyle hesitated. She needed to think this through. These men would have valuable information, but associating with them would take her too close to Cyrus. She couldn't predict what her father would do if he saw her. "I'd feel terrible if my stomach problem is a virus and they caught it from me. Can you please give them my apologies? Perhaps another time."

Luisa stared at her, the fact that she'd touched Kyle suddenly dawning in her eyes.

"Sure. I'll tell them. But don't blame me if they find someone more interesting before tomorrow."

Kyle offered a weak smile. "I'll have to take that chance." She stifled a laugh as she heard water running the minute she wheeled and started for the first-aid station. Luisa's harsh stage whisper carried over the low noise of the kitchen area.

"Why didn't you tell me she had a contagious illness?"

Kyle made a quick stop by the aid station—pay attention to details when protecting your cover, Tan said—and was sorting through this new information about a City of Light on her way to pick up her toiletries for a shower. Should she go by the shop and try to get another message to Tan? She'd been cautioned about sending anything via the d-net, but they'd lose valuable time if she waited days for Tan to return. Maybe one of Tan's networks could dig up more on this city, like a location.

She was so deep in thought, she never saw the hand that closed over her mouth or the assailant who pinned her forearms against her body, jerked her into an alley, and dragged her behind a large trash compactor. Her arms trapped, she twisted her body as a distraction and stomped downward in search of her attacker's foot. When the clever assailant shifted to avoid injury, Kyle kicked backward instead of going for the other foot. A pained grunt confirmed contact with a leg.

"Kyle, stop. It's me."

She froze mid-twist. Her lungs stilled mid-breath. And her heart seized mid-beat. It couldn't be. Could it?

"Mom?" The word was muffled under the hand still clamped over her mouth.

"Stars, I'm so glad to see you."

Suddenly released, Kyle spun and fell into the gaze as blue as her own. Then she dove into her mother's arms and sobbed into her shoulder like a child.

"I'm so sorry it's taken me this long to find you. It's going to be okay, honey. I need your help, but we're going to fix this."

Kyle's tears ended as quickly as they burst forth, but she lingered a moment longer to savor the familiar stroke of her mother's hand through her hair. She briefly mourned the child she'd been, the one whose mother always fixed problems for her. But that child was gone. She was an adult now, with a lot of other adults depending on her. She sighed and straightened, then pulled the tail of her blouse from her skirt.

"Kyle. Do not wipe your nose on your shirt."

Kyle stared at her, then raised an eyebrow, and they both laughed.

"Didn't I teach you anything?" Laine smiled, affection shining in her eyes as she dug into her pocket and handed over a handkerchief. "Use this. It's clean."

"Sorry, Mom." She took the offered handkerchief. "How'd you find me?" She gestured to her clothing. "Have trouble recognizing me?"

Laine brushed a strand of hair back from Kyle's face. "I'd recognize that boyish stride even in an evening gown." Her smile faded, and she nervously scanned the alley. "Chance. Fate. I don't know. I've been tracking your father, and I was in Killeen when I heard a bunch of believers were coming here to meet him."

"He's not my father." The words were bitter in Kyle's mouth. "Cyrus the madman is here, but the man you married left us years ago."

She saw no judgment yet no sympathy in Laine's eyes. "He's sick, Kyle. He's been sick for a long time. I have the medication he needs."

Kyle paced a few steps away, then back, stopping only when her face was inches from her mother's. They were the same height now, dark-haired, blue-eyed bookends. The few strands of gray at

Laine's temples and fine lines of age beginning to crease her face were their only difference. "So you're here to save him?"

Laine shifted back, surprise flickering across her face. "I'm here to try."

Kyle spit her words out, never wavering as she held her mother's gaze. "I'm here to torch him into his next life."

Laine cupped Kyle's face. "I can't let you do that, Kyle. You don't know everything yet."

"I know about Thomas." She wrenched away from Laine's grasp. "Lots of men lose children, and they don't go mad."

"Kyle." Laine reached for her again, but she jerked away.

"No father chains his own daughter to a tree and leaves her there day and night, giving her the minimum food and water needed to exist to make her cave to his insane ideas. No father would force his daughter to marry a stranger so she could be legally raped to bear children."

Laine gasped. "He didn't."

"I spent a month chained to that tree in the rain and heat and cold, day and night. But I'd have killed any man who tried to put his hands on me."

Anger was an inferno burning her inside and out. If medication changed him back to a sane man, he'd probably never have to take responsibility for what he'd done. He'd never pay for the people who'd died because his followers had hoarded medicines or starved because they had no food. He'd never pay for the boy whose hand was chopped off as a bloody message when he and Simon fled the dragon-horse army. She didn't care if a believer walked past the alley and saw her. She no longer cared about messages and protocol. Kyle held her hands out to her sides, palms up, and ignited a roiling blue-white fireball in each.

"He believes in judgment, and I've waited long enough. Today will be his." She would live with the consequences. This was her right.

❖

Alyssa stood before Uri's pyre, a soft breeze dancing along the long hem and sleeves of her gauzy purple robe. Han had presented her with the First Advocate's stole—a ten-centimeter band of snowy-white silk embroidered in glittering gold that draped over her shoulders and hung to her knees—only hours before. This was an Advocate's funeral, not a warrior's pyre, and her first official ceremony as First Advocate.

The night was silent except for the occasional restless snort from a dragon horse. She scanned the left half of the torch-lit training field. Next to each of the more than fifty beasts stood a bonded warrior dressed in formal battleskin. The Guard stood in formation on her right. At their command front was Jael, beautiful and fierce, and Specter, still as a statue. She swallowed and fortified her shields. Jael didn't need to hear her sudden fear that the pyre behind her could one day be her mate's. She was relieved for the distraction of the approaching trio.

Azar walked slowly, his wings unfurled and canted back as though he were holding Furcho in place. A sling cradled Furcho's right arm to his chest, but he held onto one protective wing with his free hand. Diego and Nicole flanked Azar on either side.

They stopped where Bero waited for Diego, next to the right front corner spot always for reserved for Furcho, Third Warrior. Azar knelt low on his front legs, and Furcho carefully dismounted. Diego and Nicole were instantly at his side, and Toni appeared out of the crowd that ringed the field with a chair. Furcho shook his head but sat when Jael sent a pointed glare—and Alyssa suspected a telepathic command—his way.

"Warriors." The army shifted to parade rest at Second's command.

Then Nicole, tears already streaking her cheeks, came to her side. She set Uri's familiar shoulder pack at Alyssa's feet and opened it to hand up his Advocate's stole. Alyssa fingered the material, then laid a hand on Nicole's bowed head. She'd struggled with what to say until the soundless sobs that were shaking her young assistant's shoulders also shook the words from her frozen brain. She raised her head and straightened her shoulders.

"We are not here to mourn but to celebrate the life and certain ascension of the soul we have known in this life as Advocate Uri." She paused, almost surprised at the strength in her voice as it carried across the field. Her confidence growing, she lowered her shields and poured forth the joy she felt for having known this soul.

"Uri was the embodiment of The Collective. He would have preferred to go through life quietly in the background, yet his physical size always drew notice. He had the strength to be a great warrior, but his spirit was too gentle to raise a hand against any human or beast. And, while Uri gave his life in ultimate sacrifice as a sworn Advocate for peace, he also acted with the bravery of a warrior honoring a vow to protect the life of a friend."

Alyssa climbed the light scaffolding to drape the stole over Uri's body and place his pack at his side. She returned to the ground and faced them again.

"Uri told me once that he had no regrets in this life. If there are any on this field tonight, it's only that we will miss the rumble of his laughter, his big hand on our shoulders to steady us, and the sight of children trailing him through the camp." She raised her hands. "Good speed, my friend."

Furcho started to rise but settled again when Will's clear baritone rang out. Alyssa had forgotten Will, the botanist, and Uri, the herbalist, had become friends during long debates over medicines versus natural remedies. After a moment's hesitation, a chorus of children's joyful voices joined Will's. Adults choked back tears as the youngsters warbled the "good-night song" Uri sang almost daily with them. *The stars call me, so say good night until tomorrow when the sun and I see you again.*

Parents led the little ones away, singing the last *good nights*, and Nicole helped Furcho to his feet. Alyssa went to stand by Jael as Diego and Bero took up their post at one end of the pyre and Furcho and Azar at the other. Nicole stood behind Furcho, carefully releasing the sling on his arm.

"Warriors." At Second's command, the army snapped to attention and saluted.

Furcho slowly raised both his hands, fireballs forming while Azar filled his lungs. When the dragon horse exhaled, Furcho's fire shot from his hands to join in one furious column of flame. Only after the pyre caught did Diego and Bero join in and take over. Nicole wrapped an arm around Furcho when he extinguished his flame and lowered his hands. Azar knelt and she helped him mount, climbing up behind to steady him when Azar stood and headed back to the Advocates' quarters.

"Warriors, dismissed."

Alyssa watched them go, barely registering Second's last command or the dragon horses launching into the night around her. She did feel the familiar press of Jael's body against her back.

"Will they be okay?"

Alyssa looked up, smiling at the concern in her mate's eyes. Jael valued each member of The Guard in different ways. She'd confided once that Furcho was a very old soul and she valued him most for his wise counsel. "They'll be fine," she said. "But their poor child, I'm afraid, might have to live with being named Uri."

Jael almost smiled. "That's not so bad."

"It is if you're a girl."

❖

Tan tugged the cowl of her rain slicker to conceal more of her face and cursed her bad luck. A steady drizzle had cleared the streets of Matamoros except for the occasional person dashing from building to building or from building to transport. The empty streets made it difficult for her to move about unnoticed by anyone watching from a window. It also meant that Kyle was indoors with the other believers.

Tan hadn't seen Kyle yet, but her Matamoros connections said the high-rise college dormitory that the believers had conscripted to house the single females and children was where she was staying. The dorm had a flat roof and was taller than most of the immediately adjacent buildings, so she'd waited until dark and landed Phyrrhos quietly behind the solar panels. She was counting on the curious bond Kyle seemed to have with Phyrrhos' unborn foal to draw her to the rooftop.

It was risky, but time was running out. Tan's patience was growing thin.

Phyrrhos grunted and the skin of her huge belly rippled with another shift of the foal. It was big and seemed especially restless tonight. The moon would be completely full tomorrow, and Tan expected the foal would deliver then. If not, then Phyrrhos just might burst. She'd never seen such an accelerated gestation. It'd barely been two weeks. The rapid growth was taking a toll on Phyrrhos, too. She'd been eating voraciously, especially fire rocks when they'd been back at the camp. But today, she'd eaten little— not even her favorite molasses-coated oats. Phyrrhos needed to be some place safe and quiet, not on a roof surrounded by The Natural Order believers.

Tan silently paced the roof. She frowned and massaged her back. Stars, it'd been hurting all day. But her sore back and Phyrrhos weren't the only things bothering her. She needed to be somewhere alone, just her and Kyle, where they could talk and love and heal. For the first time in all her existence, she thought maybe she could. She was tired of collateral losses like Uri or a young Ari's hand or—in her case—a young girl's innocence still damaged after many lifetimes. Kyle seemed to understand. Kyle felt like the anchor Tan could hold on to in order to quiet the storm inside.

A loud click and scrape broke through the noise in her head, and she hid behind an air duct. The stairwell door opened slowly, and a dark figure cautiously emerged. Tan smiled, then flicked a tiny fireball past the nose of the person. Kyle ducked behind the stairwell housing.

"Tan?"

Kyle's low voice played through Tan like the touch of sure fingers on harp strings. She circled silently around the staircase housing to approach from behind. Kyle stood with her back pressed against the housing, looking where Tan had been when she tossed the fireball. Tan mentally shook her head. Kyle would never make much of a warrior. She was too easy to fool. Tan had edged within inches, braced herself for Kyle's overreaction, and started to speak when a flick of Kyle's fingers lit a small flame that was a little too close to Tan's crotch for comfort. She jerked back. Kyle extinguished the flame, a grin spreading across her handsome features as she slowly turned to face Tan.

"You were getting so close, I thought you might need more light to see better."

"Punk of a sparkler." Tan's smile stole the sting from her insult.

Kyle wrapped her hand around Tan's neck and drew her close. "That's Lieutenant Blaze to you, Captain." Her lips were soft but her tongue demanding. Tan pressed her against the stairwell housing. Kyle's warmth felt good against the nagging ache in her belly.

"Sun and stars, I missed you." Kyle's hips moved against Tan's, but Tan stepped back. Phyrrhos was flashing mental pictures in her head, fast and jumbled. Pain stabbed through her side. Something was wrong.

"We don't have time." She started around the stairwell housing at a run, tossing the next words over her shoulder. "Something's wrong with Phyrrhos."

Kyle was right behind her when the heavy stairwell door swung open and slammed into her. She skidded on her back across the dark roof several meters and lay still as five believer guards emerged from the open doorway, repeating weapons firing.

"Kyle!"

Phyrrhos screamed and spewed a column of fire that ignited one gunman into a human torch. Tan's fireballs sentenced two more to the same fate. Kyle stirred. Bullets sang through the night air around them.

"Kyle, you need to get up." Tan's shout competed with the staccato rat-a-tat of the weapons.

Another gunman, tall and muscular, emerged from the doorway, followed by an unarmed man and woman. The woman ran to Kyle, but Tan's focus narrowed to the unarmed man. Cyrus. He was leaner but definitely the same crazed lunatic she'd seen strut atop the train the first time the dragon-horse army confronted him. She recognized the last gunman as one of the bodyguards the network had said set sail with Cyrus.

Phyrrhos screamed, and Tan's bond with her dragon horse blossomed with pain and fury. A graze, but a bullet had nearly found its mark. They had dared to injure her pregnant bonded. Red-hot anger blotted out any ability, any desire to reason. She raised her hands, palms out to form a nearly transparent shield of white-hot fire in front of her and Phyrrhos and pushed it toward the men. She would send them all to their next life together. Molten droplets of metal plunked onto the rooftop as most of the bullets melted. One fragment that made its way through sizzled into Tan's thigh.

Then blue arrows of flame shot into her vision, sending the men's weapons flying through the air and across the roof one by one. Each glowed red hot when it slid to a stop, melting into a fused hunk of metal. Tan withdrew her wall of flame.

The weapons gone, there was no sound but the whip of the flames from Tan's still-burning hands. The remaining believers, Cyrus, and his bodyguard stood motionless and unarmed. Kyle swayed unsteadily several meters away. Tan was relieved to see her standing but not happy about the familiar way the strange, attractive woman wrapped her arm around Kyle's waist. The excruciating pain was back in her side. Or was it her back? Enough. Jael would have to forgive her one more break in protocol. This was for Ari, for Uri, and for all those who had suffered or died because of this madman.

She raised her hands and held them to form an arc of flame over her head. "Cyrus, you have been pronounced guilty by the First Warrior of violating the directives of The Collective to hoard for your own cause at the cost of life and health to your fellow humans. You also were found guilty of heresy and conspiracy to spread heresy. As Guard for The Collective, I am here to carry out your sentence of death so you may make restitution in your next life."

Tan was aware of the woman clinging to Kyle's back speaking urgently into Kyle's ear as Tan pronounced sentence. She'd have to think about that later. She lowered her hands in front of her.

"No!"

The other men, including the now-unarmed bodyguard, flung themselves to the ground as Tan's arc of flame shot out like a heat-seeking missile toward Cyrus. Before it could reach him, a blaze of blue met and blocked Tan's death fire. She faltered. It could only be Kyle. Why?

The men hesitated for a split second, then scrambled for the doorway and disappeared down the stairwell.

She turned on Kyle and screamed, "They're getting away."

"Tan, stop. Drop your flame."

Phyrrhos screamed and pain tore at Tan. She gritted her teeth against it. Phyrrhos' connection hurt, but the jagged blade that ripped at her was the realization that Kyle was standing against her. What a fool she'd been. Tan poured her agony into her flame, but Kyle's fire was strong. When had she become so powerful? She could no longer match Kyle's strength and abruptly dropped her flame. She only hoped Kyle would be merciful enough to take Phyrrhos, too, so that her bonded wouldn't suffer the insanity of a broken bond when Tan became ashes. But Kyle's flame stopped just as suddenly. Blood trickled from a cut at Kyle's temple and from her nose. She faltered and slumped against the other woman.

"Go," the woman said to Tan. "I'll take care of her. You need to leave now before the men return with more guns. Your dragon horse is in labor."

Tan stared wordlessly as they disappeared into the dark stairwell and the heavy door clicked shut behind them.

CHAPTER NINETEEN

Jael? What's wrong?" Alyssa's hands on her back felt cold through the cloth of her T-shirt, and she knew it was because her own body was overheating. Dung. Had she lost control of everything now? She consciously turned down her body heat that had risen with the sullen and fragmented report from Tan.

"Tan is convinced Kyle has betrayed us."

Also, Phyrrhos had foaled last night, stranding Tan in Matamoros for now with Cyrus moving on to Killeen. She needed to go herself or send someone to Tan, but they were several days away and waiting for dusk to descend on the Brasília warehouse held by The Natural Order. Even if they'd been closer, she couldn't spare any of The Guard. She was shorthanded on the battlefield already. Furcho still wasn't fit for duty, but he'd insisted on guarding the train where Nicole would triage and treat less-critical patients and animals for transport back to the mountain camp.

"I don't believe it." Alyssa circled around to face her. "You don't either."

"Kyle opened her thoughts fully to me, and I found no deceit."

"I've felt nothing but sincerity from her." Alyssa frowned, wrapping her arms around Jael. "There has to be an explanation. Tan predicted betrayal from the beginning. Maybe she can't see past her expectations."

"She said she had Cyrus a millisecond away from his next life, and Kyle blocked her flame."

Alyssa pushed back from Jael to look up at her. "Wait. Start from the beginning. Exactly what happened?"

"That's all I got out of her. Phyrrhos was also in labor while all this was going on, and Tan barely got back to the barn before she foaled. She was too exhausted for an interrogation."

Soft surprise flickered across Alyssa's face. "I guess I thought the two of you were close enough that she'd let you review her memory rather than have her report what happened."

Jael shook her head. "Tan's very guarded about her memories, and I won't violate her privacy. It's impossible to know which memory you're unlocking until you review it. Almost everybody has some they'd rather not share. I think Tan has many."

Alyssa didn't push for more, but Jael could feel her concern for Tan. "Did the foaling go well?"

"A healthy filly." Jael laughed. "Monstrously big, according to Tan, but I think that's because she apparently shared labor pains with Phyrrhos." She smiled down at Alyssa. "Makes me glad I bonded with a stallion."

Alyssa slapped her on the belly. "Don't look so smug, stud."

Jael hugged Alyssa to her and closed her eyes. She wanted to remember every detail of Alyssa's clean soft scent, the silky feel of her fiery-red hair, the press of Alyssa's breasts against her ribs, and, most of all, the beat of Alyssa's heart in perfect sync with her own. Doing so soothed the battle jitters despite her growing feeling of portent. Alyssa stiffened, and Jael knew her empathic lover had sensed her concerns.

"Jael?" Fear tinged Alyssa's voice. "Honey?"

This war felt like a roller coaster screaming out of control down a steep incline before it would hopefully turn upward. She felt like a sperm pushing to get through to fertilize the egg and seed a new life. Was this about her or was it about The Collective? She'd evolved to value the needs of the many over the needs of one. Maybe the needs of the whole, however, were met only when each piece was individually whole.

Jael pressed her lips to Alyssa's in a brief kiss. "Don't be afraid. The bit of fear and worry I carry into battle will keep me alert and safe." She took Alyssa's hand and placed it over the steady throb in her chest. "Trust this, my empath. This heart has waited many lifetimes for the one that matches it." She laid her hand on Alyssa's chest. "I cannot fathom that fate would finally bring these together, only to part them. Everything will be as it should be. We are stronger together."

❖

All units in position.

Jael glanced across the rooftops to where Second, astride Titan, raised her hand and closed it into a fist to echo her mental report. She held Second's gaze, her thoughts too tangled to express. But then Second was her cousin, her clone. She was the calm to Jael's storm. She understood what Jael could only intuit.

Second lowered her fist and thumped it firmly against her left shoulder.

I'm always at your back, Jael.

Jael's nod was almost imperceptible.

It's why I've never faltered.

She returned her attention to the warehouse. The streets were eerily empty. Most of the day workers would have gone home, but a smaller second-shift crew should have been moving about, loading and unloading transports. The huge doors to the cavernous building should have been open and the lights on in the office.

The normally thriving restaurants and shops several blocks away—visible from her rooftop perch—were quiet. Their attack was expected. She activated the amplifier on her wrist IC.

"I am Jael, First Warrior of The Guard. The Collective Council has ordered the arrest of Cyrus the Prophet, his second known as Simon, and any believers who stand with them for delaying and denying the proper distribution of supplies to the general population. Cyrus the Prophet and Simon also are charged with heresy against The Collective. Come forth for judgment or we will come in and retrieve you."

Six panels on the rooftop of the warehouse slid back, and dark, unmanned weapons rose up to lock in place. Each repeating gun was flanked on both sides by an array of small missiles. Several dragon horses screamed at the perceived threat, and the guns swiveled in their direction.

The standoff seemed to take a deep breath before chaos was unleashed.

The guns sprayed deadly lead that forced the front line of dragon horses and warriors to put up a wall of flame to shield the rest. Others darted high above and flung white-hot spheres of fire to melt the delicate working of the weapons and silence them. In response, the missile arrays jerked upward and fired. Five found their mark, blowing warriors and their steeds into bits and wounding any flying nearby.

Diego flipped the amplifier on his IC and shouted orders. "They're heat-seeking. Wait until they're close, and then throw your hottest fireball skyward. They'll chase the heat."

When the next missile fired at a young recruit, a seasoned warrior flew in its path with her fireball at the ready. The missile zeroed in on her, and she waited until it was only three meters away before she flung the fireball skyward. The missile followed and exploded when it caught up with the flame. Cheers went up among her unit, and, when another launched, a young daredevil in another unit imitated her performance. Then a third. The fourth wasn't quick enough and the missile found its mark. Another warrior passed instantly to the next life, the blast blowing the warrior next to him off his steed and to his death while wounding three more too seriously to continue fighting.

The moon rose in a sky filled with swooping dragon horses. But more believers poured from adjacent warehouses and fired automatic weapons at the warriors. Angry, pain-filled screams of warriors and dragon horses filled the air. They were outnumbered at least three to one. Several large bodies dropped from the air. The gunmen jumped back, then cheered as fatally wounded warriors and dragon horses writhed and combusted into blazing pyres.

Michael's unit swept in from one end of the wide street that was filled with armed believers while Raven's blocked the other, and the warriors began a fiery cleansing of their own.

Jael circled. A gun at one corner still had five of its eight missiles to launch.

Diego. Take command. Second, with me. The back right corner. Together.

Second moved into position and raised her hands in tandem with Jael. Titan and Specter filled their lungs, and together they spewed an inferno that could likely fuse tungsten. The entire corner of the roof exploded with the missiles. Second gave a thumbs-up signal when Jael pointed to the adjacent corner. They hovered on opposite sides of the gun. It swiveled toward Jael, then jerked back to Second as though the remote operator was uncertain. They raised their hands to take out the weapon and its remaining missiles.

Jael. To your left.

Her instantaneous relay of Diego's urgent warning sent Specter into an evasive dive before he swooped back in a tight circle.

A new weapon had emerged from the center of the building. Tall, black, and sleek, the sight on its single large barrel projected a blinking red beam that scanned the sky. The beam found Second, but Titan dove to the left.

The weapon began searching again. Much heavier than the smaller guns, this one moved slower. Its red beam traveled over Diego and several other warriors without pausing, but stopped and went from blinking to steady when it found Jael. Specter deftly cut down and to the left. The weapon's blinking resumed, and it began a new scan.

Apparently, it's picky. Nothing but the best or the second best for this bad-boy gun.
Very funny. You're anything but second best, Danielle. But I do think it's scanning for my DNA. I don't think they figured you in the mix. Since it's not a danger to anyone else, we should be able to take care of the rest of these guns if we just keep an eye on it.

The street below was littered with burning corpses. Two dragon horses, wings spread, had a group of believers corralled against one building while their bonded warriors searched the misguided souls for hidden weapons. Michael looked up at Jael.

Permission to clear the building.

Jael hesitated. Normally, this would be Second or Furcho's duty as second and third in command of The Guard. But she needed Second's greater firepower on the roof, and Furcho wasn't available. The warrior looking up at her with mismatched eyes and a prancing dragon horse at his side wasn't the sullen, tentative teen Han had sent her a few years ago. This warrior stood tall, shoulders straight, head high, and clear eyes boldly meeting hers.

Permission granted. Have Raven also take a unit and enter at the other end. I want Simon, and I want this man called Xavier to question about Uri's death.
As you command.

The blinking light in Jael's peripheral vision locked on, and she looked down. The red dot targeting the center of her chest had barely registered in her mind before Specter dropped into a spiraling dive. Good thing her brain was connected to his. She frowned. She thought Second had her back...oh.

Second held a slight female warrior around the chest, legs dangling along Titan's side as she coasted to a soft landing on the next street. She bent to lower the warrior to the ground, and the woman nodded at whatever Second was telling her as she limped toward a dragon horse that was awkwardly flapping a broken wing.

Jael smiled to herself. That was Second. Always taking care of everyone. She watched Titan rise to join Specter just below the roofline.

"Ready?" Second hated mental communication, so in deference to her, Jael always spoke when it was possible. But as soon as the word was out of her mouth, she realized the battlefield had gone quiet except for the sounds of the flames and some muffled shouts inside the warehouse. She signaled Second to circle in the opposite direction, and they flew away from the building, outside the light of the flames to climb higher.

All the rooftop guns, except the DNA weapon still scanning for them, had withdrawn. Maybe Michael and Raven had taken the warehouse and found the control room. *Michael?*

Nothing here but a few warehouse workers. I'm betting there's a hidden control room somewhere. Raven's searching. I'm checking circuitry. Maybe I can disable those guns on the roof and trace the wires back to wherever the control room might be.

Jael and Second circled again, as Diego and the main contingent hovered at the ready.

A grinding noise heralded a new series of hatches opening in the warehouse's roof. Five new missiles, each four times the size of the earlier missiles.

Michael?
I didn't do that. Stars, circuits are lighting up all over down here.
Raven?
I've got nothing.

"I am Simon, President of The Natural Order." The disembodied, gravel-like voice seemed as though the building itself were speaking. "You, my magical friends, might have the impression that The Natural Order is about religion. That's what Cyrus thinks, too, but he's a little off in the head. The Natural Order is about survival of the fittest."

The missile launch pads adjusted to a steeper angle, and Jael signaled for the army to move back. They would need more room to intercept at that angle. Second circled behind the missiles, staying a mere meter ahead of the DNA weapon's red beam.

Michael, can we incinerate these?

I don't know, Jael. I can't actually see them from here, but the circuitry down here looks like some kind of programmable guidance system.

Jael, somebody's painted words on these babies.

Titan hovered closer to the roof as Second leaned in to read the inscriptions. The DNA weapon rotated, its pulsing red beam locked on her chest and turned solid.

"Actually, that's what my five little friends on the roof are about—survival of the fittest."

Second, get out of there.

Specter swept downward to confuse the gun's targeting system as Titan peeled away.

"You see, this Collective you subscribe to is allowing the weak to drag the strong people down. So, my five friends here are going to help some of those weaklings into their next life a little early, where they'll hopefully be more useful."

Jael squinted in the dim moonlight, then held a fireball aloft while the DNA weapon scanned for her. Each missile was labeled with a target—a neighborhood populated primarily by the disabled or elderly who were dependent on subsidized housing and rations, the government complex full of policy-makers and auditors, a hospital for treating the mentally ill, and the train depot where Nicole and Furcho were supervising evacuation of their wounded. The DNA weapon was locking onto her again, and Specter dodged away. She lifted the fireball again as they approached from a different angle.

The last missile's label nearly stopped her heart. It was clearly marked with the name of the private airport where Alyssa was triaging their critically wounded to be airlifted back to the base camp. How could he know about that?

"Do you like my choices, First Warrior?"

Michael, Raven, get out. Get your warriors out. Second and I are going to blow those missiles before they can launch.

"Let's see, which button to push first?"

If I can just find and cut the right wire.
Michael, out. That's an order.
I found the control room. It's empty. He's doing this from somewhere else.
Raven, out. Drag Michael with you.

"How does that child's rhyme go? Ennie, meenie, miney... Oops. I guess my finger slipped."

The missile labeled for the poor neighborhood shot from its launch pad, startling Jael with its speed. Specter might be able to overtake it in a free fall, but not ascending. Six dragon-horse warriors closed ranks in its path and joined their flames to detonate it. The explosion was tremendous, vaporizing the closest warriors and sending a dozen tumbling through the air. The night sky churned as damaged wings flailed and comrades dove to catch the warriors they could intercept midair.

Jael had to do something before she lost her entire army. The red beam played across her face. That infernal weapon was locking on her again. Specter dove below the roofline and curled around the building. Jael had to get in front of those missiles before Simon launched another.

She saw it as she rose level with the roof.

Second, get in front of them. You can fuse their fins on the underside to their pads so that when he tries to launch, they'll just implode on their pads. If Titan can hover near the roofline, I think the missiles will block that DNA weapon from finding you.
Where are you going?
I'll intercept if one gets away before you can fuse the base.
Jael—
Do it.

Specter circled in a wide arc, dipping and weaving as the DNA weapon tracked Jael. Raven and Michael ran from the warehouse to where Potawatomi and Apollo waited, and they took to the air as Diego joined Second. She'd fused the first launch pad and, with Diego's help, made quick work of the next. They'd just begun heating the third's fins when the remaining missiles launched.

Two missiles. Jael didn't need to recall the label on one, because she was certain of the other's destination.

Specter dove, wings tucked, like a bullet to intercept.

Everything happened at once, in several slow blinks of an eye. Second's yell. Diego's curse. Potawatomi's and Apollo's furious but futile ascent to help.

The timing was perfect.

The tips of Specter's magnificent wings were millimeters from each missile as he spread them to stop his dive, and Jael's blue-white purifying flame shot from her hands to engulf each deadly warhead at the same instant the blinking red beam found the ruby dragon-horse insignia on her chest and glowed steady.

Alyssa, you are my heart. In this life and always.

It was as it should be.

CHAPTER TWENTY

Second strode through the camp, ticking off lists in her mind. It was what she did best, what she'd done for Jael for years. She would keep doing it for Jael. She felt her, like a person still feels a severed limb. After all those years that Jael couldn't penetrate her thoughts, her clone's presence now was constantly in her head, adding confidence and surety to her decisions.

She'd ordered the evacuation of their Sierra Madre camp. It'd served its purpose for the training of new recruits and bonding with the nearby wild herd of dragon horses. But there were too many spies here. Somehow Simon knew when they would attack in Brasília and the location of their evacuation avenues. It was time to relocate the army. Simon and Cyrus were headed north, and so would they.

"Danielle, Tan's arrived. The Guard is assembled in the headquarters building." Furcho's battleskin showed under his open-collared shirt. None would be without theirs until Jael's death was avenged and The Collective restored.

She didn't answer but lengthened her stride as he followed her into the planning room. She stepped to the head of the table without hesitation, refusing to acknowledge Alyssa's empty seat, and looked each in the eye.

"You will continue to address me as Commander or Second. Whether here physically or not, Jael is still First Warrior and I'm her Second until The Council decrees otherwise. Are we clear?"

She looked to each for an answering nod before continuing. "We are relocating to a permanent base in the Rocky Mountains." She didn't need to add that it was a valley very close to Jael's mountain. The details already had been transmitted to their ICs. "We're transferring only personnel and what we can carry. We'll rebuild with new supplies when we arrive." She thumped the table, unsure if Tan was following along. "Tan, give us your report."

Tan looked up, her face expressionless, eyes dark, dead pools. "Cyrus and his insiders have left Matamoros for Killeen, where The Natural Order has taken control of a regional distribution center. Intel from The Network, however, says his final destination is a stronghold the believers are calling the City of Light."

Furcho, taking notes on his IC, looked up. "Do we have a location?"

"No idea, but they'll be easy enough to track."

"Kyle is still with them?" Furcho glared at Tan. "You know that Simon escaped us in Brasília."

Tan's lip curled into a snarl. "She's where she wants to be."

Furcho's scowl deepened. "She's the one who burned Simon's arm. Even if Kyle has convinced her father that she's on his side, Simon will kill her on sight."

Second slapped her hand on the table, stopping the argument before it escalated further. "We'll discuss this privately." She looked around the table. "Have your units ready to leave at dusk. Furcho, Tan, stay."

❖

The bed was empty and hadn't been slept in. Second recognized Jael's signature in the tightly stretched sheet and precisely placed pillows. The room felt empty, too, because the silent figure sitting in the dark was devoid of the vibrant aura Second had come to associate with the First Advocate. She'd been where Alyssa was now, after Saran had died. Only her links to Jael and Titan had brought her back from the black depths before she self-imploded into flame. She had no idea what would happen to an empath if Alyssa weren't strong enough to survive the loss of her soul's match. She knelt before the straight-backed chair where Alyssa sat, her eyes vacant. Second laid her hand over Alyssa's where it rested on the chair's arm. Alyssa's fingers were cold, and Second heated her hand to warm them.

"We leave tonight. I need you with us." She covered Alyssa's other hand and warmed it, too.

Silence.

"Tan thinks Kyle has betrayed us. She's a very strong pyro, and if she's at Cyrus's side, I'll need to know her intent."

More silence.

Second sighed. "I'm not going to pretend you aren't dying inside, that just breathing is a struggle right now." She paused to swallow the pain she still carried. "But I know I will be with Saran again, and when I do, I want her to be proud that I could be strong until we were together again."

Alyssa's expressionless eyes drifted to Second's, and she lifted a hand to caress Second's brow and cheek. "So like my Jael." Pain and tears finally filled her eyes and she fell forward.

Second caught and held her in a tight embrace as Alyssa sobbed against her chest. "I've got you. I've got you." Tears streaked her own face even as she offered comfort.

"I can't."

"You think you can't, but you start by going through the motions."

"I can't do it." Alyssa's sobs were slowing.

"One foot in front of the other, one minute, one hour, one day at a time. After a while, you'll realize you're going to make it through." Second held her, stroking her back and warming her until Alyssa's tears transitioned into occasional hitching breaths.

Finally, Alyssa took a deep, purifying breath. "You look so much like her." She sighed. "But you're so different—your eyes, your voice, your mannerisms." She burrowed into Second's chest. "You don't smell like her."

Second wanted to smile, but Alyssa's sadness and her own pain still filled her. "Saran liked the way I smell."

Alyssa sat back and wiped at her face. Her voice trembled anew. "I can't do it."

"Yes, you can."

She shook her head. "I mean, I can't go with you."

"Alyssa. I need you."

"You don't understand." She stood and walked to the bed. She stared down at it, then traced a tentative caress along the pillow where Jael had always slept. "Cyrus and his general, Simon, took Jael from me." Her voice broke. "Those missiles didn't leave even a trace for a proper pyre."

Second bowed her head. The explosion of the two missiles and the laser burst that had fired into Jael's chest still haunted her dreams. Jael and Specter had been there, and when the blast cleared, they were gone. Anger stabbed at Second, and she looked up into a hard, unforgiving stare.

"I'm so wounded. I know I'll hurt him," Alyssa said.

Second stepped toward her, but Alyssa put a hand up and she stopped. "Alyssa, I swear on The Collective, I'll personally see that these men are sent to their next life to pay proper restitution. No Advocate will need to take up arms as long as The Guard lives."

"You misunderstand, Danielle. I don't need a weapon. I am a weapon."

"You're an empath."

"More than a normal empath. It's one of the reasons the full power of my gift is kept secret to all but a few. Cyrus is already mad. It wouldn't take much for me to turn his emotions inward so he'd take his own life."

Second struggled to even comprehend that Alyssa would be capable of such an act. "It would scar his soul. He might never be trueborn again. Even worse, it would damage your soul for many lifetimes."

Alyssa went back to chair and sat. "That's why you have to take Nicole instead of me."

"Nicole is pregnant. Furcho won't allow it."

"Send Toni with her."

"Toni?"

"To be her shield."

❖

"Are you certain?" Second scanned the former military base, converted into one of The World Council's regional food and supply distribution centers.

"No question. For whatever reason, Phyrrhos' filly seems to be bonded to that traitor. She sprouted her first wings at dusk, and this is where she led us." Tan's words were so bitter, Second wondered what would become of all of them if they survived this. Jael had been the anchor that tethered her, Tan, and Alyssa.

It had been an arduous few days. The dragon-horse army had been traveling by train so they weren't limited to flying at night because they needed to catch up with Cyrus as quickly as possible. They'd arrived in Killeen only a day behind him. The army's support staff, except for a small contingent that doubled as medical staff and fire-rock mules, had split off for a destination in the Rocky Mountains where they would establish the new base camp.

"My network connections say Cyrus and his group are staying in that building."

"Simon?"

"No sign of him."

Second surveyed the multi-story building that curved around the upper end of a large outdoor area set up to stage public events. She worried that Cyrus had fled to a place that had been used to dismantle weapons after The Great Religion Wars. Could intact weapons still exist in the large, unused hangars?

"The network has intercepted digital traffic indicating there's going to be a huge rally tonight here. Everybody is excited that The Prophet will actually be in Killeen and speak to them. He'll be out in the open, on that platform." Tan pointed to the long, flat stage near the building. "We can take him there."

Second frowned. "A lot of innocents will be in harm's way."

"That's the best part." Tan's dark eyes glinted in the sunlight. "The network has put together a little surprise for the believers. After Cyrus starts his speech, they've got things rigged to interrupt with a holo-vid that will beam right onto the stage. It reveals what their hoarding is doing to the rest of the world, children starving and people dying without their medication. Even better, it shows The Natural Order goons using weapons to take over distribution centers and shooting women and old people who are trying to snatch boxes of pro-chow from the supply trucks."

"That's brilliant." Second regretted again that Tan had repeatedly refused a command position with The Guard. She preferred to scout and scavenge for resources. "We'll go in with a small attack force when the confusion peaks and bring in the rest only if we meet overwhelming force. I don't want a slaughter of innocents on my hands. I just want Cyrus...and that bastard Simon if he shows."

❖

"I got what you need. I think that's a personal facility there, on the right." Laine slipped the palm-sized package into Kyle's hand and pushed her toward the indicated door. "Hurry. We need to join your father." She turned to the man assigned to keep watch over them. "That time of the month. She'll be right out."

The man turned away. Men never wanted to know about women's menstrual problems.

It was easy enough to hide the tools Kyle needed in the wrapper of a sanitary pad.

Cyrus had been wary after they'd been revealed to him on the rooftop in Matamoros, but the god-complex of his madness left him vulnerable to the idea of a repentant wife and the prodigal child who had stepped in to save her father's life. He seemed intrigued by the idea of having his own personal pyro to fight pyros, but he still had ordered protective gloves to be locked on Kyle's hands at all times until he was satisfied of her loyalty.

Laine was shocked at the depth of his madness. She'd had no idea how delusional he'd become. When she looked at him, she saw the younger man she'd loved. When he spoke, she saw a stranger. That was beginning to change in the short week they'd been together.

She'd insisted on preparing his meals and waiting on him personally so she'd have opportunity to slip the medication in his food. Each day, a little of the man she knew was returning. Last night, he'd asked her to come to his bedroom, instead of the room she'd been sharing with Kyle, and they'd made love like the husband and wife they'd once been.

She'd taken advantage of their closeness to beg him to remove Kyle's gloves, but he'd withdrawn again. They would come off after he had his whole family safe in the City of Light, he said.

"Where is this city? Is Maya there?"

"On a mountain." He laughed, and the madness creeping back into his voice chilled her. "A desert, a burning bush, but no golden calf and no game of chance. Maya is coming here to go with us. Maya will bind Kylie to us, and our Natural Order will be complete."

He was gone when she woke that morning, leaving only a note and her guard outside the door. The note said he'd be preparing all day and would meet her and Kyle just before the event that evening. Before she left, she'd spied the tools. She knew they were Kyle's because she'd given them to her when Kyle was at the university, and Cyrus had confiscated them from Kyle's things when they'd been discovered. She couldn't walk out with the entire set because Cyrus would notice, so she took only the small tool Kyle would need to unlock her gloves.

Kyle reappeared from the latrine, smiling.

"All set?"

"Yes," Kyle said. "Much better. Thanks, Mom."

Laine wrapped an arm around her daughter's shoulder. When did Kyle get so tall? "It's nice to still be needed, even when you're all grown up."

"So, where are we going?"

"Your father will be busy today, so I thought we'd go help in the kitchens with the other women."

Kyle groaned. "I was hoping to have a day to look around Killeen."

Laine ignored Kyle's pointed look. "Nope. A woman's work is never done."

❖

"Prophet, Prophet, Prophet."

Nearly four thousand believers chanted as Cyrus walked onto the long platform and waved at them. His holo-image ten times his height was projected behind him so everyone could see. Kyle shuffled onto one end of the platform behind her mother, where they stood and waited for their cue in the performance.

She hated this. She'd like to burn the entire platform to the ground and end this ridiculous circus. It had taken every ounce of her control to leave the gloves in place once she'd disengaged the locks with the electromagnetic tool Laine had slipped her. Covering a pyro's hands to smother their fire was like covering another person's mouth and nose so they couldn't breathe, and Kyle had felt as though she would go insane if she didn't get them off soon.

The news that Maya would be joining them in Killeen, however, had strengthened her resolve. She glanced at the guard assigned to her and Laine. She could hold on a little longer. She knew her mother held out hope that the medication she'd been slipping into Cyrus's food would bring him around so they could be a whole family again, but too much had changed. She could never look at him and see the father of her childhood. She saw only his mental illness. She could never trust him. Cyrus had done too much damage.

Sun and stars, she hoped she hadn't destroyed her bond with Tan. As soon as Maya showed up, Kyle planned to take her and find Tan to make things right. She missed Tan every second of the day. Thinking of her was the only thing that kept Kyle from dwelling on the misery of her gloved hands. If Laine wanted to stick around and try to save Cyrus, that was her choice. But Kyle refused to let her put Maya at risk. Cyrus wouldn't force her into a marriage like he had tried to force Kyle.

"The One is with us, my friends, because we see and obey The Natural Order as it was intended." Cyrus's voice boomed from the enhanced amplifiers with which his IC networked.

The answering cheers were so deafening Kyle wanted to put her hands over her ears, but she sat with them folded in her lap, ready to snatch the gloves off.

She sucked in a quick breath. She could feel the stirring. Tan was near. Well, Phyrrhos, at least. The bond she'd felt from the dragon horse's young was stronger than ever. Had Phyrrhos already foaled? Were Jael and the army here? Kyle's modest blouse, fashionable calf-length skirt and knee-high boots concealed the silver battleskin she wore underneath. Second had supplied it for protection if Kyle found herself in battle, she'd said. There was no dragon-horse insignia on the chest. Only bonded warriors had that honor. Still, it buoyed Kyle's sagging spirit.

"We are on the cusp of great change, my believers." The crowd quieted to hear Cyrus's words. "Our numbers have grown exponentially. We have retaken control of nearly half of the world's resources so we can build healthy families and communities." Cyrus brought his hands to his chest. "I was compelled on this journey by the loss of my only son." He looked out over the faces, now silent. "My pride cost me the most precious thing in my life, but it took losing Thomas to make me turn to The One and shake my angry fist and ask 'why?'" He finished the sentence with a raised fist. "Because you have strayed from The Natural Order, The One said. I have been patient, but it is time. You will lead my people back, or I will finish the destruction I have begun and start this world anew."

A restlessness rippled through the crowd, along with quiet murmurs of "No, brother" and "We hear and obey."

Kyle closed her eyes and listened intently. Was her imagination playing tricks? In the few seconds of silence she would swear she heard the flutter of dragon wings in the dark, just beyond the spotlights.

"The Natural Order will make our families whole again. Women will serve as loving wives and mothers as they are intended. Men will be faithful providers, husbands, and fathers. Families are the cornerstone of The Natural Order."

The stage lights made it difficult, but Kyle opened her eyes and scanned the faces in the crowd. Most sat in folding chairs on the grassed field, but the people on the perimeter stood and were constantly shifting for better position. Her heart rate doubled when her eyes settled on a familiar pair working their way around the crowd toward her end of the stage. Nicole looked up, and their gazes locked for a long moment. Nicole smiled and said something into the ear of her escort. Toni glanced up at Kyle and gave her a thumbs-up signal, and then they resumed their trek in her direction.

Oblivious, Cyrus turned to Laine and Kyle. "The mudslide that destroyed my hometown and took my boy from me also separated me from the rest of my family." He motioned to them, and Laine rose to her feet. "I'm proud to make a special announcement tonight." Their guard prodded Kyle in the ribs and she stood, too. "I was joyfully reunited with my wife, Laine, and oldest daughter, Kylie, in Matamoros."

He turned back to the audience to accept their reverent responses of "as it should be" and "The One rewards the faithful." Cyrus strode over to Laine and raised her hand to his lips to kiss it, his eyes shining. "And now, I have a surprise for them, too."

Cyrus pointed to the other end of the forty-meter-long platform as a young man helped Maya up the steps. "My youngest daughter has just arrived. Our family is finally together again." Maya rushed forward and flung herself into Laine's arms, then into Kyle's.

The believers were on their feet, their cheering deafening as the images of the women's joyful reunion, then Cyrus hugging and kissing his wife towered over the stage.

Kyle held her younger sister tight and whispered in her ear. "Maya, when things start to happen, I want you to do exactly what I tell you. Do you understand? You and Mom are in danger if you don't."

Maya nodded, and Kyle released her. They both wiped tears from their cheeks. "I was afraid I'd never see you again," Maya said. "I had visions of you, but not of us together so I didn't know."

"It's okay. I'm here. Mom's here." Kyle kept her voice low. "I have friends here, too."

The hologram narrowed to Cyrus again. "This can be your families, too, when The Natural Order is restored to our society. Men are meant to lead, women to nurture, and children to learn from the roles fulfilled by their parents. "

The hologram flickered, then distorted. "Men...responsibility... up...began—" Luke frowned and waved frantically to technicians at the side of the stage as the amplification of Cyrus's message began to break up and his projected image faltered. It blinked out.

A new hologram was projected behind Cyrus. Shocked murmurs rippled through the believers as they watched a holo-vid of the first clash between The Prophet and the dragon-horse army.

Cyrus was standing on top of a train, holding a gun to the head of an Advocate. The stunningly magnificent First Warrior Jael and her dragon horse Specter challenged and pronounced sentence. Cyrus wounded, then executed the unarmed Advocate before fleeing. Burly guards fired guns at both the dragon-horse warriors and unarmed villagers alike.

While the hologram held the audience spellbound, Luke yelled at the group of digital techs trying to regain control of the holo system. Nicole and Toni skirted the stage and stood at the end. Kyle glanced their way and signaled a quick thumbs-up while the guard was watching Cyrus.

The holo images dissolved to a hospital ward of dying children and a doctor explaining that The Natural Order was withholding medicines they needed because their parents would not renounce The Collective. The next image showed guards shooting starving, unarmed people as they desperately swarmed a transport carrying boxes of food.

The hologram blinked a few times, then went dark. Almost at once, fifty spheres of flame ignited, illuminating the periphery of the gathered believers. Kyle slipped her gloves off. Twenty-five warriors ringed the crowd, holding aloft a fireball in each hand while astride a dragon horse standing with wings spread and fire shooting from their nostrils. The crowd shrank in on itself with a collective gasp.

A buckskin dragon horse landed lightly on the stage, and a blond warrior with a stern expression dismounted before the beast screamed and plunged skyward again. The warrior addressed Cyrus. "I am Danielle, Second Warrior of The Collective's Guard. You have been found guilty of violating the directives of The Collective, hoarding for your own cause at the cost of the life and health of your fellow humans. You also have been found guilty of heresy and conspiracy to spread heresy." She raised her hand and ignited a blue-white fireball. "I am here to carry out your sentence of immediate death and restitution in your next life."

Luke raised his weapon but hesitated when Laine threw herself in front of Cyrus. "No, I refuse to believe The Collective Council would execute a soul suffering from mental illness. I demand appeal."

Kyle grabbed Maya's hand and had taken a few steps toward the left end of the stage when she felt the guard's gun press into her ribs.

"I wouldn't go anywhere if I were you," the guard said.

Cyrus seemed bewildered. "Laine? Did I really kill that Advocate?" His moment of lucidity couldn't have come at a more opportune time.

"I've been medicating his food," Laine said. "After only a week, he's having moments of lucidity. He's not a bad man, only ill."

"Explain that to the boy whose hand he cut off." Tan emerged from the opposite end of the stage, sans Phyrrhos but fierce in red war paint and newly trimmed Mohawk. She raised her hand, igniting a churning fireball. "If the Second Warrior won't carry out the sentence, I will."

Kyle's heart surged at the sight of her lover. She had no time to register the intent of Tan's words, because she was focused on the three armed believers who crept onto the stage behind Tan. She grabbed the gun poking her ribs, superheating the metal so her guard was forced to drop it, and ran forward.

Tan flung her swirling, blue-white ball of death at the same instant Kyle shot a column of blue flame at three gunmen targeting Tan and Luke squeezed the trigger of the repeating weapon he aimed at Second.

Kyle's flame hit home, incinerating the lead gunman who was about to spray Tan's back with bullets.

Tan's fireball was a split second too late but also hit home. Second Warrior Danielle crumpled to the stage as Luke, rather than Cyrus, was engulfed in Tan's flame. His burning figure staggered and fell off the platform.

A pandemonium of gunfire, flame, and screams erupted as many of the men in the audience of believers rose from their seats to draw weapons and the warriors responded defensively, only melting bullets and an occasional gun, because of the women and children huddled between the seating or attempting to flee.

The two remaining gunmen spun toward Kyle, too startled by the heap of stinking, burning flesh that had been their comrade to fire their own guns. They retreated to a dark-haired man, who apparently was directing them, and they backed hurriedly off the long platform's right exit, never taking their eyes or weapon sights off Kyle and Tan.

❖

Maya was unsure what to do as the guard cursed and held his burned hand against his stomach after Kyle sprinted away. She edged toward the steps of the platform. Perhaps if she could hide among the crowd until she saw how things would sort out. Stars, where was her foresight when she needed it?

She was almost at the platform's left exit when the guard noticed. He ran over and grabbed her roughly by the arm to jerk her away from the steps.

"Where do you think you're going?" His fingers hurt where they dug into arm. "I'm going to be in enough trouble because of your stupid sister. I'm not about to lose you, too."

"Let me go," she said. "You're hurting me."

He gave her a shake. "Cyrus needs to teach his women discipline."

"Let me go." She might not be the athlete Kyle was, but she wasn't a pushover. She bit his hand as hard as she could.

"Son of a dung eater." He let go but backhanded her so hard she fell to the platform.

Maya sprawled on the rough boards, her head spinning from the blow. The screams and gunfire of the mayhem erupting around her pounded her brain. A shadow shielded her from the glaring stage lights.

"Hey, didn't anybody ever teach you not to hit girls?"

Soft hands touched Maya's cheek, and she squinted up into a boyish face and concerned eyes. She'd seen this face before.

"Get away from her." The guard stepped toward them, but her rescuer put up a hand and something stopped him.

"Hey, that burn looks pretty bad. I've got a spray in my medkit that will numb it until you can get to a clinic for real treatment."

Maya's head was clearing, and she managed to sit up to find the source of the new voice. A tall, pretty woman, flashes of an earlier vision. It was just beyond her grasp.

The woman dug around in a small pack and held up a spray canister. The guard frowned and hesitated, then put his hand forward and the woman began to spray it with medication.

"We're friends of Kyle," the shorter, boyish woman whispered. "I'm Toni. That's Nicole," she said, indicating the other woman.

Nicole suddenly shifted and sprayed the guard in the eyes. "Run," she yelled.

❖

Laine knelt next to Cyrus, who curled into a crouch, his eyes squeezed shut and hands covering his ears against the noise and confusion of the battle. She spoke quickly, but kept her tone even. "Cyrus, listen to me. You have to stop this. You have to tell them to stop shooting at the warriors. Violence is always wrong. It's never a solution. People should be allowed to believe as they wish, not threatened with starvation or sickness or violence unless they adopt someone else's beliefs."

Cyrus shook his head. "I am The Prophet. I am The One. They should listen to me."

Laine wrapped her arm around his shoulders. He was trembling. "You are Cyrus, my husband, father to Thomas, Kyle, and Maya. You are a professor of cultural history."

He shook his head, tears streaking his face. "Thomas is dead. My son is dead."

"Our son," Laine said gently. "He died a hero, saving an old woman and her small dog." Tears streaked her face as Cyrus buried his face in her shoulder and began to sob like a child, like the softhearted man she'd married.

❖

Kyle ignited her blouse and skirt to fling off the burning remnants—stars, it felt good to be in battleskin and boots—and ran to where Tan was using flame to cauterize Second's heavily bleeding head and shoulder wounds. "Will she be okay?"

"Unconscious, but vitals are good." Tan looked up, and the warmth of their connection flashed in her eyes. Then she seemed to catch herself, and distrust shuttered her features.

Kyle didn't have time to waste words. She knelt next to Tan. "I love you, Tan. You'll have to trust that fact until I have time to explain."

Hooves clattered on the platform, and Titan screamed as he landed next to his downed bonded. He exhaled flame over their heads, forcing back a group of armed believers who ran onto the platform toward Cyrus and Laine.

Azar landed lightly next to Titan, and Furcho slid from his mount. "Tan? How's Second?"

"She's stable but unconscious."

He nodded, his eyes flicking to Kyle before scanning the people running about on the long platform. Was he looking for Nicole or Cyrus? As Third Warrior and with Second wounded, leadership fell to Furcho.

Kyle decided to take the decision from him. She stood. "If you can get Azar to calm Titan before he fries us all, I'll go after Cyrus."

Tan stood, too. "Not without me to make sure the job gets done."

Kyle nodded. Tan's distrust hurt, but she understood. "Together."

❖

Maya was lifted to her feet, Toni grasping one arm and Nicole the other, and rushed off the platform. They'd taken only a few steps when they halted. Maya blinked, her world wavering between reality and vision. Not all of her foresight came to pass. This was one she'd hoped wouldn't.

"Find The Prophet and bring him to me." Xavier's white teeth shone against his dark tan as he waved a cadre of armed men around him and up onto the platform.

He and two heavily armed bodyguards who flanked him still blocked their path. Xavier's gaze flicked from the IC on his wrist to Nicole, then to Maya. "Opportunity smiles on us, my friends. We've come to collect Cyrus and a bit of leverage to control him." He pointed out Maya to his guards. "This is Cyrus's youngest daughter, our leverage." He turned to Nicole. "And fate has awarded a second gift to us. If our spies are not mistaken, this young beauty is Nicole, the fiancée of Furcho, the formidable Third Warrior we met in Brasília." He flicked his hand and one of his men pressed the barrel of a handgun against Nicole's ribs. "We'll take her with us. I think she'll prove very useful."

❖

"Prophet, you must come with us now."

Cyrus was roughly pulled from Laine, who stood. "Leave him alone. He's not going anywhere with you."

But the men already were hustling Cyrus away. Head down, he wasn't resisting. Laine couldn't let them. She ran after them and leapt, hitting the closest man in the back with both her feet and knocking him into several others. They tumbled as she scrambled up and pulled Cyrus away. But there were too many. Three large men knocked them to the ground. One dragged Cyrus to his feet again while one pinned Laine's arms so the third could tie her kicking feet together. She was thrown onto her stomach and her arms wrenched behind her back while they tied her hands. Laine was desperate. She raised her head and screamed for her only remaining weapon. "Kyle!"

❖

Tan and Kyle were at least twenty meters away when Laine's cry for help rang out. As they sprinted forward, Tan threw up a protective wall of bullet-melting flame while Kyle's exploding fireballs took out two of the eight men with laser-like aim before the group disappeared down the platform stairs. They ignored the stairs and leapt off the platform, only to skid to a halt.

Xavier stood next to a large transport, holding Nicole in front of him with a gun pressed to her ribs. "Ah, more warrior friends. I don't believe we've had the pleasure." He jerked his head at the men. "Get in the transport." He smiled at Tan and Kyle. "I hate to be rude, but we don't have time for introductions. Here's what's going to happen. Nicole is our get-out-of-Killeen-free card. In fact, she's going to be our guest for a while, our insurance against further attack from your irritating little army. We'll be in touch when we're ready to negotiate her release."

"No," Nicole said when Kyle raised her hand. "He's very serious. Tell Furcho not to worry. I love him."

Xavier backed them into the transport, and the door closed. Tan touched the communication device in her ear and murmured quick instructions. The vehicle had barely moved when Phyrrhos, along with Michael and Apollo, landed next to her. A stunning, red-gold filly also landed beside Kyle, her red elliptical eyes pulsing and wings fluttering. Kyle was mesmerized as the filly danced around her.

"No time." Kyle barely registered Tan's growl before she was jerked up onto Phyrrhos' back behind Tan. "You two can get to know each other later." Then they were aloft, Michael and Apollo on one side and Raven and Potawatomi on the other. Furcho and Azar streaked past, and the night sky filled with dragon-horse warriors as they shadowed the transport to an airstrip. Kyle closed her eyes briefly as she wrapped her arms around Tan from behind. This wasn't the time or place, but the soft brush of Tan's Mohawk against Kyle's cheek and the buttery scent of skin was like coming home. She nuzzled into Tan's neck and kissed her ear. "Stars, I missed you."

Tan stiffened, then silently rested a tentative hand over Kyle's.

The transport sped down a long dark road to a remote airstrip and stopped next to a sleek silver jet. After a moment, Xavier stepped out with Nicole held tightly against his chest, his gun pressed against her ribs.

Azar, red eyes pulsing, blue flame spurting from his nostrils, landed several meters in front of them. Apollo, Phyrrhos, Potawatomi, and Bero touched down behind Azar.

Furcho dismounted and stalked slowly toward Xavier, his face a mask of fury, his voice low. "If you do anything to hurt her, I will burn you so slowly you will feel every layer of your skin blister and char black."

"Protective, aren't we, Third Warrior?"

"We have you surrounded. It will be simple for us to disable your plane. Let your hostages go and meet your judgment like a trueborn."

"That's where you're wrong, dragon boy. The way I see it, I hold all the cards." He turned his head and raised his voice without taking his eyes from Furcho. "Juan."

Another man stepped out of the transport, dragging Maya roughly by her arm when she stumbled as he held a gun on her with his other hand. She cried out when the hard tarmac scraped the skin from her knees.

Kyle rushed forward. "You bastard." Furcho's upraised hand stopped her charge.

A second guard appeared in the doorway of the plane, roughly holding Toni by her collar.

Xavier smiled again. "If you touch my plane, I'll start by shooting the girl." He shrugged. "Next will be Cyrus's daughter. We still have the wife to keep him in line." He narrowed his eyes. Nicole flinched as he grabbed her hand and shoved the gun's barrel against her knuckles. "Then for every minute you continue to delay our departure, I will shoot off a piece of your girlfriend, starting with her pretty hand."

Nicole's eyes were wide with fear, and Furcho cursed.

Maya swayed, her eyes blank and unseeing. Her guard grabbed her around the waist to hold her up. "What the crap?"

"Maya?" Not now. Kyle had to think fast. "It's a medical condition, probably all the excitement. Take me instead of Maya. She'll be more trouble than you want for a hostage."

Xavier eyed her. "Who are you, her girlfriend?"

Maya straightened, her pupils pinpoints in pools of iridescent green. Her voice was high and wispy as she began to speak.

"Moon's magic, sun's fire, Ghandi's heart, and Odin's sword. But first a trade, same heart, two souls will pay a debt long owed."

Her pupils expanded, and Maya seemed to return to awareness. She looked directly at Furcho. "Do not be afraid. The shield will protect. Everything is as it should be for now."

Furcho held her gaze for a long moment, then touched his ear to activate his communicator. He murmured instructions for the army to withdraw.

"Furcho, no." Kyle was stunned. "Maya." But Maya's eyes were closed now, and she slumped against the guard as he half-carried her toward the plane. The others departed the transport and boarded the plane. Several men carried her mother, still bound, while her father followed meekly behind. She moved to go after them, but Furcho's hand closed around her forearm. His fingers dug into her arm to silence her when she opened her mouth to call out.

Xavier watched them closely, waiting until everyone else was on the plane.

Furcho held Nicole's tearful gaze. "Trust Maya, baby. Keep her and Toni close."

Nicole nodded, offering a small smile. "We'll be fine. I love you."

Xavier backed away from them, feeling his way up the boarding steps so that Nicole was always between him and The Guard. Kyle had never felt so helpless. Who was this man? Where were they taking Nicole, Maya, and her mother? Simon had to be behind all this. She shook off Furcho's grip and stepped forward.

"You wanted to know who I am?" Her shout rang out above the hum of the plane's engine gearing up.

Xavier stopped in the doorway of the plane.

"I am Kyle." A calm filled her so deadly, she felt as if she could shoot lasers from her eyes to his. Her voice had no tremor, no fear. Only resolve. "You tell Simon that Kyle is coming for him."

Tan's warm hands gripped her shoulders as the hatch slid shut and the plane taxied unchecked down the runway.

Chapter Twenty-one

Though daylight had come almost an hour before, the sun was just showing over the high peaks of the Rocky Mountains as Kyle followed Furcho in the line of weary warriors making their way down the steep trail to the new encampment.

Alyssa, frantic, met them where the trail emptied into the valley and construction of their permanent camp was already well underway.

"Furcho, what is it? I could feel it the instant you landed in the meadow."

Furcho rubbed his eyes. Kyle had never seen him look so weary. "They took Nicole. She's okay and Toni's with her, but that bastard took her."

Alyssa glanced at Kyle. "Cyrus?"

"No, Xavier. The guy Simon recruited in Brasília," Furcho said. "I don't think Cyrus is running the show anymore. Simon is."

Kyle stopped next to Tan, who was watching Alyssa as her eyes went to the stretcher Raven and Michael carried that bore the still-unconscious Second Warrior.

"No, no, no." Alyssa's hand went to her mouth. "Not Danielle, too." Tears flooded her eyes.

Tan grabbed Alyssa's shoulders and shook her. "Listen to me. She's unconscious but stable. I need you to help me, not panic, eh?"

Kyle could feel Alyssa's overwhelming fear, her despair, and marveled at Tan's strength in the face of it.

"You're broadcasting, Alyssa. I need you to shield before we walk into camp," Tan said softly.

Alyssa closed her eyes, and the anxiety that had gripped Kyle a moment before receded.

"Good. Now show us where the new clinic's located." Tan released Alyssa, and Kyle hurried with her to follow when Alyssa ran to catch up with Raven and Michael.

❖

Kyle slumped against the doorframe. She didn't have to be an empath to feel the defeat that permeated the camp. She still couldn't believe Jael had been killed in Brasília. The possibility that Tan could also die in battle chilled her to the very core. She didn't know how Alyssa was surviving. She sighed.

She knew the dragon-horse army had slept little over the past week as they traveled to catch up to Cyrus's group, and not at all in at least the past thirty-six hours. Yet Furcho sat on the porch of the new headquarters building, staring at the setting sun. Alyssa still kept vigil at Second's bedside, holding her hand and constantly watching the vitals monitors for a flicker of change. At the end of the ward, Tan was hunched over the medical scanner, searching for something, anything she might have missed in Second's newest scan that would explain why she remained unconscious. Kyle pushed off the doorframe and went to her.

"Tan, come shower and lie down for a short while." She massaged the tense shoulders. "You won't be any good to Commander Second if you collapse from exhaustion."

She took Tan's hand and led her to the headquarters building. Since this was to be a permanent camp, separate rooms and personal facilities had been built for each of The Guard. She pushed open the door to Tan's assigned room.

"No furniture yet, but I managed to find a double airbed, some sheets, and basic toiletries for the personal facility." She tugged open the closure of Tan's battleskin, exposing the beautiful brown skin of her strong back. "You'll sleep better if you shower first."

Tan turned and her hands grasped Kyle's, stopping her. "You expect after all that's happened to pick up where we left off?"

"No," Kyle said softly. "We both need to heal, but we can only do that together, Tan. It hurt me, still hurts that you were so quick to believe I would betray you."

Tan turned away again. "If you hadn't stopped me, Cyrus would be dead now. Second wouldn't be in a coma, and Nicole would be here, safe."

Kyle toed off her boots, then unfastened her battleskin and stepped out of it. She wore nothing underneath. It was a risk. Tan could throw her out in the hall naked. She padded to where Tan had gone to stare out the window and slowly peeled the garment down to expose Tan's shoulders. She reverently kissed the curve of her neck. "Mom had just told me Cyrus had my younger sister stashed somewhere. If you'd killed him then, I might have never found her. I didn't have time to explain that to you." She wasn't going to give up. She continued kissing along Tan's shoulders, wishing she could read Tan's thoughts as she stared out at the dying light.

After several long minutes, Tan closed her eyes. "On the platform, when Second hesitated to execute Cyrus, you left your sister and mother unguarded to save me from the guy shooting at me from behind, didn't you?"

"Yes, and I'd do it again."

Tan turned in her arms and searched her eyes. "Why, Kyle? Why would you do that?"

Kyle held her gaze. "Because if you left this life, you would take half of my heart with you."

Tan dropped her forehead to Kyle's shoulder. "I'm not worth it, Kyle. I didn't trust you."

Kyle cupped Tan's sculpted cheeks, lifting her face and brushing her lips against Tan's full mouth. "Stop punishing yourself, Tan. You hurt the people around you only because you keep punishing that poor little girl from the hut so many lifetimes ago. She did the best she could." She caressed Tan's face and kissed her again. "And she grew into a beautiful soul who repairs a little boy's hand, heals the sick, defends The Collective, and is a fantastic lover."

Tan blinked back tears as her hands began to roam tentatively over Kyle's back, then along the slope of her hips. "I don't know."

Kyle smiled at her uncertainty. "Try for me? For us. Stop hurting yourself, and let me love you, Tanisha."

Tan wanted to…desperately. Kyle's soul was the one that matched hers. But did she dare? She swallowed, then cleared her throat. "You're naked."

"I thought maybe we could shower together."

"Saves water. You're into that kind of thing, aren't you?"

"Yes. Efficiency of resources is a big part of creating a successful agri-community."

"I don't mind saving water."

"Good." Kyle started toward the shower but stopped when Tan didn't follow. "Is there something else?"

Tan glanced away, a rare shyness warming her neck and ears. "In the cave, you know, the first time—" No more secrets. Kyle had to know everything if this was going to work. She looked up and met Kyle's gaze. "That was kind of hot. The truth is, sometimes— not a lot, but occasionally when I'm in a certain mood—I like it a little rough."

"I was afraid I had, you know, overstepped." Kyle ducked her head, her lips curling in a small smile. "It was really hot." Then she looked up and frowned. "Just don't ever ask me to do anything that would damage you. I don't want to ever see lashes on your back like you had then."

Tan's eyes filled with tears. She took Kyle's hand in hers and brought it to her lips. "I don't think the little girl from the hut is going to need that any longer."

❖

Wildflowers swayed in the warm, gentle wind as Alyssa glided through the forty-fourth movement of the long eighty-eight-movement form, seeking her center in the familiar patterns Han had taught her. It had saved her from near madness when she was an unshielded empath. She hoped it could help her survive the rest of this life with only half of her heart still beating. The movements now were a painful reminder of the many times she and Jael had practiced Tai Chi together. Still, it was a memory she didn't want to forget. As she moved into the fifty-sixth pattern, she could almost feel Jael's strong and steady presence behind her, matching her flow with unerring precision. It felt so real, her heart beat loud in her ears with the anticipation that Jael would actually be there as she rotated with the next—

Alyssa jerked up, torn from her dream by a terrible scream. Pain shot up her back and she thought it might be her own, until another rattled the windows of the hospital ward. She recognized it as dragon horse, rather than human. It must be night again. Second was still unconscious and unmoving on the bed. She groaned as she stood and stretched. Another agonized shriek sounded, more terrible and closer than the first two. Running footsteps pounded down the hallway outside the ward.

Will skidded through the doorway, breathless. "It's Titan. I think he's looking for the commander. Maybe she's calling him. Is she waking up?"

Alyssa scanned the vitals monitors. No change. She shook her head. "I don't think so."

The screams were growing more frequent, and other dragon horses joined in a tortured chorus. Alyssa put her hands over her ears.

"I'll go see what's going on," Will said, shouting to be heard over the deafening noise.

Alyssa studied the monitors for any sign of a change. Instead of waking, they seemed to be slowing. That couldn't be right.

Will returned and hugged her to him. "Michael said for us to stay inside."

"What? No. What's going on, Will?" She pushed him away. She knew her lab chief was developing a relationship with Michael, but he obviously didn't understand yet how arrogant warriors could be when it came to dealing with non-warriors.

"Alyssa. Don't. He said you should stay with the Commander."

This wasn't right. Something wasn't right. What didn't they want her to know? To see? She charged through the door and outside.

Second's buckskin dragon horse, Titan, nostrils flaring and spewing flame, paced in the wide lane outside the hospital, beating his wings against the ground without taking flight. People peeked out of windows and from between buildings. Only the remaining members of The Guard and Kyle stood in the lane, circling the distraught animal. The dragon horses of The Guard hovered along the rooftops of the camp, still adding their voices to Titan's.

"What is it? Does he need to see Second?"

Titan breathed a long column of flame into the sky, then screeched out a wounded sound that slammed Alyssa so hard she nearly collapsed. She didn't usually sense animals, but she felt his despair as real as her own.

Furcho bowed his head, unable to speak.

Kyle grabbed Alyssa's arm to steady her but looked to Tan. "Tan, what's happening?"

Tears trickled down Tan's face, but her voice was steady. "If a warrior passes this life and the bond is broken, the dragon horse usually goes mad from the pain. A lone horse will fling himself against cliffs until he dies. The lucky ones have a herd that will gather and end his pain quickly. That's why the others are here."

Titan flung himself to the ground, got up, and charged the building to fling himself against it like a rabid animal.

"Stop him." Alyssa grabbed Furcho's arm. "Do something. He's hurting himself." Then Tan's words sunk in. *If a warrior passes this life...* She ran into the hospital. The vitals monitors were silent and dark. "No, no. Not you, too. I can't make it without you." She hit the code button. Everybody was outside. She sprinted back outside.

"Tan, she's coding." She tried to drag Tan toward the door, but she wouldn't move. "You're a doctor. You have to come."

Tan turned to her, her eyes pools of pain. "She's gone, Alyssa. Their bond is broken. Second made me promise if this ever happened...her greatest wish has always been to be with Saran."

"I don't understand what they're waiting for," Furcho muttered. "Azar just keeps showing me the wild stallion. I don't understand."

"There's your answer," Kyle said.

Dark Star's wings spanned the entire width of the lane as he coasted to a landing several meters from Titan. He breathed pure blue flame. Titan reared and cried out, a pitiful sound. As he launched into the air, Dark Star bellowed a huge column of flame, and Bero, Azar, Potawatomi, Apollo, and Phyrrhos joined their inferno to his. Within seconds, Titan was ash floating away on the wind.

Alyssa sagged against the building. It was done.

She could hold back her sobs of grief no longer and ran inside, closing the door to the ward and locking it. She had no other patients and wasn't ready to light another pyre. The hand she took in hers was still warm. She smoothed back the blond hair as she cried and stroked the cheek so like her lover's. She wasn't Jael, but with Second's help, Alyssa was beginning to feel that she just might make it, find some purpose in this life until she could be with her love again. "I needed you, Danielle. I know you wanted to be with Saran, but without Jael, I needed you to stay with me."

She wished that people were as merciful as dragon horses and would send grieving souls to follow the ones to whom they were bonded. When they lit the pyre for Second Warrior Danielle, Alyssa would lose the last tiny piece of Jael, the other half of her soul. She sobbed as she laid her head on the still chest. She cried for the days no longer filled with the expectation of her warrior surprising her at the hospital and the laughter they shared. She mourned the wondrous starry flights and possibility of children they'd talked about one night. She dreaded the lonely nights ahead without that strong, valiant heart beating under her cheek as she lay draped over Jael's long body to absorb its warmth.

Her sobs quieted and her breath hitched as she rubbed her wet cheek against the solid chest. Maybe she was going mad like Titan. She could have sworn she heard the thu-thump of a heart. Madness might be better than waking each day with reality. Wait. She heard it again. A gasp sounded as the chest under her cheek rose and fell. She jerked up. Sun and stars. She was crazy. She blinked. The monitors over the bed lit up, and readings climbed into normal ranges. Color flooded into Danielle's gray face. She ran to the door, unlocked and flung it open.

"Tan." She ran outside. No one was there. She turned to go back and collided with Tan in the hallway.

"Alyssa." Michael and Raven were right behind Tan. "I know you—"

"She's alive. Come quick." She ran back to the ward without waiting to see if they'd follow.

The monitors still showed normal readings. Thank the stars. She wasn't hallucinating.

"This is impossible," Tan said, feeling for a pulse in the wrist and neck.

Eyelids rippled with movement, and monitors measuring heart rate, body temperature, and brain activity began to elevate.

"She's waking up," Michael said.

Tan had flicked on a penlight and started to lift an eyelid when a clomping ruckus made them all turn toward the door.

"What the—get that animal out of here," Tan said.

Dark Star wedged himself through the doorway and stood at the foot of the bed, rattling his wings in warning when Raven moved toward him. He extended his arched neck, and his red, elliptical pupils pulsed as he touched his nose to the figure in the bed.

Alyssa stood very still until a groan drew her gaze back to the bed, and she touched the warm cheek as the eyelids fluttered. "Come on. You can do it. Open your eyes and look at me." The monitors quieted and the numbers dropped, and Alyssa held her breath. Her throat tightened with tears she didn't think she had left to cry. "Please don't leave me again."

"I'm here." The voice was hoarse but the inflection familiar. The numbers rose and steadied again. "It just took me a while to get back." The eyelids fluttered, and thick blond lashes lifted to reveal eyes as blue as the summer sky. Jael swallowed and licked her dry lips. "We're growing old together. They promised."

THE END

About the Author

D. Jackson Leigh grew up barefoot and happy, swimming in farm ponds and riding rude ponies in rural Georgia. Her passion for writing led her to a career in journalism and North Carolina where she edits breaking news at night and writes lesbian romance stories by day.

Her awards include a 2010 Alice B. Lavender Award for Noteworthy Accomplishment, a 2013 Golden Crown Literary Society Award for paranormal romance, and a 2014 Golden Crown Literary Society Award for traditional romance. She also was a finalist in LGBT erotic romance in the 2013 Rainbow Awards, and a 2014 Lambda Literary Awards finalist in traditional romance.

Write to her at author@djacksonleigh.com or follow her at facebook.com/d.jackson.leigh or www.djacksonleigh.com.

Books Available from Bold Strokes Books

Love on Tap by Karis Walsh. Beer and romance are brewing for Tace Lomond when archaeologist Berit Katsaros comes into her life. (987-1-162639-564-0)

Love on the Red Rocks by Lisa Moreau. An unexpected romance at a lesbian resort forces Malley to face her greatest fears where she must choose between playing it safe or taking a chance at true happiness. (987-1-162639-660-9)

Tracker and the Spy by D. Jackson Leigh. There are lessons for all when Captain Tanisha is assigned untried pyro Kyle and a lovesick dragon horse for a mission to track the leader of a dangerous cult. (987-1-162639-448-3)

Whirlwind Romance by Kris Bryant. Will chasing the girl break Tristan's heart or give her something she's never had before? (987-1-162639-581-7)

Whiskey Sunrise by Missouri Vaun. Culture and religion collide when Lovey Porter, daughter of a local Baptist minister, falls for the handsome thrill-seeking moonshine runner, Royal Duval. (987-1-162639-519-0)

Dyre: By Moon's Light by Rachel E. Bailey. A young werewolf, Des, guards the aging leader of all the Packs: the Dyre. Stable employment—nice work, if you can get it...at least until silver bullets start to fly. (978-1-62639-6-623)

Fragile Wings by Rebecca S. Buck. In Roaring Twenties London, can Evelyn Hopkins find love with Jos Singleton or will the scars of the Great War crush her dreams? (978-1-62639-5-466)

Live and Love Again by Jan Gayle. Jessica Whitney could be Sarah Jarret's second chance at love, but their differences and Sarah's grief continue to come between their budding relationship. (978-1-62639-5-176)

Starstruck by Lesley Davis. Actress Cassidy Hayes and writer Aiden Darrow find out the hard way not all life-threatening drama is confined to the TV screen or the pages of a manuscript. (978-1-62639-5-237)

Stealing Sunshine by Tina Michele. Under the Central Florida sun, two women struggle between fear and love as a dangerous plot of deception and revenge threatens to steal priceless art and lives. (978-1-62639-4-452)

The Fifth Gospel by Michelle Grubb. Hiding a Vatican secret is dangerous—sharing the secret suicidal—can Felicity survive a perilous book tour, and will her PR specialist, Anna, be there when it's all over? (978-1-62639-4-476)

Cold to the Touch by Cari Hunter. A drug addict's murder is the start of a dangerous investigation for Detective Sanne Jensen and Dr. Meg Fielding, as they try to stop a killer with no conscience. (978-1-62639-526-8)

Forsaken by Laydin Michaels. The hunt for a killer teaches one woman that she must overcome her fear in order to love, and another that success is meaningless without happiness. (978-1-62639-481-0)

Infiltration by Jackie D. When a CIA breach is imminent, a Marine instructor must stop the attack while protecting her heart from being disarmed by a recruit. (978-1-62639-521-3)

Midnight at the Orpheus by Alyssa Linn Palmer. Two women desperate to make their way in the world, a man hell-bent on revenge, and a cop risking his career: all in a day's work in Capone's Chicago. (978-1-62639-607-4)

Spirit of the Dance by Mardi Alexander. Major Sorla Reardon's return to her family farm to heal threatens Riley Johnson's safe life when small-town secrets are revealed, and love may not conquer all. (978-1-62639-583-1)

Sweet Hearts by Melissa Brayden, Rachel Spangler, and Karis Walsh. Do you ever wonder *Whatever happened to...*? Find out when you reconnect with your favorite characters from Melissa Brayden's *Heart Block*, Rachel Spangler's *LoveLife*, and Karis Walsh's *Worth the Risk*. (978-1-62639-475-9)

Totally Worth It by Maggie Cummings. Who knew there's an all-lesbian condo community in the NYC suburbs? Join twentysomething BFFs Meg and Lexi at Bay West as they navigate friendships, love, and everything in between. (978-1-62639-512-1)

Illicit Artifacts by Stevie Mikayne. Her foster mother's death cracked open a secret world Jil never wanted to see...and now she has to pick up the stolen pieces. (978-1-62639-472-8)

Pathfinder by Gun Brooke. Heading for their new homeworld, Exodus's chief engineer Adina Vantressa and nurse Briar Lindemay carry game-changing secrets that may well cause them to lose everything when disaster strikes. (978-1-62639-444-5)

Prescription for Love by Radclyffe. Dr. Flannery Rivers finds herself attracted to the new ER chief, city girl Abigail Remy, and the incendiary mix of city and country, fire and ice, tradition and change is combustible. (978-1-62639-570-1)

Ready or Not by Melissa Brayden. Uptight Mallory Spencer finds relinquishing control to bartender Hope Sanders too tall an order in fast-paced New York City. (978-1-62639-443-8)

Summer Passion by MJ Williamz. Women loving women is forbidden in 1946 Hollywood, yet Jean and Maggie strive to keep their love alive and away from prying eyes. (978-1-62639-540-4)

The Princess and the Prix by Nell Stark. "Ugly duckling" Princess Alix of Monaco was resigned to loneliness until she met racecar driver Thalia d'Angelis. (978-1-62639-474-2)

Winter's Harbor by Aurora Rey. Lia Brooks isn't looking for love in Provincetown, but when she discovers chocolate croissants and pastry chef Alex McKinnon, her winter retreat quickly starts heating up. (978-1-62639-498-8)

The Time Before Now by Missouri Vaun. Vivian flees a disastrous affair, embarking on an epic, transformative journey to escape her past, until destiny introduces her to Ida, who helps her rediscover trust, love, and hope. (978-1-62639-446-9)

Twisted Whispers by Sheri Lewis Wohl. Betrayal, lies, and secrets—whispers of a friend lost to darkness. Can a reluctant psychic set things right or will an evil soul destroy those she loves? (978-1-62639-439-1)

The Courage to Try by C.A. Popovich. Finding love is worth getting past the fear of trying. (978-1-62639-528-2)

Break Point by Yolanda Wallace. In a world readying for war, can love find a way? (978-1-62639-568-8)

Countdown by Julie Cannon. Can two strong-willed, powerful women overcome their differences to save the lives of seven others and begin a life they never imagined together? (978-1-62639-471-1)

Keep Hold by Michelle Grubb. Claire knew some things should be left alone and some rules should never be broken, but the most forbidden, well, they are the most tempting. (978-1-62639-502-2)

Deadly Medicine by Jaime Maddox. Dr. Ward Thrasher's life is in turmoil. Her partner Jess left her, and her job puts her in the path of a murderous physician who has Jess in his sights. (978-1-62639-424-7)

New Beginnings by KC Richardson. Can the connection and attraction between Jordan Roberts and Kirsten Murphy be enough for Jordan to trust Kirsten with her heart? (978-1-62639-450-6)

Officer Down by Erin Dutton. Can two women who've made careers out of being there for others in crisis find the strength to need each other? (978-1-62639-423-0)

Reasonable Doubt by Carsen Taite. Just when Sarah and Ellery think they've left dangerous careers behind, a new case sets them—and their hearts—on a collision course. (978-1-62639-442-1)

Tarnished Gold by Ann Aptaker. Cantor Gold must outsmart the Law, outrun New York's dockside gangsters, outplay a shady art dealer, his lover, and a beautiful curator, and stay out of a killer's gun sights. (978-1-62639-426-1)

White Horse in Winter by Franci McMahon. Love between two women collides with the inner poison of a closeted horse trainer in the green hills of Vermont. (978-1-62639-429-2)

Autumn Spring by Shelley Thrasher. Can Bree and Linda, two women in the autumn of their lives, put their hearts first and find the love they've never dared seize? (978-1-62639-365-3)

The Renegade by Amy Dunne. Post-apocalyptic survivors Alex and Evelyn secretly find love while held captive by a deranged cult, but when their relationship is discovered, they must fight for their freedom—or die trying. (978-1-62639-427-8)

Thrall by Barbara Ann Wright. Four women in a warrior society must work together to lift an insidious curse while caught between their own desires, the will of their peoples, and an ancient evil. (978-1-62639-437-7)

The Chameleon's Tale by Andrea Bramhall. Two old friends must work through a web of lies and deceit to find themselves again, but in the search they discover far more than they ever went looking for. (978-1-62639-363-9)